Bloodied Mind

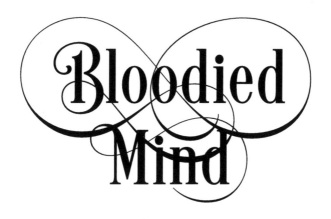

Bloodied Mind

RAYMOND HUGH

MORNING MIST

Poole

Dorset

BH16 6FH

Email - info@morningmist.co.uk

A CIP catalogue record for this book is available from the British Library

ISBN 9781068714801

Printed in Great Britain by

Biddles Books Limited, King's Lynn, Norfolk

My thanks to all who helped me in my research for this book and understandably wish to remain anonymous. You know who you are.

Dedicated to all those who have suffered whilst I have been writing this book

Continued from *Bloody Conscience*

To fully understand the story you will have had to have read
Bloody Waters and Bloodied Conscience first

CHAPTER
−1−

Marck, France

The rain had been falling relentlessly for hours and there was no respite in sight. There were no clouds overhead, just a dark grey mass giving no clue to the brisk wind that blew in from the sea. The sea that Mukhtar had been trying unsuccessfully for months to cross.

He pulled up the collar on his coat and turned his back to the wind. His coat was of good cloth, a donation from someone who cared in Calais. There weren't too many of those anymore. When he had received the coat, it still had a label attached. It was new. Now, no more than a couple of months later, it was in a sorry state. The result of days of 24 hours wear. His coat too quickly had become a blanket for his cardboard bed. And there were too many days where he never removed it from his badly stained body.

For hours now his sodden clothing had offered no protection from the torrent of water descending from above. The first trickle descending the back of his neck had felt uncomfortable, now all his clothes were clinging to him as though they were extra layers of skin. Discomfort was the new norm, He was past caring, he hardly noticed. Partly because he had become used to it and partly because he was waiting for what he hoped would be his salvation.

He stamped his feet, partly because he felt the need to move and partly in frustration. He had been waiting for over an hour now and still there was no sign of the promised van. In the surrounding shadows he glimpsed other movements. He had no doubt that they were people like him, waiting for their salvation. He had been told to find a place to wait on his own, on no account must he gather with others and not to bring attention to himself. If anyone approached, he had been instructed to walk around the block and find an alternative place to wait. He looked around him. Facing and to his right, white painted houses with faux Flemish brick lined the road. All had meticulously manicured gardens. Light shone out from many of the windows. The polluting rays weren't a threat, they were mostly soaked up by extensive lawns. If anything the escaping light helped to enhance the shadows affording valuable cover for those who had no desire to be seen. Behind him lay open ground, ripe for development. In the distance moving lights gave away the busy A16 Autoroute and a cluster of motionless brighter lights at the lorry park known as Transmarck.

Transmarck had once been a popular target for those looking for a free ride to the promised land, the UK. But for several years now security had been really tight and drivers were aware of where to look for unwelcome and uninvited passengers. Although lorries were still a target for passage, most, despite the risks, favoured trusting their luck in small boats, even dinghies. News of every death by drowning spread quickly among the significant population of migrants waiting to try and cross to the UK. There would be mourning and prayers said for those who had lost their lives but it did nothing to deter. Nearly all waiting to cross had been to hell and back, most several times and living in the camps around Calais was a living hell in itself. People placed their lives in God's hands and if he wanted to take them then so be it. God knows best. He would have a reason.

Gazing at the houses before him, the cosiness within so effortlessly displayed, Mukhtar reflected on his own life and how he had ended up on the outside looking in. He had been born and brought up as a child in the Badakhshan province, Afghanistan. Badakhshan to him was paradise on earth, nowhere, since he'd left, had he witnessed such natural beauty. Life had been simple, sometimes hard but always joyous. Then came the rise of the Taliban, life had started to change. Freedoms were steadily taken away. His parents, wanting a better life for their only son, had paid people to transit him to the UK where they had friends and relatives. The voyage had been hard but compared to today, easier. Within three months of leaving his home he was in a strange place called Birmingham. He remembered he had, at first, hated it. His home in Afghanistan had been surrounded by natural wonders. Smells and sounds delivered by God. His new home, Birmingham had been created by the hands of man. Nothing was natural, the constant noise offended his senses and the air he had found disgusting, fouling even his tongue. However the human body and mind is quick to adapt, one reason why homo sapiens is so successful, and within months not only had he come to accept his new surroundings, he'd come to enjoy them.

At first he worked in an ethnic supermarket. His employment there had been poorly paid and strictly cash in hand, but cash in one's hand was a new luxury. In Afghanistan, life tended to be lived through bartering, by the exchange of goods. Cash in one's hand was a luxury. Living in a crowded house had been nothing new to him being able to buy clothes had been and he'd quickly embraced the consumerist lifestyle that dominated his new found society. The constant desire for goods had bred ambition and a desire for a lifestyle, which in Afghanistan would be impossible. In this new found society, nothing was impossible. You just had to work hard to achieve it.

From the supermarket he'd gone to work at a garage, owned by a Syrian mechanic. He'd been keen to learn and learnt quickly. After several years he was the garage's main mechanic and gained a reputation for being a hard and above all , honest worker. His new boss had recognised his value and in return had paid him well. Better still the

Syrian had connections and one day an Afghani passport was delivered into his hands. He knew not to ask questions, as a result a national insurance number quickly followed and a personal bank account. He was living the dream but never forgot his family who regularly sent him messages via friends and relatives. In return, using an unregistered Hawala, (money broker), he had been able to send money back to his parents. Not too much, that would have brought them unwanted attention. Just enough to bring them a little peace.

Then came the rise of the Taliban, al Qaeda, Osama bin Laden and September 11th. The West in 2001 invaded and as the war unfolded he'd felt a growing desire to return to his country, to help rid it of the Taliban and give his birth place the freedoms he had enjoyed in the West, more specifically to, in some form, pay back the country who had given him such a good living. As the years passed his desire had grown stronger and eventually they'd grown so strong that it was inevitable that he'd return to his country of birth.. In 2017 he'd taken a flight from Heathrow to Quetta in Pakistan and with help had crossed the border into Afghanistan. Travel through his country had been extremely difficult and it had taken more than 5 months before he'd found himself back in his home village. His parents, though delighted to see him, had feared for his safety. The Taliban hadn't gone, they were everywhere, you just couldn't see them. With such strong connections to the West he would have been a target. No more than a day later he'd found himself on the road again. This time heading for Kabul. Weeks later, he was working for the British as an interpreter. His colleagues there had nicknamed him Muck, he knew what it meant but didn't care. It was all in fun and he was enjoying doing valuable work for the country who had given him so much.

Years later, without warning the Americans announced they were pulling out and with them the British and every other Western nation. The result was chaos and with it panic creating even more chaos. He'd expected the British to look after him but instead found himself abandoned. As the military exited he was left to the mercy of the informers, to those who wanted to cosy up to the Taliban. Life as a consequence had been lived in the shadows, not knowing from one day to the next whether it would be his last. His only hope was to return to the UK. The one place where he had ties. Returning to his village was out of the question. He would almost certainly be captured and suffer a long and torturous death, worse still his presence there may have resulted in the same fate for his family. No, his only choice had been to return to the UK. The problem was, doing so today was a lot harder than it had been all those years ago. To ease his passage crossing borders, he'd paid a lot of money to a lot of people. Some had taken his money and done nothing to ease his passage. As a result, it had taken him almost two years to slip out of Afghanistan, to cross central Asia into Europe and finally to where he was now, Calais, almost within touching distance of the country he considered his home. ALMOST. That slither of water the French called La Manche and the English, the English Channel was proving an almost impossible obstacle. On a clear day, the white cliffs were visible and at night the lights that lined the English coast day or night, the English coastline was nearly always visible, teasing and at the same time daring him to try again. And try, try, try again he had. Money had, before every attempt, passed hands, with promises of deliverance to the fabled land for that was what the country he considered home had become. On every occasion his attempts had failed and the people he'd paid money to vanished into thin air. There was always another to take their place with the same empty promises. Common sense was to ignore them, but when your position was hopeless you had no choice, you wanted to believe in the man offering you hope. And in reality that was what you were paying for, hope, but hope was the end of the rainbow when compared to despair. Common sense thus went out of the window and he'd put money into the next man who'd come offering him hope.

His last attempt to cross was by rubber dinghy. The dinghy had been hopelessly overcrowded and his attempt to climb on board had been in vain; he had been pushed back by those already on board. Perhaps had been watching over him, for little over an hour into the dinghy's crossing, it had sunk and over half of those on board had perished. 'God's will' was the only consolation.

His last attempt though had cost him the last of his money. He'd had nothing left except the clothes he stood up in and a few Euros for food. To add insult to injury, the recent so-called 'storm of the century' had destroyed his makeshift home. After the storm, his home had been little more than flattened cardboard.

Then came hope. For weeks, perhaps months, there had been growing rumours of a team of local sympathisers who were willing to traffic people to the English coast for free. People who found themselves in an impossible situation. People like him. Their cover was a food station, an unofficial one so somewhat clandestine. The food station's next location was always delivered by word of mouth and only to those who had been chosen to be helped. The one public face for the food station was a somewhat wild local woman with red streaks in her hair. It was she who appeared to select who needed to be helped and made contact. Nobody she'd made contact with had returned to the camps circling Calais, evidence of a100% success. The same couldn't be said of those who demanded money. Many like him had paid only to find themselves back where they'd started with no offer of a refund. The people who ran the clandestine food station offering salvation, hope to those who had run out of hope, were considered by many to be angels sent by God. They were of legendary status.

One day, and quite unexpectedly the wild woman with red streaks had approached him. Word, she'd told him had reached her of his predicament and there were people who wanted to help him. And as a direct result of that initial contact, here he was, standing in the shadows, soaked through, waiting for the magic van to arrive. He was on the verge of giving up and seeking shelter when a fading white, rather old looking Peugeot Boxer with a refrigeration unit pulled into an unplanned layby. Seconds later, a second van turned up and from this van a food station was quickly set up. Within minutes, a hot meal was being served along with fresh baguette and cheese. Around twenty-five people, including children seemingly from nowhere, appeared from the shadows. Mukhtar was amazed he hadn't spotted them before. Months, perhaps years of having to hide in the shadows had probably made them experts. From the refrigerated van someone was walking around serving coffee. He was approached, offered a cup. As he took it the man uttered using a loud whisper, "Montez dans le van." It came across as an order not a request. Mukhtar did as he was told. Somebody else was holding one of the rear doors open. He quickly climbed in to find six other people already waiting inside. The six included what he assumed to be a family of four mother, father and two young girls, no more than eight in years. As he moved to sit down, two more aspirants climbed in behind him. They were to be the last. The man holding the door smiled and silently closed the door. There were nine of them Mukhtar had counted, five men, he being the oldest, two women and the two young girls. He felt strangely sleepy, with all the excitement and expectation he assumed he'd be electrifyingly alert, the opposite was coming true. He was struggling to keep his eyes open. He took another sip of his coffee; it was strong but strangely sweet. The van shook as someone started the engine. Seconds later, they started to move. The movement caused him to slide sideways, he struggled to push himself up. He thought he could hear a light hiss and the air had a strange perfume about it. It wasn't unpleasant but he sensed it wasn't right. Mukhtar did his best to fight the weight that was sending him to sleep, but it was to no avail, his eyes closed and he slumped to the floor, his head coming to rest on the feet of one of the young girls. And so the van drove on, its cargo in the hands of the angels sent by God.

Mukhtar had no idea how long he had been asleep, all he knew, now that he was awake, was that the light hurt his eyes. He tried to move but something was preventing him. Not a restraint but his muscles wouldn't obey the instructions sent by his brain. He felt he should feel scared, but he didn't, he felt strangely at ease. Happy even and he sensed he was smiling.

"So you're awake Mukhtar, good, how are you feeling? Not too uncomfortable I hope?"

The stranger, Mukhtar, couldn't see him, didn't wait for an answer.

"I hear you've travelled a long way, and that you've been trying to reach England." The man paused and a face appeared in Mukhtar's vision. A round smiling face, with a strong nose and dark eyes. There was a hint of satisfaction in the man's eyes.

"Well we can help with getting you to England, it's just a shame it can't be all of you." The man laughed. As he did so Mukhtar felt a prick in his arm. His eyes started to close, he still felt strangely content. Whatever he was lying on started to move. He assumed it was some sort of trolley. This must be the start of his crossing to England. Mukhtar felt himself smiling within.

R.I.P. Mukhtar.

CHAPTER
–2–

Gendarmerie Nationale, Calais, France

Not a million miles away and around the time Mukhtar had arrived to wait for his salvation, Capitaine Olivier Vendroux was leaving his gendarmerie to visit Cap Blanc Nez. Not an official visit, though if asked he would declare it was. No, a visit to satisfy his morbid curiosity. To see where two men had recently fallen to their deaths, one being his predecessor, Thierry Maubert.

The weather was disgusting. Wind and rain assaulted the capitaine as he walked to his car, a shiny Alpine A110. Opening the car door, he stood for a second to look back at the building he, not by choice, was in charge of. He found it offensive, disgusting, boring, a monstrosity that offended his senses. Looking around him he found, just like the weather, the whole scene depressing. No wonder, he thought, the people who worked inside were so grey. It would take a lot to shine a light with so much greyness. Boring and depressing people working in a boring and depressing building. No one he'd talked to so far had he found challenging or cultured. Apart from Colette, his secretary, whom he found had a certain charm, everyone else he found simple, uncultured, boring and, worst of all predictable. He hoped to God that the organisation didn't have long term plans for him in Calais.

Turning on the ignition, he put his foot down on the accelerator enjoying the roar from the direct injection 1.8 litre engine. A satisfied smile played on his lips, at least they hadn't taken his car from him. He'd been worried that it may have been replaced with a greyer, boring model. One that would blend in better with his new surroundings. But to his relief they hadn't, at least in his car he could shine.

Deftly reversing out of his designated parking space, he accelerated joining the rush hour traffic lining the road outside. Despite the traffic, it wasn't long until he was on the coast road that ran along Calais Plage. He was amazed to see that there were quite a number of people on the beach. Every one of them was mad, he considered. The sea looked angry and it was obvious the ferries crossing La Manche were having a tough time of it. The rain drew heavier and the capitaine increased the speed of his wipers, at the same time turning on his radio. Light pop music filled the Alpine's interior. He was now passing the seafront's Hotel de la Plage. Though brightly lit, no doubt to draw attention, the hotel somehow retained something of the innocuous. Perfect perhaps for a professional femme fatale to seduce, and use, the town's unsuspecting head of the gendarme. The smile played further on the lips of the capitaine. With his smile accelerating to a laugh, the Alpine accelerated too. He didn't care that he was breaking the speed limit. He was the powerful capitaine of the town's gendarme. He was untouchable.

Minutes later after passing through the coastal towns of Bleriot Plage and Sangatte the Alpine A110 was enjoying the open road and the climb to Cap Blanc Nez. For the first time since being posted to Calais, Capitaine Oliver Vendroux was impressed. The approach to Cap Blanc Nez was impressive, something he hadn't been prepared for and the Cap itself quite magnificent. As he approached the summit, the ground became pockmarked with craters, evidence of the intensive bombing by the British RAF during WW2 and, close to the cliff edge, the remains of German Blockhaus. So much death must have occurred here. A cruel smile this time played on the capitaine's lips. Swinging right, he pulled into the roughly surfaced car park for the Cap. Two other cars were parked there, both with their windows steamed up indicating their occupants had been there for some time. After pausing for a few seconds, he pulled into a space away from the other parked cars and facing the sea. He was in no hurry to get out, instead he sat staring at the ribbon of lights that mapped the English coast. The wind chucked the rain against his windscreen at the same time erratically rocking his car. The noise outside almost deafened the music playing on the radio and instinctively he turned up the volume. A retro song was playing, 'Mon papa a moi est un gangster', he'd forgotten who it was by. He liked the song and sat back to listen, enjoying the rocking of his car by the wind. The song finished too quickly to be replaced by a more recent number, 'Tahitialamaison by Keen'V. As he listened he began to feel uneasy, it made no sense but for some strange reason the song unnerved him. Switching off the radio he did the same with the ignition and stepped out into the worsening weather. The wind and rain hit him hard and he took in a sharp breath as the damp air penetrated his lungs. Far from being cowed by the weather, he relished in it. The weather was challenging him and he was up to the task. With the tails of his coat flying behind him, taking bold deliberate strides, he made his way passing the monument to the cliff edge. Bracing himself, he raised both arms and stared up at the sky. Wind and rain battered him but he didn't care. He relished in the exhilaration the wild weather brought and the wind was blowing in from the sea offering protection from the rocks below. Only if the wind dropped suddenly was he in danger of toppling over the edge and he relished in that risk. Slowly he brought his head down to gaze on the waves crashing against the white chalk some one hundred and thirty-four metres below. What a magnificent way to die, he whispered to himself imagining the two men who had not long before met their deaths on the rocks below. He was almost jealous.

A sound startled him, a sound coming from behind. Not of the wind, the sound was too deliberate. The capitaine spun round almost losing his balance as he did so. Before him stood three men, two were several metres back and had a Mediterranean appearance. The one in front, standing so close, if it weren't for the wind the capitaine would feel the man's breath on his face, was Caucasian. He had no outstanding features, however his stance warned that he knew how to handle himself. All three men were dressed in black. For several seconds everyone stood motionless, each trying hard not to take a step forced by the wind.

The man only inches away spoke. "Bonsoir Capitaine Olivier Vendroux."

Ardres, France

Around the time Capitaine Olivier Vendroux was stepping out from his hated Gendarmerie to visit Cap Blanc Nez. Lieutenant Beaufort, the capitaine's second in command, was dropping his ex-capitaine's widow and her daughter off at their house in Ardres. The funeral, he considered, had gone well, far better than expected. Especially considering the circumstances. The downfall of his ex-capitaine, from pillar of the community to complete and utter shame, resulting in him taking the cowardly way out, must have been playing on the minds of all those in attendance. Yet, only respect had been on display and support for his grieving wife and daughter. Even his new capitaine, Capitaine Vendroux, had ensured the gendarmerie had played a modest but important not to mention respectful role in Capitaine Maubert's burial. A lot could have gone wrong, but nothing had. The farewell to his ex-capitaine had been perfect, almost joyous.

Before starting his engine he watched Vivienne, Madame Maubert) and her daughter walk up the garden path to their house. Was it him being male or a gendarme that made him want to see them safely inside? A bit of both he thought. He couldn't drive off without seeing them open and close the door behind them. As they approached the open porch which protected the front door, two people appeared out of the shadows. They looked young, teenagers possibly, a boy and a girl. The lieutenant thought they looked familiar. He rested his hand on the door handle, in readiness in case he was needed. Watching, he started to rest easy, the four appeared to be in conversation. Seconds later all four entered the house. The lieutenant let out a sigh of relief, all good. Now to take Colette home, he leant over his seat and closed her mouth. He smiled, he'd never seen Colette drunk before. He wouldn't forget this in a hurry, and he knew already that she'd hate that. His smile broadened. Turning on the ignition he made to put his car into gear when there came a scream. Then another from inside the house. Leaving the engine running and the keys in the ignition he kicked open the driver's door and started running up the path. The sound and violence of the door being thrust open woke Colette. Struggling with her consciousness she tried to remember where she was. Capitaine Maubert's, she recognised the house. She'd been there on more than one occasion. Focusing her mind fixated on the lieutenant. He was frantically banging on the front door. Sobering in seconds Colette opened the rear door and started walking, half running up the path. Her heels wouldn't allow her to do anything else.

"Lieutenant, Qu'est-ce que? Qu'est-ce que?"

The lieutenant either didn't hear her or chose to ignore her, instead he continued to knock on the door repeatedly shouting Vivienne, Vivienne. Without warning, the door opened. Standing in the doorway wasn't Madame Maubert or her daughter but a young man. His youthful face was freshly weathered by fear. The lieutenant was just about to ask who the fuck he was and what was going on when Colette's voice came from behind.

"Jean, Jean. What are you doing here?"

The young man's face crumpled; he struggled to speak but nothing came out. Instead he almost fell on the door handle for support. The lieutenant stood, stunned into motionless. Colette pushed past him grabbing the young man she'd called Jean. She shouted at the lieutenant.

"This is one half of the couple I told you about, the couple who came into the gendarmerie to report they'd seen Thierry pushed off Cap Blanc Nez. Why are you here Jean, what are you doing here?"

Before Jean could answer, the lieutenant leaped forward to help Colette. The young man's legs had given way and without the support of the two would have ended in a heap on the floor. With difficulty, they half carried and half walked him into the lounge. There they found a young girl, barely a woman sobbing uncontrollably on the couch. Madame Maubert, her face etched with confusion, was pacing up and down whilst her daughter, her face full of thunder, stood with her arms folded at one end of the sofa.

Colette with the lieutenants helped manoeuvre Jean onto the sofa, where he rested both his hands supportively on the girl's left thigh.

"And this is Camille," Collette motioned to the girl sobbing on the sofa. "Why are you both here?" She repeated.

Camille wiped her face and looked as though she were about to speak when Jean managed to make his mouth work.

"Your capitaine, your gendarmerie wouldn't listen to us, what were we to do? Jean opened his palms upwards. "We felt it was only right that they," Jean waved his hand in front of his face. "That Madame Maubert knew the truth, what really happened."

"It's my dad's fucking funeral, show some fucking respect, as if we haven't been through enough. My poor fucking mother." The daughter violently rubbed her sleeve across her face. Furious that she'd allowed tears to escape her eyelids.

"We didn't know." Camille sobbed.

There came another scoff. "MENTEUSE. Didn't know! My dad's funeral has been all over the fucking media, where have you two been? Mars?

Her mother waved her hands in a gesture of calm yourself, however when she spoke it was not to her daughter but to both Colette and the lieutenant.

"Is it true what they say? That my husband was pushed, that he was murdered, that he never committed suicide.?"

Colette looked at her feet, the lieutenant struggled to find the right words.

"Well?"

"I promise we didn't know it was the funeral today." Camille repeated. This time her statement was barely a whisper and everyone standing ignored her.

"I haven't had a chance to interview them Vivienne, I don't know."

"But you knew of their accusation?"

The lieutenant nodded. "Yes."

"They told me" Colette cut in, trying to support her lieutenant who looked like he was praying for the ground to swallow him up.

"They told you and you never had the courtesy to tell me, his wife?"

"I haven't had the chance to interview them" the lieutenant repeated.

"But your capitaine interviewed them, he must have told you."

The lieutenant nodded, struggling to decide how much he should say. He counted Vivienne as a friend but he was still a gendarme. He couldn't reveal every conversation in the gendarmerie.

"And?" Madame Maubert's expression was starting to change from let's all keep calm to one of anger.

"He didn't believe their story; he didn't think it was worth investigating."

"He wouldn't listen to us," Jean's battered, beaten disposition had changed to one of anger. "He treated us as though we were stupid little kids."

Colette moved to calm him. Lieutenant Beaufort spoke across everybody.

"Look, Vivienne, I know how you feel".

"Do you? Do you really"? The daughter scoffed

"No, no, you're right, it's impossible to but you must see that I couldn't come to you with some story that I haven't even had a chance to investigate. The lieutenant paused. "Especially one that my boss has told me it's not worth bothering with."

"Then you wouldn't have interviewed them, lieutenant?" He was conscious she used his title rather than his first name.

"No, Vivienne you're wrong I probably would have done".

"Why would your boss, Capitaine Vendroux, have told you not to?"

"He didn't actually say that, just that it wasn't worth bothering with."

Sounds of contempt came from the sofa. The lieutenant ignored them, his ex-capitaine's wife had cornered him and he could see that she knew it. To interview the two after what his new capitaine had said, meant that he didn't trust his new boss. And that was the elephant in the room. He didn't trust his new boss, Capitaine Vendroux. Prior actions had already demonstrated this, the difference now was he was having to face the fact. But was it professional mistrust or something worse, far worse?

"Look lieutenant, I understand your difficulty, but don't you see, if I'd known this before I could have we could have buried my husband with pride. Even if it had only been internal pride. I would have known that there was a strong possibility that he hadn't taken the coward's way out. Whatever he's done, what stupid foolish things he's done, my husband was never a coward, lieutenant. You've worked with him. You must know that." Madame Maubert, Vivienne was struggling to hold back her tears.

Lieutenant Beaufort lowered his head. "I do and I'm sorry." He knew he had to get a grip of the situation and fast. What was being said between these four walls must never get outside. At least not at this time. Not until he was ready. If it did the consequences could be catastrophic and the truth never discovered. Whatever the truth was. He was becoming increasingly uncomfortable that whatever the truth was, investigating it was far beyond his paygrade. Worse still, how he felt, if he didn't investigate it then no-one seriously would. Never in a professional capacity had he felt so alone. Not knowing who to trust. Staying with trust, somehow he had to gain the trust of all those in the room with him. Turn things around and move on, somehow snuff out the raw emotion that had been displayed so far and persuade everyone present in the room, from here on to work together, and at his pace and importantly, always with him in control. It was quickly dawning on him that to do this it would almost certainly mean that, on occasion, probably several, perhaps even frequently, it would require him to work outside his official capacity as a gendarme. That he'd have to tread carefully, not to attract suspicion. His work would have to effectively be clandestine. He knew he'd be putting his professional reputation and his position as a gendarme on the line, but he owed a lot of people, not just the people in the room but everyone involved in the investigation, since the storm. And everyone touched by the investigation since the storm. Many of whom were dead or missing. In particular, he owed it to his ex-boss, Capitaine Maubert and his widow who he was conscious of, was staring at him intently, no doubt trying to second guess his thoughts. In fact, so deep had he been in thought, it was only now he realised the whole room had fallen quiet, that everybody had their eyes on him. This was his test, his moment, the moment of no return. He either had to grasp it, move everyone present in one direction, side by side or risk lighting a fire that could spread who knows where.

"I think we could all do with a drink," he smiled at Vivienne. No one had expected this, the lieutenant could tell by the expression on every face. Vivienne's intense stare moved to a look of surprise to a smile of relief.

"You're right, lieutenant, shall I make some tea?"

"TEA!" It was the daughter. "Maman, when have you ever made tea? You'll be suggesting roast beef next."

Her mother laughed. "I really don't know why I said tea, coffee then?" She looked around the room for approval.

"We're all French, Maman, we need a real drink. Papa has a bottle of cognac in his office, a very special bottle. He showed it to me once. He told me he was keeping it for a very special occasion, though he'd no idea what or when that would be. Well I say we break it open and toast Papa. And", the daughter looked around the room ending with Colette and the lieutenant, "and make a start finding out what really happened to mon père." She finished with a grin. Smiles filled the room.

And to finding out what the fuck is really going on the lieutenant said to himself but in silence. His deliberately broad smile covered his thoughts, "Excellent idea".

"If everyone agrees," Madame Maubert smiled at her daughter, then to the young couple on the sofa. Jean and Camille both returned her smile, each with a single nod, "excellent, then I'll get the glasses". Her daughter quickly disappeared in search of the promised special bottle of cognac. In under a minute she returned with an unopened tear shaped bottle. Holding the bottle at eye level she read aloud the label.

"L'Essence de Courvoisier-Lunar."

"I remember your Papa being given it. It was a present from the mayor to celebrate the millennium. I believe the mayor received it from his friend Pierre de Fauw". Madame Maubert placed her finger horizontally under her nose. There came a scattering of laughter from the room.

"It looks expensive", expressed the daughter.

"If it had anything to do with Pierre, it will be".

"Anybody care?" The daughter made an exaggerated move to open the bottle.

"Noooo." A unified cry went up from the room and the bottle was opened. One by one the daughter, with deliberate slowness filled everyone's glass. As she did so the rain outside became noticeably heavier. The lieutenant lifted the glass to his nose, he was no expert but his senses told him that the liquid in his glass was truly special.

"To Papa," The daughter took a long sip. "To Theirry," Madame Maubert did the same. "To my beloved ex-boss Capitaine Maubert," the lieutenant raised his glass before tasting the liquid within. "To Capitaine Maubert," everyone repeated and drank. Madame Maubert mouthed a silent merci to the lieutenant who bowed his head in response. Nobody except Colette spotted their silent communication. When nearly all were well into their second glass, the lieutenant drew himself up making it obvious to all that he wanted their attention.

"Speech," the daughter said frivolously. Still holding the bottle it was more than obvious she was way beyond her second glass.

"Merci", the lieutenant waved to the daughter then in exaggerated fashion across the room. "Before we go any further I want you to be able to remember what I have to say." The room laughed, exactly what he had wanted. They were at that moment, 'all for one and one for all.' He had to make the most of it. Quietly he raised his glass and took a gentle sip. "To all of those who have passed and are missing from the day of the storm." The atmosphere in the room changed, changed from laughter born out of a quick release from stress, to one of solemnity. All wanted to hear what the lieutenant was going to say next.

"Since the storm," he started, "my job as a gendarme has been something of a living hell. A hell that has been played out in the national and sometimes international media." You could hear a pin drop. "I have faced horrors I never expected to face as a gendarme in a small town like Calais. I've lost a colleague, people who I am close to calling friends and in the capitaine," the lieutenant threw a smile at both the daughter and Madame Maubert, "both a respected colleague and a close, very close friend. Now… " The lieutenant paused. "Now, this is where it becomes even more difficult." The lieutenant let his gaze fall on everyone in the room. "It is pretty obvious, I think, to everyone here that there are avenues of investigation that are being ignored by my gendarmerie." There came a murmur of agreement, from one or two a strong murmur of agreement. The lieutenant held up his glass free hand. "There may be legitimate reasons, reasons I've not been told. Conspiracy theories will not help anyone in this room. Having said that, it is evident that Camille and Jean have a story that needs to be investigated. And if I am going to put my neck on the line and investigate a line of inquiry outside that of the gendarmerie I must have everyone's word that not a word of this gets outside this room. You must not discuss it with anyone, your best friend, your lover, your closest relative, even your dog." There came a trickle of laughter. "If one word gets out, I will drop everything and deny everything. Is that clear?" Once more you could hear a pin drop. "Is that clear?"

"Yes." One by one those present offered their agreement.

"Good and thank you. Firstly, Jean, Camille, you need to tell me what you saw or think you saw." Jean made to speak but the lieutenant stopped him. "Not now, not after this delicious cognac." The lieutenant turned to the daughter. "It really is very good."

The daughter waved the bottle above her head. "Merci Papa."

"Merci," the room chanted.

"As I was saying," the lieutenant spoke quickly, he didn't want to lose the room. "As I was saying, not now and not here. You must promise to never come back to this house again. Someone will see you and start asking questions. Is that clear?" Both Camille and Jean nodded. Colette will take your contact details."

"I already have them." Colette cut in.

"Have they changed"?.

Both Camille and Jean shook their heads, "Non".

"Good, then I will be in touch, as soon as it is convenient to do so. Don't be impatient and go and do something stupid if I haven't been in touch in the next few days. Is that understood?" It was. "Good, now I must thank you for your hospitality, Vivienne, and bid you good evening. You two need to get going too." Camille and Jean in response both finished their glass and stood up. All kissed the hosts on both cheeks. As the lieutenant did so, he whispered his promise to do what he could. Both daughter and mother gave the lieutenant a tight hug. Outside the lieutenant escorted the two to their car. It was still raining heavily but no one appeared to notice. "I will be in touch," he promised. "For now, drive bloody carefully, you're well over the limit, Jean, as am I and I don't want one of my gendarmes picking you up and questioning you." The lieutenant said it with a grin but both knew he was serious.

"We'll take the back roads, we always do."

"Yes well, I don't want to know." The lieutenant held out his hand. When he had finished Colette did the same.

"Bonne chance," she offered as she shook.

Both Colette and the Lieutenant watched as the pair drove off. As they disappeared over the rise, the rain that had been falling thick and fast got their attention. Using his key fob the lieutenant unlocked the doors and both slid in.

"Are you ok ,Colette? You've had rather a lot to drink"?

"Are you lieutenant"?

"I've only had the cognac".

"I didn't mean that".

"What?" The lieutenant paused and for a few seconds there was only the sound of the rain. "You mean what happened back there?"

"Yes, you could lose your job".

"I know".

"Maybe even worse." For a few seconds more there was only the sound of the rain as both contemplated what was meant by this.

"I know," the lieutenant said slowly. "But I'm not a coward, I cannot turn my back on this. I owe too many people. And you Colette, are you happy with it, you didn't say a word inside. Will you help me? Or at least turn a blind eye?"

"I will help you, lieutenant".

"You mean that?"

"Bien sûr". Colette grinned.

Not another word was said. The lieutenant switched on the ignition, started the wipers and a little over carefully moved off.

Not far away another car, smaller, was navigating the standing water in the narrow lanes referred to recently as the 'back roads.' The young couple drove in silence until Camille could bear the silence no longer.

"For God's sake, Jean, put some music on." Jean did as he was told. Leaning forward he turned on the radio. It was already tuned to her favourite music station. A song was just beginning, a song they both recognised. 'Tahitialamaison by Keen' V. Camille turned to her boyfriend who had his gaze fixed straight ahead.

"Fuck, Jean, what's going on, c'est pas normal".

Back at a house in Ardres a mother and daughter were enjoying another glass of cognac.

"What do you think"? Madame Maubert asked her daughter.

"What do I think mother? What do I think? I think I'm going to put some music on".

"What music"?

"Whatever's on the radio. The radio was always tuned to Calais' Radio 6 and connected to a Bluetooth speaker. Madame Maubert enjoyed doing the housework whilst listening to the radio. Seconds later both mother and daughter were standing still with a glass in their hand waiting for the adverts to finish and the music to begin. An English voice came over the speakers and seconds later a tune they both recognised, 'The Funeral,' by Yungblud. At first both stood in shock before breaking into laughter. Neither recognised the significance of the next song, 'Tahitialamaison,' by Keen' V.

Fate works in mysterious ways or is it God. Or are they one of the same?

Chapter
—3—

NCA's Temporary Offices, Gladstone Park, North London, England

Roger Denton of the NCA stood staring at the box on his desk brought to him by security. The guard who had delivered it stood back shocked by the expression on Roger's face.

"Is everything ok, sir? The box has been scanned for explosives or for any kind of booby trap device".

"Who delivered it"?

"Courier, the one always used by the Met, the package is from the Met, Scotland Yard."

'Bollocks' Roger thought to himself and kept the thought to himself. "The delivery will have been captured on CCTV"?

"Yes of course sir".

"I want the footage streamed to my office and I want it now, not tomorrow".

"Yes, sir," the man from security had never seen Roger like this. He looked as though he were about to explode.

"Is there a forensics team still in the building?"

"Yes I think so, I can check."

"No, don't worry, I'll do it, get me that security footage will you".

"Yes, sir", the man from security paused.

"Anything else?" Roger forced his gaze from the parcel.

"Do you want me to leave the parcel with you, is it a threat?"

Roger forced a smile, "No not a threat, more of a message of sorts. That's why I want to know who delivered it and who sent it. If it's from the Met, you can find out?"

"Yes should be a doddle, sir, everything internal from the Met is recorded and tracked".

By 'internal' Roger knew he meant any of the security services. "Then find out will you"?.

"Yes, sir," the man went off looking pleased that he had something to get his teeth into.

Roger watched him go, he hadn't the heart to tell him that his search would probably be fruitless. He walked around his desk examining the parcel with his eyes only. If he was right it wasn't what was in the parcel but whom. And there was something much worse to consider, much, much worse. If the contents of the parcel was whom, and not what, then whoever had sent it was aware of the NCA's temporary offices. Despite all the efforts, the double checking of backgrounds of all the staff, a much-restricted staff at that, despite all of the extra precautions, someone, or worse an organisation, a terrorist group or unfriendly country knew where the NCA were, every step of the way. And perhaps more worryingly for himself, where he was.

He buzzed through to Nick. It was late, he may have gone home.

"Are you alright, boss, I was just about to go home? Want another coffee"?

"No, no coffee Nick, but if you can spare a minute I'd be grateful".

"Coming." Nick put the receiver down. Something was wrong, he sensed it. And it wasn't the blowing up of his house, as if that weren't enough. What the fuck could it be now? He'd promised his wife a night out. Shit, she'd never understand. Whatever his boss wanted he knew it wouldn't be a five-minute affair. 'Married to the job,' was that the expression? He was married to both the job and his boss. That's what it felt like anyway. He wouldn't be married to the woman he loved for much longer that was certain. And who could blame her. Anyway, perhaps it was for the best. With what was happening, no one felt safe anymore. He didn't particularly care for his own safety but he did that of his wife. He'd much prefer to see her re married and happy than in pieces to be scraped off the pavement. Someone or something was playing with them and if everyone was honest they hadn't a bloody clue who it was and just how far they could go. And the question on everybody's lips, why, why, what was their end game? That was the question nobody wanted to ask. And the answer may just be too unpalatable to contemplate.

Ignoring what his boss had said, Nick picked up a couple of cappuccinos on his way. As he entered his boss's office, Roger had evidently forgotten what he had said for he automatically held out his hand and took the coffee.

"What is it, boss"?

"That, Nick". Roger nodded towards the square box sitting on his desk.

"Fuck, you don't think it's a bomb do you?" Nick took a step back; a fruitless gesture and he knew it. If it were a bomb a step back wouldn't save him. It was purely instinctive.

Roger shook his head, he almost laughed. "No, no it's not a bomb. Anyway, security has scanned it."

"Then what?"

"Not what, who. I've seen a box like that before Nick, in fact, two boxes. It's identical to the two that were delivered to my house. One of which I was unfortunate enough to open. The one that contained John's head, the debt collector we'd been looking for." Roger looked at Nick directly in the face.

Nick didn't flinch." Shit, and you think there's a head in there?"

"Not think, Nick, I'm almost certain."

"But whose?"

"I've no idea but we're going to have to find out and there's only one way to do that."

"Not over coffee," Nick managed a smile.

"No, not over coffee," Roger agreed.

"Security will have the delivery logged, and there will be CCTV footage."

"I've already asked for it, Nick, and according to security, the parcel was sent by the Met."

"Crap."

"Yes, I know and security are following that up but we both know they'll never find anything. Whoever is messing with us, Nick, really knows what they're doing and everything about us. Even the fact that we're now located here. This place is meant to be top secret."

Silence fell between the two men, each asking the uncomfortable question, did they trust the other.

"Are you worried for your safety, Rogg?"

Roger stared at the floor, hands in pockets. Nick had called him Rogg, not sir. Had it been meant genuinely, a kind of recognition that they were close colleagues, in this mess together or was Nick a man not to be trusted? A deliberate attempt at getting closer for the wrong reasons. For now, he'd accept the former. He needed a friend and he hoped Nick would be just that. "Do you know, I'm not. Whoever is doing this appears to know everything about me. They've had ample chances to kill me but haven't. It's almost as though they're enjoying playing with me. Like a cat playing with its prey. It's not a nice feeling Nick and why? What are they getting from it? Why are they keeping me alive?"

Nick didn't answer, instead he looked at his boss then across to the parcel and back to his boss.

"When are you going to tell Jane?

"After I've finished my coffee." Both men smiled.

"You didn't answer my question Nick, why are they keeping me alive? Why are they playing, taunting me and the NCA?"

Nick shrugged his shoulders. "Classic reason, they must see some use in you, perhaps one day soon you'll be approached." Nick shrugged his shoulders again. "Who knows." He looked straight at his boss. Roger stared straight back.

"I was worried you might say that." Both men took a sip of their coffee, welcoming the warm distraction. "Nick, how many people work in this building?"

"I've no idea, 150, 200 max, there's the specialist teams, forensics, secretaries, typists, cooks, I could go on."

"And how many do you know personally"?

Nick thought for a second, finishing his coffee but keeping hold of his cup. "To say hello to, to have a chat with, I'd say around sixty to eighty. Who I know well, who I work closely with." Nick shrugged his shoulders again, "perhaps thirty to forty, around ten of those I count as friends, close friends. Why do you ask"?

Roger shook his head, "I don't know, someone in here is passing on information MI5 and this guy that I've been in contact with from the upper echelons of security, believe it must be more than one person. A team working within. But who? I honestly haven't a clue, have you? And how were they recruited? Security have run extensive checks on everyone working here and yet this arrived today, addressed to me personally." Roger actually tapped the offending box sitting on the desk.

"You shouldn't have done that Roger, forensics and all that".

Roger sighed. "I know, it's pure bloody frustration, I'll be honest Nick I'm not sure which way to turn next. Who is recruiting these people, not to mention how and why. Both the bombs at our offices and my house were apparently planted years ago."

"Your house?" Nick cut in. Roger realised he'd said too much.

"Yes apparently so."

Nick spared his boss by not asking any awkward questions. There hadn't yet, as far as he knew, been a full examination of his boss's' broken house', the bomb scene, so how the hell did he know the bomb had been placed there 'years ago'? He stored the question at the back of his mind. "Talking of explosions, the media are going nuts. The Met is still blaming gas leaks, and that it's just unfortunate, but it doesn't take an idiot to see that they're not. MI5 are rolling out gas experts on TV and insisting that the heads of utilities grant interviews and admit that the explosions may be poor workmanship by contractors. The fact that there have been several explosions in a short space of time is simply bad luck. An unfortunate coincidence, but how long they can string that line along I don't know. Thank our lucky stars that nobody so far has picked up that you work for the NCA. That would really cause a storm."

"Jane's seeing to that, any media exposes that association and she'll have their liver on toast for breakfast"

Both men laughed at the image. Roger fondled his empty cup.

"Nick, how many people work here overnight?"

"Skeleton crew, security, until dawn when the teams start arriving. Well you know sir, why are you asking me?"

"I know, just wanting reassurance. Listen Nick I want no one to know about my delivery. I'm going to take it down to my quarters and put it in my fridge. We'll behave as though nothing has been delivered. Thank god security was late with it. Few people would have seen him carrying it through."

"Then what?"

"I'll put a forensics team together, a team I can trust, well feel I can trust, and we'll have them open and examine the parcel in my kitchen. No one else needs to know about it. It'll keep whoever sent it guessing for a while. Their informers won't be able to report back."

Nick pulled a face, "You know sir, the informer may simply be somebody in the typing pool, possibly even a cleaner. All they may know is the address, where we are now and who you are. That's it."

Roger scoffed. "Do you really believe that Nick?"

Nick grinned, "No, no I don't. You do realise your apartment's almost certainly bugged."

"Certainly, not almost," Roger smiled, "I'm very careful where I get changed. Seriously, I don't care. The team I choose will be sworn to secrecy. If anyone asks a question, that person will be put under suspicion. Plan?"

"I'm not sure it's a good one, but yes it's a plan I pose." Personally, Nick couldn't see the point.

"We need to ensure security keeps this under wraps as well." As Roger spoke, the man who delivered the parcel appeared at the door. The door was open but he knocked anyway. Roger motioned for him to come in. He did so, and after acknowledging Nick's presence handed Roger an A4 sheet of paper.

"With the new security measures, I can't send you the CCTV footage electronically, I need special authorisation. I can print you off a still, though. Nuts". The man from security finished with his opinion. Roger took the paper making a noise that translated, I agree fully. He held up the paper so Nick could see too, on it was a photo of a Luton van with the livery of a London courier, used as the man from security had said, by the Met. The van was parked in the front yard and the image captured the driver stepping out of the van.

"Have you checked the registration"? It was Nick who asked.

"Yes", the man from security handed over a second sheet of paper. It was a printout from the DVLA's database. His arms beginning to ache, Roger placed the paper on his desk. The man from security intending to help went to move the parcel, to allow more room. To his surprise Nick grabbed his arm.

"No it's ok, leave it where it is." The man from security drew back, doing his best not to express his shock. "Forensics need to examine it," Nick explained. "We don't want anybody else touching it."

"I don't bloody believe it." Roger's outburst drew both men back to the printout. "The van is registered to Peter fucking Fitch, Peter 'fucking nothing to do with me' Fitch. This guy's taking the piss. He's got to be involved, he's just very clever. He's probably laughing at us now." Roger walked around the room waving in exaggerated fashion his arm in thin air. "Hello, hello Mr Fitch, are you laughing?"

"I really don't think he's involved Roger, someone's using him, just as they're using us."

Roger dropped his arms, "Well if they are there must be a reason why they are, we just need to dig deep and find it."

"There's something else." The man from security was holding up a third sheet of paper, he looked nervous. "I took the liberty of downloading and printing a copy of Mr Fitch's driving licence, and you're not going to like it."

Roger grabbed the paper from the man's outstretched hand and placed it on the desk. The two detectives quickly realised what the security man meant. All the details on the licence were correct, that wasn't the problem. It was the photo. Instead of Peter Fitch, the photo was unmistakably a very good image of the Russian president. President Putin.

A House Somewhere in Mayfair, London

Jane couldn't help being mesmerised by the clear cube held by Orme in the light of the moon. The tiny object floating inside, whatever it was, appeared to be organic and quite dead, though for some reason, Jane suspected it wasn't. It was simply suspended in life. Orme placed the cube on the central table and walked back to the window.

"I love the light of the moon," she let her right index finger slide gently down the glass. It's so pure and its rays, their magnetism affects the human mind, to an extent that some people, when the rays are at their strongest, behave completely out of character. Legends abound worldwide of the power of the moon, look at the European werewolf. Seven thousand years before your Jesus was meant to walk on this earth, people like you and me were respecting the werewolf. An animal that came alive bathing in the light of the moon." Orme turned to look at Jane. "And only now are we truly once again beginning to appreciate its power and how to use it." Orme's dark eyes, the only human part of her form visible shone bright with excitement. Her eyes softened on seeing Jane's expression. "Forgive me Jane, you look tired. Tea? Or would you prefer something stronger?"

"Tea would be lovely." Secretly, Jane craved a brandy or something equally as strong but in Orme's company she needed to keep every wit about her. Jane didn't see Orme give a signal, but the next second the door opened and a slight woman in bright Arab dress entered.

"Chayee," Orme said softly, and the woman in response backed out of the room. 'Chayee was the one word Jane recognised, it was Persian for tea. Before that Orme had been speaking in a language she didn't recognise and yet she somehow understood. And when Jane spoke, she spoke the same language. How was that possible? She thought in English but her words came out quite differently and Orme understood them. Because of this she felt a certain bond with Orme, one she couldn't explain and she sensed it worked the other way around though she had no doubt that unlike her, Orme understood why.

"Everything appears to be going to plan Jane, do you see it that way?"

"If you mean to spread chaos and confusion, yes. Those involved as far as I know haven't a clue what or who they're dealing with. They're running scared."

"Good, which is exactly what we want." Jane was sure could feel Orme smiling beneath her veil.

"What now? Why have you summoned me here?" The door opened and the slightly Arab dressed woman carried a Turkish tray on which sat an elaborate tea pot along with a bowl of cubed sugar and a bowl of fresh mint. Placing the tray on a side table she expertly poured, and without asking, stirred two cubes of sugar along with the mint into each cup. After passing each woman a cup, she left in silence leaving the tray behind. Orme after inhaling the sweet smelling vapour from the tea walked back to the window without drinking. Jane knowing the tea would be good took a long hard sip. It was delicious and somehow revitalised all her senses. No longer did she feel heavy with guilt, she was doing the right thing. Orme, continuing to stare out of the window, spoke softly, slowly and with purpose.

"How much longer will your NCA be in operation?"

Jane took a moment to think. "After today, when I receive a call I'm expecting from Roger, I'll recommend the agency be disbanded, keeping only the mundane operations and those recording data under the NCA banner. All existing files/operations I'll then recommend be passed to MI5 and the Met or relevant authorities."

"What about the agents?"

Jane smiled. "I'll recommend that extra security checks be done on the key agents, mainly those who are friendly and that they be transferred where they will be most needed and most helpful to us. Already some are 'assisting the Met. You chose well with the NCA as we have connections of some sort with all the other agencies."

"What about this Roger Denton, will he come over to us?"

Jane shook her head, "Not a chance." I'm keeping him close to me, he trusts me implicitly but that doesn't mean he tells me everything. Like everybody else he's lost in the confusion you've created." Once again Jane could sense Orme smiling.

"I think we may be able to use Mr Denton and others like him." As she spoke Orme, worked a pattern with her finger in the glass.

"You need to be careful, they've worked out the difference with the beheadings. They'll soon discover who has been responsible for the gangland jobs and will be searching for who is responsible for the others. No matter how careful your operators are, by the nature of their activities, they'll start leaving clues".

"No, we don't want that. "Orme's finger started to move across the glass in a more forceful fashion. "I will be putting an end to that." Jane was sure she heard Orme laugh. A heavy silence fell between the two. Jane knew when not to speak. "I think the ideal opportunity for you to recommend disbanding the NCA will come early tomorrow. I'm expecting a COBRA meeting to be called and you will almost certainly be invited. At that meeting you will have the ear of everyone that matters including the PM. We are slowly weaving our way into the heart of your government, Jane. Their weaknesses are everything we despise. Your people deserve better and we will give it to them. The whole world deserves better and we will deliver, I promise you." At that moment a phone rang. Orme opened a door in a highly polished side cabinet and pulled out a shelf on which sat a large phone. A light flashed in time to the ring. Orme motioned for Jane to come over. "It's Stephan Sands, your Home Secretary. You left your phone with your double back at the safe house?"

Jane nodded, "Yes of course".

"Good then if there's any sort of tracker your phone and presence will be confirmed at the safe house. His call has been diverted from your phone to here but nobody will be aware of that."

Jane picked up the phone. "Stephan?"

"Jane," Stephan's deep aristocratic voice was unmistakable. "Jane, you need to get some shuteye. The PM's called a COBRA meeting for 7am tomorrow morning, usual place."

"That's an ear....."

"That's all, Jane, don't be late, this is serious." The line went dead. Early had been the word Jane had been trying to get out. Once again she could sense Orme smiling. Before she had a chance to ask a question, the phone rang again. The caller ID flashed on a screen. Roger Denton. Jane took a deep breath.

"Roger".

"Jane". Jane already knew one of the reasons why Roger would be ringing her but she sensed there'd be something else.

Orme continued to stare out of the window listening to the intense dialogue between the two senior members of the NCA. They'd got this far. To anyone looking in, it would appear that her organisation was on the verge of total success. But Orme knew that not to be true. Infiltrating and controlling the government was relatively easy. The fact that those who supposedly ran the country were allowed to accept gifts said everything. Those that mattered would be corruptible in some form. The elected were supposed to serve those who voted for them, not those bearing gifts. It was a corrupt system and the reason her organisation in Europe had started with the United Kingdom. The real target though and the hardest to crack would be the upper levels of security. The country had seven levels of security. MPs were only on the seventh rung as were most of those in the NCA. The Prime Minister even was only on level 5. That meant there were four tiers of security and secrecy above him. Secrets that he wasn't authorised to see. Secrets and security he was in complete ignorance of. The people in the top four layers were the real people who ran the country. The men in 'grey suits,' Princess

Diana had called them. These were the people she had to have on her side, even if they weren't aware of it, if her mission was to succeed.

A Wine Bar and Restaurant near Harrods, London, England

After the introductions Charles took charge.

"You, ladies and gentlemen, choose your food and if you don't mind I'll choose the wine. A bottle of red and white so everybody's happy, ha-ha"

Fatima or Ariana as those at her table knew her, had noticed that Charles as well as laughing at his own jokes tended to laugh at the end of every sentence. She gracefully laughed with him whilst equally paying attention to the Home Secretary and his wife. Deliberately she would frequently ask the other man sitting next to her for advice regarding the menu. After all she supposed that they dined there before. Which they had frequently. When asking for advice Fatima would discreetly lean into the man in charge of the Home Office allowing him an enticing brush of her body and a whiff of her perfume, a magic handed to her by the pharaohs of ancient Egypt. Charles decided on a red, Guado al Tasso and for white, a bottle of Bramito della Sala. Glasses were expertly filled and quickly emptied to be silently filled again. Fatima was enjoying the table talk. Charles was full of anecdotes and Henrietta had an incredibly sharp wit. Her husband was less so but he wasn't boring and Fatima could feel the hormonal male inside him desiring her. It was a good start.

Every now and then, she'd glance across at the table with Cuiping and the three women. Not once did Cuiping acknowledge her but every now and again she felt, rather than saw a glance thrown from the table. And instinctively she knew it was Cuiping.

Halfway through the main course everything changed. Stephen, yes it was Stephen now received a call. On taking it, his manner changed completely. Frivolity changed within seconds to sobriety . He stood up.

"Charles, Ariana, it's been a pleasure", he turned to his wife. "Henrietta, I'm sorry my job calls. Will you please all excuse me, there's a car waiting outside for me". He turned to Charles, "Charles, will you…"?

Charles broke in, of course, of course. We'll make sure Henrietta gets home safely won't we Ariana.? Boudicca and wild horses won't stop us ha ha." Henrietta nodded her thanks and grinned at Fatima. Her husband then made a hurried exit, unnecessarily brushing against Fatima as he left. Men are so adolescent, so predictable, how did men ever come to dominate the world? Fatima kept the thought to herself.

"This often happens." Henrietta made to assure Fatima.

"It comes with the territory, anyway more wine for us ha ha." Charles started pouring.

With her target otherwise occupied, Fatima found she was able to unwind and enjoy the remaining company, which somewhat to her surprise, she did. The atmosphere in the wine bar helped. The air was filled with loud talk and bursts of raucous laughter from members and associates of the government letting off steam after the stresses of running the country. Mrs Sands, Fatima soon came to realise, was the stronger of the two in their marriage, and from what she said it was obvious that her husband, the Home Secretary, not only turned to her for advice but to great extent depended on her. What was the Percy Sledge classic? 'Behind every great man there's a woman'. The song was well known both in France and Persia and from what Fatima could see that song epitomised the relationship between the Home Secretary and his wife. She would definitely have to work on Henrietta as well, enter through the back door so to speak.

Charles' chauffeur drove them all home. Henrietta was dropped off at a flat in Belgravia. Fatima, still at work, quickly became aware of a dark coloured saloon with two men in front parked a little way away. Very inconspicuous, and she smiled to herself, looking in the other direction. Next the chauffeur dropped Fatima off at her hotel. She'd half expected Charles to try something on but he didn't. He remained the perfect gentleman, all charm and laughter. As she took the lift to her floor she found herself smiling. She'd had a really good, a really really good evening. For the first time in years she felt happy, contented. Was this what normal life was like? How she longed for it.

NCA's Temporary Offices, Gladstone Park, North London, England

Roger had ushered both Nick and the man from security out of his office before he made a call to Jane. He wanted the call to be confidential. It was probably all a waste of time, whatever method of phone call he chose to use, going by recent events somebody was almost certainly listening in. He started to wonder 'why bother at all' and immediately admonished himself. Self-defeatism wasn't an option, if he let that take over him he and they, the NCA had lost. To whom? Well he was sure they'd soon find out.

Picking up the secure line he put a call through to Jane.

"Roger."

"Jane, how's safe house living?"

"Boring. Despite the risks I think I'll soon be returning to my house. Here, and perhaps I'm doing MI5 a disservice, but it feels very much as if I'm staying in the Big Brother house. That I'm being watched."

Roger made the appropriate noises relating to sympathy and understanding. And his sympathy was very much genuine, he knew exactly how Jane felt. It was beginning to feel as though the NCA's new super-secret offices were taking part in Big Brother too. And worse he was beginning to feel that someone, or more than one person, was watching his every move. It was not a nice feeling.

Jane, not sensing Roger's discomfort stared across at Orme, who remained standing by the window staring down at the softly lit park below, apparently oblivious to her conversation with Roger. Even so, Jane was feeling more than a little uncomfortable having a conversation with one of her closest colleagues with her standing so close.

"What is it, Roger?" The question was voiced in a hushed tone. Roger assumed it was because of her Big Brother comments earlier. In equally hushed tones, he explained about the package on his desk. How it was almost identical to the two delivered days ago to his house, the two that when opened it was discovered contained heads. Heads and genitalia. That he was sure if he opened it, the contents would be the same or similar. Jane pushed him, if it were a head, who it may be, but he genuinely had not a clue and found he had difficulty convincing her of this. He told her that he wanted to keep his delivery quiet and have a specially selected team of forensics examine and open it. And, if the parcel did contain a head to have forensics go over every square millimetre before it was sent to the pathologist.

"You do realise, Jane, that the fact the parcel was sent for my personal attention at this office, at our supposedly secret location, that our security has been compromised. It means somebody, almost certainly someone not particularly friendly to our cause, knows where we're located, where I work and worse still may be following our/my every move. Somebody may even be listening to us".

Jane couldn't help looking across at Orme who was still, apparently nonchalantly, looking out of the window. Was she listening in? If she was, there was nothing she could do about it, and it didn't matter anyway. She had no secrets where the organisation was concerned.

"I doubt it", Jane eventually responded; "MI5 are there to stop anything like that happening. Anyway, Roger, if you're right this is a security breach too far. I've been called to a COBRA meeting tomorrow morning. Whilst there, I'm going to suggest that the NCA be disbanded, for the time being anyway. We'll keep certain teams going, those keeping the records and running the mundane stuff. The more serious stuff we'll have to look at, it may be that we pass our more sensitive files on to MI5."

"Does that include what I'm working on?" Roger could feel his blood rising. Everything Jane said made sense but the thought of passing all his hard work over to some gloating bastard in MI5 brought out something primaeval in him.

The next ten minutes were spent calming Roger's sense of injustice and how what she was suggesting may work. Whatever action was taken they both agreed it must be swift before the worm burrowed further. Roger then went on to talk about Peter Fitch, the ANPR search on the delivery vehicle bringing up his name once more and finally to the DVLA record of his driving licence having, instead of his photo, the photo of President Putin. This confirmed their earlier suspicions, the CCTV evidence supposedly placing Peter Fitch at the Sky Bar at the top of the Hilton, Park Lane, had in fact been taken from a still stored in the DVLA database. That the DVLA database had somehow been hacked. The photo of President Putin on a British citizen's driving licence confirmed not only that the database had been hacked, but much, much worse that whoever had hacked it, could, it would seem, play with it at their will. The two on the line recognised the seriousness of this, it had already been discussed. The DVLA database was for all intents and purposes the UK's unofficial identity card. Proving who you were was harder for a driving licence than it was for a passport. The DVLA database was the main reason why no government, despite all the terrorist threats, had introduced a national identity card. If the database had been hacked and worse still whoever had hacked it could move information around at their will, not only would it create chaos, but it would be an unprecedented threat to national security. And whichever government was in power at the time would almost certainly have to fall on their sword.

Jane instructed Roger to conduct another security search on Peter Fitch, 'There must be a reason why,' she insisted. 'You may even want to interview him yourself,' something Roger had already decided he would do. The next twenty minutes or so were spent going over finer details. At the end, each offered the other good luck and to take care, Jane promising to contact Roger as soon as she came out of the COBRA meeting.

"Keep your head down," were Jane's final words before she rang off.

After she'd gone, Roger sat back in his chair letting his mind wander. Never in his life had he been in a situation like this. In the past with any investigation, there had been a suspect. What he, and the agency were involved in now, was the biggest challenge he, they had ever faced, and he had not one, not even half a suspect. If he was honest, he hadn't a bloody clue who was playing with them. He picked up the printout of Peter Fitch's driving licence. At President Putin staring back at him. Was this intended as a deliberate message from the Russians' that they were responsible? That was the suggestion but using his experience it felt too obvious. It wasn't the Russians' style, they never suggested anything and denied everything. No, it felt to him as though whoever it was wanted them to think that way. To cause an unnecessary diversion. A signpost pointing in the wrong direction, to waste the NCA's resources searching for something that wasn't there.

Why did he think of the expression 'signpost'? Who used that term? Jason bloody Mortimer of, 'I haven't a bloody clue'. What did he call himself now? Roger pulled out his wallet and from his wallet the man's latest card. 'Donald Anas'. How did this man simply walk in here?

Entry was meant to be strictly invitation only and yet he simply walked in. And yet he could be 'batting for the other side' as he had put it to him. Standing up, Roger decided to find out. Closing and locking his door he made his way to the security office. Walking past the various offices, very few people remained at work. Who were they, he wondered, and what were they doing. Scouting each open door, he began to realise how very few people in the building he knew personally and what a narrow view he had of the work that was done here. Where were the leaks coming from, which office, how many offices. As he passed offices that were still occupied the people in them almost always looked up to see who was passing. Some smiled, some simply stared, when it was the latter, he immediately felt guilty. For many, he too must be a suspect, it was not a good feeling. Never had he felt so uncomfortable in his work, and he had been in some tight situations in his career, if career is what you could call his mish mash of operations.

The security office was an almost all window affair. No hiding here. The windows afforded a one-hundred-and-eighty-degree view of the front yard and there were cameras at every corner. A bank of televisions offered the staff in the office a view of virtually every square inch outside. Instant replay was available, and everything caught on camera was automatically recorded. His security level allowed him inside, a rare privilege, most weren't. He buzzed and placed his ID card against the scanner. The door lock clicked noisily, and he pushed hard. The man who had delivered the parcel was there with two colleagues, one scanning the bank of televisions. Rather embarrassed Roger realised he didn't know any of their names. Thank God there were three of them then. He could address them collectively. He'd always been aware how important it was to address people correctly and knowing a name went a long way when wanting respect, or more importantly information.

"Evening gentlemen, may I have a word?"

All three turned to listen, perfect. Behind them he noticed it was raining, that persistent rain that no matter how hard you tried, eventually found a way inside your waterproofs. Living in a bunker you lost track of what was happening on the outside. At first, he'd welcomed the security of living underground, now he was starting to resent it. He was beginning to yearn after the smells of autumn, the dampness in the air and the chill that hinted at winter's dawn. The smell of decaying leaves and the steady patter of rain relieving the drought that was summer. Seeing the outside for the first time in days, Roger made up his mind. Once he'd finished with security, he was going to take a trip. Sod his safety, if whoever was playing him wanted him dead, he'd be dead by now. The poor bugger who committed suicide blowing up his house demonstrated that. He chose to blow it up when he knew he wasn't there. Why? Not wanting to go down that road again he turned his attention to the three men who were standing waiting.

"That parcel I received earlier, the one you've dropped off, Jim," Roger had managed to tag his name badge, he nodded to the man. Jim gave a small smile, the other two didn't move a muscle. "I don't want anyone in this building to know I've received it. I'm not asking you to deny I received it; I know everything must be recorded. I'm simply asking you not to talk about it.

"Why would we?" It was the man who'd been manning the cameras.

Roger realised by his answer that he may have made a mistake by mentioning the parcel. After all, it was just a parcel. By asking them not to mention it, he'd drawn attention to the bloody thing, and it was human nature to talk about the forbidden. He decided to use the gospel where security was concerned.

"It's a matter of national security, the fewer people who know about it the better."

The air tensed as he said this, all three drew themselves up. It had worked.

"Of course," Jim spoke for all three, and the other two echoed their colleague's promise.

Roger put on his best smile. "Thank you, now I need your help. I need the footage of the delivery like yesterday. Did the courier deliver any other parcels?" All three shook their heads. No one spoke. Roger asked another question. "Did you guys spot anything suspicious? The driver's clothes, his manner. Anything about the van?"

Again, all three shook their heads, Jim looked thoughtful.

"Jim?"

Jim shrugged his shoulders "Nothing really, only that the delivery was so ordinary, so slick. The driver hardly said a word. The paperwork was perfect, clean, I signed, and he was gone. And it was a morning delivery, the van should have been full but yours was the only parcel. I thought nothing of it at the time but now that you're asking questions, that was weird.

"Thank you, Jim. I think you guys realise by my questions that we believe this was no ordinary delivery. It's imperative therefore that our conversation remains in this office, especially after what happened to our old offices."

All three men looked deadly serious. They had all lost colleagues, perhaps close friends in the bombing of their old offices. Unless one of them was complicit, Roger had gained, by using one simple phrase, their complete loyalty.

"Good if you can get the CCTV footage for me by the morning, that would be a real help."

The guard who had been scanning the television screens spoke up. "I can't send you the footage, not without clearance but you can, if you want to watch it back, you can do it in here. I can play it back to you now if you want." Roger really needed a still so he could try face recognition, but it wouldn't do any harm to look, there was a remote chance he may even recognise the man. Five minutes later his heart had sunk. He recognised the driver ok. It was a schoolteacher from Wellingborough, he was already known to the security services. It was Peter bloody Fitch. Roger did his best not to show his disappointment and asked the footage to be sent to him anyway. He'd have digital forensics look at it. Not that they'd find anything, he was pretty sure of that.

Roger moved on to his next topic. "I had a visitor today. From my understanding visitors can only be invited and must be registered with you guys first. You let this guy just sail in. I had no idea he was coming. How come you let him in?" The man who hadn't spoken so far spoke now. He was tall, around Roger guessed, sixty years of age with a muscular physique. It was obvious this man worked out regularly. A well-manicured beard only half covered a scattering of scars, and if you looked hard enough his eyes betrayed the fact that this man had witnessed the darker side of life. It was obvious to Roger he was ex-military and almost certainly at one time special services. And it was obvious now he spoke that he was in charge of the shift.

"I can explain that, sir," his voice was steady, hard as granite. It matched his physical appearance. "The gentleman who visited you has the highest security clearance possible. They don't need an invite".

"And his name"? Roger was curious to see which name he had registered under. Jason or Donald.

"I've no idea, sir. Those with the top level of security, for us anyway, simply need the code. We go through a process using their security pass followed by fingerprint, iris and face recognition to confirm their identity and security clearance. All we're given is a number, never a name".

"Can I see the number"? Roger had no idea what he could gain by knowing a number, but you never know.

"I'm afraid not sir, it's classified information".

There you go. Well, if whoever was playing with him could access the CCTV, then it was possible they had access to their security system including security clearance. It would be a much harder nut to crack.

He knew that, but from what had happened in the last week nothing would surprise him.

Thanking the three, he left, to his surprise Jim followed him out.

"Sir, you asked me to trace who had sent the parcel from the Met, Scotland Yard."

"So, it was Scotland Yard?"

"Yes sir, except the officer who supposedly sent it left the force over six years ago."

Roger had half expected that answer. "I don't suppose you asked if anybody over there knows where he is now?"

"Yes, but nobody knows. Or they wouldn't tell me."

"Ok, thanks for trying, Jim." Roger made to move off and stopped.

"What was the officer's name?"

Jim had no hesitation, he was good. "A Superintendent Hulbert, Johnathan Hulbert."

Roger froze. No wonder Jim hadn't managed to get an answer from the Met. Superintendent Hulbert was an ex-colleague. He'd been a plant in the Met, MI6 had placed him there. Not only was he an ex-colleague but he'd once been a colleague of the recently deceased John Mitchell. Was JH, as everyone used to call him, complicit in all that was happening or was whoever it was simply playing a cruel game. Almost certainly the latter and if so, where was JH now? They must know his and John's connection. Somebody was bloody playing games, especially with him, why him? Why the fuck were they picking on him? Was anybody actually who they said they were, especially Mr Donald bloody Anas. Was he for real or someone placed to wind him up even further. To plant diversionary signposts in his brain. And Jane was right to disband the NCA, whoever it was playing with him had got into the NCA's CCTV system. The NCA had become a colander, full of holes. It might as well cease to function. Where he'd go, heaven knows. MI5 were welcome to his files; he no longer gave a shit.

By the time he'd returned to his office, Roger had calmed a little. Just a little but enough to allow his training and loyalty to kick back in. Pulling on a pair of disposable gloves, he gingerly picked up the offending parcel and holding it at arm's length marched over to the lifts. Half a minute later, he was in his apartment. Luckily the fridge had been designed to hold a large number of supplies, even so, Roger still had to remove every shelf before the parcel fitted. He wondered whoever was watching, made of his action and whether they'd report it. Satisfied, he searched for and after more than one curse of frustration, located his car keys. Minutes later, he was approaching the exit longing for the taste of fresh air on his lips. Taking out his pass he placed it on the scanner and waited for the door to open. It didn't, the door remained hard shut. He tried again, same result. He was just about to try 'third time lucky' when the stocky man, the one in charge of security approached.

"I'm sorry, sir, but we're not allowed to let you leave the building until we know where you're going."

"You mean you're holding me prisoner here?" Roger was furious.

The security guard kept his calm, he was used to dealing with extreme reactions. "No sir, you're free to leave, we just need to log where you're intending to go. It's for your own safety. After all, with recent events the measures are in place to protect, where possible, everyone who works here. I'm hoping you understand? Especially with your background."

Roger silently counted to ten, he didn't like the idea of being tagged, especially considering the obvious breaches in security. Logging his intended movements was like broadcasting to whoever it was his diary for the day.

"Look to be honest I just fancy some fresh air, a bit of a drive to clear my head and a burger."

The man from security grinned. "I'll log you're going to McDonald's, according to my log we must be their best customer." The guard chuckled.

"Thank you," Roger grinned back. Two men with similar pasts acknowledging how ridiculous the new security measures were.

Sitting in his car, Roger wound down the window and breathed in, the odd droplet of rain lashing his face. Everything tasted good. Refreshed, he turned on the ignition. He was ready, he knew exactly where he was going, he wanted to see what they had done to his house. The one last bastion of stability in his life gone forever. The bastards, whoever they were, knew what they were doing.

A Street in Ealing, West London.

After she'd come off the phone to Roger, Jane had spent a rare half hour with Orme discussing operations. Orme never gave much away, simply hints of what had been achieved and more importantly what they wanted to achieve next. Jane through their rare conversations quickly came to realise that nearly all Orme's most trusted operatives were women. In fact, she could only ever recall her once ever mentioning a man, and even then, it wasn't by name. Simply that he lived somewhere in Belgium but was becoming increasingly important as part of their operation in the UK. Her role had always been to destabilise the security services, to help spin confusion everywhere. So far, she had managed to achieve that and if she also managed to have the NCA disbanded then, with a little luck and, if she played her cards right, she would have greater access to both MI5 and MI6. At least that was the plan. Other people she knew were in this plot, but she had no idea who they were. Since joining the 'organisation', she'd never been allowed to communicate by phone. It was always by private message, face to face and even then, only after hearing the signal, 'Pitgam'. She had no idea what it meant. She thought it was a strange word.

Driving, she was now approaching her road, or rather the road of her double. The planning by the 'organisation' was ingenious. The road where her double lived ran parallel to hers in leafy Ealing and her actual house backed onto hers. Her double was a respected citizen, Carole Morvan, a regular church goer and the biggest laugh of all, worked at the Met as a police profiler. It was a common joke that she lived so close to the head of the NCA. No one suspected that they were, when needs required, each other. A wig, neckerchief and a touch of makeup and, within minutes Carole Morvan, became Jane, head of the NCA. Not only that, her voice, her mannerisms even how she thought was her, Jane. It was like watching a hologram of herself. The same couldn't be said in reverse. She could look like Carole, but that was it. As a result, she only portrayed Carole at a safe distance. In any case she rarely played Carole, it was always the other way around. When she needed to contact the organisation. When she needed to escape her real self.

With a deftness that demonstrated years of habit Jane pulled Carole's car, a 2013 Ford Focus into the drive. The house as far as the authorities were concerned was inherited from Carole's parents. Parents who existed on paper only. It was far too big for a single person, and for appearances sake Carole was always moaning about its upkeep and that one day soon she would downsize. For as long as Jane lived on the other side of the fence, that would never happen. Once inside the house, Jane turned on several lights as well as the television. Anyone watching - there wasn't - would simply think the occupier was settling in for the evening before retiring to bed. After making a cup of coffee, she sat down to watch the news. The explosions in North London were still news but not headline news. Both were still being peddled as gas explosions and it looks as though the media were accepting it. A documentary would play in an hour asking, 'How safe is our gas'? Jane decided not to watch it. There was nothing about the hacking of the DVLA database, worse still the taking over of it, but the security agencies wouldn't be able to gag the media for much longer. It was all over social media. After only a few minutes on Facebook she had seen driving licences with photos of monkeys, sheep, Highland cattle, all types of dogs, as well as famous people, mainly politicians and world leaders. In particular Kim Jong Un, the 'Supreme Leader' of North Korea appeared to be very popular. Jane smiled at the thought of the politicians trying to sort this mess out. They would be blaming everybody but themselves. Orme had told her this evening that the hack would only last for a couple of days after which they would allow the database to return to its original status. She'd gone on to say that no matter how hard they tried, they'd never discover where the hack came from. That they wouldn't be searching for anything organic. What Orme had meant by that, Jane hadn't a clue.

The next moment 'breaking news flashed up on the television screen. 'DVLA database hacked'. The female presenter went on, after announcing what was a very serious hack to detail the various examples/ consequences of the hack. Photographic specimens of the hack sent in by victims were presented on screen. The owner's personal details were always blacked out, leaving the offending photo. After a series of animal faces the slide show finished with an image of Kim Jong Un. Returning to the newsreader it was obvious she was trying not to laugh. Jane found herself doubled up and laughing too. No one could see her, but millions were watching the newsreader. No doubt when the transmission had ended, she would get a serious bollocking.

Recovering herself, the presenter went on to highlight the seriousness of the situation and that the Prime Minister recognising this had called a COBRA meeting early tomorrow morning, after which there would be an announcement. That was all for now. The next article was on students still needing counselling due to not being able to attend college or university during the pandemic. Jane scoffed. Your grandfathers were almost certainly fighting in WW2, and you need counselling because you couldn't go to school. Pathetic, Jane turned the television off in disgust. She looked at her watch. It was almost 10pm. She yawned, she needed her bed, not a bed in this house. Her own bed. The organisation had devised a system where via the rear gardens she could enter her house without being seen. A vine covered walkway encircled Carole's garden. From a side door which wasn't overlooked, she could enter this and follow it around until it met the fence separating the two gardens. One of the fence panels was on gliders, sliding this across she stepped into her garden closing the panel behind her. A carefully placed collection of shrubs then provided her a clandestine route to her cellar. Twelve steps led down to the cellar door. A typical motion activated security light protected the entrance picking out anything that moved but Jane had a fob which turned it off and on again only when she was inside. After locking the door behind her Jane climbed the stairs to her hallway. The only light was from the streetlight outside, there was a full moon, but low clouds were only allowing the occasional ray to pass.

Jane shivered; her house was cold but she dared not put the heating on. If anyone was watching a little green light might, if they were profes-sional, attract unwanted attention. Doing her best to avoid the windows she climbed the stairs to her bedroom. Her bed was a welcome sight. Silently she undressed until she stood only in her knickers and the scarf around her neck. Standing at the bottom of her bed she gazed out of the wide bay window onto the street below. The first thing she noticed was her hedge had been trimmed, the tiny front lawn mown and her bins put out onto the street. Her gardener had been, Jane smiled. The fact that he had was a symbol of both normality and regularity. Jane craved both, nothing in her life was regular or normal. She turned her attention to the street; cars were parked but there was no sign of anyone sitting in one. Evidently the Met's budget didn't stretch to keeping an eye on the house of the head of the NCA. Jane smiled again; they would live to regret that. Early tomorrow morning she would walk out of the front door, and no one would suspect that the woman entering the house was not the same woman exiting. Just as they hadn't suspected anything yesterday evening.

Shivering again Jane broke her gaze from the scene outside and walked over to a full-length mirror behind the bedroom door. Slowly she untied her scarf and let it drop to the floor. Taking a step closer, she examined her neck. The scar was brighter than usual, a sign she'd come to understand that she was either in a state of stress or excitement. Probably both, she admitted to herself. Gently with her right little finger she followed the scar left to right around her neck. She sighed, closing her eyes. It was as though it had happened yesterday. She relived the shouting, the excited babble of voices. The sand abused her mouth. Knees belonging to several men held her down. She tried to spit, to rid the sand from her lips but nothing came out. The man with the knife laughed. He misunderstood. He thought she was trying to spit at him. He spat back, more than once, his foaming saliva blurring her vision. That with hindsight had probably been a blessing.

"Allahu Akbar" the man holding the knife shouted. He raised the knife high above his head. Through the man's spittle Jane could just make out the blade flashing as it caught the light of the Afghan sun.

"Allahu Akbar", the small but over excited crowd chanted. What they lacked in size they made up for with fervour.

Jane knew what was coming and someone pulling her hair, so her head arched back exposing her neck confirmed it. To her surprise, it didn't hurt. She felt something hard slide across her neck, and then something warm and wet against her skin. Whoever had been pulling her hair let go and her head fell sideways. Pain racked her body as several of the crowd presumably kicked her. She tried to cry out but found that she couldn't. Then came the spittle as one after another the ensemble unloaded their disgust on her. There came more shouting, then silence. More silence then the buzzing of flies, flies she soon felt on her exposed skin. At that moment, she actually wanted to die and die quickly.

Jane once more touched the scar that remained a constant reminder of that day. A single tear slowly rolled down her left cheek. She didn't bother to wipe it away, instead she watched it until it lost its grip on her face and fell to the floor. It was the organisation who had saved her. They had realised her value and therefore saved her for their own purposes perhaps, but nonetheless they had saved her, which was more than she could say for the elected politicians. She spat at her mirror watching her spittle slowly slide down the glass. Corrupt self-serving bastards, with no experience of real life. She hated each and every one of them and she wanted to bring each and every one of them down. They had abandoned her in Afghanistan, used her and left her to die. As she did every time she looked at her scar, Jane's mind wandered back to the beginning of where she was now. The day she started at Hendon, training to become a police officer. After only years in the force, she had found herself yearning for more. Adventure was what she wanted, there was a huge wide world out there and she wanted to see it, experience the people who lived in it. She had joined the army, and her wish had been granted. She had been sent to places far and wide, some of which she never knew existed. Maybe because of her dedication and sometimes blind loyalty and in particular her acumen she had been approached to transfer to the military wing of the security services.

She had jumped at it and had quickly found herself working undercover in many of the hellholes on earth. Her last placement had been Afghanistan. Her mission, to recruit local women to work undercover in their country, reporting back to the British government. Her translator was a lovely man whose name was Mukhtar. When he spoke English, it had been with a Brummie accent which had on occasion made Jane laugh out loud. Every day she wondered where he was now, had he too, like her, been abandoned by the British government? One day she hoped to find him, to be reunited. Her efforts with the Afghani women had met with great success. Then without warning it was announced, led by America, all the Western powers were pulling out. What followed can only be described as panic and chaos. She'd found herself alone, without any sort of escort, in a remote part of the country close to the border with Tajikistan. Her reason for being there to recruit and report on the trafficking routes from and into the county's northern neighbour. Up until then she had built up a good rapport with many of the locals, both men and women. With the departure of the West, many of those she recruited felt betrayed and one of those, being disillusioned, gave her up to the Taliban. The result, the scar on her neck.

If it hadn't been for the organisation, as everyone she knew who worked for it, called it, she'd have died an inglorious death. Her corpse was cleaned to the bone by flies and anything else that took a fancy to her decaying flesh. Days after her attempted execution she had woken in a reasonably well-equipped medical establishment, she still didn't know where. And she had no idea how long she'd stayed in its care, a long time, that's all she knew. And that it had taken weeks to get her voice back, possibly even months, time had simply ceased to exist.

She had no idea how she'd got there, but one morning she woke up in a different room and it turned out she was in a hospital in Turkey. Within hours, a representative from the British Embassy in Ankara had visited her, interviewed her and arranged for her passage home. Upon her arrival in the UK, she had been taken to a military base where she'd undergone some intrusive medical examinations and an equally intensive debriefing. Surprise surprise the government now cared. Not for her though, they'd wanted information. They wanted to know who had helped her, how she had managed to get from where she'd been left for dead to a hospital in Turkey. The answer was she genuinely didn't know. An answer they refused to accept. Eventually she was however allowed to go home and at the same time, told because of her neck injury the army no longer had a place for her. They abandoned her with very little thanks or ceremony.

For a while she had been lost until one day a complete stranger stopped her in the street. He told her he was from the people who had saved her and helped her get out of Afghanistan and that the people he worked for wanted to help her once more. The only condition was that in return she had to promise to help them. With nothing to lose she had agreed. The next day she had been taken to a house in Mayfair, a house she now knew belonged to Orme; she doubted that Orme actually lived there. There, after a welcome cup of tea, mint tea she had been led to a plush room somewhere in the basement. She had no memory of what had taken place there, only that when she had left, she'd felt like a million dollars, that the world was her oyster. Days later she had applied to rejoin the police force and had immediately been accepted. Because of her background after only weeks, she'd been promoted and transferred into a specialist unit. Months later the NCA came knocking and she transferred there and put in charge of her own department. Only at this point did she get the feeling that a person or persons were pulling strings for her. Around six months went by during which her team had been regularly praised for nearly always returning good results, when her predecessor was tragically killed in a road accident. The search went out for a new head of the NCA, she was approached and on advice of the organisation immediately accepted. The rest is history; something of a meteoric rise from an angry lost soul to head of the NCA.

She'd had no qualms about accepting the organisation's mission and the role they wanted her to play in it. She hated the establishment and everything it stood for. Now, a couple of years later, she was beginning to wonder what the organisation's goal was. She knew her mission and to some extent Orme's but what was the eventual aim, the end goal? To rid the world of corrupt and incompetent leaders especially men.

To let women have the dominant role in how the world was managed. Orme had once said to her, 'religion is often blamed for wars and warfare, but in truth it is never religion, it is the male species. They are almost entirely responsible for every war staged on this earth since the beginning of history. And who suffers most? The planet and every innocent living creature on it. If this male madness is not stopped there will soon no longer be an earth, at least not a habitable one'. This had hit home with Jane; she couldn't agree more. And she still did agree, she was beginning to question some of the organisation's methods and who were their backers, where did they get their money from? Orme, by her dress, was obviously of the Islamic faith but many others she'd met from the organisation were not, they were from all kinds of faiths. And she'd quickly learned that the organisation was pretty extensive, that it had operatives everywhere including not a small team in the NCA. The organisation, organisation, organisation, that's all she ever heard. What was its name? She knew it had one, as someone within its ranks had once told her. The woman had then clammed up and refused to say any more. Why was the name such a big secret? Jane let out a long sigh, whatever her misgivings she knew she had no choice but to keep with the long haul. Any attempt to jump ship she had no doubt would result in her losing her place on the earth that the organisation was wanting to save.

Tearing herself away from the mirror Jane climbed into bed. She had to be up, washed, dressed and ready by 5.30 in the morning when she was expecting her double. She knew exactly which outfit she had to wear; her double would be wearing the same. Welcoming the false feeling of security the quilt gave her, Jane's eyes slowly closed. Her last thought before she fell asleep was of Roger. Roger was one of the good guys. Roger had experienced the same horrors as she, just as his ex-colleague John had, God rest his soul. Just like her, Roger had been thrown by His Majesty's government into the world's cesspits with little, sometimes, no reward. After all the abuse he was still fiercely loyal. He would never take the path Jane had chosen, if he found out, he would probably kill her. Jane's eyes closed shut.

A Street Somewhere in Bushey

It felt good being behind the wheel of his car. His car was the one thing left in his life that gave him any sense of normality. The car was his and the contents within it his, even rubbish and an old coffee cup at that moment he considered friends, good friends. They were a memory from a normal day and right now a normal day felt a long time ago. The M1 was still busy and the rain prevented the human desire to speed. Roger didn't care, as long as he got to where he wanted to go haste could take a back seat. Fiddling with his car stereo, Roger found REM and pressed play. The sound of 'Losing my Religion' soon filled the car's interior. Most appropriate, Roger actually smiled, that's exactly how he felt, cornered. He just wished he knew by whom.

The next song, 'Everybody Hurts', dampened his mood and he turned the music off. Another time. The rest of the way he'd drive in silence. Roger exited at Junction 5 turning left and at the next, right, to pass the entrance to Costco. As he did so his mobile rang, glancing down at his phone on the passenger seat, he immediately recognised the caller, D.I. Johnson of Havant Police Station. Reaching for the phone, he pressed, 'I'll call you back'. Returning his concentration to his driving, he immediately became aware that his two second phone action had caused him to veer into the lane of oncoming traffic, and there was lots of it. A startled female driver swerved left to avoid him, her male passenger with both hands in the air, 'what the fuck.' At the sound of several horns Roger swiftly pulled his car into the left lane. Shit, he needed to concentrate, his visit to his former residence he wanted to keep low key. A head on collision would, if he was still alive, blow his visit out of the water and the media quickly connect him with the destroyed house. They would dig and it wouldn't take long for them to discover where he worked. After that there would be more digging and the gas explosion would be revealed for what it really was, a lie, and the truth revealed that it was an explosive device. The Met would be bombarded with questions, something they really didn't need right now.

Steadying his nerves, Roger slowed so that he was within the speed limit. He had to be careful or Jane would ban him from leaving his quarters in the NCA's bunker. A fate he couldn't bear thinking about. For the rest of the way, which was only eight minutes, he drove as though a police car was following him, impeccably. Approaching his road, he half expected it to be taped off but it wasn't. Bracing himself he, with precision driving controlled entirely by nerves, swung right. Roger immediately saw the police presence where his house had been, as he approached the pile of rubble which had once been his home came into view.

"Move along, sir, please," A policeman in a high visibility jacket waved his arm. He was tired of morbid spectators, 'disaster tourists' his boss called them. And here was another. He couldn't understand why the entire road couldn't be closed. "Move along, sir, come on there's nothing to see here."

Roger thought about producing his ID, instead he decided against it, accelerated, turned left at the end of the road and left again down one of the many roads parallel with his. Finding a parking space, he got out and after grabbing a raincoat from the boot walked briskly back to his road putting the raincoat on as he went. As he turned into his road his pace slowed, it wasn't deliberate but a nervous reaction. He hadn't expected to feel like this. His Majesty's government had trained him to deal with every kind of crisis, however this was personal. He didn't expect to feel like this. He was amazed to see the pub next door to his house open. He'd been sure the authorities would close it for a few days, citing safety or to use it as a temporary base, but no. The lights were on and looking through the windows it looked as though they were pretty busy. He immediately remembered his last night there, when he was drunk and returning home to discover the head of an ex-colleague, a man his entire department had been looking for, in a box in his garage. The memory caused acid to rise in his throat and he determinedly swallowed. He was not going to allow himself to be sick. Coming to a standstill he stared at the blackness that had once been his home. He'd expected it to be floodlit with an investigation team crawling all over it, but it wasn't and there wasn't. The area was fenced off but that was all. So dark was it, he could hardly make out what was left. The rain continued to fall but he was oblivious to it. This was his moment, staring at the blackness he deliberately recalled his last moments in his lounge. Glass in hand watching the revellers in the street where he was now standing and listening to Ane Brun singing his favourite version of 'All My Tears'. The memory was now so vivid he was virtually reliving it. He wanted to cry but his training wouldn't allow him. 'Under torture you must not show emotion.' As he played the song through his mind, some would claim God was listening, the clouds parted and moonlight flooded the ground. Roger stared at the pile of crumpled masonry that had once been, according to the estate agent, a desirable Victorian dwelling in a sought after location. The moonlight somehow gave Roger a new found peace, the light he found respectful. As though an invisible hand were pulling them, the clouds closed and the moonlight blotted out. It was enough, Roger had no desire to ever come back here.

"Sorry, sir, do you mind moving on, there's nothing to see here." It was the same policeman who had moved him on earlier. This time Roger pulled his ID.

"This is my house," he whispered. The constable's face was a picture, his mouth frozen. "I don't want any fuss." This time Roger's whisper was a little more urgent.

"One minute, sir." The policeman walked over to one of two police cars parked outside. After a conversation through the driver's window, a tall man in plain clothes got out. With what Roger recognised as a 'put on' casual gait, the man approached.

"Roger Denton?"

Roger nodded, "Yes I just wanted to see for myself what was left".

"Not much, I'm really sorry. I was warned. Sorry, wrong word, but you know what I mean, that you may be coming".

Roger refrained from asking by whom. "Stupid I know, I just wanted to see."

"I would, if it were me." There followed an uncomfortable silence.

"I thought the place would be lit up like a stadium and crawling with investigators. And I'm amazed the pub's open." Roger nodded in the pub's direction.

The man in civvies looked across. "Those who know better than us, don't want it to be seen that we're making too much of a fuss. I assume you know why." The man looked straight at Roger. "The reason why this," the man waved his head, "the street is open, the pub and why we're sitting outside."

"Sorry," Roger managed a smile.

"Don't be, why don't you go and have a drink? If you want more than one, if you're not daft I'll have one of my officers escort you back."

"Thanks, but it'll be just the one."

The officer in civvies nodded once. "Ok, enjoy it." And he moved off returning to his car having never disclosed his name or rank.

Roger watched him until he was back in his car and the door shut. Only now did he notice the rain, he was soaked. Without taking another look at the mess that had once been his house he moved swiftly to the pub. The pub was busy, those who recognised him looked up, surprised. Roger nodded to a few, whilst avoiding chatting. At the bar he had to wait until three other customers were served, including one ordering for a large table. The landlord, seeing him, nodded.

"I'll be with you, Roger."

Roger smiled his thanks. He pulled at his soaked trousers, they were clinging to his legs. Behind him he could feel several pairs of eyes watching him, no doubt talking about him. He silently prayed they all stayed in their seats. The last thing he wanted was sympathy coupled with embarrassed small talk. He pulled out his phone and leant heavily on the bar playing with the digits. He wasn't looking for anything in particular, just sending a message, 'leave me alone'.

"Just coming, Roger."

Roger smiled again. "Take your time, you always have done in the past".

The landlord laughed, "Thanks", and reached for the card machine.

As he did so, a call came through on Roger's phone. Once again it was D.I. Johnson of Havant police station. And once again, Roger pressed the automatic, 'I'll call you back'. Havant police station, to an extent where all this mess had started. He didn't trust his phone, he had little or no doubt that someone was listening to his calls.

"What will you have, Roger"? The landlord had finally got to him.

"The usual".

"Which is?" Roger was just about to tell him when the landlord cut in. "Just joking, Neck Oil?"

Roger smiled, yes, the landlord was ex-military, humour was important in a situation such as his. Roger welcomed it.

"There you go," the landlord slid the beer onto the bar. Roger reached for his wallet. The landlord stopped him. "This one's on the house mate, but don't tell anyone or you'll ruin my reputation".

Roger laughed, "thanks".

"I won't ask how you're feeling, I know you're feeling like bollocks".

"Thanks".

The landlord leaned close signalling for the girl filling the washer to serve. "It wasn't gas though was it, someone planted something nasty in your house?"

His question took Roger completely by surprise, and his hesitation was a giveaway.

"You know I'm ex-army, Roger, I know the difference between, gas, explosives and a bomb and what they did to your house was a neat job, very neat. I don't expect you to tell me anything, I get that and I've no idea why you're here, but if ever you need my help, I still have contacts." The landlord tapped his nose, "And we look after each other, anything you tell me won't go any further. You know that." The landlord tapped his nose again.

Roger took a sip of his beer, his phone was ringing again. D.I. Johnson, once more he pressed, 'I'll ring you later.' He looked up at the landlord. "Thanks, why am I here? I just wanted to see, that's all, just to see".

"I get that".

"And thanks….."

"Doug," the landlord helped.

For all the years he'd been drinking in the pub, Roger realised he didn't know the landlord's name. He'd probably been told on more than one occasion but it had never registered. "Thanks Doug," Roger looked at his phone, "actually there is something you can help me with, have you got some paper and an envelope, just one sheet of paper?"

"I've no idea, I'll ask Sally."

Roger assumed Sally was his wife. The landlord disappeared out back, he could hear him shouting. A couple minutes later he returned, "There you are, it took a while. I can't remember the last time we posted a letter and I assume you'll need this". The landlord handed Roger a biro.

"Thanks, safer than electronic."

The landlord nodded his agreement and pushed himself off the bar to serve.

After wiping the bar dry Roger placed the paper on the bar. Taking a sip of his beer he paused to think. Music entered his ears, up until now there hadn't been any. The landlord had turned the music on, he was good, very good. He knew all the subtleties when dealing with trauma. 'Getting away with it all' by James played over the speakers. And that's exactly what was happening, they were getting away with it all. More determined, he took another sip of beer and started to write. ' Hi Detective, sorry I missed your calls. Can't call on this phone neither must you on yours. Go and buy a 'burner' phone. (Hate the expression,) write down its number and post it to me first class. This address, The Hare and Hounds. Roger stopped.

"Doug."

"Hang on," the landlord passed his customer to the girl who had worked for him as long as Roger could remember. He walked over, "Yes?"

"What's the address here?"

The landlord looked surprised, "Well you should know, you've lived next door for years. Same road, same post code, just The Hare and Hounds".

Roger slapped his head. "Of course, sorry".

"Don't let the bastards get to your head or they'll win." The landlord went back to serving.

He was right. The Hare and Hounds, Greenland Road, Bushey, WP23 2HA. Roger folded the paper neatly and slid it into the envelope the landlord had given him. Sealing it he addressed the envelope. 'For the personal attention of D.I. Johnson, Havant Police Station, Civic

Centre Road, Havant, PO9 2AN'. Satisfied, he went back to his pint. The landlord sidled over.

"All good?"

"Thanks, yes, can you do me a favour?"

"I said I'd help if I could."

"You did," Roger held up the sealed envelope. "Can you post this tomorrow, guaranteed next day delivery?"

"Consider it done, and I won't take your money."

Roger removed his hand from his pocket. "Thanks and is it alright if the recipient posts a reply to me here?"

"Of course." The landlord, Doug, took the envelope from Roger's hand. "How will I let you know when a letter's arrived?"

"You won't, I'll be back to pick it up in a couple of days."

"Fair enough."

Roger finished his pint. "Thanks and thanks Doug. Duty calls." Roger pushed himself from the bar.

"Look after yourself and remember, I know people."

Roger nodded and walked out, nodding to the same people he'd nodded to when he'd walked in. Outside to his annoyance it was still raining. He buttoned up his coat. He couldn't help but glance over to where the police cars had been parked. The one with the man in civvies had gone, replaced by a marked police car. He didn't care, someone was up to silly games, let them play, see if he gave a toss. Pulling up his collar, he half walked and half ran back to his car. Inside he turned on the ignition and the fan to clear his windows which were already steaming up. His mind went to the landlord, Doug. Could he trust him? He hoped so. He realised there was virtually nobody he trusted anymore. Only Jane perhaps. Windows cleared, he pulled out, going back the way he came. All the time he kept checking his mirror. He was pretty sure no one was following him.

In just over half an hour, he was pulling into the secure parking at Gladstone Park. Security acknowledged him as he entered, they were a different team to the one that saw him leave. Most of the lights were either off or dimmed, a sense of calm descended at night. A false sense of security. He stopped by his office, no messages. After taking the lift he entered his apartment. He waved to the cameras he believed were there. He couldn't resist opening his fridge. The box was still there, it hadn't been touched. Roger gave an involuntary shiver and closed the door. After taking a strip wash, he made himself a coffee and retired to bed. Turning on the tv he tuned to Sky News. The explosions in north London were old news. All over the news was the hacking of the DVLA database. The Prime Minister had made a speech. Roger watched it. 'Rest assured' was basically the message, we're dealing with it and everything will soon be rectified and back to normal. Crap, Roger grinned. "You know fuck all", he shouted at the telly. "Typical politician bullshit". Next came a bit of fun. Images of various affected driving licences were displayed on the screen. Which animal are you?, the presenters laughed, 'or bird'. The picture of the head of a chicken flashed up on screen. 'Perhaps you can ask for your favourite pet to be displayed on your licence'. Both presenters laughed again. 'Of course there is a very serious side to all this'. "The producer's had a word in your ear." Roger shouted at the screen. Next, a face Roger recognised filled the screen, the assistant commissioner of the Met. His message was for people not to take advantage of the hack. His officers would prosecute anyone driving illegally. 'Good luck with that', Roger had some sympathy. If the hack wasn't solved quickly all hell could break loose on the roads of the UK. 'Not my problem.' Roger's coffee cup slipped from his hand, the warm liquid quickly spreading across his quilt. He didn't notice, his eyes were closed. He was no longer conscious.

CHAPTER
—4—

Cap Blanc Nez, Near Calais, France

"Bonjour Capitaine Olivier Vendroux".

The capitaine stared in disbelief, rain battered his face and the wind battered his body. There was no mistaking he was at the mercy of the three men before him. Was this how his predecessor had died? He didn't know the details but those two stupid children who had entered his office were right. His predecessor had been pushed. Was this now going to happen to him? The wind whistled past him, below he could hear the waves battering the chalk wall that was Cap Blanc Nez.

"What the fuck do you think you're playing at?" To his surprise, the man before him held out his hand. He had little choice but to take it. The man doing the talking gripped it hard and pulled him close so their faces almost touched. Capitaine Vendroux felt himself go limp an action that was embarrassingly involuntary. "Are you mad?" The man whispered through clenched teeth. The capitaine struggled to find a response, he didn't really understand what this man meant. Without warning the man loosened his grip and at the same time gave a little shove. The capitaine felt himself falling backwards, this was it, this was the end. His hand hurt as the man gripped him hard. He let out a yell. "Is this what you want?" The man softened his grip a little. The capitaine looked down wildly.

"S'il vous plait, non," his plea for mercy was hardly more than a whisper. It felt like minutes, tens of nauseating minutes, when in fact, it was seconds. There came a jerk and he felt himself being pulled and then thrown to safety. The capitaine tripped and fell forward onto the sodden earth. The two men accompanying the speaker hauled him to his feet. And when upright held him steady by his arms.

"Find his car keys."

One of the men expertly searched the capitaine's pockets. After only seconds the keys were thrown to the speaker's outstretched hand.

"I'll drive his car, you two take him inside. And no resistance, you've already caused enough trouble." The latter phrase was directed at the capitaine. The capitaine didn't argue, instead his reply was to retch and vomit, where a short while before he'd been lying on the ground.

The speaker pulled a face "Get him inside."

Capitaine watched helplessly as the stranger who did the talking walked off with his keys. Seconds later, he recognised the familiar sound of his Alpine roaring into life. The next minute the two men holding him started marching him towards the road, always he noticed out of view of the carpark and the track feeding it. At the road, the D940, they waited until they were sure there was no passing traffic and ran him across. After the road, the two guarding him led him beneath the restaurant on the summit of Mont d'Hubert directly below which shone the lights of the village of Escalles. For a fleeting second, he thought about making a run for it, but the thought rested only for a second. He had to simply wait and discover his fate. Anyway if they'd wanted to kill him they would have done so when he was being dangled on the top of Cap Blanc Nez. After passing beneath the restaurant they started to climb. The going underneath was rough, the ground with the rain treacherous, and the wind and rain together, draining. It wasn't long before the capitaine could see where they were leading him. It was the restaurant on the summit but not the public entrance, the service area.

After bundling him down a bank, he found himself standing between a number of rubbish carts, each labelled a different colour.

"Par ici." It was the first time one of his captors had spoken and was followed by a rough push. The end of their adventure, the capitaine could see was a simple paint peeling door. There was an industrial bell push, unlit, to the right of the door and the man who still hadn't said a word pushed it. The capitaine could hear the bell ringing inside. They didn't have to wait long before the door opened. A man of North African appearance stood inside. He looked distinctly displeased.

"Mon Dieu, Mon Dieu," he waved his arms, signalling for the capitaine to come in. "vite, vite."

The capitaine did as he was told. He was soaked through, his mouth full of the taste of vomit and he was shaking with cold. No matter what awaited him inside, it had to be better than where he was now. The push wasn't needed but he received one anyway. The door closed behind him and he was left alone with the displeased looking North African.

"Follow me," the man half trotted down the brightly lit corridor ahead. On the walls were a number of posters mainly detailing workplace practices, and many of those official, supplied by the Ministere du Travail. The capitaine guessed rightly that he was in the staff area of the restaurant on the summit of Mont d'Hubert. "You can clean up in there." The North African opened a door to a washroom, "there are clean towels. And be quick, I am very busy. I'll wait here."

"Merci," the capitaine just about managed his thanks. He wasn't used to being talked to like this, especially from a North African, a 'Beur'. The capitaine, realising he was no longer in danger, was beginning to regain his confidence and with it his natural arrogance. Capitaine Olivier Vendroux would soon be back.

A House in Coulogne, near Calais, France

Lieutenant Beaufort sat in his lounge staring out at the rain running down the glass patio doors to his garden. In his hand he held a bottle of 3 Monts beer. So deep was he in thought he was hardly aware he was holding it.

There had hardly been a word exchanged between him and Colette on the way to dropping her off. Both of them had been too deep in thought, something that had stayed with him. The one question both had asked the other, 'are you sure about this?' Both knew, although it was unspoken, that they could lose their jobs if it was found that they were a) disobeying orders and b) running their own investigation. Worse still, under French law they could both spend some time in prison. It may be seen as betraying the state.

The lieutenant took a swig of his beer. Thankfully, his wife had already gone to bed by the time he'd got home. She would have immediately spotted something was different and interrogated him until the truth came out. He didn't want her to have to share his burden, not yet anyway. There may be a time in the future when she may have to. He'd cross that bridge when it came.

His mind went back to the so-called 'storm of the century'. That had been the start of everything that had happened since. The mutilated body of the girl on the beach. The severed heads, all, according to Monsieur Hubert the pathologist at Boulogne, were surgically removed. The migrant who claimed his fellow migrants were being kidnapped, that they never arrived in the UK. The same migrant whose decapitated head ended up being delivered to his wife in London. Where was the rest of him? Here in France or in London where the poor man's head is resting in a police morgue? The poor man's claim after the death of Capitaine Maubert had been dropped, no longer investigated. He made a note to look into the claim again. Then there were the bodies of the poor mutilated children found on a boat in La Manche, in a boat registered in the UK. Their investigation had barely begun when their bodies were shipped back to the UK. In secret and under heavy guard. An operation he had been part of. He made a note to speak to the pathologist, Monsieur Hubert. That wouldn't be easy, the pathologist was of the old school and adhered to every rule, even those that weren't there. He'd have to be very careful in his approach, the last thing he wanted was him contacting their new capitaine. Thinking of London, he remembered the missed calls from London. From the offices of the NCA. He couldn't remember the man's name but Colette would have it listed. He'd ask her tomorrow. His mind dwelled on the missing dead moving to the missing living. What the hell had happened to Marie? One of their own, a colleague of his. Both vanished into thin air. As had the couple harbouring the migrant whose head had ended up in London. Ismail that was his name. What had happened to them. Because of his country's liberal laws on the 'right to disappear', their disappearance had only been a cursory investigation. They may even be mixed up in all of this. He made another note. His mind went back to his missing colleague and to Pierred de Fauw, who had been seen in the vicinity of his colleagu's last known location and had been questioned. He'd have to check the notes. His mind travelled to a connection, the no doubt very expensive bottle of cognac they'd all enjoyed earlier. Apparently a gift from Pierre de Fauw to the mayor. The two were very cosy and Pierre, following a hefty grant from the local council and a virtual land gift, was investing in a new hospital and technology plant. Why? What was he to gain and why Calais? Did it have anything to do with anything? Probably not but it was worth a look at. The lieutenant made another note. Who else had disappeared? According to the migrant Ismail, possibly hundreds, thousands even, but they were just migrants, no one really cared. His gendarmerie, when it had been put to them by Marie, had felt a sense of shame. It was still with him. But they were almost impossible to investigate, lack of identity was their first line of defence. No, who else had disappeared, the man from the BRB, Baptiste. Only apparently he wasn't from the BRB, he had been an imposter, where was he now? How was he involved in all this? And all this 'nonsense', according to Capitaine Vendroux, about the 'Red Market'. Why had he pointed the gendarmerie in that direction? For what purpose? To deter them from what was really going on? If so, what? Was his new boss right? Was it all to do with drugs? It was an easy assumption. Too easy? Too simple? There'd been no reports from the UK or Interpol with reference to drug cartels operating in the Calais area. That didn't mean though that there wasn't. What about the surgically mutilated bodies, how could they be related or were they being used as mules for drugs? He made another note and another referencing Baptiste. Why had he apparently duped his gendarmerie? Why? Why? Why? Anyway the Red Market scenario was stupid, his officers were right. How would you hide an operation like that? Somebody would see something, report it. And the smell would be impossible to hide.

From the disappeared the lieutenant returned to the dead, in particular his late capitaine, Capitaine Maubert. Why was a professional Femme Fatale sent to seduce him. Knowing his ex-capitaine as he did, she must have been highly skilled. His ex-capitaine had never been one to let his head be turned by a woman. He was totally devoted to his family and his job. Why was his ex-capitaine targeted, and by apparently, according to his seniors a well - known professional of her trade. And where was she now, who had employed her, and were probably protecting her. And the ultimate question again, WHY?.

The lieutenant stood up. All this thinking was making him restless. Why, why, why and not a hint of an answer to any of them. Cap Blanc Nez, his ex-capitaine had had a fixation on the place. He'd even ordered the Tunisian restaurant on the summit to be raided. All in vain, they'd found nothing. It turned out to be a very expensive exercise, nothing more. Cap Blanc Nez, Cap Blanc Nez, Cap Blanc Nez. The place where, if the young couple were to be believed, his ex-capitaine was murdered. What was it about Cap Blanc Nez. It was just a place where shit happened, the lieutenant dismissed it. It was just coincidence. If he could have seen his new capitaine, Capitaine Vendroux, known his situation, his location at that very minute, he would have a very different view.

Tunisian Restaurant on the Summit of Mont d'Hubert, near Calais, France

After cleaning up and drying himself down the capitaine was led into a small office. Two steaming cups of coffee were waiting on the central desk. One of them was for the man sitting on the other side. The man who had dangled him over the cliff.

"I don't like these bloody games, they're dangerous. I'm trying to run a restaurant. I don't want the bloody gendarmerie up here again."

"Tell him that." The man nodded to the capitaine, "He's in charge of it, I just wish he'd behave as though he was. Sit down." The command was directed at the capitaine. The man who was obviously either the owner or in charge of the restaurant, looked at the capitaine with visible distaste.

"I liked your predecessor, he was a good man, professional. It was a great shame he had to die." He turned to the man behind the desk. "I'll shut the door, and get his bloody car out of my fridge, I need it."

"Oui, oui, dix minute". The man waved his arm impatiently. "Sit down," he repeated to the capitaine. "Have some coffee, it's strong. You look like you need it."

The capitaine did as he was told. He sipped at the dark liquid in the cup. The man was right, it was good and he did need it. "Merci." It was all he could manage.

The man sitting on the other side of the desk drank his coffee in one go and leaned forward. "Now tell me, what the fuck do you think you were playing at.?" The capitaine looked embarrassed.

"Quoi?"

"Quoi!" The man stood up. "Quoi! Standing on the bloody cliff edge, where your predecessor met his death. With your arms out as though you were on the bloody Titanic, and in full uniform. In full bloody uniform, are you trying to bring the world's media down on us? If it hadn't been for the inevitable publicity, I'd have pushed you off there and then. Thank God you weren't visible to those in the cars in the car park. Thankfully they were both otherwise occupied." His voice softened. "You were sent here to be our eyes and ears inside that bloody gendarmerie, to steer them away from what we're doing here. And all you've done since you've arrived is behave like a spoilt little prick. Remember we have other eyes and ears in that building. And the word is most people working in your gendarmerie think you're a bit of a dickhead, a jumped up pompous git from Paris. Now tell me, what were you doing skylarking on that cliff edge and in weather like this?"

Capitaine Vendroux shrugged his shoulders, embarrassed. Like a bolt between the eyes he realised that what he had done was madness, how could he have been so stupid. He had no choice but to tell the truth, he could offer no other explanation. Head down, he struggled to get the words out of his mouth. He felt like a scolded schoolboy, a far cry from the big cheese in charge of a gendarmerie.

"I needed a thrill, that gendarmerie, everyone who works in it bores me silly. They have little minds and boring little lives. The whole town simply depresses me." He knew it sounded crass, but it was the truth.

The man opposite leant back, running his fingers through his hair. "So you decided to play 'dare', like two little kids running in front of a moving train. Pathetic. It's you who has the little mind." The man shook his head. "I can't believe you're so bloody stupid. If I had my way I'd take you down below, have bits of you shipped all over the world. But I can't, it would bring too much unwanted attention. And two capitaines of the town's gendarmerie disappearing within weeks of each other, no, no, and who knows who may have seen you drive up here. You probably own the only Alpine in Calais, that car's a pain. Someone is bound to have spotted you. No sadly we have no choice but to let you remain in your role, but from here on in try and behave like an adult. Gain the respect of the people who work under you and they'll follow you wherever and where we want them to follow. NOW, do you follow?"

The capitaine nodded, he'd never been spoken to like this and the worst part, he knew he deserved it.

"I didn't hear you?"

"Oui." Being forced to say it out loud was the ultimate humiliation.

"Bon," the man opposite leaned back in his chair, for the first time since their meeting on Cap Blanc Nez he appeared to relax. "Now, I understand, you had a young couple come to see you, claiming they'd seen your predecessor pushed off of the cliff?"

The capitaine nodded, "Yes, that's right."

"And you sent them away with their tails between their legs?"

"I wouldn't put it quite like that?"

"How would you put it? You let them walk out of your gendarmerie probably, after being dismissed by you, wanting to shout their story from every Calais rooftop. The last thing we bloody need. We'll have the world's press back on our doorstep. Do you want that?" The man was no longer looking relaxed, he was now leaning forward with his forearms resting on the desk. Do you bloody want that"?.

"Non, of course not." For the second time that evening he realised how stupid he had been.

"Non. Then call them back in, apologise, listen to what they have to say, treat them like adults. Once you have their trust, convince them to keep what they think they've seen a secret. Tell them it's imperative to your investigation that no-one hears about this or the perpetrators might go underground and never be caught. Got it"?.

The capitaine nodded, "Oui, I'll do it first thing".

"Good," the man on the other side of the desk actually smiled. He stood up, "right you'd better get going, your car's outside. You've never been here ok." The man held out his hand.

The capitaine did the same and winced as the stranger gripped his hand hard. "And no more foolishness, understand? One more cock up from you and I promise no matter what the risk, you'll never see daylight again. Got it?"

The capitaine nodded, this time with short forceful jerks of the head. "He wanted the man gripping his hand to let go. Such was the pain he felt tears welling up in his eyes. No way did he want them to escape, they had to stay where they were. "Oui, oui, his head continued to nod.

"Bon", the man let go. "Bon", he said again. "Get a good night's sleep Capitaine Vendroux, you'll need it if you're going to make things work tomorrow. Bon nuit, exit the way you came in." The man made it clear that he had no intention of escorting him out.

Capitaine Vendroux needed no further encouragement, it was as much as he could manage not to run down the corridor. The exit door was on a very strong spring and for a split second his heart sank. He thought the door to be locked, that it was a sick joke. He was never going to leave this place. Then the door came open and splashes of rain wetted the capitaine's face. Never had rain been so welcome. He pulled open the door and stepping outside heard it slam beside him. There waiting was his beloved Alpine. Driving back down the D940, never had the lights of Calais appeared so welcoming. Neither had his bed, when he eventually crawled into it, he could learn to love Calais. It was his last thought as his eyes closed.

On top of Mont d'Hubert, from an office window the man who'd never introduced himself watched the Alpine's lights disappear. The man's a prick he thought to himself. A danger to their whole operation here. He'd only got the position because of a favour. If he'd had anything to do with it the man wouldn't have got within a hundred miles of Calais. And favouritism wasn't the organisation's way. In the organisation, everybody got where they were through merit. Favouritism was a curse of the corrupt world they were wanting to extinguish. Well, if that prick of a gendarme put one more foot wrong he wouldn't be held responsible for his actions.

Too much was at stake here. The reason why after his stint as Baptiste of the BRB he'd not travelled far but underground. This evening was the first time he'd stepped outside since his last visit to the gendarmerie in Calais. The organisation had establishments all over the world but here, he was often told, was the most important. It was the forerunner and therefore experimental. What he'd been made very aware of was, if the experiment succeeded here then it would be laid out at all their other sites. He wasn't sure exactly what the experiment was, his security clearance meant he wasn't privy to that information, nor was he allowed in the really sensitive part of the complex under Mont d'Hubert. His job was to oversee the security involving the construction workers further excavating and modernising the tunnel complex created for Rommel during the second world war. He knew there was extensive work going on underneath a hill close to Wissant called Mont de Couple. That the tunnel connecting it to the complex where he was now under Mont d'Hubert had been excavated years ago and modernised in the last year, but that was it. Security was tight, very tight and that was his responsibility. Because of his previous experience in the DRM, BRGE and lately the BRB, he was considered ideal for the post. Bizarrely it was his experience with these agencies that had driven him into the arms of the organisation. He had hated the way they operated, the damage they did. When he was approached he hadn't hesitated to jump ship. Although he wasn't entirely sure what the organisation stood for he felt a unique sense of belonging. Something he'd never experienced before. This was strengthened by a language he hadn't until he joined the organisation knew existed let alone speak it. Yet with selected people he could converse fluently. One was entering the office now, someone who he was told would never see daylight again. A man called Antanois.

"Axsti".

"Axsti".

The New Dawn Hotel, Bayswater, London, England

Rania looked around her room. It was compact, but clean and most importantly safe.

She couldn't quite believe she was where she was. In a foreign country, with work, good work and a salary a couple of years back she would have thought to be only fantasy. Now not only did she have that salary but the organisation, nobody ever told her its name, had promised her an apartment to boot. She had to pinch herself, scared she might wake up to discover it had all been a dream.

Lying in bed she closed her eyes remembering how she had got here. Where it had all started. Her journey had begun in her country of birth, Libya. Her father had been a doctor and it had been his dream for her to follow in his footsteps. Being the dutiful daughter she'd entered the medical profession and had been training with the LNHS, (Libyan National Health Service) when, what the West called 'The Arab Spring' came to Libya and as a result the assassination of Gaddafi. At first there had been ecstatic celebrations quickly followed almost inevitably by civil war. The medical system virtually collapsed overnight, despite this her father was determined to practise where he could, supporting the people and the country he loved. Eventually his loyalty cost him his life and she, her mother and her two sisters were driven from their home. They'd been given shelter by her extended family but it hadn't been easy. Slowly things started to settle down and, in 2017, a peace agreement was signed. It wasn't perfect and there had still been conflict but it was a hundred times better than the years immediately before. As a result, outside agencies had entered Libya to help, one being the NRC, (Norwegian Refugee Council), which she had joined as a medical assistant. It was whilst she was there that she had been approached.

One day a woman whom she recognised as a helper with the agency, sat with her whilst having tea. She had told her of an organisation which was looking to recruit foreign medical professionals and assign them in hospitals all over the world but mainly the western world. That they would, as she had already gone through basic training, complete that training and help her to pass the relevant exams needed to practise wherever her final destination would be. If that hadn't been enough to tempt her, the final salary she'd quoted was. It had been eye watering. The very next day she left the NRC and days later was taken with several others over the border into Tunisia. She knew this as they'd passed through Dhehiba, a Tunisian frontier town her family had taken shelter in at the height of the conflict.

From Dhehiba, their windows had been blacked out. When they were removed they were underground, about, Rania speculated, an hour from the border with Libya, so somewhere in the rocky terrain that runs up from Dehiba to Tataouine. A region famous for Berber cave dwellings. So maybe no surprise that they were underground. The temperature underground was much more bearable and easier to control. A fact that people who lived there had understood since biblical times.

For the next couple of years, she wasn't sure exactly, the underground was where she had lived and trained. The only daylight she and others training with her saw were in specially constructed chambers where carefully angled shafts allowed sunlight to flood in. It was where everyone went to relax. The medical facilities were like nothing she'd ever seen and she was astonished that she'd never heard of the place. Her teachers too, were very highly skilled and whatever she was taught stayed with her, never to be forgotten. In her last six months, she specialised in brain surgery and was after that time, declared a competent surgeon. Quite incredible, for normally such competence would take years to achieve.

She was allowed to sit her final exams without having to travel to the capital Tunis. She'd passed with flying colours and was told that the organisation would prefer her to take up a position that had become vacant in London. London sounded exciting and she had readily agreed. Next had been an intensive course on the English language and after just six weeks she found herself fluent. She even spoke English with a French accent, something the organisation promised would open doors for her. The next step had been to travel to Cairo where she had sat an exam called PLAB 1. Again she had passed easily and, as a consequence, travelled to London to sit the second part of the exam, the practical, called PLAB 2. Today she had received her results and had passed with near perfect marks. The organisation she had been told were delighted and tomorrow she would not only start her new job with an eye watering salary but would also be shown the apartment she had been promised. An apartment, all to herself, she could hardly believe it. She couldn't wait.

As she drifted from reflection into sleep, her mind travelled back to her time underground in Tunisia. Though bizarre, she had really enjoyed her time there. The one black spot, if you could call it that, had been during her first week there. She had got lost in the myriad of tunnels that made up the complex and ended up in an area, she was told afterwards, forbidden to students. After passing through a set of double doors she had found herself in a tunnel that hadn't been sanitised. The walls were in the main of roughly hewn rock, mixed with plaster that in places was crumbling to dust. The tunnel had been lit with caged lights, a harsh unforgiving light, nothing like the soft but clear light of the area where the trainees lived and practised their profession. She had seen lettering stencilled on the walls and signs with similar lettering on some of the doors, doors that led off of the main tunnel. Heavy solid metal doors. She didn't recognise the language but assumed it to be German as also stencilled frequently was an image of a four legged cross, a swastika. They had learned of the swastika at school and the war that had been fought across North Africa. She had only been there for a couple of minutes when a man she assumed to be some sort of security guard had found her and unceremoniously marched her to her principal's office. There she had undergone some pretty unforgiving questioning, at the end of which everyone was all smiles again. The doors through which she'd passed she'd been told should have been locked and that was for their own safety. That the tunnels beyond were unsafe.

Rania rolled over so that her left cheek was nestling into the folds of her pillow. Her left cheek was the one her father would always squeeze when he was happy with her.. If only her father could see her now, he'd be so proud. Perhaps he could see her, perhaps he was watching now, at this very moment. The thought made her smile and Rania remained smiling as she drifted into sleep. Swastikas and roughly hewn tunnels forgotten.

A Safehouse Somewhere in South London, England

The time was 9pm. Time, that day, for the shifts to change. Shifts varied so as not to attract unwanted attention. Although a changeover was routine, the hour was not. That evening a team of three, all male, tasked with keeping Jane, head of the NCA safe were to be replaced by a night shift, consisting of two men and a female. All employed by the Met. Each parted and arrived individually, again so as not to attract unwanted attention. Once settled in, the female member of the night team volunteered to make coffee, offering to check on their client at the same time. The two men readily accepted her offer and settled down for the night.

The female officer bound up the stairs two by two and at the top gently knocked on Jane's door. The door opened.

"Coffee?" the female officer asked loudly.

"Yes thank you, that would be lovely, milk and two sugars."

"Pitgam," the word was spoken in a whisper, "5.30am."

The woman nodded and closed the door. The officer returned down the stairs and made her way to the kitchen. Minutes later, she returned to the lounge with two mugs of steaming coffee. She was just about to take a coffee to Jane's room when one of the male officers stood up.

"I'll take it, I want to take a look around anyway."

A Street in South East London, England.

At just after two in the morning, a rusting white transit style van pulled up outside a nondescript house in a nondescript street somewhere in south east London. The garden didn't look as though it had been cared for, for months and outside three bins were overflowing with rubbish.

The driver got out and slid open the side door. Leaning inside he pushed to one side the pile of newspapers he was paid to deliver. First though, he had to collect a far more valuable cargo. After looking left and right he knocked on the door. A camera above filmed every move. It was a good minute before someone opened the door. A man he knew to be Romanian stood before him.

"Three," the man who had opened the door held up three fingers.

The driver did the same. "Three, ok. Good." He walked back down the short path to the street and again looked left and right. "Ok, bring."

The Romanian stood back to allow three men half-carry half drag three scantily clad women, two in their mid-twenties and one in her teens, possibly early teens, so no more than a girl, down the path to the van. The eyes of all three were set deep into their sockets and devoid of life. Their arms were covered in tiny puncture marks from months of drug abuse. On reaching the van each was unceremoniously bundled inside. The driver after a quick look slid the door shut.

"They won't wake up?"

The three men laughed, the tallest amongst them spoke.

"No, don't worry, no."

"Ok." The driver gave each a roll up before sliding one between his own yellowing teeth. With a cheap lighter, he lit all four cigarettes before and without another word, climbing into his van. His next stop was a local garage. It wasn't open 24 hours so he left the tied bundles of paper on the front step. The second garage was open 24 hours and he enjoyed a few minutes conversation with the two staff along with a free coffee. Two hours later the only cargo left in the rear of his van was one bundle of papers and the three females. His destination now was a building in South Kensington. Being a creature of habit he always filled his van ready for the next day at a petrol station under a quarter of a mile away. Always his last stop before delivering his most valuable cargo. A police patrol car sat in the forecourt. It was always there. Inside the station two uniformed policemen were enjoying a coffee before finishing their shift. They greeted the driver of the van as though he were an old friend.

They even knew his name, 'Badij'. The open familiarity was from years of meeting at the same place, same time. Minutes later Badij was at his final destination, an underground parking area. There was the odd car but the majority of vehicles parked were ambulances. Opening the rear door he hauled out the last bundle of papers and delivered them to the security office. When he returned to the van he knew the three females in the back would be gone. A quick check confirmed this. Climbing into the driver's seat he picked up an envelope left on the dashboard. He wouldn't open it there, that would show a lack of class. Instead he placed it between his legs, driving till he pulled up in a quiet residential road. Never the same one, that could attract unwanted attention. Tearing open the envelope he counted out the notes inside. £700, not bad for a night's work. It was a pity this little side line wasn't a daily affair instead of just now and again. He never questioned the amount of money left for him, that he knew would be a stupid move. Normally it wasn't more than £200 a body. He guessed the extra £100 was for the youngest of the three. Older and more deteriorated bodies, he was sometimes lucky to get one hundred a piece. Today's cargo was good, £700 was close to the maximum amount he'd ever received. He never questioned what happened to the bodies once they'd been delivered. Only once had he delivered a dead body, they were always alive, either unconscious or so drugged up that they hadn't a clue where they were. He liked to think that the medical institution where he delivered them would look after them, bring them back to health, though he knew this to be unlikely. Who was he to ask questions, he was simply doing his job.

Chapter
–5–

The Next Morning

NCA's Temporary Offices, Gladstone Park, North London, England

Roger was woken by his mobile ringing. Waking from a heavy sleep, with his eyes half closed, he waved his right arm searching for the object responsible for the offending noise. His knuckle made contact first and he heard his mobile fall to the floor. 'Shit', forcing his eyes open he hung over the bed feeling for his phone which had stopped ringing. Had the caller rung off or had the drop killed his phone? 'Shit, shit, shit'. Swinging his legs over the side of the bed he scanned the floor with tired eyes. They were useless in such dense darkness. 'Shit', he swore again, reaching for the light. As he switched it on, the landline rang, this time Roger answered before the second ring.

"Roger."

"Morning Roger, Jane." Jane, it had to be, and he was only half awake.

"Morning Jane, this is early even for you." Roger wished he'd had a coffee before she rang. Jane was sometimes like Zebedee on speed. He rubbed his headboard scalp.

"Got a meeting, or had you forgotten?"

"No, of course not. You told me you were going to call me after the meeting."

"That was before I'd heard about your little excursion last night." Shit she knows, he wanted to tell her himself. "Was that a sensible thing to do Roger?"

"I just wanted to see it." There came a short silence. He heard Jane sigh.

"Roger, it's just a house, bricks and mortar. And don't worry about the insurance. I've thought about it and the last thing we need is insurance investigators crawling all over the place. They'll soon work out it wasn't gas. I've already cleared it. The government will pick up the tab for your house and loss of contents. Just name your figure. Providing you're sensible they won't quibble and they've already promised me that they'll be more than generous. You'll be able to live in something of a palace in comparison."

"That house was more than bricks and mortar, Jane. That house was all I had to show for my sad, sad existence. Everything inside was personal to me, how can you replace that? How can you replace my memories? Or has His Majesty's government managed to insure them? All I have now, Jane, is my car and the few clothes I have with me. Oh and what's inside my head, which believe me, isn't great."

"I know Roger, I kind of know how you feel. Living in a safe house, I have virtually nothing of my own with me. Just a couple of photos I collected last night." She instinctively held her hand up to stop him, even though he wasn't there to see her. "And before you say anything, I know it's not at all the same thing, I'm just trying to say, I do understand as far as I can."

"Do you feel safe in your safe house, Jane?" There came another pause.

"As much as I can, yes. Why do you ask?"

"Because I have a nasty feeling that I'm only safe here because whoever is doing this wants to keep me alive and, in a way, knowing that is in a way worse than being dead. Whoever it is knows about this place, they know I'm living here and worse they've infiltrated our CCTV security. Peter bloody Fitch has appeared in our front yard. I wouldn't be surprised if someone is listening in on our conversation now."

"This line is secure, Roger".

"You really think so, Jane? Until now would you have believed that someone could have not only hacked but played silly games with the DVLA database? Whoever's doing this has abilities we're still only dreaming of".

"We still have our trust, Roger," Jane felt herself blushing as she said it. "Listen I have to go, my car's here. Keep your mobile with you, I'll call as soon as I get out with a heads up. I may even come over".

"I'll look forward to welcoming you to the 'Big Brother' house."

Jane didn't hear him, her car had pulled up outside and her double was already getting out. She glanced at her double, yes she was wearing identical clothes, she hoped that went as far as her perfume. Good security officers were trained to pick up on things like that. She rushed to the mirror checking every last detail. She was good, Next she picked up a file and her briefcase. Jane would never leave her briefcase in a car, even for a minute and she was pleased to see her double was carrying hers. Each briefcase would contain notes for the other. Jane waited on the stairs out of view of the front door. The door opened and her double entered. They passed on the stairs.

"Axsti," both whispered. Jane counted to ten and walked out of the front door. "Got it," Jane waved the file above her head. "Whitehall here we come."

"Yes, Ma'am", the driver shut the door and got in as did his front seat passenger, an armed officer. "Whitehall it is". And the card sped off. From the front bedroom window a woman watched them go. She smiled. Perfect, no one suspected a thing. After splashing her face in the bathroom she removed her wig and silk scarf. Minutes later, she was in her own house. She had to hurry as she had an early meeting at Scotland Yard that morning.

Roger replaced the receiver, he remained sitting on his bed deep in thought. He wondered why he hadn't been invited to the COBRA meeting, after all it had everything to do with the NCA. Maybe the government wanted higher authorities dealing with it. There could be another reason, one that was very unpalatable. That the higher authorities didn't trust him. He hoped Jane trusted him, they'd worked closely together ever since she'd become head of the NCA, he'd find himself really upset if he ever learned she didn't.

Standing up he walked to the kitchen. He needed a coffee, a good coffee. He turned the Nespresso machine on, filled the water tank, dropped in a capsule and listened as the machine went to work. Before he drank, he used up valuable seconds breathing in the fumes. Sighing with contentment he cupped his spare hand around the top of the cup and took a long sip. 'Ahhhhh', just what he needed. The world could take away his life but it hadn't as yet taken away one of his greatest loves, coffee. Taking steady steps around the kitchen, he savoured every sip. On finishing, he rinsed the cup and put it to one side. Filling the kettle, he switched it on and placed a mug upright. The last coffee was good but rich. He could never manage more than one. What he needed now was a mug of the instant stuff. He enjoyed his first mug of coffee sitting on his bed watching the morning news, 'World Business Report'. It had almost finished but he was pleased he'd managed to spend ten minutes with Sally Bundock. He'd never met her, was never likely to meet her but even so, counted her as one of his friends. The news was all about the hacking of the DVLA, the explosions never got a mention. Not quite true, they were part of the traffic report.

Finishing his cup, he returned to the kitchen. With the events of the last few days, he'd forgotten his three coffees routine. Maybe that was why he'd inherited so much bad luck. It was nonsense of course but a significant part of him believed it to be the case. He'd have a shower first though. True to his belief, straight after his shower Roger made himself his third coffee of the morning. Sipping continuously at the steaming liquid, he walked over to the fridge. He suddenly experienced an unsettling feeling that the box was no longer there. He needn't have worried, it was and with it a sickly sweet smell that almost caused him to vomit. He closed the fridge door quickly and took another long sip of his coffee. The coffee worked, he immediately felt better.

Humming, he got dressed, he even put a tie on. The three coffees had worked. Despite all that had happened he felt positive this morning they were going to achieve something. He was determined that would be the case. Picking up some papers, he marched purposefully to the lift, got in and pressed the button for the floor with his office. The lift came to a halt and the doors opened. To his surprise standing there was Nick and two members, Roger could tell from their uniforms, from security.

"Bloody hell am I late or something, it's only," Roger looked at his watch, "it's only just gone seven".

It was Nick who answered, he looked nervous. "No sir, there's been another explosion."

"Shit, where?" The three men before him appeared unable to talk, they each stood motionless staring at him. "Where Nick? Casualties?" Roger looked at his watch again. "Bloody hell it's rush hour." It didn't bear thinking about.

"No casualties sir." Nick was holding something back, Roger could tell.

"Then where Nick, what the bloody hell is the matter with you?"

"In our front yard." It was one of the security guards who offered up an answer."

Nick swiftly cut in. "It's your car Roger, someone must have put a bomb under it."

"I need to see it," Roger started to move forward but the two men from security closed ranks, stopping him.

One of them spoke. "We can't let you do that sir. It looks like you may have been a target. We can't let you leave until we're sure it's safe, and I'm going to post someone on your office door. With your house and now your car it looks as though someone has it in for you sir."

I'm not in any danger Roger was pretty sure of that, whoever had it in for him had had plenty of opportunity but he wasn't about to argue the point. And the last thing he needed was an armed officer guarding his office. It would send out all the wrong signals, however, he knew again that arguing the point would be fruitless. Security, whatever his wishes, were going to give him armed security. At least while he was in their building.

"The EOD, (explosive ordnance disposal) are checking all the other vehicles parked now, but it looks as if it was just your car that was targeted. Staff are starting to arrive for work, I need to know what you want us to do. Do we let them in or send them home?" The security guard was doing his job.

Roger thought swiftly, "How sure are you that there are no other explosives waiting to be detonated?" The question was unfair and everyone there knew it.

"Another ten minutes and the EOD will have finished checking the yard. They've already given us the all clear on the underground parking. They checked that first as it could, if a bomb went off, have caused structural damage. As for the building, well...." The security guard paused, he held his hands open. "But then, our old building. We thought that...." Roger stopped him.

"You just said EOD, they got here a bit bloody quick?" Although phrased as a statement, the man from security as well as Nick knew it was a question. "Well?" Roger sensed a rat.

"The bomb went off at exactly two am." The EOD were called immediately, they arrived within twenty minutes."

"And" Nick cut in. "Before you ask sir, officers from the FEL (Forensics explosives laboratory), now the EOD have declared it safe have already started examining your car. They may even have a preliminary report ready for you some time this morning. The area's been screened off so no one can see the damage. After initial checks, I've been told that your car will be transported, undercover sir, to the FEL's lab at Porton Down". " Roger didn't know where to start. He was meant to be in charge and yet he felt as though he were being worked by a thousand ropes.

"Two am? Why the fuck wasn't I told? And you're talking about letting staff in, shouldn't we be evacuating the building?"

"You weren't told because we were worried that you were a target, that the bomb was meant to go off while you were sitting in your car. We couldn't have you running outside if you get my point, sir. We thought it better to let you sleep. You were perfectly safe in your apartment. As for evacuating the building. This building", the security guard looked about him, "this building has been constructed to withstand a nuclear attack. You could argue that it is safer to be inside than out. Much safer. Especially under the circumstances".

"They notified Jane and she called me. I promised her that I'd come in. You know me sir, I'm not normally one for the bird's chorus. I was here by three, pretty impressive!" If it was meant to be funny no one laughed. " Jane said she'd come but she has an early morning meeting. I promised her we'd keep her informed, and she also asked me to keep what's happened under wraps. She doesn't want the great British media getting hold of this."

Jane! He had only spoken to her a little over an hour ago. Why hadn't she said anything? He'd bloody well ask her. Roger was seething.

"The staff sir, shall I let them in? I'm sure a queue's starting to build. It might not look good."

Roger's mind was racing. It would appear that he was the last to know and yet in the last few seconds everybody was looking to him for a decision. "Is there a fire engine up top?"

"Yes sir, it's procedure in an event such as this, in fact there's two." The man from security recounted the information as though it were a training exercise.

"Good then tell everybody waiting that there's been a small fire and because of where it is full security checks have to be completed before the all clear is given. Everyone will understand that." The man from security stepped into an office to relay Roger's instructions to the ground.

Roger turned to Nick. "Nick, do you know who is in charge of the EOD team?"

"Yes, a guy called Anthony McDonald." Roger knew him, he was an ex-marine and almost certainly at one time special forces.

"Can you ask him to pop down to my office?"

"Will do, I'll go fetch him"

Roger tended to trust anyone who was military or ex-military. They tended to be fiercely loyal to their country and therefore much harder to corrupt. Their heads were rarely turned by the promise of money or fanatical idealism. The man from security returned to join his colleague.

"My men are letting everyone waiting know about the fire. I've told them to act as though it were a minor incident."

"Which it is." Roger attempted to play down the fact that his car had just been destroyed. "Can you guys wait here, I just need to speak to the guy in charge of the EOD team before I make a decision."

"Yes sir."

Roger returned to his office. He gazed around the room. This was his life now, his office was the only thing he had left. At that moment he felt like the loneliest man on the planet. Through the glass he saw the two men from security retrieve a couple of chairs from an office. They were obviously expecting a long wait. Roger smiled, he had to find humour in the tiniest situation. It would keep him from going mad. Moments later he saw through the glass Nick returning with a man wearing what Roger always described as 'bomb fatigues'. Anthony McDonald had ex-military written all over him. His stature was always bolt upright even as he walked. John had once said to him, 'you win over your enemy by demonstrating that you're stronger than they are, that you're not afraid of them'. Everything about this man's stature echoed John's advice. Nick knocked on the glass.

"Anthony McDonald, sir".

"Pleased to meet you, Anthony". Roger held out his hand. Anthony gripped hard and gave a single shake. I wouldn't want to get on the wrong side of this guy was Roger's first thought. Thank god we still have people like him.

"Sir."

Roger looked him up and down, his bulk was bulked out by his bomb fatigues. He had removed his head gear to reveal a hard-nosed face with a square chin, an obviously once broken nose and a haircut so short it was almost shaved. His eyes were haunted from the horrors of battle but still retained a twinkle.

"You once did service with John Mitchell didn't you?"

Anthony McDonald visibly relaxed. "John," he almost laughed. "That ole rascal, what's he up to now?"

"I hear he's in the debt collecting business."

"I've heard something along those lines too. Well, good luck to him." It was obvious to Roger that the man knew nothing about John's demise. Either that or he was a bloody good actor. Roger relaxed.

"Yes, good luck to him." Roger managed a smile. He hoped it was convincing. "Anthony, what do you make of the situation up top? And are we safe, can I give the all clear for my people to come in?"

Anthony looked straight at him. "My boys are just finishing off, there's definitely nothing in the parking areas. As for your building," Anthony shrugged. "I can't guarantee that."

"I doubt if anyone could get a bomb past security here. I sometimes even have a job getting in and out."

Anthony's lips curled into a smile that was tinted with sarcasm. "Never underestimate those who intend you harm, you managed to drive in with a bomb under your car. Unless that is, someone planted it whilst it was parked. Either way it proves your security is fallible". Anthony graciously made no mention of the NCA building that had been flattened in Vauxhall. Roger looked through the glass to the two men from security waiting outside. Anthony McDonald wasn't going to say it directly, that wasn't his pay grade but he was hinting strongly that the bomb under his car could be an inside job. If that was indeed the case, appointing an armed guard outside his office didn't exactly fill Roger with confidence, if anything it made him more vulnerable.

"Can you tell me anything about my car? The explosion?"

"That's not my job…"

Roger cut in. "I know, your job is to ensure the surrounding area is safe. But from one ex-soldier to another".

Anthony McDonald looked at the ground, it was obvious he was uncomfortable about saying anything. Roger thought he had lost, when.

"The FEL will fill you in but to me it looks like a very controlled explosion. A professional job. Most bombs let everyone in a couple of miles radius know that they've exploded. But this one to me, looks as if it was deliberately designed to be low impact. Not to be noticeable. Even if you were sitting in the car when the bomb exploded I think you may have survived. From what I've seen the driver's seat is still intact."

"Then why go to all the trouble?"

Anthony McDonald smiled. "That's your job sir, but I have seen this sort of thing before. It's normally done as a warning. A bit like the Mafia delivering a horse's head to your door." At that moment the internal phone on Roger's desk buzzed. He picked it up.

"It's for you," Roger passed the phone to Mr McDonald. The phone conversation lasted no more than two minutes.

"That's it, my men have finished, the parking areas have been given the all clear, we've found nothing to worry about.

"Thank you," Roger held out his hand again. This time the man from the EOD's grip was a lot more bearable.

"Not at all," Anthony felt beneath his fatigue and pulled out a card. He handed it to Roger. It had the EOD's insignia on it along with the name, 'Anthony McDonald', and a mobile phone number.

"From one ex-military to another, if ever you need help." Anthony looked about him. "Outside of here, give me a call. I still have contacts." Now where have I heard that recently, Roger thoughts wandered back to his excursion yesterday evening.

"Thank you, I will." Roger pocketed the card.

"Shall I see myself out?"

Roger tapped the glass, "Nick show Mr McDonald out will you." He watched as the two men disappeared down the wide corridor. When they were out of sight he turned to the two from security.

"Right the EOD have deemed the parking areas to be safe so we can start letting people in. Underground parking only though, I don't want anybody driving into our front yard. And tell your men to keep calm, to stay relaxed, we have to keep an appearance of everyday normality." Whatever that may be, Roger kept the thought to himself.

The two security guards left in a hurry, one barking into his radio. Roger returned to his office and dropped into his chair. Placing his arms behind his head he let out a long sigh. Nick returned, looking very uncomfortable. Roger put him out of his misery, "Join me in my office Nick."

"Coffee?"

"Yes, yes please," perhaps his three coffees needed to be elevated to four. Roger couldn't believe it. His car. His bloody car, who was trying to destroy him without actually killing him. Who knew that his car was so important to him? Who?

Gendarmerie Nationale – Calais, France

Capitaine Olivier Vendroux was in early that morning. After last night his pride had taken a beating. He was determined to show them what he could do. If the organisation wanted a boring, well behaved capitaine they would have one. He could play that role, he had no doubt.

Colette arrived, surprised to see their new capitaine's car parked in its designated parking space. She was early herself that morning and had expected to be one of the first in. She definitely hadn't expected to see their new capitaine till much later. Placing her personal effects in her office she mounted the stairs and knocked on the door with the newly fitted sign. 'Capitaine Olivier Vendroux'. He had insisted on the sign being personalised whereas her old boss had been happy with a sign that simply read, 'capitaine'. To her surprise their new capitaine opened the door. He had a beaming smile on his face.

"Morning Colette."

"Bonjour capitaine, can I get you a coffee?"

"That would be excellent, merci." Colette was about to turn to make one when the capitaine stopped her. "Colette, that young couple that came to see me early the other morning, what were their names"? Colette knew exactly who he was referring to.

"You mean Jean and Camille?"

"Oui, oui, have you still got their details?"

"Oui, bien sûr."

Capitaine Vendroux looked pleased, very pleased. "Perfect. Colette, do you think you can contact them? I might have been a little hasty the other day. Rushed to judgement too quickly. I'd like to interview them again. Can you see if they're willing to come and see me again? I'll send a car if it helps."

"Of course, capitaine." Colette, shocked, turned to leave and once again the capitaine stopped her, this time by holding her forearm.

"Oh and Colette," the capitaine put a finger to his lips. "I don't want this to go beyond us, ok?"

"Bien sur," Colette said for the second time. And this time the capitaine let her leave.

A House in Coulogne, near Calais, France

Lieutenant Beaufort adjusted his tie in the mirror. Happy he looked at his watch. He wasn't late, it was only a twenty minute drive to his gendarmerie. He walked through to the kitchen where his wife had prepared coffee and plated two fresh butter croissants along with a knob of butter and a small bowl filled with his favourite confiture. He kissed her on the cheek, she'd been to the boulangerie. His wife never failed him.

"Since when have you preferred the sofa to me?" The sofa was where the lieutenant had unwittingly spent most of the night. His wife had found him in the early hours cradling an empty 3 Monts bottle in his arms. 'You were holding the bottle as though it was a new born baby', his wife had teased. 'Are you trying to tell me something'? Definitely not that! If she were honest his wife was a little disappointed.

Grabbing his notes from the night before he sat down to enjoy his breakfast. His wife had the radio on, a song was playing, Tahitiala-maison by Keen V. Normally the radio didn't bother him but for some reason that song did. He looked up at his wife who was standing at the kitchen sink, her hips swaying to the music.

"Cheri, do you mind turning the radio off, I'm trying to concentrate."

"Then try drinking less bierre." Rather than turning the radio off his wife took it with her and she along with the music disappeared upstairs.

The lieutenant returned to his notes. Yesterday slowly came back to him and with it his thought process whilst drinking several bottles of 3 Monts on his sofa. He stopped at his note for the English detective and with his own detective's mind circled his note 'pathologist'. The bodies of those poor children found on a boat drifting aimlessly in La Manche. And the bodies of the two murdered men found with them. They'd never been properly investigated and now the bodies, as far as he knew, were back in the UK and the whole thing hushed up. The whole thing stank, he needed the pathologist's report. He needed to compare it with the report on the severed heads also found in La Manche, along with the torso and the body of the poor little girl found on the beach at the foot of Cap Blanc Nez and the village of Escalles. Would he be able to tell if all the mutilations were made by the same hand? He'd decided yesterday evening whilst enjoying several beers on his sofa to contact the pathologist at Boulogne, Monsieur Hubert. Now in the dim Autumn morning light, over a sobering coffee and croissant he made the same commitment. If he was honest, the thought of speaking to Monsieur Hubert on such matters put the fear of god into him. But it had to be done. He decided to make it the first thing he'd do when he arrived at the gendarmerie. NO. Something inside made him change his mind. He had no idea what but something was telling him that wasn't a good idea. He'd phone him now from home.

Trembling, he looked up the number on his mobile and from his landline dialled it. After three rings, a young sounding voice answered, a young male voice.

"Hello?"

"That's all the young voice answered.

"Have I got the right number? Is that the morgue at Le Hospitalier Boulogne Sur Mer?"

"Oui", The lieutenant wished he was there so he could give the young man a slap.

"Can I speak with Monsieur Hubert s'ilte plait".

"Oui, one moment". The line fell silent. The lieutenant drummed the kitchen table as he waited, planning in his mind how best to phrase his questions.

"Oui, Monsieur Hubert."

The lieutenant took a deep breath. "Monsieur Hubert, it's Lieutenant Beaufort from the gendarmerie nationale at Calais. Have you got time to talk? I know you're always very busy." The lieutenant crossed his fingers.

"Lieutenant," the pathologist's reply sounded unexpectedly cheerful. "Lieutenant, please call me Jean-Paul. I was about to ring you. However I don't think it wise to speak on the phone. Can we meet?"

The Royal Lancaster Hotel, Lancaster Gate, London, England

Fatima stood at her hotel window gazing over Hyde Park. The sky overhead hung heavy with a blanket of slow moving dark grey clouds. To Fatima it was the most depressing grey, but at least the rain had stopped. How she longed for the blue sky that normally favoured

Marseille. She just couldn't understand how people managed to live day in day out under such miserable conditions.

Returning to her room, she threw herself on her bed. The tv was on and her new target, whom she'd met for the first time last night was all over the news. Him the minister for transport and the prime minister. Each had made announcements overnight regarding the hacking of the DVLA database. Fatima didn't know what the 'DVLA database' was and had had to look it up. She'd laughed out loud when images of people's driving licences were presented on screen. Images of Trump, Putin and Kim Jong Un appeared to be very popular along with a huge variety of animals. She wondered if the organisation had anything to do with the hack but she couldn't see why they would want to do such a thing. If anything it had a detrimental effect on her mission. How was she going to target the man if he was battling what the newsreader had called, 'The UK's biggest ever breach of security'. He simply wouldn't have time no matter how tempting or available she made herself. The thought of seduction made her think of her last target, the gendarme in Calais. How he had unexpectedly made her orgasm for the first time. She quickly pushed the memory from her mind. Her orgasm had made her vulnerable, not in full control. It must never happen again. Standing, she disrobed and headed for the bathroom. She needed a shower, a cold shower.

Whitehall, London, England

Jane was glad to be in the open air. The COBRA meeting which had been all over the news had been fraught and embarrassing for the collected security agencies who hadn't come up with a single credible answer to the hacking of the DVLA and the obvious infiltration of the

NCA. As the prime minister had so delicately put it, 'so none of you have a fucking clue'?

What no one had dared to admit, was that they were at the mercy of whoever was responsible and they hadn't a clue even who that was. Russia had been mentioned but the chief of MI6 or SIS had told the room that he had spoken to the Russians and they had assured him they had nothing to do with the NCA or the DVLA hack. Indeed they were beginning to experience similar problems of their own. The chief had gone on to say that he believed them and the fact that they were beginning to experience similar problems suggested that they might have an even bigger problem. They may be facing a global enemy, an enemy with financial backing and sophisticated technology. Even worse, no one had a clue, whoever it was, what was their raison d'etre? Whoever was responsible had made no political or financial demands, it just didn't make sense. A full hour had been wasted on discussing who it may be, at the end of which, much to the frustration of MI6, Russia remained the main suspect.

The prime minister had gone on and on about what he was to tell the media and the great British public. What had taken place had made his government a laughing stock, he'd kept repeating this line. Eventually it was accepted that all they could do for now was report that the hack was being dealt with and that normal service will soon be returned. In the meantime, the government was sorry but no further licences would be issued until the database had been secured and checked. That they were sorry for the obvious inconvenience this would cause but, at the same time, issue a warning to those who weren't qualified to drive or had been banned, do not attempt to take advantage of the situation or they would feel the full force of the law. Under the circumstances everyone thought this was the best they could come up with. The media would of course ask some very awkward questions but for now any questions were to be stalled with the classic 'no comment whilst the situation remains fluid'. That they would be the first to be told if anything changed. Good luck with that Jane had thought, inwardly smiling at the image of politicians and ministers squirming on sofas. A press conference would be arranged for 3pm that afternoon where, it was unanimously agreed, that invited journalists would be there to take notes only and not to ask questions.

The question of the NCA came up last. Everyone present had been previously advised of the internal problems of the agency. It was unanimously decided that the agency would have to be dismantled but using a step by step basis. That the other agencies including the police would have to take up some of the roles currently the responsibility of the NCA. The relevant ministerial departments along with the chancellor will look at budgeting these extra responsibilities. It had also been unanimously agreed that, for now, the public would remain ignorant of the fact that the NCA was being disbanded.

The meeting had lasted a little over four and a half hours, and at the end of it no one could say they had arrived at any kind of satisfactory solution. Never had Jane seen such a collection of deadpan faces following a COBRA meeting. Normally a clear path of direction would have been decided on. But not today. Today had simply confirmed that somehow they would have to muddle through and keep that they were muddling from the media, the great British public and most importantly other sovereign nations. Jane had almost felt sorry for them.

As for her role, the near future would be an intense one. Dismantling the NCA in secret would be no easy matter. And her role after that? The prime minister himself had promised her a role in one of the agencies, but which one? Nothing had been said.

Now standing outside, she actually found herself enjoying the noise and the buzz of the traffic, travelling between Trafalgar and Parliament Square. As she stood her car turned up. Her security got out and opened the rear door. Jane shook her head.

"No, I need some fresh air, wait for me here. And I need a decent coffee, not the muck His Majesty's government provides."

The security made to object but Jane cut him dead.

"I'll be alright. Follow me if you like but keep your distance. I've been at close quarters all morning, I need some space." Her security nodded.

"As you wish, ma'am, but I won't be far away should you need me."

"Thank you." Jane started to walk up Whitehall to Trafalgar Square. She saw her security instruct the driver and start to follow. He was far enough back. Tourists, lots of them, flooded Trafalgar Square. They all looked so carefree. How lucky they were that they weren't aware or involved in the affairs of state. Knowledge brought weight on one's shoulders that was sometimes difficult to manage. She held a great secret, so did others she worked with. How many secrets were held by those crowding Trafalgar Square. Hundreds? Thousands possibly. But how many of those secrets may be world changing? Now there was a question, and one she didn't want to know the answer to.

After crossing Northumberland Avenue, she turned right and then left passing under Charing Cross Station. In Villiers Street, she entered Gordon's Wine Bar. It had only just turned twelve and yet the vaulted cellar was already busy. Busy but busy with locals, not tourists and somehow Gordon's always managed to retain an atmosphere of untroubled serenity. An oasis she had heard many people describe it. And that it was, an oasis from the swarm of 'emmits' outside. Inside Gordon's, you were transported to another time and another place. London and all its noise was completely shut out. Sitting at a small table she ordered a small glass of merlot from the extensive wine list along with a pork and duck pate. Both arrived with quiet efficiency, the waiter recognising her, asking the usual questions as to her wellbeing.

Looking around Jane was relieved to see that her security hadn't followed her in. It was well known that she enjoyed this bar and nearly always visited when attending meetings in Whitehall. He probably hadn't felt the need. After finishing her pate, Jane visited the ladies washroom. Almost at the same time a lady, forty-something, enjoying a drink with a similar aged male got up and followed her in. Apart from the two of them the ladies was empty, Jane had completed a quick check.

"Pitgam".

"Axsti," Jane replied.

"Axsti."

"As planned, they haven't a clue."

The forty something woman smiled at Jane's few words. Nothing more was said, she waved her hands to activate the hand drier and left. Jane followed her moments after, returning to her table to finish her wine. The woman after ordering another glass of wine continued in deep conversation with her male partner. It was obvious to anyone watching that they were lovers, their undisguised intimacy was on public display. Minutes later Jane finished her wine, paid her bill and left. Outside her security was waiting, he looked cold and fed up but to his credit smiled as she joined him.

"Rather than follow me you can walk me back," Jane smiled broadly linking her arm in his. Jane feeling confident, her security feeling most uncomfortable.

Inside the wine bar, a man wearing a dark blue open necked shirt and off white chinos watched her go. Folding his newspaper he asked a waiter for his bill. Standing he nodded to the couple at the adjacent table but they didn't see, they were too interested in each other. After paying his bill, he stepped outside into the mass of movement in Villiers Street. It was cold outside but he didn't notice. He rarely felt the cold and therefore rarely wore a coat. He was happy in just a shirt, and rain hadn't been forecast. The lady he'd been watching had turned right. He turned left towards the Embankment. He felt no desire to follow her, he knew exactly where she was going.

Chapter 5

Maastricht Aachen Airport, Holland

Pierre sat back cradling his complimentary glass of champagne. It was never too early for champagne. The English felt the need to add orange juice as an excuse but not the French, the Flemish neither. They'd just been given the all clear for take-off. His pilot had told him it should be a straight forward flight, that they should arrive in Tenerife early afternoon, two thirty pm to be exact.

Perfect, it would give him time to relax and enjoy a little sun as well as sample something of the local cuisine. Tomorrow he had a full day. An inspection of a hospital they were about to open, meeting a number of his team followed by a press conference in the afternoon. He was looking forward to the press conference, he already knew that the local people idolised him. He took another sip of champagne, it tasted good.

"We're clear for take-off", The capitaine looked back through the cabin door. Pierre raised his glass.

"I'll take that", the French hostess took his glass. "You can have it back when we're in the air".

"Along with the bottle"?

"Along with the bottle". The hostess gave him a wide smile.

Pierre lent back further, enjoying feeling the thrust of the engines. He was determined to enjoy the flight and he had made a good start.

NCA's Temporary Offices, Gladstone Park. Cricklewood, London

Nick returned with two freshly brewed cappuccinos.

"This is the best bloody thing about this place", Nick commented, placing a mug on the desk.

105

"It's the only bloody thing." Roger quickly retorted, gesturing to Nick to take a seat.

"I don't know, I wouldn't mind your apartment". Nick sat down, crossing his legs whilst taking a noisy slurp of coffee.

"I need to speak to your mother, Nick. As for my apartment, would you like to live in a 'Big Brother' house"?

"You think you're being watched?" Nick sounded genuinely surprised.

Roger laughed, "Of course I do. Don't you?"

"It would explain it."

"Explain what?"

"Why security have nicknamed you fanny."

"Fuck off." Roger aimed a scrunched napkin at his colleague.

Nick ducked, "At least if you get into the wrong hands you won't have to worry about your manhood being displayed in your mouth, there wouldn't be any point". Nick laughed again. This time an empty coffee cup hit the intended target. His face changed. "You've still got that parcel in your apartment, what are going to do with it?"

"Who's in from forensics today?"

"Skeleton team, most are out and about, do you want me to check?"

"In a minute, you haven't mentioned my car, Nick."

"I know," Nick's smile was one of sympathy. "I was waiting for you." Roger knew the earlier banter was Nick's way of taking the sting out of the situation. It was the way of the services. Find humour when you're in a tight spot and you'll get through it.

"Why didn't you wake me, Nick, when you got the call?"

Nick shrugged his shoulders. "Jane called me, told me not to. To let you sleep. She said your emotions would probably get in the way of those trying to do their job. She said in your state of mind you may be something of a liability." Nick paused, he felt embarrassed. "Sorry sir. For what it's worth I think she was wrong, but you can't argue with Jane."

"No you can't", Roger managed a smile.

"How are you feeling"? Nick finished his coffee. "I mean you've lost everything, I'm not sure how I'd cope if it was me."

"What have I lost Nick? A car and bricks and mortar. They're easy to replace and Jane has already assured me that the NCA will cover everything I've lost and more." Silence fell between the two men, not an uncomfortable silence, a silence created by men lost in their own thoughts.

"It's not just that," Nick looked at the floor before raising his head. "Someone's out to kill you. I'd be shitting a brick if it was me."

Roger gave Nick a rueful smile. "You really think so, Nick? Haven't we had this conversation before? If somebody was out to kill me, they'd have done it by now. No, someone's trying to send me a message but what or why, I've no bloody idea. Perhaps whoever it is are trying to demonstrate that they're in control. And if that is the message, they're right, they bloody well are. We have teams out there", Roger waved his left arm in the general direction of the offices outside, "investigating and searching for what? I haven't a clue, have you?"

"I wouldn't say that, whoever it is, has made at least one mistake. Look at Peter Fitch."

Roger scoffed, "Peter Fitch? I'm beginning to believe Peter Fitch, the poor bugger, is their idea of a joke".

"You can't just write him off".

Roger's stance changed. "No, I know, and I'm not. In fact I'm thinking of interviewing him myself. When he's not expecting it and at his place of work".

Nick frowned, "Just go easy, the guy's got a shit hot solicitor and he's already threatening legal action citing harassment. Have you told Jane"?

"No."

"I wouldn't if I were you." Roger was surprised to hear his colleague say this. Nick was always one for adhering to protocol. He decided not to push him on it though.

Roger looked at his watch, it was gone ten. "Speaking of Jane, I wonder when the COBRA meeting will finish, I'm expecting a visit."

"They've got a lot to talk about, she won't be in the best of moods after listening to a load of hot air for hours."

Roger grinned, "No she won't, I'm bloody glad that we haven't been charged with investigating the DVLA hack."

"Bloody right", Nick concurred, "what's your take on it?"

Roger leaned back in his chair, arms behind his head. "Got to be the same people we're looking for, but why have they made public what they've done? It simply doesn't make any sense". How many times has he said that recently? "All they've really done is embarrass the government and caused a certain, ok, significant degree of chaos. But what have they gained from it? Surely they'd have a much stronger advantage if they'd kept their hack secret."

Nick pursed his lips. "A warning?"

Roger thought about this, "To whom and why"?

Nick, like Roger, leaned back in his chair. "To the government I guess. As to why, well I expect we'll find out in time." Nicks statement remained hanging in the air. Roger knew this was what all the agencies were afraid of. What was to come. That stranger, the one who kept changing his name. Donald something. His card was in his pocket but he chose to leave it where it was. What had he said? That the agencies were rattled, that whatever was coming it was going to be big? Something along those lines. He'd also hinted that France might be involved somehow. To investigate. He'd tried that and the new capitaine in Calais had cut him dead. Maybe he should try the back door so to speak. And under the circumstances to trust no one, Donald had pushed that line again and again. He looked across the desk at Nick, for the second time he wondered if he could trust him, was he working for anyone else?

"Nick, how did you know I was coming up in the lift earlier, you and the two guys from security were waiting for me"?

Nick was puzzled, why had his boss suddenly asked that? "Security contacted me, they have a control which lets them know every time the lift is operated. Where it was called from and where it's going. They knew you were coming up, they wanted me there when they met the lift." Roger hoped that was the case, that security along with Nick hadn't been watching his every move down below.

"I just wondered". Roger answered the question etched on Nick's face. "Right, do you want to see who's in from forensics? Let's get this over with".

Roger watched Nick go, he wished he'd asked for another coffee first. Never had he been in a position as to what to do next, which direction to take. But he was there now. A lot he knew depended on what Jane had to say after COBRA. It was interesting that she preferred to visit than phone. Especially with the apparent security risks. What did that say? That she was worried they'd be listened to too? Nick tapped on the open door.

"Three only in, all fairly new. Do you want to wait for someone more experienced to return?"

"No", Roger's reply was emphatic. "Let's do it now but three's a crowd, two will do. Ask them to get their kit will you, and meet me, ah no you can't. Bring them back here and we'll all go down together. And Nick."

"Yes?".

"Softly softly, low key, I don't want a fuss. Oh and don't let them contact anyone on the outside. This is strictly in house."

"Gotcha", Nick disappeared again.

Roger hoped he was doing the right thing, he knew he could be disciplined but sod it. This was his one chance of taking a step ahead of whoever and he was going to take it. Could it really get any worse? Almost certainly not.

It was a good ten minutes before Roger returned with two men, suspicion etched all over their faces.

"Roger, this is Laurence and Jamie, they're ready when you are." Nick introduced the two as if they were friends.

"What exactly is it you want us to do? And if it's a body of some sort, why isn't a pathologist here?"

Roger frowned at Nick, he hadn't wanted to divulge any more than the fact that what they were to examine was a suspicious parcel.

"Come in gentleman, Nick shut the door will you." Nick did as he was asked.

Roger looked at the two, he could see they were both nervous as well as suspicious. He wanted to put them both at ease whilst at the same time putting the fear of god into them, something of a contradiction.

"Gentleman, Laurence, Jamie. I've received a parcel, here at our temporary HQ. It's almost identical to two parcels that I received at my house not long ago. Now I'm going to be honest with you, both those parcels contained a mutilated head. One was an old colleague and friend of mine." The two men looked at each other. "Now I suspect this parcel contains the same or if not something similar. If it is a head, at the moment I've got no idea who it could be. Anyway none of that is your concern. What I want you guys to do is to try and find out who packed and sent this parcel. The tiniest thing that may help us take a step in the right direction. I want the parcel thoroughly examined before, if there are human remains inside, before it's handed over to a pathologist. Now, the reason the circumstances are a little different is that this is a matter of national security, worse we may have a mole, more than one actually in this building. Therefore I hope you'll understand, I do not want this matter getting beyond the four of us in this room. You're not to say a word to anybody you understand? Now I trust my colleague here." Roger gestured to Nick, so if this gets out I'll know it'll be because of one of you two. Do you understand"? The two men nodded before replying in unison.

"Yes sir."

"Good then follow me."

Not a word was said in the lift and all stood in silence again as Roger opened his fridge. The only item inside was an ordinary box, square and just big enough to hold a football.

"There, that's the package I want you to examine."

"Have you a bathroom we can use?" It was Laurence

"To scrub up and change," Jamie explained

"I hope you're doing the right thing." Nick commented whilst the two men were getting ready.

"So do I, Nick." Roger gave Nick his widest grin but it was less than convincing.

The two men returned wearing coveralls. The first thing they did was put plastic sheeting on the kitchen table.

"Now I need you two out of the way." Laurence's voice was commanding, this was his domain. He was in charge.

Roger and Nick did as they were told. And watched as the two men went about their task. For little over half an hour the two appeared to examine every square millimetre of the package. Now and again samples of some type were placed in small self-sealing evidence bags for more detailed examination in the lab. In under an hour they declared they had finished and were they to open the parcel? Roger confirmed that they were to do just that. Neither looked too happy about this but proceeded, carefully slicing the top of the box with a scalpel. If anyone is watching by a television monitor, and if I'm right, they're going to have one hell of a nasty surprise. Roger kept the thought to himself.

The first thing to hit was the smell. As the top was pulled apart it hit as though a grenade had been exploded in the room, bursting to escape. The gas given off by whatever was rotting inside rushed into the small space which was the kitchen enveloping everything and everyone. Jeremy staggered back and was instantly sick down the front of his coveralls. Laurence stayed in position but the colour of his skin said it all. He was doing his best not to do the same as his colleague. Both Roger and Nick had experienced the smell of rotting human flesh before, too often if they were honest, but even for them they found the foul tasting gas this time a little overpowering. Both placed their hands over their mouths.

"Want me to continue"? Laurence was doing his best to remain professional. His colleague had shut himself in the bathroom where by the sound of it he was continuing to suffer.

"Can you see what's inside?"

Laurence frowned at Roger. "For the moment only newspaper."

"Then take it out".

Laurence pulled a face and using a pair of tongs carefully removed the paper placing it in a large evidence bag for further examination. Seeing the contents for the first time he took three steps back, retching, but to his credit managed to keep the contents of his stomach inside him.

"You need to take a look, but don't touch anything." Laurence just about managed to get his words out.

Roger and Nick approached the table, they both knew what to expect but that didn't make it any easier. Peering inside, Roger immediately recognised the scenario, he had seen it all before and Nick had seen photographs. A man's head, his mouth forced open and stuffed with his genitalia. It was a grotesque sight made worse by the fact the face was beginning to decay.

"Recognise him"? Roger turned to Nick, swallowing as he spoke.

"I'm not sure." Nick took a step back, turning his head away.

"Cold water will help".

"I know". Nick went to the kitchen sink and turning on the cold tap let the water splash over his face, in particular his nostrils. Not bothering to wipe himself dry he returned to the box and once more peered inside. "He looks familiar as though I should know him but I can't remember where from."

"Ditto". Roger shook his head in frustration.

"Can we take the head out?" Roger turned to Laurence. His colleague had returned wearing a new set of coveralls and looking somewhat embarrassed. His apology was quickly dismissed by Roger.

"We should really wait for a pathologist, it'll need to be stored in a specially insulated body part bag."

"We haven't got time for that. You have an evidence bag big enough don't you"?

Laurence looked uncertain, "Yes but......

"No buts, let's get this done." Roger looked as though he were the only one there who wanted to get it done, but the others to their credit accepted their fate without argument. Laurence took a relatively large clear plastic bag from his holdall.

"I'll need you two to hold this open." His request was directed at the two NCA officers. Dutifully they each took a side and stretched the bag open. "Jamie I'll need your help, using tongs we need to deliver the head into the bag. Whatever we do we mustn't drop it. Everyone felt their stomach's rise on hearing this. The job was made more difficult as the decaying flesh tended to move as pressure was placed. As a consequence it took several minutes before the decapitated head was nestling in the bottom of the bag. Roger held it up for Nick to see.

"Recognise him now?" Nick shook his head before rushing to the sink and emptying the contents of his stomach. Jeremy did the same but this time he managed to make it to the bathroom in time. "I feel like I know him", Roger stared at the obscenity in frustration. He shook his head. "Right in the fridge you go". He put everybody out of their misery by placing the head carefully back in his fridge. He saw the expression on Laurence's face. "Don't worry, as soon as you're gone, I'll call the pathologist to come and collect it. Laurence didn't look convinced but had no choice than to accept Roger's word.

"I'll need to take the box for testing."

"It's all yours, that's why I wanted you here. Exactly for that."

Laurence appeared not to be listening, now accustomed to the smell apparently, he was busy examining the interior of the box. Taking a pair of tweezers he reached inside. "I think I may have found the identity of your head." He held up a bloodstained card, white and blue in colour. Both Nick and Roger recognised it instantly. It was a Metropolitan police warrant card. Someone had taken it out of its holder, almost certainly the someone who had placed it in the box. Why do that? Nick, forgetting his raging stomach for a moment, walked over to take a closer look. Both officers recognised who the card belonged to.The allegedly corrupt officer both the NCA and the Met were desperate to find. Clearly printed on the card was the officer's name. Detective Constable Havers. From the photo they could all see that it was Haver's head they had in the fridge.

"You silly boy", Roger muttered, "what did you get yourself into? Just who did you piss off"?

"I'm going to need to take this." Laurence reminded the two NCA officers, you may wish to photograph it as evidence before we've finished with it and can return it to you.

"Of course, thank you". Using his mobile phone, Roger took a number of photos, each from a different angle.

"And you may wish to take some photos of the head", Laurence motioned towards the fridge. "I've no idea how long you intend to keep it in there but the fridge will not stop the process of deterioration, it will simply slow it down. And do you want me to send a police photographer down? It'll be better than using your mobile".

"No". Roger was adamant. "What you two have witnessed stays with the four of us, is that clear? I have my reasons for being a little unconventional with this and as I told you both earlier it may be a matter of national security. If I hear that either of you have been discussing this with a third party you will have me to deal with and you won't like it, I promise. Understand"?

For a split second the two forensic officers glanced at each other before nodding. "Yes".

Roger, unconvinced, stared hard at each of them.

"You have our word, sir", Laurence looked to his colleague for confirmation.

"You do".

Roger relaxed, Nick returned to the sink to splash more water on his face. "And I value your concern and I understand where it comes from, but you've no need to worry. After you two have left, I'll be contacting a pathologist." Roger meant it too.

Going back to work the two from forensics bagged the warrant card and then the cardboard box. Roger went into his bedroom returning with a large holdall.

"You can't leave here carrying that lot for all to see. Use my bag".

Dutifully, the two carefully placed the bagged cardboard box in the holdall. "If that's all sir we'll make a start."

"Before you go, one question"? The two forensic officers looked at Roger, their expressions betraying their thoughts, 'What'?

"The warrant card, it has blood on it, would you say that occurred when the guy was killed or from laying in the box with the poor bugger's head"?

Laurence shrugged his shoulders. "Hard to say, the bottom of the box is lined with plastic which in turn has a thin layer of blood, which would suggest that blood was still running when the head was placed so quite possibly the stains are from that. But then again the blood could have been there already. It's hard to say at this stage, then of course it's a possibility that it's the mix of the two".

Nick looked thoughtful. "What does the fact that the blood was still running when the head was placed in the box tell you?"

Jeremy looked at Laurence who in turn nodded. Jeremy answered Nick's question. "That's really a question for the pathologist, but to me, both of us, I think Laurence will agree with me. It would indicate the head was severed soon after the victim was killed or possibly severed when he was still alive." Jamie once again looked across at Laurence.

"I would agree with that", Laurence backed his colleague up, "but as Jeremy said that's really a question for a pathologist".

"I understand". This time it was Roger who spoke, any more questions Nick"? Nick shook his head.

"Ok gentlemen, you'd better get out of those coveralls and I'll show you out, you'll need one of these to work the lift", he held up his key. "And I have the only one so I'll have to go up with you".

Ten minutes later the officers from forensics were back in their lab and Roger in his apartment. The first question Nick asked was, 'What do we do if the lift fails? How do we get out of here'?

"Do you know, I've no idea, I've never thought about it".

"Well I think you should, I couldn't sleep at night not knowing. You could be held prisoner down here". Roger ignored him though he mentally filed Nick's question for later. He really hadn't thought about it. But he needed to, he wasn't sure now if he'd be able to sleep that night not knowing.

"Well, what do you think"? Roger pushed Nick's question from his mind by asking his own.

"Think"? Nick let out a long sigh. He pushed himself away from the sink where he'd been leaning and grabbing a chair sat down. "Think, well the possibility that Havers was beheaded whilst he was still alive would suggest an element of Muslim extremism".

"Or someone wants us to think that way".

"Yes possibly, but that's a hell of a lot of barbarism simply to throw us off the track".

"True but look at Langstone, look at Spain, brutal beheadings, almost certainly gangster related, no suggestion of Muslim extremism".

"True", Nick conceded but the others and the head in your box, did you see the neck? To me, and I'm no expert, but that didn't look like a hatchet job. That looked like a clean cut. By someone who knew what they were doing or by someone using a very sharp knife at close quarters. Similar to the videos we saw placed online by Isis."

Roger thought about this, certainly a suggestion of an Islamic involvement had raised its head from time to time. His mind went back to the Hilton on Park Lane. The disappearing Arab women, his warning from Ishaan, head of the hotel's security. The severed head delivered to an address in North London, Muslim related. Could what they were dealing with, be a more sophisticated version of Isis? If it were, the thought scared the shit out of him. These people didn't think in any reasonable manner. They were dedicated and loyal only to their own narrow beliefs. And worse, if they were from the Middle East they would have access to shed loads of money. And their traditional way of communicating, word of mouth would explain why the listening agencies hadn't picked anything up. It was worth following up. He needed to speak to Ishaan again too. Any day now they will need to start forensically examining every room at the hotel. It would be a gigantic operation and privately, Roger felt, a fruitless one. A massive waste of resources.

"We need a pathologist to examine that head". Nick's statement tore Roger from his thoughts.

"Yes, yes we do, I'll book one to come and collect it".

"That won't look good, a pathologist coming down to your apartment carrying an insulated body part box or bag. You'd be the talk of the office if you aren't already".

Roger gave Nick a wide grin. "No it wouldn't, I hadn't thought of that. I'll have to think of something, it can't stay here much longer".

"No it can't and definitely, not in your fridge. You heard what forensics said".

"I'll stick it in the freezer, in fact I'll do it now." Roger went to his fridge, took out the wrapped head and placed it in his small chest freezer. He found the whole operation surprisingly painless. Nick he saw, had turned his head the other way.

"Done, Nick, shall we go up"? Nick needed no encouragement; he made for the lifts. He didn't want to spend another minute in Roger's horror apartment.

In the small sparsely equipped NCA 'in house' lab, Laurence and Jeremy gave the exhibits from Roger's flat a rudimentary examination.

"We can't do this here" Laurence after a small hour conceded. "We don't have the equipment needed. It'll have to go outside. I'll book it into the usual lab."

Gendarmerie Nationale, Calais, France

Lieutenant Beaufort was still struggling to make sense of his conversation with Monsieur Hubert the chief pathologist at Boulogne when he arrived at the gendarmerie to start work. The famously prickly pathologist had been uncomfortably charming, first names. WHAT!!! Before today he'd always insisted on addressing him using his title and surname. This morning's conversation had flowed as though they'd been buddies for years. The pathologist had asked the lieutenant to meet him at Les Baigneurs, a very traditional and therefore simple cafe in

Ambleteuse. A large village, famous for its Napoleonic fort on the coast road, the D940, to Boulogne. 'Twelve thirty sharp' the pathologist had told him. Sharp, he hadn't changed completely then. He'd better not be late and he somehow had to keep their meeting from his new capitaine. He knew he would never agree to it.

As he walked through reception, Colette tapped on the glass. Sitting in her office she was waving frantically, signalling for him to come to her. Looking around him, he didn't know why, it was probably after what happened the night before. He was already feeling guilty, under suspicion. He had to block his feelings out, act naturally or he'd quickly attract unwanted suspicion. Forcing a smile he waved and, after tapping the door, entered Colette's office.

"Why are you knocking"? was Colette's first words. "You never knock, just push". She laughed realising how that might be interpreted.

"Bonjour, Colette, I know". The lieutenant shook his right hand in frustration. "What is it"?

"Sit down," she waved to a chair, "you'll never guess what"?

"What"? the lieutenant sat.

Colette recounted her conversation with Capitaine Vendroux earlier that morning. And the fact that she'd been asked to contact Jean and Camille to come back for a second interview.

"What do you think? Perhaps we've got the capitaine wrong after all".

The lieutenant hardly heard her, he was worried what the two might say to his boss. Would they reveal their meeting last night? If they did, no it didn't bear thinking about.

"What do you think"? This time Colette's question was a decibel or two higher. It worked, she once more had the lieutenant's full attention.

"Think?, I'm more worried about what they might say to the capitaine".

Colette laughed, "Rubbish, they'll be fine. They're not kids".

"Only just".

"Have faith", Colette scolded him. "What do you think?"

The lieutenant shook his head. "To be honest, Colette, I don't know what to think. Since that bloody storm everything seems to have gone mad around here".

"Well I think we should give our capitaine a chance, perhaps his early behaviour was just nerves, being in a new place and all that".

"We shall see". He couldn't believe Colette, what a change from yesterday. It looked like he may be on his own after all. Leopards don't change their spots that quickly, something has happened to bring about this change of heart. He had to find out what. How he hadn't a clue. "Anyway I'd better go and see the great man, let him know I'm here."

"Sarcasm will get you nowhere, lieutenant".

"Shame". the lieutenant grinned, shutting the door behind him.

The capitaine's door was ajar. The lieutenant knocked once and entered. His boss was at his desk, reading through a pile of papers. He looked up on seeing the lieutenant enter.

"Ah lieutenant, I thought I'd catch up. I'm reading through all of the files created since that storm everybody keeps talking about. I've asked those two kids to come back in to see me. I fear I might have been too hasty. Perhaps they have something worth investigating".

"Maybe", the lieutenant hoped he sounded nonchalant. The last thing he wanted was to sound nervous. "I'm off to interview a couple of fishermen who think they may have spotted something unusual out to sea". It was a lie, they had no new leads. His teams were simply plodding, going over old evidence.

"Good, good lieutenant, well keep me informed".

"Will do sir".

"Leave the door open, it gets stuffy in here". The lieutenant did as he was told. He was relieved his new boss hadn't asked him to sit in on the interview.

The capitaine watched the lieutenant go. He was relieved his lieutenant hadn't asked to sit in on the interview. He hoped to keep the two kids under his wing, to himself. He needed to convince them that his gendarmerie was taking their evidence seriously and following up on their story, when in truth they were doing nothing. The last thing he needed was them talking to anybody else.

The lieutenant, after leaving the capitaine's office, visited the various teams doing the plodding. It had been discovered that the gendarme who had gone missing was secretly on a number of adult dating sites. It was looking increasingly as though he may have grown too fond of one and crossed over to someone in his second life. Hopefully they would soon find him and close off one of the avenues of enquiry. If they did, someone would have to tell his wife. In some ways revealing that he'd been found and was living with another woman was harder than revealing that he had died. The latter though hard, was in a way, easier to accept than being rejected for somebody else.

Le Week-End Cafe/Bar, Sangatte, France

It was close to ten am when Jean received the call, he was just finishing serving breakfasts. He quickly dumped the plates he'd been collecting on the bar and accepted the call as he walked outside.

"Hello."

"Jean?"

"Oui".

Colette took a deep breath, why didn't schools teach youngsters how to answer the phone. "Jean, Jean, it's Colette. Colette from the gendarmerie, remember"?

"Oui, bonjour Colette".

Colette took another deep intake of breath, you'd never believe they'd been in deep conversation the night before. Slowly and clearly she explained that the capitaine who had previously dismissed them now wanted to see them. To hear their story again. Apparently she explained to him that their capitaine thought there might be something in their story after all. It changes nothing where we're concerned, she assured him.

After her call, Jean sat down stunned. He didn't know what to think. How he regretted that they'd been intimate in his car on Cap Blanc Nez that night. He needed to speak with Camille. He called her, for the first time since he could remember, she wasn't picking up. Where was she? Camille always picked up, her phone was an extension to her body. Where the bloody hell was she?

The Royal Lancaster Hotel, Lancaster Terrace, London

It was mid-morning and Fatima was still in her room. She knew one day soon she would be shown the most important part of her new identity. It might even be today. That was how the organisation worked. For the last hour she'd spent her time between her bedroom window, admiring the view across Hyde Park and the television, always the news. Her new target was never often off it. Even Al Jazeera. Now close to eleven am, she was beginning to become sick of the Right Honourable Stephan Sands, and this was before she'd even begun to target him. Fatima walked back to the window. For the first time since she'd started working for Pierre and the organisation she was feeling nervous. She was confident she could seduce Stephen Sands but why did she feel she was getting in over her head? She'd hived a lot of money away and before this job she'd been thinking about retiring. Of trying to lead a normal life, maybe find a nice Muslim man, settle down and have a family. Now she was beginning to wonder if this would ever be possible. Would the organisation ever let her retire. Was she too valuable and, after this job, would she know too much? Too much for the organisation to let her go. She had to do some serious thinking before it was too late.

At that moment the room telephone rang. Was this it? Was she going to be shown her new home? She picked up the receiver. It was reception.

"Madame, sorry to disturb you, there's a Mrs Henrietta". She heard the person on the front desk turn and speak to a woman. "A Mrs Henrietta Sands to see you. She's told me to tell you that you're not expecting her and it's fine if you're busy. She only stopped by on the off chance, as she's in the area".

"No it's fine, please tell her that I'm on my way down".

"Certainly"."

"I'll be five minutes". It was too late the receptionist had gone.

Henrietta Sands, the woman whose company she so enjoyed last night. The wife of the Home Secretary. This was completely unexpected. What on earth could she want? There was only one way to find out. Fatima quickly examined herself in the mirror, her mix of black and purple with a touch of silver braid expressing her Persian roots she decided was perfect. Sobriety with a hint of glamour. As tended to be her signature she finished by wrapping a deep purple scarf over her head and around her neck letting the tassel ends flow loosely about her broad shoulders.

Ten minutes later Fatima exited the lift stepping into the spacious hotel foyer. She immediately saw Henrietta. She was standing beside the reception desk looking very anxious. She smiled warmly as she recognised Fatima, Ariana to her. Meeting in the middle Henrietta kissed Fatima warmly on the cheek.

"I hope you don't mind me coming". Her anxious expression had returned.

"Not at all, in fact I'm glad you've come, I've been wondering what to do for the last hour".

"You're being honest, I hope?"

"Perfectly". Fatima smiled broadly. She was immediately feeling the attraction she'd felt the night before. Henrietta despite all her wit and power, being married to the Home Secretary, was naturally defenceless, vulnerable almost. Completely unassuming, too often she'd come across women who were full of self importance purely because they were married to a successful or powerful man and vice versa. Henrietta, going by first impressions was nothing like that. Completely the opposite.

"I'm so glad", the relief was clearly visible on Henrietta's face. "I just had to get out, with all this driver's licence nonsense, Stephan will be utterly unbearable. He's cooped up in Whitehall somewhere now, in a meeting with people he confides to me that he can't stand. After that, the media. Stephan's a clever man but he can't handle stress. He'll be an absolute nightmare, WHEN he comes home". Henrietta paused, for the first time Fatima noticed how small Henrietta was, five foot two, not much more."So I needed to get out, and I thought of you. I so enjoyed your company last night, your background". All a lie, Fatima to her surprise found herself feeling a little guilty. "We're so dull and grey here in England, and you're so exotic. So I wondered if you fancied spending a few hours, possibly a day with me. I can show you London, if you're buying a house here, you'll need a guide, a friend too". Henrietta touched Fatima's arm. "London, without a friend, can be a very lonely place. Only when Londoners have had a drink, do they socialise".

"Of course, I'd love to". It was a golden opportunity for her to find out about the man who was her target. Targeting via the back door so to speak. If the organisation had been planning to show her her new house, they would simply have to wait. "But how did you know I was staying here"? Fatima carried that professional suspicion, a suspicion that spoke, 'trust no one'. A suspicion that also stemmed from her life experiences.

Henrietta was the wife of the Home Secretary. A master key in the cog that was the establishment. Henrietta could be just another cog, sent to find out more about the 'exotic' Ariana.

Henrietta responded immediately. "I called Charles. He wouldn't give me your number but told me you were staying here until your house was ready to move into. That he was sure you wouldn't mind me stopping by".

How very astute of Charles, no doubt he too had seen the opportunity. Attacking her target via the back door. Fatima was sure Charles wouldn't have revealed where she was staying if he'd felt it to be a risk. She relaxed. "So what now"?

"Coffee or tea", came Henrietta's immediate response.

"Here"? Fatima motioned to the hotel's lounge.

"No". Henrietta grabbed Fatima's arm, "No, I'm going to show you London, there's a lovely little tearoom around the corner. You'll love it".

NCA's Temporary Offices, Gladstone Park, North London, England

Roger sat in his office deep in thought. Playing between his fingers, a card. On it a name, 'Donald Anas' and a mobile phone number. He needed a pathologist to examine the head of Detective Constable Havers currently stored in his freezer. After everything that had happened he was nervous about using the usual pathologist. On whose side was he batting? On whose side was anyone batting for that matter? Mind made up he stopped fingering the card. Placing it upright on his desk he opened a drawer and pulled out a pay as you go phone. A phone he'd taken from John's flat in Drury Lane. After turning it on he called the number on the card. The ringtone seemed to go on forever and he was just about to give up when a man's voice answered.

"Donald, Donald Anas".

"Donald? It's Roger, Roger Denton".

"Change your name Roger or never use it when speaking to me". It was not the answer Roger had been expecting. The line went silent, not dead, just silent.

"Are you still there?" He didn't have the time to waste on silly agency games.

"Yes, just checking something. All good. How can I be of help"?

Roger explained the situation with the head, how he wasn't sure if he could trust one of the Met's pathologists and how he'd much prefer an independent examination. He finished by asking."You gave me the card of a good forensics lab. Have you a pathologist you can recommend, and am I doing the right thing"?

"You certainly are"came the immediate response. "So tell me again, who knows about what you've got stored in your freezer"? Roger told him. "That's already too many but can't be helped, the Met aren't aware"?

"No"."

"Keep it that way. Let them carry on looking for Mr H". Roger assumed he meant by Mr H the unfortunate Havers. "Listen I'll come and collect the head, your security there hasn't the level of clearance to search anything I carry. I'll bring a pathologist with me. You can absolutely trust him". There came a pause. "He's not cheap though and the Met don't have an account". There came another pause. "Oh, we'll sort that somehow, now we'll be with you in around an...". There came a third pause, this time Roger could feel him looking at his watch. "Jane's coming to see you, I've no wish to bump into her. Call me after she's gone and we'll be with you within the hour". The line went dead. How the hell did he know that Jane was coming over?

Roger didn't have time to try and work it out. There came a knock at his door. He quickly returned the phone he'd been using to its drawer.

"Yes?"

Fiona, an accomplished officer currently working with a team coordinating with the Met in the search for Detective Constable Havers entered his office. Roger felt himself blushing, he prayed it didn't show.

Fiona appeared not to notice. "I've the file from the constabulary in Cornwall, on the raid at Bodinnick. It makes interesting reading, sir". She placed a thin folder on his desk. Roger picked it up and opened it. There wasn't much but Roger could see, at a glance, that what was there, was relevant to everything that they'd been investigating since the discovery of the murder in Langstone.

"The inhabitant of the property sadly is dead. The armed response team had to shoot her as she opened fire on our officers. To be honest, I think there was no way we could have taken her alive. If we hadn't killed her, I think she would have killed herself."

"And she is"?

"Confirmed sir, Claire Flynn. One of the nastiest gangsters to have come out of Manchester. Responsible, we believe, to have ordered dozens of killings but none were ever proven".

"And what do we think she was doing in", Roger peered at the file. "Bodinnick"?

"Uniform have interviewed close neighbours and the staff at the local pub, The Old Ferry Inn, and all say she'd told them she'd moved town to retire". Fiona scoffed. "Retire, she'd never be able to retire, not with her record".

"Well, she has now". Roger threw a thin smile.

"Yes,sir, she has". Roger had stopped flicking through. He was examining a number of photos. They showed an image that was becoming far too familiar. Several were taken from several angles and were of a decapitated head. As before the victim was male and had had his genitalia unceremoniously stuffed in his mouth. Two more were photographs taking facing and after the genitalia had been removed.

"What's this and who is he"?

"That's the main reason I came to see you, sir. Just before the raid, a courier delivered a parcel. When it was opened, this is what was found inside. I know you received something similar". Fiona's voice faded as she finished.

"Thank you". Roger gave a reassuring smile. He was picturing the officers opening the box, their shock when they had peered inside.

"Have we checked the courier and who sent it"?

"The courier involved denies ever having a van in the area and there's no CCTV in the local vicinity. We're scanning further afield but so far nothing; the van appears to have simply disappeared". Sounds familiar, Roger kept the thought to himself. "Mrs Flynn had cameras all around her house. They got a good shot of the driver", Fiona helped Roger find another photo. It was a very clear shot of a man ringing a doorbell. Roger recognised him immediately. "We've done a face recognition check and according to the DVLA database he's a Mr".

"Peter Fitch, I know, except it's not, is it"?

"No sir, Peter Fitch at the time was".

Roger cut her off. "Feeding the bloody thousands or something equally bloody public".

"Teaching", Fiona said quietly. "And before you ask, sir the facial recognition check was before the DVLA was hacked".

"Knowingly", Roger pointed out.

"Yes sir, knowingly. What will be of interest to you, the image you have there of the delivery driver was shown to the officers at the scene. All have said that the photo taken from Mrs Flynn's CCTV is nothing like the driver they witnessed. But how is that possible? Digital forensics are currently examining the house's security system but the last I've heard, they've found nothing. They can't explain it". Sounds familiar, Roger thought again. Fiona reached across the file and pulled out another paper. "This is an artist's impression after talking to three of the officers present at the time. They all say it's a pretty good likeness".

Roger looked at the drawing, the image shown looked nothing like the man in the photo.

"Have we tried putting this through 'face recognition'"? Sometimes if the sketch was good enough the system could find a match.

"Yes, and the system has come up with over ten thousand probables and thousands more possibles. We're just starting to check each one". The pain in Fiona's voice was obvious. Roger returned to the photo, taken directly of the decapitated head. After the genitalia had been removed.

"Have we tried face recognition using this"? To Roger's surprise Fiona confirmed they had.

"Yes sir, and it's not perfect, but we're pretty sure it belongs to one Ryan Hedges. The man we had under surveillance. His house was bombed, if you remember".

"Yes, yes of course, we're still investigating". Roger wanted to move on quickly. "Well we're pretty sure it's him. Samples have been sent to a lab for DNA testing. Anything else?

Fiona looked nervous. "Yes, sir, but like everything else it's very odd. We recovered Mrs Flynn's mobile phone. We knew she made calls with it as she was under surveillance. And yet when it was checked there was only one number listed on it and when we called that number all we got was someone laughing at the other end".

"And did you try tracing the number"? Roger already knew her answer.

"Yes, but apparently the number doesn't exist. How does that work"?

"I wish I knew; we've already come across this with someone else's phone". It was the first Fiona had heard about it. "And the landline"?

"Almost the same thing sir. Mrs Flynn has been paying her bills regularly and she's been making and receiving calls and yet the phone company has no record of any of them. They can't understand it".

All this was sounding, frustratingly, all too familiar.

"We're still looking for Detective Constable Havers, sir. All the ports and, any way out of the country have been alerted to look out for him. He appears to have simply disappeared. Somebody must be helping him. We'll keep looking sir".

"Thank you Fiona, keep me up to date will you"?.

"Of course sir". With that Fiona left, leaving Roger feeling extremely guilty.

Gendarmerie Nationale, Calais, France

Colette recognised him instantly. Secretly she always liked to admire young men but this one was special. It was Jean and he was alone. Without his girlfriend Camille. Seeing him in reception, she tapped on the glass wall beckoning him to come to her office.

"Jean, where's Camille? Why have you come alone, I believe the capitaine wanted to see both of you".

"I know". Jean looked despondent. "I can't get hold of her, she's not answering her phone. If I'm honest I'm a little worried". Jean looked it, Colette thought to herself. In fact he looked ill with worry.

"Then why have you come now Jean; it could have waited".

"No", Jean shook his head. "I want to get this over with, why has the capitaine changed his mind"?

"I've no idea, Jean, the capitaine doesn't tell me everything. Perhaps someone else has come forward I don't know about. I simply don't know. It's good that he wants to see you though, isn't it"?.

"Is it"? Jean looked doubtful. "Do you think he knows about yesterday"?

"Of course not". Colette hoped she sounded convincing. She'd wondered if that was the real reason Capitaine Vendroux wanted to see them again herself. "Do you want a coffee before you go up"?

Jean shook his head. "No, I just want to get this done". Colette nodded.

"I'll see if he's ready for you". Colette buzzed using her desk phone. Jean heard her announce that he was here. "He's ready", Colette replaced the receiver. "Do you want me to take you up"?

Again Jean shook his head. "No need, I know where it is".

"Ok, as you wish, oh and Jean", Colette put a finger to her lips. "Not a word about last night".

"Of course not". With that he bounded up the stairs three at a time and after turning right along the corridor soon arrived at a door proudly displaying a newly fixed sign. 'Capitaine Olivier Vendroux'. Taking a deep breath he knocked, how he wished Camille were with him. Was he, he wondered, simply going into the lion's den. He had no reason to trust the gendarme. Was he doing the right thing?

"Entrez". It was too late now.

Jean pushed open the door.

Les Baigneurs Café, Ambleteuse, France

Lieutenant Beaufort spotted Monsieur Hubert, the pathologist immediately. He hadn't dressed down for the occasion which arguably he should have done. Les Baigneurs was a good old traditional cafe without frills. It was arguably the only cafe of its type left on the coast between Calais and Boulogne. Nearly everywhere else along the coast had been smartened up to please visitors from England and Paris. As a result, it tended to serve the local population, a population clinging to the past. When he'd been an adolescent, a number of the cafe/bars along the coast had what was referred to as a 'fisherman's licence'. These cafes used to open in the early hours, allowing in theory, the fisherman returning from sea to wash the salt out of their mouths with a beer or two. Often more. As a youth, if he hadn't managed to pick up a girl he and his friends used to visit these cafes to carry on drinking after everywhere else was closed. There were still a few cafes that did this but they were fast disappearing. Les Baigneurs didn't have a 'fisherman's licence', but it was somewhere where working people could go, have a chat, enjoy a drink and a bite to eat in an environment they were familiar with. Not only familiar with, comfortable with. The lieutenant had sensibly removed his uniform, replacing it with jeans, a tee shirt and fleece. He fitted in perfectly. The pathologist however was in a smart tan suit and as a consequence was attracting the odd glance.

The lieutenant walked across to his table and heartily shook the pathologist's hand. He deliberately made it look as if they were old friends.

"I'm a bit overdressed," were the pathologist's first words.

"You are a little". The lieutenant had never seen the pathologist look nervous before and it was obvious he was, very. What was this all about? "But don't worry a beer will help you fit in".

"I'm driving", he couldn't help noticing the lieutenant's scowl. "Ok, just the one". The pathologist attempted a smile.

"Pelforth"?

"Oui, merci". The pathologist nodded weakly.

Lieutenant Beaufort went to the bar to order. The service was quick and it wasn't long before he had rejoined the pathologist. They clinked glasses.

"Sante."

"Sante", Jean-Paul Hubert attempted to smile and failed miserably. The lieutenant couldn't fail but notice that the man sitting opposite him wasn't looking at him but beyond him to the bar.

"Jean-Paul," the lieutenant, although invited to, still felt odd calling the pathologist by his first name. "Are you ok, is something wrong"?

"Pardon", Jean-Paul did his best to concentrate on the lieutenant. "Pardon, I'm scared someone might be following me".

Scared! Following! What the hell was going on?

"Following you? Jean-Paul, let me sit where you are. We're trained in the gendarme to spot people following us". It was a lie, but it worked, the pathologist allowed him to swap places. Once settled the lieutenant deliberately made out that he was scouring the bar. Focusing once more on Jean-Paul.

"What is it, Jean-Paul, what's spooked you. What is it that you can't tell me on the phone"? Jean Paul no longer looked nervous, he looked petrified. The lieutenant once more scoured the bar. Hoping to put the man sitting opposite him at ease. "No one's following you Jean Paul, now tell me what is it, what's happened"?

Jean-Paul couldn't help taking one quick look over his shoulder.

"You remember escorting the bodies of those poor children to Calais so that they could be returned to the UK"? How could he forget?

"Yes of course. "But what's that got to do with anything"?

"You didn't find it suspicious, the involvement of the GIGN"?

The lieutenant pursed his lips. "Of course but it was government business. Nothing to do with us. Is this what all of this is about"? Had he come all this way for nothing.

"Yes", Jean-Paul couldn't help taking another look over his shoulder. "But there's more lieutenant". The pathologist went on to explain what had been demanded of him. To delete all digital records of the twelve mutilated children along with the two adults found with them. How he'd been forced to hand over the physical files too of his post mortems.

That if anyone asked, to tell them that he didn't have the space or time to carry out so many post mortems and that they'd been transferred to a morgue in Paris.

"We both know that's not true lieutenant, oh, though not having the room IS true". For a moment, Jean-Paul looked lost in thought.

The lieutenant smiled, you could never take the pathologist away from his work for long.

Jean-Paul was back. "They gave me a number and an address in Paris to give out if anyone asked and was insistent. Here", Jean Paul unfolded a small square piece of paper, on it in ultra neat handwriting was an address in the Chaillot region of Paris and a phone number with an 01 code, Paris.

"Have you tried dialling it"?

Jean-Paul shook his head. "No,no I wouldn't dare, and they threatened me lieutenant".

"Threatened you"!

"Yes, yes". Jean-Paul finished his beer. "Yes, they told me that if I breathed a word of this that I would not only lose my licence to practise but my pension as well. I'm taking a huge risk telling you lieutenant, a huge risk, in fact I'm risking everything I've ever worked for but I'd prefer to die with a clear conscience than a nice house".

"I think we both need another beer". The lieutenant stood up. This time the pathologist made no protest. The bar was busier now and he had to wait. Pinned to a shelf behind the bar was a curled photo. It had obviously been there for a long time as it was beginning to fade. The photo was of Frank Ribery, a footballer born in a working class suburb of Boulogne who, despite many challenges, including a near fatal car accident had finally realised success. The photo was of him playing in a Bayern Munich shirt. The lieutenant thought about what Jean-Paul had just told him. He had a new found respect for the man. Jean-Paul bore a conscience, one that he held as a torch above anything else. Who knew the struggles he had gone through to become chief pathologist and he was prepared to throw it all away. Just so he could sleep at night. How many people were prepared to do that? Not many and if he were faced with a similar situation, wasn't sure he could either. Jean-Paul had been disturbed by the removal of the twelve mutilated children and the cover up that had followed. Whereas to a great extent he had simply accepted it. True he had made a couple of notes to call a detective in London, but that was it. PATHETIC, he scolded himself. He had to make amends.

"Monsieur"? It was the barmaid. He ordered two more Pelforths and returned to the table where Jean-Paul had gone from distinctly nervous to fiercely determined.

He'd gotten the hardest part over with, he'd told somebody. There was no going back now. From here on, it was all or nothing.

The lieutenant placed both beers on the small table. Instinctively he scoured the bar. After what Jean-Paul had just told him he understood why he felt nervous. The stakes were obviously very high and it was very possible that the pathologist WAS under surveillance. That he wasn't exaggerating. He couldn't see anyone who didn't look as if they should be there. Once more the two men clinked glasses. This time though 'sante' wasn't shared.

"Tell me Jean-Paul, why are you meeting me? Why aren't you telling what you've just told me to my boss"?

"I don't trust him". The lieutenant was surprised by the pathologist's bluntness.

"Don't trust him"? So here was someone else who didn't trust Capitaine Olivier Vendroux. It wasn't just him and Colette.

"No I don't, I think he's in with them."

"Them?"

Jean-Paul looked directly at the lieutenant. "Yes them, don't ask me who they are. The people who sent the GIGN, who organised the address and number in Paris. Probably some government department, just them". And then a bombshell. "It wouldn't surprise me if 'them' had orchestrated your old boss's death so they could move their new man in. Nothing would surprise me after what I was threatened with". The pathologist's observation hit the lieutenant as though it were a bullet between the eyes. Jean-Paul had thought this and he wasn't even aware that two young people thought they'd seen Capitaine Maubert pushed to his death, that it wasn't suicide. Could Jean-Paul be right? It sent a shiver down the lieutenant's spine.

"Of course I don't really believe that they'd go as far as murdering someone, but knowing Capitaine Maubert as I do, I never and still don't believe him capable of suicide". The pathologist looked thoughtful. "Then again I never thought him capable of betraying his dear wife. Perhaps I'm just a stupid old man being overly suspicious".

"You're not". The lieutenant was quick to reassure him. "Now tell me about the twelve mutilated children and the two adults that were found with them and sent back to the UK. What do you think was so special about them"?

"How long have you got, lieutenant"? The lieutenant looked at his watch.

"Now? Not long, but we can carry on this conversation another time. Give me a synopsis"

"Ok", the pathologist furrowed his brow as he thought where to begin.

"To start, how were they all killed? Did you identify that"? The lieutenant helped him.

Jean-Paul took advantage of the prompt. "The two men, easy. Gunshot wounds. The twelve children? There were no signs of physical wounds that would have led to their deaths and that would have been hard to cover that up. Having said that, on three of the children I did discover a prick on their arms suggesting a recent injection. I wanted to investigate further but of course the bodies were taken away. But they may all well have died due to a lethal injection, a deliberate act".

"So murder".

"Yes, lieutenant, murder". No wonder whoever it was wanted this covering up. If this got out it would be the shock of the year. What really pissed him off, if Jean-Paul was right, was that he'd helped take part in the cover up. The state, if that's who it was, had used him. He felt his blood rising.

"Anything else, Jean-Paul"?

"Yes, plenty. The two men had been shot recently, perhaps only hours before they were found, whereas the children had been dead for much longer, perhaps even weeks longer. And after they were shot dead the two men hadn't been touched whereas the children had been mutilated, professionally mutilated".

"What do you mean by 'professionally mutilated'"?

The pathologist took a very deep breath. "It's only my theory you understand, based on my professional opinion as chief pathologist, having said that I will never put what I'm about to tell you in a professional report".

"Go on, Jean-Paul, I promise I'll never ask you to do that".

The pathologist leant over the table as though he was worried somebody might be listening. What followed was spoken in a loud whisper.

"If you want my professional opinion, lieutenant, the children were cut apart for their body parts. It was quite evident that a competent surgeon or surgeons had removed everything that could be transplanted. All had had their eyes removed and some had even been scalped. It wasn't just internal organs, some had had their feet, hands removed. All with a surgeon's knife. It looked almost as though they were being kept so their bodies could be mutilated to order. A shop selling human parts. Your old boss hinted at such a possibility after the discovery of those heads and the poor girl's body on the beach.

"Have you still got those?"

"Yes, yes. Nobody's ever claimed them, poor souls.

"You say you've got no records Jean-Paul, how much can you remember? Can you write what you remember down? Don't type it up at the morgue. If someone is keeping an eye on you, the discovery of that could get you into very hot water".

Jean-Paul looked pleased with himself. "I can do better than that, lieutenant". He reached into his inside jacket pocket pulling out a small machine.The lieutenant recognised it instantly as a hand held recording device. The pathologist handed it over. "I record everything on there before I type up my reports. The GIGN never asked for it and no way was I going to offer it. All my observations and thoughts are recorded on there. You'll need to find another pathologist to make sense of them. And someone you can trust. But I daren't help you more than that. With any luck, I'll keep my licence and pension. To the GIGN and their puppet masters, I'm still a good boy". The lieutenant took the offering and zipped it tight in the chest pocket of his fleece.

"If you're sure, Jean-Paul".

"Quite sure". The pathologist was looking nervous again, glancing over his shoulder.

"Do you want something to eat"? The lieutenant hadn't had lunch and his stomach was beginning to tell him so, he guessed the pathologist hadn't either. Jean-Paul shook his head.

"Non merci. I have sandwiches waiting in my office. I ought to get going or my staff will wonder where I've got to. I rarely leave my place of work lieutenant, not during office hours". Both men stood up and shook hands.

"Take care, Jean-Paul, I'll be in touch". The lieutenant tapped the pocket concealing the voice recorder.

"No offence, lieutenant but only if it's absolutely necessary". He waved before opening and closing the door to the outside. Looking out of the window the lieutenant watched him drive off. Well, well, well, what a turn up. He'd had no idea what to expect but certainly not what had just taken place. He touched his chest pocket needlessly confirming the presence of the handheld voice recorder. How on earth was he going to investigate what the pathologist had told him, especially his suspicions, without arousing the suspicions of his capitaine? Taking a sip from his almost empty glass, he again unfolded the small square of paper. He stared at the address, it was in a very smart part of Paris. Hardly where you'd expect to find a morgue. He knew someone in Paris, another gendarme. They had trained together and remained friends ever since. He reached into another pocket for his phone. He'd give him a ring. Something inside told him not to be so hasty. He glanced around the cafe, was he being watched? He'd wait till he was in his car. For now he was hungry. He signalled to the girl behind the bar who in turn signalled to someone else. A traditionally dressed woman, the lieutenant guessed in her mid-sixties, arrived at his table.

"Oui, monsieur, vous avez choisi?"

The lieutenant glanced at the no nonsense menu. "Andouillette frites s'il vous plaît". And after a second's thought he added another Pelforth to his order.

Jean-Paul Hubert was deep in thought. The road between Ambleteuse and Wimereux was in places stunning and something he always enjoyed. Today, after his meeting with the lieutenant, he hardly noticed. So deep in thought was he, he was oblivious to the car hanging onto his tail. He still didn't notice when the car, on a rare short straight stretch of road, pulled out and accelerated until it was alongside. Two young men stared across at Jean-Paul who remained oblivious to their presence. The sounding of their car horn brought the pathologist bolt upright. For a second, he saw their two faces grinning and then took evasive action as their car swerved towards his. His car shook violently as the inside wheels left the road and then swerved as the inside right wheel hit a patch of sand. The car that had forced the pathologist's sudden manoeuvre sped off disappearing round the corner ahead. He could see the two men inside looking back and laughing. Using his gears rather than his brake Jean-Paul managed to steady his car back onto the road. Another car pulled up behind him, slowing, until there was only a few inches gap between the two bumpers. Another horn sounded. The pathologist this time realised why, he was hardly moving and he was on a bend. Putting his foot down on the accelerator, he raised his hand in an apology. Pulling out of the bend, the car behind accelerated and passed with the driver, this time a woman holding up a single finger in his direction. At the next available parking area the pathologist pulled over. The parking area, on a bend afforded views out to sea and back along the coast to Cap Gris Nez. It was quite beautiful, even under a grey sky.

Life was beautiful as well as wonderful. Working with death all of his working life he realised only now, moments after he thought he was about to die, how he'd ignored God's wonderful gift. From here on, he was determined to change, to loosen his control of his morgue, to get out and see the world. Or to simply enjoy the odd beer as he had today. Leaning his chair back he allowed his head to drop back onto the head rest. He closed his eyes. Seconds later the pathologist was asleep.

Lieutenant Beaufort after leaving the cafe decided not to ring his friend in Paris straight away. Instead, he drove slowly back along the coast, deliberating on how he was to explain what he needed. On reaching Cap Blanc Nez he pulled into the parking area positioning his car so that he had a view of the monument erected by the English to commemorate their navy's patrol of La Manche during the first world war. He now knew how he was going to phrase his request for a favour. Taking out his mobile, he dialled. A familiar voice answered. After exchanging pleasantries the lieutenant launched right in, his pre-planned approach forgotten.

"Marcel, I need you to do me a favour".

Chapter 5

Gendarmerie Nationale, Calais, France

Whilst Lieutenant Beaufort and the pathologist, Jean-Paul Hubert were enjoying a beer in Ambleteuse, Jean, the young waiter at Le Weekend cafe/bar in Sangatte, was sitting nervously in Capitaine Vendroux's office. Try as he might, he couldn't stop himself from wringing his hands and when he did he found himself tapping the floor with his feet which brought a frown from the man in uniform sitting across the desk opposite him.

He wished Camille was with him, only now did he realise how much he depended on her support. He always acted the strong man but sitting alone in an office of the capitaine of the gendarmerie made him realise that between the two of them, she was probably the stronger. That his perception of her being weak was drawn from the fact that she was simply more relaxed than he was. He would never underestimate her again, where the hell was she?

As it turned out, the interview was a lot easier than Jean had dared to imagine. The Capitaine was all smiles and patient with his questions as well as Jean's answers. Jean didn't reveal anything new from their last interview. The only difference was this time the capitaine appeared to be listening and made notes at regular intervals.

At the end, the capitaine stood and shook his hand. He also gave Jean his card.

"We need to keep this between ourselves, Jean. I will get the right people to investigate your story, ask awkward questions but discreetly you understand. If what you have told me reaches the wrong ears, you could be putting both yourself and your girlfriend"....

"Camille", Jean helped him.

"Camille, yes. You could, if word got out, both be in serious danger. If what you have seen is true, the murder of a capitaine of a gendarmerie. Imagine what the same people could do to both of you. They'd probably torture you before killing you. From here on, for your own safety you must only speak to me about this, no one else. Is that understood". Jean nodded. The capitaine had wanted to put the fear of God into the young man and he could see from the expression on Jean's face that he had succeeded. He would show that jumped up prick who had threatened him last night. "And if anyone else talks to you about this, no matter who it is, you must let me know immediately, is that understood?".

Jean nodded fiercely, it was.

The capitaine was all smiles again. "Good, now if you want another coffee, ask Colette to get you one. She's very good at that sort of thing. Our reception can be quite entertaining sometimes if you fancy drinking it there, real cabaret stuff, but if you don't I'm sure Colette won't mind you sitting in her office. I'll call her now". Capitaine Vendroux reached for one of the phones on his desk.

"Merci capitaine". Jean made to leave.

"Rein". The capitaine's smile was the last thing Jean remembered from his visit. It was perhaps a shame that he didn't recognise it for a smile of gloating satisfaction.

As Jean stepped from the stairs into reception he saw Colette waving at him, at the same time mouthing coffee. He pretended not to see her. He had no wish to stay a second longer in the monstrosity that was the gendarmerie. Exiting, he almost ran for his car. Starting up the engine, he'd changed gears three times by the time he'd left the car park. He rang Camille again, where the fuck was she? He'd kill her.

NCA's Temporary Offices, Gladstone Park, Cricklewood, London, England

Minutes after Fiona had left, Nick entered Roger's office.

"Was that about Cornwall"? Roger sighed.

"Yes, want me to fill you in"?

"I've already got the report sir, as have half the team".

"What do you make of it? And yes go ahead". Nick had made a questioning gesture to a chair. Nick pulled it towards him and sat down.

"Well I think we've found the person responsible for the hatchet jobs in Spain and Langstone. Mr Ryan Hedges, ex-military as you know, it turns out had a reputation as a hit man to hire and his methods apparently were always a little untidy. Perfect for the likes of Claire Flynn. And Claire, Havers and Mr Ryan complete a nice little circle. Two questions stand out, three for the teams out there". Nick nodded to the door of the office. "What did Mrs Flynn want from Havers, or what was she getting from him. And why have Havers and Mr Hedges been murdered by what looks like the same people responsible for all the other heads, including your ex colleague. What were they involved in, that we don't know about. And I'm assuming here, perhaps wrongly of course, that the people responsible for the beheadings are the same people responsible for all of the technical stuff, the DVLA, the non- existent phone lines that work, the corruption of CCTV images and Pet..."

"Peter, bloody Fitch, yes I know. In fact, I've definitely made up my mind to go and see him".

"Good luck with that sir, I think it'll be a waste of time".

"We'll see".

"Yes, we will", Roger spread the Cornwall files across his desk. So we're really no further forward, we still haven't the foggiest. WHO and WHY"?

"It looks like we've solved the murders in Spain and Langstone and somebody has done us a favour with Clair Flynn".

"Yes, Nick, but that pales into insignificance when compared to the big picture. It feels to me as though someone is trying to bring our country down and so far they're bloody succeeding". Nick pulled a face.

"With respect, sir, that's not really our fault is it? It's not our remit. It's MI5 or whoever else is creeping around in the shadows for His Majesty's government". Roger immediately thought of Donald or Jason, whatever his bloody name was. Whose shadow was he under?

"We all have to pull together on this, Nick".

"Yeah sure, as if MI5 would share anything with us". Roger ignored him.

"Apparently Jane's coming over, she'll fill us in".

"Yeah and give us loads more impossible tasks". Nick was in a particularly negative mood that morning, perhaps it was because of events earlier and him throwing up.

"Try and be positive Nick, you're dragging me down and if anyone's having a shit time it's me. Your world by comparison is all joy and happiness".

"Yeah and I'm really feeling it. Sorry sir". Nick responded quickly to his boss's glance. A knock at the door, broke their mood. Gary, one of the team investigating the Hilton on Park Lane poked his head round the door.

"Sorry for interrupting, sir but the PM's just about to make a broadcast after the COBRA meeting. We thought you might like to watch it. We've got it on in the office.

"We would, come on Nick, the PM will put you in a good mood". Nick made a vomiting sound not dissimilar to the noises he was making earlier in Roger's apartment.

When Roger and Nick arrived, there was a fair crowd gathered gazing up at a television screen suspended from the ceiling.

"There will now be a formal broadcast by the prime minister regarding the situation with the DVLA." The one-colour screen with words confirming what the announcer had just broadcast gave way to a solemn looking PM backed on either side by perfectly curled Union Jacks.

The message was almost identical to the one yesterday, except today the prime minister was promising the great British public that those involved were close to solving the problem and that normal service will soon be resumed.

"News to me". A woman's voice called from the doorway. Everyone turned to see their boss, Jane dressed in a sharp salmon pink two piece suit and on her face wearing a sarcastic smile, standing in the doorway. The room erupted in laughter. It was what everyone needed. Some light-hearted release.

"Roger"?

"Coming", Roger pushed his way to the door. As the two left a round of spontaneous clapping broke out. Jane responded by giving two air punches with her right fist.

"I wonder if they'll still be cheering me when they're told what I've come to tell you". Jane pursed her lips. Roger offered Jane his chair but she declined. This is your office, Roger, I'm the visitor, I'm happy sitting here. Jane sat in the chair recently vacated by Nick.

"So are we any nearer to finding out who is behind the hacking of the DVLA"?

"Nobody's got a fucking clue", Jane threw back her head and laughed. "If they have, nobody is telling me and they're certainly not telling the PM. The COBRA meeting on that front came up with a big fat nothing. Nobody's admitting it of course but we're at the mercy of whoever is responsible and the scary thing is, they haven't contacted us to explain why they've done what they've done and what the fuck do they want"? It wasn't often Jane swore.

"On that front you said, Jane. And the NCA"?

"Can we have some coffee, Roger, I'm parched. The stuff they serve at Whitehall is like lukewarm dishwater". Roger grinned, he agreed with her totally, it was bloody awful.

"Hang on". Roger left his chair, he caught Nick in the corridor. "Nick can you get someone to bring us two coffees, cappuccinos both and no sugar, both".

"I'll do it, Jane might even ask me to stay".

"In your dreams". Nick laughed

Of course he wasn't invited.

Over the next hour Jane revealed the unanimous decision as to the fate of the NCA. As they'd expected, those at the meeting had accepted Jane's proposal that it be disbanded. That, with the obvious infiltration by those presumably hostile to the UK, it was no longer fit for purpose. Worse still, it's continued existence could well pose a risk to the country's security.

With everything else that was happening it had been decided that it was not in the country's interests to inform the general public. As far as they were concerned, the organisation would continue to exist and therefore the phone lines will still be manned. And teams gathering and organising data would continue under the umbrella of the NCA though their budget would be taken up by MI5. The PM had promised the head of MI5 that his agency would receive more money to cover the extra cost, which almost certainly meant they would receive nothing.

What would happen to the rest of the agency was less clear. Everything would continue as they were for now though outside agencies would no longer hand down information. The NCA would be on its own. When people left, they wouldn't be replaced and as resources dwindled, it was hoped more people would leave. Especially those who had infiltrated the NCA. With no new information to feed on, it was hoped they would depart sooner rather than later, to be among the first to leave. All those who left from the investigating teams would be tracked by outside agencies. 'Or so I'm promised' Jane had said. It was obvious she doubted they would be. There simply weren't the resources.'It's hoped', Jane had finished, 'that the NCA will be completely disbanded within three years. That until then the agency will be closely monitored, that there may even be the possibility of MI5, even MI6 planting their own moles'.

"I won't blame you, Roger, if you want to leave".

"Do you suspect me"? It was a question Roger felt he had to ask.

"God, no, you're too stupid".

Roger laughed, "Thanks".

"You're welcome, Roger. Anyway, please tell me truthfully. How are you? First your house, now your car. Someone has it in for you. I thought you'd be safe here".

"I am", Roger gave a wry smile. "Obviously, my car wasn't".

"The agency will pay for it of course", Jane held up her hand. "I know, I know that's not the point".

"No, it's not".

"You can have use of an agency car, of course".

"I know". The last thing he wanted was an agency car. They had tracking devices. Those who wanted to would be able to track his every move. "Thank you".

There followed an uncomfortable pause which Roger broke.

"What are you going to do Jane? You can't live in a safe house forever".

"And I don't want to, Roger, I hate it. I think I'd prefer to take my chances than live like a chicken in a hen run".

Roger laughed, "Imagine what it's like for me, oh, and do you know what happens if the lifts fail. How do I get out? If they did, I can't remember security telling me". More likely, someone didn't want him to know but he kept this to himself.

"I haven't a clue, there must be one". Roger, changed the subject.

"So what are you going to do, Jane, will you stay with the agency till the end? In my opinion that will be a waste of your talents. Somebody has to stand up to those idiots the Great British public voted into power".

"You forget, Roger, they're simply the face of power, they don't hold the real power". Roger smiled, an all knowing smile, he knew she was right. "As for what I'll do, I don't know. I'll see what I'm offered. I'm hoping for a role in MI6, God knows I've done enough dirty work for them in the past. They owe me". This was news to Roger but he knew better than to ask for details. "Changing the subject Roger. The legal stuff has come through allowing us to search the Hilton". Roger laughed again.

"It's never going to happen, is it, Jane, where are we going to find the resources? With what we have at our disposal it'll take close to a year to go over every room and that's without us being disbanded. There's no way the Met will agree to taking it on".

"You could start with rooms on the floors you first suspected".

"It's too late", Roger shook his head. Too many people will have stayed in those rooms, they'll be too far contaminated, and there's no obvious evidence John Mitchell or our man were murdered in any of the rooms. It would have been too difficult to clear up. No, I think they were taken out alive and killed later. How? Please don't ask me how, Jane. To be honest I haven't a clue".

"I wasn't about to. Why don't you start by examining the guest list, that might throw something up and get digital forensics in there. See if they can find how their CCTV system was doctored".

"It's worth a go", Roger admitted, though going by everything else, the DVLA etc. I don't think we'll find anything. These people, whoever they are, are very clever, very sophisticated".

"So you think what happened at the Hilton, to your ex-colleague John Mitchell, you think they might all be linked"?

"I can't prove a thing, Jane but my gut from the beginning tells me they are and I trust my gut as much as I do evidence".

"Don't we all, it's how we've solved most of our biggest challenges. What about this missing detective? Has he been found".

"You mean Detective Constable Havers, no nothing, he's somehow managed to disappear without a trace". Why was he lying to Jane? Roger's questioning of himself was saved by a knock at his door.

"Come in", Jane answered for him.

In stepped an armed uniformed security officer along with a late to middle aged man, dressed all in black.

"Sorry", the security officer apologised. "I've been ordered to guard your office sir, and this gentleman is from the bomb squad, it's about your car, sir".

"If now is inconvenient, I can wait", the man introduced as being from the bomb squad offered.

"No, come in, I want to hear this. Close the door will you". Jane's last remark was directed at the security officer, who did as he was ordered. He knew it wasn't a request.

The man in black made to speak but before he could Jane proffered him a chair. The man sat looking most uncomfortable. It was obvious he would have preferred to have remained standing.

Leaning forward, he held out his hand to the two already in the office. "My name's Pete, Pete Collier and technically I'm from the FEL but every security department calls us the 'bomb squad'. I think they like the drama the name projects". Both Roger and Jane smiled at this. Pete Collier turned to Roger. "Am I to assume that you're Roger Denton, owner of the car involved"?

"You assume correctly, Pete".

The man from the FEL turned to Jane. "And may I ask who you are, madam"?

"She's my boss", Roger hoped his intervention would prevent Jane from exploding. Jane didn't, smiling sweetly she simply reached into her handbag and presented her identity card. Pete examined her card. Completely unphased he handed it back to her.

"Thank you",

"Call me Jane".

"Jane".

"So what can you tell us"? Jane asked.

"It's only a preliminary observation you understand, we're going to have to take your car to our lab for a thorough examination". Both Jane and Roger nodded, get on with it, we knew that already. "What I can tell you is that this is a very professional job, possibly the most professional I've ever come across.The explosives were very carefully calibrated and positioned to do a specific amount of damage with the minimum of fuss. Whoever was responsible was not looking for effect, they were not looking to gain attention. If you want my opinion which is unscientific, I guess the bomb was planted as a warning. If you'd been sitting in your car, sir, when the bomb went off, I think you may well have survived. This bomb in my opinion was not planted to kill. Indeed it's possible, if you'd been in the driver's seat when the bomb exploded you may even have escaped without serious injury. The car imploded, not exploded". Jane and Roger looked at each other. Roger had no idea what Jane was thinking but he was thinking what another man had recently told him. Anthony McDonald from the EOD. Explosions such as this are normally used as a warning, or something along those lines. Two experts in the same field were telling him the same thing. That the bomb is a warning. A warning about what? Not to stay out after seven? Roger wished he bloody well knew.

"There's something else, something you may find more worrying". Mr Collier hadn't finished.

"And that is"? Jane raised her eyebrows.

"This was a close quarters ignition. Whoever set off the bomb did it using a fob". Pete Collier of the FEL held up a small black fob. "And we've found it, hanging on a key hook in your security office. I hate to tell you this but it is my belief that the bomb was detonated by someone standing in your security office. Almost certainly by one of your security staff. I think you might have a problem".

"Have you discussed this with our security"?

"No", Pete replied to Jane's question. "That's your job, though they know we have this". Once again the fob was held up. "I'm afraid we'll have to take it away for forensics to examine it. The fact is that whoever set the bomb off could clearly see your car. And therefore knew you weren't sitting in it sir. This fact would support my theory that the bomb was meant as a warning, nothing more". The man paused, it was obvious he hadn't finished. "There's something else. I am also the officer who was in charge of the explosion at your house sir. Obviously the bomb was very different but the way it was detonated is the same. A close quarters detonation using a fob. At your house it meant suicide for whoever pressed the button. The only reason I can see why you would want to use a close quarters detonation would be to make bloody sure the bomb exploded. There are all sorts of things that can go wrong with a long distance detonation".

The next half an hour was spent asking the man from the FEL questions but they learned almost nothing more.

As he closed the door behind him Jane turned to face Roger. He had never before seen the look on her face that he was witnessing now.

"If you ask me, Roger, it's my belief that someone is suggesting to you that you retire".

"Nobody is going to force me to retire, Jane".

"I might, if you don't. Don't try to die a hero, Roger. You've done more than enough for your country, and if you do die in the line of duty, you'll be lucky to be remembered longer than five minutes. Anyway for now I suggest you check out that security office, and quickly but keep it low key".

'Low key'! How the hell was he to keep a search of the front security office low key?.

"By the way, after the COBRA meeting the Home Secretary caught me. They're planning on holding a memorial service for all those who were killed in the bomb blast at our old offices".

"That's nice of them". Jane ignored what she believed to be sarcasm.

"And they're already discussing building a memorial on the old site, similar to 9/11. When they feel the time is right they're going to ask staff and the general public for ideas".

"I'll give it some thought". Again Jane ignored him.

"Keep me informed, Roger". With that, after adjusting the scarf around her neck Jane got up and left.

Roger watched as she disappeared down the open corridor nodding to people as she went. He couldn't have known at that moment how her words, 'don't try to die a hero', would, not in the too distant future, come back to haunt him.

The Royal Lancaster Hotel, Lancaster Gate, London, England

Fatima had had a most enjoyable day. She'd also loved the company of Henrietta Sands. Fatima had expected a shopping trip to one of London's world famous department stores but no, not at all. Henrietta had taken her to a place called Camden Market.She had loved it. Camden had reminded her a little of the bazaars in Persia, Like the bazaars Camden was vibrant, full of noise and bright colours. There the similarity ended. Camden had a weirdness that was absent in bazaars. Possibly absent anywhere else in the world. 'My husband would kill me if he knew we were here', Henrietta had confided in her. 'When we go out it's to boring, stuffy shops or equally stuffy restaurants. That's why I wanted to see you. I wanted you to see the real London'.

Chapter 5

Together they had visited every conceivable type of shop. Enjoyed listening to a wide variety of street musicians,'buskers', Henrietta had called them, and enjoyed a meal in a huge building that could have been straight out of Africa.

Henrietta was a completely different woman to the one she'd been introduced to the night before. The one thing that was the same from the night before was Henrietta's attire. The way she was dressed. For such an energetic personality, for someone with razor wit, Henrietta dressed down. Her image was dowdy, a 'plain Jane' she knew the British described it as. She had approached her on the subject, attempting to persuade her to buy some of the exotic wear that was to be found on sale all over the market. 'My husband would never allow me to wear it', Henrietta had eventually confided. 'I have to play the part of a wife to the Home Secretary. And it's bloody boring', she'd whispered in Fatima's ear. They had both laughed out loud.

To end the day, the two had enjoyed a cocktail in the hotel's swish Park Lounge Bar, both with a little persuasion from the bartender had chosen a 'Madame Nipa'. It had been a good choice. It was whilst enjoying a cocktail that Henrietta revealed her political brain. Her grasp of world as well as home affairs Fatima discovered, was broader than anyone she'd met. Except perhaps for Pierre. She also discovered that she often strongly disagreed with her husband and his government on policy but would never say so in public. Despite everything, Henrietta was fiercely loyal to the man she was married to. In that way, she could almost be Persian.

Fatima had seen her off in a taxi. 'Goodbye, Ariana', she had called from the taxi window as it drove off. We must do this again'.' Yes we must, Fatima found she was fiercely determined they would.

Not wanting the day to finish yet Fatima returned to the Park Lounge bar, ordering another Madame Nipa. Sitting cross legged in a lounge chair her vocation, the reason why she was in London took

153

over her thoughts. What had she learned about her target from her day with his wife? Not much except she was even more determined to execute her mission as efficiently as possible. She felt no desire to seduce this man, even in her professional role. Something she had never felt before. Finishing her cocktail she left the bar, ignoring the glances of at least three men as she did so, and took the elevator to her floor. As she entered her room, trapped under the door she discovered a crisp white sheet of paper folded in half. Sliding it out from under the door, Fatima opened it. She knew it would be some sort of message. The organisation never used phones. She was right, and it was on hotel headed paper and neatly typed. She read.

'Order room service for eight pm, your choice'.

Fatima read the message several times before placing it on the bed. She had been here before.

Hervelinghen, Near Mont d'Hubert, France

After leaving the gendarmerie, Jean had driven to his place of work, Le Weekend cafe/bar in Sangatte. There, he'd asked the owner for the afternoon off, citing personal reasons. The cafe wasn't busy, it was that time of year and Jean's request was granted immediately.

The owner watched him go. He recognised that, at that moment, Jean was a troubled young man. He hoped he wasn't in trouble with the law. He knew he had been in the past but that had simply been adolescent hormone stuff. Responding to peer pressure. Jean was a good lad at heart, he worked hard, his regular customers liked him and he was never late. He also spoke a smattering of English, always useful being so close to Calais.

After leaving the cafe Jean drove straight to Camille's family house in Hervelinghen. On arrival, he was disappointed to find there was no one at home. The family, trusting him, had given him a key. Using it, he let himself in. Everything was as it normally was, why shouldn't it be? Sitting at the kitchen table, he rang Camille again. The sound of a mobile ringing came from somewhere within the kitchen. Jean looked about him? It was coming from a corner close to the old kitchen fire. It was where the family hung their coats. Jean stood up and walked to the corner. The ringing tone stopped. Frustrated, he went back to the kitchen table and rang her number again. This time he went straight to the corner, phone in hand. He recognised Camille's hooded jacket. He reached for it, her phone was in the right side pocket. His number was flashing on the screen. He stopped it and scrolled down her missed calls. All his calls were displayed, she hadn't had her phone with her at all that day. Now he was really worried. Camille never went anywhere without her phone. Jean pondered what to do, sit and wait or go out and look for her? He'd look for her. On opening the door he froze. Parked outside, there was a patrol car. A patrol car belonging to the gendarmerie. The front doors opened and out stepped two gendarmes in full uniform.

The driver spoke. "Jean? Jean Fournier"?

Jean wanted to reply but he found he couldn't. He couldn't move his mouth.

NCA's Temporary Offices, Gladstone Park, Cricklewood, London, England

After he was certain Jane had left the building Roger called Donald. He responded after the first ring.

"She's gone", Roger felt as though he were behaving like a naughty schoolboy. Though this was serious, grown up stuff. Why was he trusting this man? Because security did? After what he'd just learned, security was a joke.

"Ok, I'm going to be in and out, Roger, that's it. Have everything ready for me. I'll be there in around forty five minutes". The phone clicked dead.

He buzzed through to Nick. "Nick, have you got a minute"?

"On the phone or in your office"?

"In my office".

"Now"?

"Now".

"Coming". Roger recognised the exasperation in Nick's voice. A few minutes later, he was sitting in the chair he had not long before vacated. It was beginning to feel to Nick as if he and the chair were a permanent fixture.

"Sorry, Nick, but this is important".

"Isn't everything"? Roger ignored him.

"It's about my car Nick". Nick sat up.

"Oh".

Roger went over what he had just been told by the man from FEL. Most importantly, the bomb that had destroyed his car had been detonated using a simple fob by someone in the security office.

"Shit", was Nick's immediate reaction.

"We need to obtain the list of who was on duty last night, surely there must be a CCTV camera covering the security office. You know the time the bomb went off. Check the internal cameras, the external ones as you know have already been checked. We may just see who did this".

"It was probably Peter Fitch". Roger threw him a look.

"If it is, he's coming to London, hot shit lawyer or not. I don't believe he's entirely innocent".

"Hundreds of others say he is". For a second time, Roger ignored him.

"Anyway, check the internal CCTV footage Nick and the log, confirm who was on duty last night. There's normally only three of them so it shouldn't be difficult.

"Do I have authorization sir? After all they're security, where do we stand when it comes to investigating them?". Roger thought, Nick had a point, where did they stand?

"I'll give Jane a call," he finally decided. Like Donald, Jane answered after the first ring.

"Sorry Jane, it's about s.."

"Security, I know. I've already contacted them, they're expecting you."

"Than…." Jane had already gone. "They're expecting you Nick, Jane's already authorised it. Well not you personally but someone".

"I'm on my way".

"Take someone, maybe two people with you, Nick, and make sure they're armed. The security guys won't like being investigated and, on top of that, we no longer know which side they may be on". Every security guard was a trained marksman and since the bombing of their HQ, they were allowed to hold guns in their offices. They should be locked away but Roger wasn't willing to take that chance.

"Gotcha". Nick made to leave.

"Oh and Nick".

"Yes"?

"Jane said to keep it 'low key'".

"What! Yes ok, shit". With that Nick left.

Roger lent on his desk. He looked up at the armed security officer outside his office. He hoped to God he was friendly or he was a sitting duck. What the bloody hell was going on. Weeks ago he would have sworn on a bible that the offices of the NCA were one of the most secure places on earth. And now, only weeks later that assumption had been blown apart, literally.

He saw Nick leave with two officers in tow. Would they find anything? Why did he doubt that they would? It should be straight forward enough, except that nothing was anymore.

When they were out of sight, Roger got up to take the lift underground to his apartment. He was very conscious that as well as the guard outside his office, security from their control panel would know what he was doing, where he was going. Would they be waiting for him when he came up? He bloody hoped not. He hoped with Nick being there they would be otherwise occupied. He would have a lot of trouble explaining the contents of his bag.

"I'm just popping to my apartment to get something". Roger had no idea why he felt obliged to explain where he was going to the guard outside his door, he just did. Perhaps it was his feeling of guilt.

"None of my business, sir, my job is simply to protect you from anyone intending to do you harm whilst you're in your office". Roger looked him up and down.

"Well if you're going to be outside my office all day, do you think you can do it in civvies? Wearing a uniform is not good for morale". The security guard grinned.

"I'd love that, I hate wearing a uniform". The guard raised both elbows slightly to demonstrate how uncomfortable it was.

Once in his apartment, he went to the freezer, Roger half expected Haver's head to have disappeared, to somehow have been magicked away. To his relief, it hadn't. It was still there, eyes staring up at him. Looking at it he wished now he'd placed the head so it was facing in a different direction. Carefully, he lifted it out and closed the lid. Why the fucking hell hadn't he found a bag to put it in first?

In the security office, Nick and his team found the two guards more than cooperative. They were the same two that had been on duty the night before, the night of the explosion. The third hadn't turned up yet.

"How late is he"? barked Nick.

"Fifteen minutes", both guards answered.

"Late enough, do we have his address? Have you tried ringing him"?.

"He's not answering and yes, it's here". The guard who answered the question turned the page in a book to reveal an address in EC1, Islington. Fuck Nick thought, they have all this state of the art equipment and the details of the officers working security were kept in a manual address book. God help us.

Grabbing a phone, he dialled a number he knew well. It was a direct line to the Met, avoiding the need to go via the operator. "It's Nick Hunter, NCA. He read out his ID number. There really wasn't any need, the operator knew it off by heart. "I need an armed response unit to", he read out the address. We're sending our own team now". He waited while the operator directed his request to the right people.

"More details please, units on their way." Nick filled her in. "Thank you Nick, four officers attending, they'll see you there, Chief officer attending, Superintendent Collins".

"Thank you".

"Good luck, Nick".

"Thank you, hopefully we won't need it". The line clicked dead. "Come on you two, we're going walkies, I'll fill you in on the way". As they drove out of the yard Nick radioed back instructing another team to review the CCTV. He tried Roger but there was no answer. Shit, He needed to know what was happening, his mobile wasn't responding either. Bloody hell, I bet he's in his flaming apartment.

Nick was right. Roger was cursing, searching for an appropriate bag in which to transport Haver's head. He couldn't find one, bloody hell where was his brain? He should have thought in advance. He glanced at his watch, shit Donald could arrive any minute. There was a supermarket carrier bag in his kitchen, it was all he had. He could hardly go back to his office wheeling a suitcase. Grabbing a jumper he wrapped it around the plastic containing the head and placed it in the carrier bag, it only just fitted. Fuck, it looked so bloody suspicious. What else was there? He glanced at his fridge, it was all he could think of. In it were a few snack-like items, most bought by his female staff who worried about him living in a 'bunker'. He grabbed a few items and stuffed them carefully in the bag. It would have to do. Ready to leave, he wondered how Nick was getting on in the security office. It made no sense, why leave the fob used as a detonator hanging on a hook? There must be a reason? Was it left so it could be used to detonate something else? Shit he had to get back to his office.

As Nick and his team of two raced to the address in Islington, a call came in from Superintendent Collins requesting more details. They needed to know exactly what they were dealing with. Nick went over everything he knew which, on reflection, wasn't much.

"So explosives could be involved, therefore, there's a strong possibility there may be explosives at the address we're attending"?.

"Yes". Nick had to admit there was.

"Well, from what you tell me, I doubt if we'll find the individual at home but the address may be booby trapped. We don't want another Enfield or Bushey".

So the super knew the real reason for the explosions. Before Nick had a chance to reply, the superintendent came over the radio again.

"I'm going to call in the bomb boys as well as the fire guys. We need to be prepared for the worst. This is a much bigger operation than just us. The first thing we need to do is close off the road and evacuate all nearby properties. I'll make the call now".

"Roger. Nick looked at his screen, "ETA for us is sixteen forty eight". Shit really, even using lights.

"Noted, we'll be there in ten, see you there." There was the brief sound of static as the radio went dead. Swearing Nick pulled into the right hand lane as he approached the Archway bridge and put his foot down.

"Get out of the bloody way", he swerved as a moped driver delivering pizzas pulled out of the queue of cars into his path.

Back at The NCA's temporary offices in Cricklewood Roger stepped out of the lift and ran to his office. No one seemed to notice that a supermarket carrier swung wildly from his left hand. He quickly scanned his desk, had the man from FEL left a card? He couldn't remember, anyhow he couldn't waste any more time looking. Not bothering to sit, he picked up the desk phone and buzzed through to reception. A woman answered, he recognised her voice. Mary, she'd been with the NCA for years, thank God.

"Mary, put me through to Dstl at Porton Down will you. Tell them it's extremely urgent. I need to speak with one of their agents. A Pete Collier, could be Peter Collier. He attended an investigation here not long ago".

"Stay on the line Roger, I'll contact them now." Roger tapped his desk with the fingers of his spare hand as he waited. Thank God there wasn't hold music, that may have sent him over the edge. "Roger", Mary was back on the line.

"YES".

"Dstl says he's on his way there. They wouldn't give me his mobile, they're calling him now to tell him to contact you urgently. I've given them your mobile as well as this number. They've promised me they'll stress that it's extremely urgent. To wait for his call".

"Wait, shit. Sorry Mary. Ok, thanks". Just as Roger put the phone down, there came a tap at his door. Roger, every nerve tight in his body, spun round. Standing before him was a man in an open neck shirt. Donald. In his right hand, he was carrying a wide tattered peeling leather briefcase.

"You have something for me"?.

Roger lifted the supermarket carrier from the floor. Donald stared in apparent disbelief. It was the first time Roger had seen him anything but calm.

"You aren't kidding are you"?. Roger shook his head.

"No, I'm not. That's all I could find".

"Good job I brought this then", Donald clicked open the briefcase and placed it open on the desk. "Put everything in, bag and all". Roger made to protest and changed his mind. He placed the carrier bag complete with D.C. Havers head and the snacks from his fridge in the briefcase. Donald after checking to see nobody was watching them closed the lid and snapped the locks shut. Roger's mobile rang, mouthing, 'got to take this', he answered. It was Pete Collier.

"Just a minute", he turned to Donald who, by his expression, looked as if he were waiting to be given something else. "This call is important, anything else"?.

"Yes, I need to take a photo of your credit card".

"What? fuck, why"? Donald tapped the briefcase. For the pathologist. The NCA won't pay his sort of money. He'll want some sort of guarantee."

"You've got to be joking", he heard Pete on the phone. "Two secs Pete. Here". Roger threw a card on the desk. Donald using his phone took a photo and after turning the card over took another.

"Thank you, I'll be in touch. Oh and I won't be coming back here again. I don't like being familiar to people. Especially people I don't know". With that Donald left, closing the door behind him. Roger watched him say goodbye to the security guard then returned to his phone.

"Pete, sorry".

"That's fine, what's the panic? What's all this about"?.

Roger alerted him to the fob, his curiosity as to why whoever it was had left it on site, why hadn't they taken it with them. It seemed under the circumstances to be the obvious thing to do. But they didn't. Why leave it? Unless they wanted it to be found?

"Pete, you said you were the one to investigate my house".

"Correct".

"A little bird told me that the explosives had been there for some time, probably placed when I'd had building work done. I'd had a chimney taken out a couple of years back".

"I'd like to know who that 'little bird' was but yes, that's correct. We're still investigating but that's almost certainly the case, yes".

"When was the last time Porton Down had building work done"?.

Roger heard Pete chuckle,"Building work here never stops, or so it feels. But you know of course, there was years of building work to facilitate our move from the fort at Halstead to where we're heading now." (In 2020, after years of delay due to construction the FEL moved from Fort Halstead near Sevenoaks in Kent to the Defence Science and Technology Laboratory at Porton Down in Wiltshire).

"What if, during that building work, a bomb was hidden somewhere amongst the infrastructure"?.

"Impossible". Mr Collier's answer was emphatic.

"It's what your colleagues believe happened at our offices in Vauxhall". The line went silent.

"What are you suggesting"? Roger clenched his fist, he had Pete's attention.

"How well are you guys searched when entering DSTL"?.

"Very".

"Would a fob for setting off a bomb get through"?.

"Definitely not". Again Mr Collier's answer was emphatic.

"What if it were in an evidence bag"?. Again the phone went silent.

"I see your point".

"Where's the fob now"?.

"With us, we'll be at Porton Down in under half an hour".

"I suggest you keep that fob somewhere very safe and persuade the powers that be to get your building thoroughly checked over".

"That won't be easy but thank you for your advice".

"Let me know how you get on".

"Roger, Roger". Roger smiled, his name was the butt of many jokes when using the radio, even when using the phone as now. He put the receiver down and dropped into his chair. He felt exhausted. Something caught his attention on his desk. It was his credit card. His mind immediately went back to Donald. Fuck he had to be kidding. He quickly went to his phone to check his balance.

Pete Collier remained deep in thought. The man from the NCA, his theory had unnerved him. His theory, if you could call it that, was far-fetched. The stuff of James Bond, but what if he was right? Was it sensible to drive into the DSTL with a possible detonator or should they alleviate any risk by taking it somewhere else? His thought process was briefly interrupted as he concentrated manoeuvring the car off the A303 onto the A338. They were on the last stretch before they reached Porton Down. If he was going to make a decision he would have to make it quickly. Eyes on the road, he asked his passenger.

"Mick, where's that fob we picked up as evidence? Is it in the back"?. Mick didn't answer. Pete turned to his colleague to see if he was asleep. He was well known for it.

"It's here". In a raised hand, Mick held the fob. His mouth was curled up at the sides, not into a smile but a self-satisfied smirk. It was the last thing Pete Collier was to witness on this earth.

No sooner had Pete Collier rung off when Roger's phone rang again. This time it was his next in command, Nick. And he had a lot to say.

Chapter 5

A Street in Islington, EC1, London, England

When Nick finally arrived at their target address in Islington, London's emergency services were already demonstrating their well-oiled efficiency. Not only had the road with the house belonging to the suspect been closed but the two roads running adjacent too. The Met, along with their advisers were obviously taking no chances. Uniformed police officers were busy escorting confused looking, Nick assumed, residents, out and under the tape barriers. Their already difficult job, made harder by the inevitable gathering of curious bystanders. The roads feeding the closed off roads were already beginning to experience traffic build up and the Met's traffic officers were busy trying to keep things moving whilst attempting to put in place a signposted diversion. Nick pulled up on a double yellow placing an NCA official ID pass in the windscreen. Not that, going by the past, the local wardens would take any notice.

Pushing through the fast growing crowds, it was evident that amongst them were many of London's journalists. Unless this was sorted quickly, the tv crews would soon be attending. 'Low key', is what Jane had wanted, some hope. Flashing their NCA passes the three men were escorted by a uniform to where a group of men were standing. Represented in the group were the London ambulance service, the local fire brigade, the Metropolitan police and the EOD. Representing the EOD was a man called Anthony McDonald, not long from running an operation at the NCA's temporary offices in Cricklewood. Recognising each other they each returned a nod.

"Superintendent Collins.SFCO, I assume you must be Mr Ley". A man dressed all in black and with a Heckler and Koch G36C, slung over his shoulder stepped forward holding out his hand. Nick shook it along with the other two men from the NCA. "Are you guys carrying a weapon"?.

"They are", Nick confirmed that his men were both carrying a Glock 26 but that he wasn't.

"Well, if there's any shooting to be done I ask, unless I request your help, that you leave any shooting to us."

"Granted", Nick was more than happy to grant the super's request. With that sorted he was introduced to the heads of the other emergency services.

"Never a dull moment with you guys is there"? Mr McDonald half joked when they shook hands.

"You'd better meet my chief". Nick followed the super to a man standing several metres from them. He was standing bolt upright and his uniform was immaculate. Nick recognised him immediately as the Met's deputy assistant commissioner.Shit, he wished Roger was here.

"Hello, Nick", the commissioner made no sign that he was going to offer his hand. "I have to say I'm beginning to become a little tired with having to attend a crisis related to the NCA. Not that I'm blaming you of course". It looked as if he immediately regretted his words for he now offered his hand. "Let's see if we can sort this one without any of our guys or yours getting hurt shall we? Want to fill me in"?.

Nick went over what he had already told the super. The chief had already heard it from his super but he wanted to be sure the latter hadn't missed anything out.

"So we suspect this guard to have been involved in blowing up a car in your backyard".The use of the word 'backyard' sounded like a dig to Nick. "Have we any evidence, or reason to suspect that this guy may be armed?"

"Only from our experience, those involved with explosives often are".

"Fair enough. Superintendent Collins, any comment"?.

"I agree with Mr Hunter's caution. Explosives and guns tend to go hand in hand".

"As do I", the deputy assistant commissioner actually managed to smile. "So gentlemen, where do we go from here? We're ready to deal with the worst outcome but let's try and avoid that from happening shall we? What do the bomb boys, the EOD say"?.

It was the super who answered. "They've set up digital equipment which hopefully will seek out and stop any remote control signals attempting to detonate a bomb. Before they're prepared to send any officers in to search for booby traps etc, they want us to ensure there is nobody with a gun inside".

"Looks like a bit of a 'Catch 22' then gentlemen'. What do you advise Collins"?.

"That, for now we sit it out, try and make contact. See if we can find out if there is actually anybody inside, or whether the place is empty".

"Empty except for a possible explosive device".

"Yes".

Nick listened to the two whilst studying the house in question. It was his view, and unofficially of the NCA, that the house would be empty. Why would you hang around, knowing the world and its wife would come gunning for you? The house in question was very ordinary, there was nothing exciting about it. It looked a typical seventies build, and may, by its frontage, have once been a small industrial unit or lock up. It was now a centre terrace, a terrace consisting of three and from what Nick could see, the only post war dwellings in the street. Nearly all the other buildings were elegant Georgian and Victorian town houses, with a vine covered pub at the western end.

As he watched, there came a sound of rushing air, similar to when lighting a gas hob, except this was louder. Seconds later, a bright light appeared through the windows of the house in question and, seconds after that, flames could be seen lapping at the glass.

"That looks to me like an incendiary device".

167

"Agreed", Anthony McDonald of the EOD responded to the fire officer's comment.

The services reacted immediately. The fire brigade, ready for something like this to happen, opened up with their hoses, spraying the roof. But from a distance dictated by the EOD, there was concern there could be other explosive devices not yet detonated. The one SCFO officer not in position ran to take his up, waiting with his colleagues, guns trained on the front and back doors in case their target, with nothing to lose, exited guns blazing. They would take him down before he had a chance to fire a single shot. Despite the fire department's best efforts, flames could soon be seen exiting the roof and at the same time windows started to shatter.

What a bloody mess. Nick looked around him. There must be, counting all the services present, more than one hundred highly trained service personnel, and if you include the bomb teams, ambulance, fire brigade and the various security services close to thirty vehicles. All because of one man, an NCA employee, it was senseless but he actually felt guilty. With nothing to do but stand and watch he tried Roger again. This time he got through.

The NCA's Temporary Offices, Gladstone Park, Cricklewood, London, England

Roger listened intently as Nick described the scene unfolding in front of him and events since he was asked to check out the CCTV in security. He could hardly believe what Nick was telling him. What a bloody day. It felt almost as if they were at war and their enemy had a distinct advantage, they were invisible. The NCA hadn't the foggiest who they were fighting. 'Midge is checking the CCTV from the early hours', Nick went on to explain. On learning this Roger couldn't resist smiling, he was their CCTV nerd. He had been with him at the Hilton and appeared to be the only one of them enjoying the experience. Midge wouldn't miss a trick.

"How long do you think you'll be there, Nick"?.

"How long is a piece of string? The three of us are standing here as though we're spare parts. There's nothing we can do except perhaps identify a dead body if they find one, and I'm pretty sure they won't. I think it's pretty certain our man is long gone, and looking at the house, the way it's burning there'll soon be nothing left but cinders. I can't see the special boys finding any useful evidence. How the hell did this guy get through our DV checks,(Developed Vetting), surely the checks should have picked something up"?. Roger was in full agreement. How did any of these people that have infiltrated the NCA get past the security checks in place precisely to prevent this sort of thing from happening. Not only that, it was known the enemy was working within but the NCA hadn't a clue who they were. Repeated vetting had thrown up nothing still. For all anybody knew he, Roger could be one, Nick, even Jane. Roger laughed inwardly at the idea. In the past they had looked down on the Met for very publicly having their vetting procedures or lack of, exposed. Now who were they to criticise?

"Are you still there, sir"?.

"Yes, sorry. I don't know Nick. As far as I'm aware, we're all now being vetted again by MI5, but what they'll find if anything, God only knows".

"In that case, you'd better hand in your notice now then sir"?.

"Very funny Nick, so how long is your piece of string do you think"?.

"As I've told you, sir, there's nothing we can do here really except stand and watch. I'm not sure if anybody would notice if we quietly slipped off, but if someone did notice it wouldn't look good. Especially as all this fuss is because of one of our boys. By the way, the guy who's in charge of the EOD operation is the same guy who cleared us this morning".

"Anthony", Roger looked for his card.

"McDonald". Nick helped him out.

"Bloody hell, what must he think of us"? The thought was depressing. "Anyway Nick, you'd better stay there to the end. Who's the public figure there"?.

"The assistant commissioner".

"Really? He's going to love us too. Well when he leaves I suggest you consider your next move".

"Thanks a bloody lot ,sir".

"Good luck, Nick". Roger replaced the receiver to find the officer they'd just been discussing, Midge, standing in his doorway. How long he'd been standing there, waiting, he had no idea.

"Come in, Midge, you have something for me? Please say yes, and please don't tell me it's Peter Fitch". For a moment Midge looked puzzled.

"I've sent you the relevant footage you needed. I've had it signed off. If you log on, you'll be able to access it". Roger did as he was told. Within seconds, on his screen, there was an image of the front security office. The image wasn't brilliant but it was in colour and a better recording than many he'd seen. The time in the right hand corner read 1.58, Roger knew it to be a 24 hour clock. At almost 2am, one of the security officers was seen to raise his arm and for a split second there was a flash of light. Immediately after, all three officers could be seen automatically taking up their specific roles. Roles they'd been trained for. "Now watch sir". Midge had obviously cut the recording for the time was now ticking over at 3.58. Almost two hours later. The security guard who had been caught on camera raising his arm could now clearly be seen hanging a fob on a key hook. Roger had expected that but he hadn't expected what came next. The security guard turned straight towards the camera and grinned. Worse still Roger recognised him. He'd regularly checked him in and out. He felt like punching the screen.'You smug bastard, If I find you, I'll take your testicles and put them through a grinder'.

"Anything else"?.

"No, sir, that's it".

"How come the guards, after this, were simply allowed to walk out when their shifts had finished"?.

"Search me, sir. I guess nobody thinks of checking security". And that's a big bloody mistake, Roger was furious.

"Ok, Midge. Thank you". Midge turned to go and stopped.

"Any more news on the Hilton, sir? I don't mind going back there if you need me to". Roger sighed, shaking his head. The guy was a glutton for punishment.

"No, nothing. And I don't think there'll be a need but thanks for the offer",

"No problem sir". Midge left, at the same time, Roger's desk phone rang. He could see by the indicators that it was Jane. What the hell could she want, she'd not long left. He picked up the receiver.

"Roger, it's Jane", There was no need, he already knew.

"Jane".

"Pete Collier, the guy from FEL. Have you heard"?.

"The guy who's in charge of investigating my car, oh and my house? No. Heard what"?.

"He's dead". There was no easy way of saying it. "Or rather he's been killed".

"Killed"! Roger, having served with the military and during his time at the NCA was used to death but Jane's news threw him. He wasn't ready for it. He was struggling to respond.

" It looks like his car was blown up on the A343 travelling back to Porton Down".

"Blown up? Bloody hell, what the fuck's going on Jane"?. Jane ignored him.

"Obviously, this is very sensitive. The government, to their credit, has immediately put a gagging order on the media, but people talk, Roger. I fear the news will get out sooner than later. There were witnesses, they have been made to sign the Official Secrets Act or face jail".

"Can we do that"?. Again Jane ignored him.

"The local constabulary are there in name only, MI5 have taken control. They're starting to ask questions and they have a major one, Roger". Roger could see what was coming and he didn't like it.

"Apparently you put an urgent call to Mr Collier, seconds before he was blown to bits. What was the purpose of that call? I need to know Roger and leave nothing out".

Roger gritted his teeth. Shit, he knew MI5 were, for the moment anyway, marking him as a suspect. With everything else that was going on within the NCA this could potentially place him in a very uncomfortable situation. He went over all that had happened, the CCTV footage of the suspect, the fire at the suspect's registered address. His questioning as to why the fob would be left on site, that to him it had made no sense. That there had to be a reason for leaving it. And then his theory as to why. He had phoned to warn Mr Collier. Jane listened in silence. When Roger had finished her silence continued for several seconds before asking.

"So, if I understand you correctly you believe that there are explosives waiting to be detonated in the FEL's newly built labs at Porton Down. And that you believe one of the builders involved in the construction placed them there".

"Correct".

"Jesus Roger, if you're right this will rattle a few cages. It will take some convincing. Do you know the hoops these companies have to jump through to win a contract such as this"?.

"I know, but it's what happened with my house"... Jane cut in.

"Is it? Can we be sure? I haven't seen a report yet Roger, have you"?. Roger realised he had said too much. He was digging an enormous hole for himself. No one had corroborated what Donald had told him yet and the only evidence that the 'bomb guys' had touched on so far was that it had been a close quarter detonation.

"Sorry, I'm thinking of our office, Jane. In Vauxhall".

"Are you?". It was obvious she wasn't convinced. "But yes if you take Vauxhall, you have a point and a credible theory. I'll contact the powers that be. They're not going to like this, not at all".

"Jane".

"Yes".

" Was it an explosion that killed Mr Collier"?.

"Yes, a big one, some of his car ended up one hundred metres plus in adjacent fields". Roger thought.

"Was anyone else with him when he died"?.

"Yes, one of his team that was investigating your car, why"?.

"I'm wondering if it was he who set off the bomb, using the same fob. It might be worth checking him out".

"Noted, Roger".

"And Jane, how the hell did they manage to get a bomb under that car".

"That's the question everyone's asking Roger. Expect a rough ride. Are you sure you won't consider retiring? I'll back you and ensure you're retired on full pension. You could find yourself a woman and enjoy nice holidays".

"Sounds like hell, Jane".

"Idiot. Keep your head down Roger and keep me informed". The phone went dead. 'Keep me informed', it was Jane's signature phrase. If ever he was responsible for her epitaph he would find room somewhere for, 'keep me informed'.

Roger leaned back in his chair. What a bloody day. Surely that must be it. He wasn't sure if he could cope with anything else. It was a good job his gun was locked away. If it wasn't it was very possible he would commit mass murder. A knock at his door interrupted his thoughts. Looking up he saw one of his investigation team standing with two unceremoniously dressed gentlemen. He recognised them instantly. 'Digital Forensics', shit he'd forgotten.

CHAPTER
–6–

The Same Afternoon in France
Wissant, France

The lieutenant's call to Marcel had gone well. His old friend and colleague had willingly agreed to visit the address given to Jean-Paul by the GIGN.Increasing his suspicion, Marcel who had lived and worked as a gendarme in Paris for close on fifteen years, couldn't recall ever hearing of a morgue in the Chaillot region of Paris.Not unless it was one the government wanted kept a secret, and from his limited experience the government had plenty of those, secrets that is. Yes he'd take care and anyway he'd ask around first, see if anyone he worked with knew of the morgue before he paid a visit.

The lieutenant then asked if Marcel knew anything about their new capitaine. Capitaine Olivier Vendroux. Again his friend's response had been negative. Never heard of him, then again capitaines in Paris were ten a penny, they were like ants. So it was hardly surprising that he had never heard of him. 'What's he like'? Marcel had asked.

The lieutenant had given him his honest opinion, he's a 'dick head'. 'Must be Parisian born and bred then' had been his friend's response.

On that note they had said their goodbyes. After he had gone, the lieutenant found himself worrying whether he had done the right thing in asking his friend to help him. By doing so was he putting Marcel in danger.? To involve the GIGN there must be serious players at play. Players who were possibly above the law.

The thought stayed with him as he drove the coast road back to Calais. On approaching Wissant he turned off. He couldn't face returning to his gendarmerie, not just yet. He needed to think. Approaching winter, Wissant was something of a ghost town and he was able to park close to the seafront. Buttoning his coat against the stiff sea breeze, he walked the short stretch to the promenade. A cafe, its windows steamed up, looked very inviting but he'd never be able to think in there. No, he needed a walk. Facing the sea he turned right along the promenade passing below Maureen's empty apartment. On the beach, work was taking place on repairing the restaurant that had taken such a battering in the storm. He knew that an employee had been killed whilst trying to batten everything down. The memory only dampened his mood, his worry for Marcel. Should he phone his friend back and tell him not to bother? His conscience was telling him that it was the right thing to do but he needed to know. His need to know won, at the end of the day it was Marcel's decision whether he went or not. His feeling of guilt satisfied, the lieutenant started to walk.

Car Park, Pointe aux Oies, Wimereux, France

Jean-Paul was woken by the sea wind. Its strength over the hours had increased enough to cause his car to shake. Turning to face the sea he winced, his neck felt as though someone had placed a rope around it and pulled hard. He slowly rolled it the other way hoping that the pain would go but it didn't. Sitting upright, he slowly turned his neck, left, then right. It wasn't moving easily, he'd have to take care when driving. Driving, he remembered the idiots almost running him off the road. They had found it funny. At least it was youths playing the fool, for a moment he'd thought it could be something far worse. His pent up relief made him laugh. He was overreacting. His imagination was encouraging him to believe he was mixed up in a web of spies. Spies that were happy to kill him if he didn't play their game. He laughed louder, Jean-Paul, what is the matter with you? This is France, you're not living in a James Bond movie.

He wondered whether to get out and stretch his legs for a few minutes. He shivered, no. It looked cold outside and it was getting dark. Dark! What was the time? He turned the ignition so that his car dashboard lit up. Gone five, Christ he'd been asleep for just over a couple of hours. The taste in his mouth reminded him of the beer he'd had whilst with the lieutenant. He never normally drank during the day and he was regretting it now. His head felt heavy and his mind fuddled. Adjusting his posture and securing his seatbelt the pathologist turned on the car's engine. Pushing down on the accelerator he enjoyed the roar of the engine. As he pulled out of the car park he wound down both windows. He needed to wake up, to be alert.

In Wimereux, the shops were just closing. Soon they would be preparing for Christmas. For once, he found he was actually looking forward to it. Normally he hated Christmas, he would find an excuse to stay in the morgue. The dead didn't bother him. Not this year though, this year he was determined to enjoy it. A few hours ago, believing he was going to be joining the corpses in his fridge had made him wake up. Wake up and smell the beer, he laughed out loud again. After passing through Wimereux he turned left thus leaving the coast. He considered going back to his morgue but no, today he was going to break the habit of a lifetime. His staff he knew would be wondering where he'd gotten to. So worried they might actually report him missing. The pathologist laughed out loud again at the thought, he was completely unaware that he was putting his foot down.

Hervelinghen, near Wissant, France

Jean had his heart in his mouth as the two gendarmes exited their car. Every image in his head of Camille was not good and very bloody. What sort of accident had she had? Had she been murdered? He couldn't imagine life without Camille.

"Yes I'm Jean. Is this about Camille? Where is she? Where's Camille? Is she dead"?.

To Jean's surprise both officers started to laugh.

"Dead? no, why do you say that"? It was the officer who'd asked him his name. Jean felt his legs start to give way. Thank god, but why were they laughing?

"Why are you laughing"?.

"Because of you, you wally", this time it was the other officer. "Your family has been trying to get hold of you. All their calls have been going to voicemail and when they contacted your work they were told you'd left. We're friends of your dad and when they couldn't get hold of you, he asked if we'd do him a favour and come and see if you were here. They've been ringing here too". Jean's head was a heady mix of relief and confusion. What was going on? Why were Camille's family trying to get hold of him? Why didn't Camille have her phone with her?

"I've only just got here", as he spoke he heard the phone in the farmhouse ring. Without apologising he rushed inside before whoever it was rang off. Outside the two officers broke into another round of laughter.

"Hello, hello".

"Jean where the fuck have you been"? It was Camille, Jean felt like crying.

"Been? Where are you, why haven't you got your phone? You always carry your phone, I've been ringing you non-stop. Where are you"?.

"In hospital".

"HOSPITAL, which one? Why? What happened? Are you ok? I love you Camille". Turning he saw the two officers grinning in the doorway "This is personal, what do you find so funny"?.

"You", it was the driver. "Talk to your girlfriend".

"Camille"?.

"Jean will you fucking listen to me". Such was the force of Camille's voice both the officers heard her every word and retreated outside to relieve their mirth. "Jean"?.

"I'm here, where are you"?.

"I told you, in hospital and stop panicking, where have you been, you're not at work"?.

"I went to, oh never mind", Jean thought better of it. He needed to tell her when everything was calm. In hindsight he didn't think she'd be too pleased about him going to see Capitaine Vendroux on his own. In fact now, hearing Camille's voice he was beginning to regret it. "Never mind, I've been ringing you all day".

"I know sorry, it was all a panic, BUT I'M ALRIGHT JEAN, come and see me we're at Le Centre Hospitalicr de Calais.

"Boulevard des Justes"?.

"You've got it."

"I'm on my way", Jean replaced the receiver before Camille had a chance where to go when he arrived.

"He's such a bloody dick head sometimes", Camille laughed from her bed.

"We know", both her parents agreed in unison.

"So she's told you"?. It was the driver, and he had the biggest grin on his face.

"Yes, that's she's in hospital in Calais". Both gendarmes looked at each other.

"So where have you been"?.

"Seeing your capitaine, Capitaine Vendroux". On hearing this both gendarmes stopped smiling.

"Vendroux, WHY?" It was the driver. Shit, Jean cursed himself, why hadn't he kept his mouth shut?

"He's a dick head", added his colleague.

"He is", Jean replied instinctively. The laughter was back.

"So do you want an escort? Blue lights and all, after all it is an emergency. You can follow us, we'll get there in no time". They saw the look of shock on Jean's face. The driver stepped forward and cupped Jean's face with both hands.

"She didn't bloody tell you, did she? Well I will. Your darling Camille is pregnant, you're going to be a dad. God help the little one". He slapped Jean across the face. "Now come on young man, follow us. No speeding now". Both gendarmes got into their car whilst still laughing.

Gendarmerie Nationale, Calais, France

It was almost five pm and Capitaine Olivier Vendroux had had enough. He'd seen that young idiot this morning and had spent the rest of the day trying to take or rather show an interest in the various investigations his gendarmerie were acting on. He found them all entirely boring and his staff equally.

Nearly five pm, he decided he could get away with leaving a little early, after all he was the boss. He could do what he liked. Anyway his lieutenant was around to….., ah his lieutenant wasn't around, he remembered now. He'd gone to interview some fisherman about something or other. The capitaine looked at his watch. He'd been gone a bloody long time, his lieutenant was taking the mickey. He'd have words tomorrow. Secretly he was glad. He couldn't stand the man. Like the rest of his gendarmerie, he found him boring and worse he didn't trust him. He sensed all the time the lieutenant was holding a torch for his old capitaine. The last capitaine as far as he could see had been an idiot. He was dead now and his lieutenant needed to get over it. To accept the fact and move on.

After slipping some papers in his case and folding his coat over one arm he descended the stairs to reception. Colette saw him and waved, he waved back and then he was out of the door. Freedom at last. The capitaine drew in a deep breath. Many found the air carried in from the sea refreshing. He didn't, he found it cold and disgusting. After wiping the salt from his lips with his tongue he climbed into his beloved Alpine, his rose in a desert. Where to go? He didn't fancy going back to his accommodation yet, it was depressing. No he needed a drink, bright lights. Calais Nord he'd been told was where the nightlife was to be found. In particular Rue Royale.

In under ten minutes he'd parked in Place d'Armes, the main square of Calais Nord. Looking around it didn't have the sophistication of Paris but he had to admit it wasn't as depressing as the rest of Calais. He chose a bar on a corner close to the square. The Cafe de Paris. Managing to grab a table by the window, he ordered a bavette, (flank steak), with frites and salade. Instead of wine he decided to do as the locals do and ordered a beer.

Three hours later the capitaine was still there and enjoying himself immensely. He'd lost count of the number of beers he'd consumed and he was past caring. He wouldn't be able to drive and he didn't care about that either. There were plenty of hotels and they were bound to have rooms. Who the hell would want to stay in this shit hole anyway. Other clients of the Cafe de Paris watched on, some with shock, some with amusement. They'd never seen a gendarme behave in such a way. Certainly not when they were in uniform and certainly not having the rank of capitaine. Their last capitaine, Capitaine Maubert, was never seen drunk in public. Those who were commenting on such a fact

Cafe de Paris, Calais

couldn't even imagine their old capitaine being drunk at home. God rest his soul.

Finally the owner's had had enough and they discreetly told the capitaine that as well. Swearing loudly he left in search of a hotel. A man smartly dressed and with a close cut beard watched him leave. After counting to ten, he paid his bill and left. He stayed some distance from the capitaine and stayed with him until he was confident that he'd booked into a hotel. Satisfied he got into his car, parked not far from the capitaines and headed for the coast road. On reaching the top of Mont d'Hubert he pulled into the car park serving the Tunisian restaurant at its summit. Turning the car's lights off he drove slowly around the back and into the service area. Parking, he walked to a door in a side wall. There was no need to ring the bell, the door opened for him. Inside he took a deep breath, The man waiting for him was not going to be pleased by what he was about to report.

Centre Hospitalier, 1601 Bd des Justes, Calais, France

The drive from Hervelinghen to the hospital in central Calais, under any other circumstance Jean would have found thrilling. The gendarme car in front of him with lights flashing and siren blazing were his personal escort. Never before would he have believed that it was possible to cut through Calais so quickly. Once he was safely parked both gendarmes had shaken his hand and wished him good luck. For the first time he had seen the human face of the gendarmerie. His distrust of them still wasn't shaken though.

In the hospital reception, he found Camille's father waiting for him. He approached Jean grinning all over his face.

"You didn't give her a chance to tell you where she was, and this place is like a small town. She called you a dick head", her father slapped him on the back. Jean smiled ruefully, it wasn't the term 'dick head' he minded. It was the fact that it was the same term used not long ago to describe the new capitaine of their gendarmerie. The thought of being compared to a gendarme made him feel queasy.

It was a very, very long walk until they were in the room where Camille was resting. In the room, apart from the bed, other furniture included a table and three chairs along with a comfortable looking arm chair with a small table by its side, on which sat a lounge style table lamp. On the walls were tastefully framed paintings depicting local scenes. Jean had experienced worse hotel rooms, a lot worse!

He immediately went to Camille and gave her a gentle hug. He wanted to hold her tightly but was afraid he might hurt her or even the baby. The baby, Christ who'd have thought. He was going to be a father. Finally letting her go he stood up to see both parents smiling at the scene, Her mother wiped a tear from her cheek, and stepping forward gave Jean a motherly hug. Stepping away she looked him directly in the face.

"Where the hell have you been Jean"?. She shook him by the shoulders.

"Maman."

"Come on, let's leave these two love birds alone for a while, they have a lot to discuss". Her father took his wife gently by the elbow to lead her outside and to the small maternity waiting room.

"Oui, oui, pardon Jean", her mother caressed his cheek and then kissed him on the forehead before allowing her husband to lead her away".

"Dix minutes", her father warned the two as he left.

"Quinze", Camille begged.

"Douze", Camille laughed.

"D'accord" This time it was her parent's turn to laugh.

After they'd gone, Jean had a thousand and one questions. They were jumbled, in no order and often repeated in a different form. Combing through them, they basically boiled down to no more than four. What had happened, how come she'd ended up in hospital, why hadn't she left her phone behind and how did she feel about the baby?

Camille's answers, given in the same order. That morning she'd experienced severe abdominal pains, so severe her parents had rushed her to hospital. She had been in too much pain to think about her bloody phone. A doctor had examined her and soon discovered she was pregnant. 'Three months, Jean'! 'Three months'! She'd been passed to a gynaecologist, who after examination had declared that he could find nothing wrong. That sometimes women experienced severe pain and that he could give her something for that. But just to be sure there was nothing wrong, he was going to keep her in overnight for observation. As she talked Jean kept stroking her, a look of adoration on his face. At first Camille tolerated it but in the end she found it too much and pushing his hand away told him.

"Jean I'm your girlfriend not your fucking dog. Anyway where have you been? My parents have been trying to contact you. They even phoned your work and your boss told them you'd left early. What's going on, Jean"?.

Jean put his head down. He knew she wasn't going to be happy and this was not the situation that he wanted to tell her. If anything it was the worst situation. Camille knew the signs, there was something he was hiding. Something he didn't want her to know. Jean was crap at keeping secrets. It was one of the reasons she loved him so much. His character in many ways was very similar to a dog's and she wanted it no other way. You could trust a dog and no matter what you did to it would remain loyal to the end. Even lay down its life for you. She was very very confident that if it came to it, and god forbid it wouldn't that Jean would do that. Lay down his life. Looking at him now, seeing his struggle, a single tear rolled down one cheek. Putting one hand on the back of his neck and massaging gently, she whispered.

"What is it, Jean? Tell me. It can't be that bad. Where were you? Where did you go"?. Jean lifted his head. He still couldn't quite bring himself to look at her.

"The gendarmerie".

"The gendarmerie"? Camille hadn't known what to expect, certainly not this. "The gendarmerie but why"?.

Jean, rambling again eventually got round to telling her about Colette's call. Him trying to get hold of her. Deciding to go anyway followed by his conversation with Capitaine Olivier Vendroux.

"He was so nice Camille, he kept apologising for his attitude before. He told me he'd been wrong and that he should have taken us seriously. He promised me he'd look into it but using the right methods".

"What are they"?. Jean shook his head.

"I've no idea. He also said not to tell anyone else about this. That if Capitaine Maubert had been murdered, the people responsible wouldn't hesitate to kill again if they found out there were witnesses. That we had to keep this to ourselves, to tell no one but him".

Silence fell, there was a massive elephant in the room and it was making its presence known.

"But we've told the lieutenant, and that lady with him plus his widow and his daughter, any one of them could have ordered his murder. Especially Vivienne. She had every reason to want him dead after embarrassing her with his affair that the whole of Calais knew about. What if they're all in it together. They told us under no circumstances to tell anyone else. Maybe that's why".

"Capitaine Vendroux told me the same thing", Jean pointed out.

"Yes but he gave you an explanation why. They didn't. If you were his widow, wouldn't you want the whole world to know? Not hide it away". Jean had to agree, he'd been thinking along the same lines himself".

"I'll give Capitaine Vendroux a call tomorrow, he gave me his card". Camille took one hand in hers and squeezed.

Chapter 6

"You do that Jean, we're doing the right thing" .At that moment the door opened. Camille's father poked his head through.

"All right you two? Can we come back in? It's been fifteen minutes"

The Promenade, Wissant, France

The lieutenant, as mentioned before, adored Wissant. For him it was the most beautiful place on earth. Now, pacing along the promenade, deep in thought with the sound of the sea in his ears, despite the death the town had witnessed his opinion hadn't changed. Ahead of him Cap Blanc Nez rose majestically from the sea. During and since the storm, Cap Blanc Nez has been the centre of so much and his late capitaine had been obsessed with the place. But why? What could a chalk cliff hide? His late capitaine's obsession had been ridiculous. For him it was simply a cape, which, through sheer bad luck happened to receive currents that brought shit in from La Manche. To blame the Cap itself, to him, seemed ridiculous. Looking at the Cap now, he couldn't help but be impressed. Darkness was descending and the iridescent light from the strengthening moon picked out whispers of sea mist giving the impression the cliff face was wearing a cloak. All this death and you still manage to look majestic. The lieutenant turned to walk back. Remembering the young girl, her body mutilated, found at the foot of Cap Blanc Nez, he felt guilty for his admiration. Cap Blanc Nez was her headstone. He must never forget that.

He forced his mind to turn around. He was a gendarme. He had to concentrate on the job in hand. Immediately his mind went to his meeting with the pathologist. If he didn't know him, he'd tell himself the man was fantasising. But Jean-Paul was the last person on earth to fantasise. And if he wasn't fantasising then this could be a somewhat risky, if not dangerous investigation. It looked as if governments may

187

be involved and although they made the law they often considered themselves above it, sometimes resulting in fatal consequences. He really needed to go back to his superior with what he knew, except that he couldn't. Capitaine Vendroux had already told him not to ask questions.

And after last night, there was now a second issue he couldn't go to his superior with. The apparent murder, not suicide, of his ex-boss, Capitaine Maubert. To do so, would mean the betrayal of the young couple who had confided in him and that would never do. The lieutenant, hands in pockets, turned to face the sea. In the distance the lights thread along the English coastline were beginning to shine. It looked as though both investigations were to fall on his shoulders. Investigations that he would have to carry out in secret. At that moment he felt as if he was the loneliest man in the world.

The End of the Day, England

The NCA's Temporary Offices, Cricklewood, London, England

Roger Denton of the NCA almost lay in his chair staring at the wall opposite. What a bloody day. He'd had some bloody awful days in the past but this one must count as the worst. He considered it to be the longest day in his life and it wasn't over yet. Nick was still out there and there was no way he could clock off himself until Nick had finished, and he may still be asked questions about Pete Collier. The people who did this sort of thing worked twenty four seven. They had no respect for the normal working day. He knew it was very possible that he may receive a call in the early hours and under the circumstances that it probably wouldn't be a pleasant one.

Digital forensics had been a waste of time. They'd admitted that they had little that was new to report. In a way he had been relieved, he wasn't sure if he could get his head around much more. 'Little that was new', he suspected was digital forensic speak for bugger all but to be sure he'd sent them to conduct an interview with his team. They could thank him later. His last words to the two was that he would almost certainly need a team shortly to investigate a possible hack into the CCTV at the Hilton on Park Lane. And to be prepared. The expression on their faces had been akin to two young children waiting to open their Christmas presents. If he was able to send them in and it still wasn't certain that he'd be given permission to, he hoped that they'd have more luck than the team investigating the hacking of the DVLA and the other team, this one from an outside source investigating how their own CCTV out front had been hacked. Word was that the team investigating the DVLA, the so-called creme de la creme of the intelligence services, had so far found zilch. The same with the team investigating the security CCTV. If this was indeed the case, the powers- that-be, will be shitting themselves and the prime minister will have egg all over his face. To such an extent that he may have to resign. What a bloody mess and those responsible for it appeared to have a personal vendetta against him. Why? he asked for maybe a hundredth time. What had he done to so piss them off.

His mind wandered back to Jane's visit earlier and her subsequent phone call. She was the absolute master at hiding her feelings. It was almost impossible to know what she was thinking but she'd looked visibly irked by him disclosing that he knew about the bomb and when it had been placed in his house. He couldn't be sure but he felt it was almost certain that she already knew which meant Mr bloody Donald had been telling the truth. A step on the long ladder to trusting someone. Concentrating on Donald, his mind went back to the day he'd first met him. at Vauxhall Pleasure Gardens directly after the explosion at their old offices. Back then he was calling himself Jason, now it was Donald. Roger wondered if Donald even knew what his birth name was. He was almost certainly living life using an alias. What would he be calling himself next week? Tomorrow even? He concentrated once more on their previous meetings. The next time was at Whitehall where he had been an unannounced member of a COBRA meeting and then the Lamb and Flag in Covent Garden. On each occasion they'd spoken, Donald had spoken about the possibility of a French connection. If anything he'd pushed it. On a blank sheet of paper, he wrote French Connection. Then gendarmerie, Calais. The last time he'd phoned them, they, or rather their capitaine had been less than helpful. Maybe he should try again. Perhaps speak with somebody else. He doubted whether it would do any good but 'nothing ventured, nothing gained'. He tended to live by the saying. He made a note to ring them again.

Then there were the bodies of the dead children. Bodies that had mysteriously disappeared. According to the capitaine, he looked up his notes, according to Capitaine Vendroux in Calais they were in a morgue in Paris. Maybe he should attempt to contact that morgue, after all, the poor children may not be British but they were last known to have been on British soil. Under the protection of the British government. Roger scoffed, that was a joke. However, that must give him some sort of right to see them and his own government, a minister, had told him directly that they wanted the children back. He made another note. 'Contact morgue in Paris'. He paused, then added another. 'Ask Jane to speak with Stephan Sands, get him involved'.

Staring up at the ceiling Roger searched for the French connections he knew of already. Maureen Fowlis was the first to come to mind. The woman his ex-colleague had contacted him about, and almost certainly had a close relationship with. He had been worried that she may have been some sort of honey trap. Had she been? They still didn't know. Her registered address was in Wissant, France but she was known to have travelled to the UK. And according to Border Force, she still hadn't left the country. So where the hell was she? Roger brought up the CCTV footage of her entering the Fielding hotel in Covent Garden. Watching it he smiled, as before she reminded him of Mrs Fox, a character from Dad's Army. She looked to him like the last person to be a professional killer, yet death appeared to follow her everywhere. Both in France and over here, including that of his ex-colleague, John, who was not only killed but decapitated. Maureen, Mrs Fowlis was the one proven connection with France and the UK. But how did she fit in with all this mess? Roger made a note of her name and then added, 'where is she'? He'd have her face distributed, he still had the photo John had sent him, see if face recognition cameras picked her up. Why hadn't he done this before? He cursed. If he had, they might have found her by now. Before he'd finished with Maureen he listed all the people he knew of who had either met her and were known to have died or gone missing.

His ex-colleague, John, had been beheaded, beheaded it looked like using a surgical knife and by someone who knew what they were doing. The first evidence of something similar happening was the poor chap whose head was delivered to his wife in north London. Roger tapped on his computer, Ismail. He looked up the latest report. There wasn't much and he made another note to follow it up. There should be more by now, much more, why wasn't there? He was apparently a migrant trying to reach the UK so he was very much the NCA's responsibility. He made another note. Ismail was another connection with France, and the first as far as he was aware, of the surgical beheadings. Who was doing this and why? Unlike the gangster related beheadings, these were neat, professionally done. Possibly by a trained surgeon even. Were these gangster related too? Perhaps someone had found a surgeon willing to take dirty money or were they copycat? Roger made another note.

Once more his mind went back to his meeting with Donald Anas in the Lamb and Flag. There was another French connection Donald had highlighted, what was it? It came to him. The Arab woman. The suspected femme fatale, professional enough to seduce the head of the gendarmerie in Calais. Fatima, he had made a note, almost certainly not her real name. Where, if she was, involved in all of this? And where was she now? Donald had asked him about the two Arab women he was sure he'd seen in the Hilton, apparently removed from the hotel's CCTV. Had Fatima been one of them, and if yes what the hell was she doing here? Again it was all circumstantial but too much of a coincidence, surely? And why had she been sent to seduce the gendarme? What was he investigating at the time? Donald had mentioned the 'red market', really? Did that really exist? It had come up before. Roger made another note, and added who sent her? Just like the mess now, who? Who and why?

The most unpalatable connections were the missing children and the severed heads found floating in the English Channel, now stored in a morgue in France. Reports received from the said morgue suggested that the heads had been surgically removed. There the similarity with the adult heads ended. Were they connected somehow? Roger felt they must be. He made another note. He really needed to speak to France. If necessary involve Interpol.

Roger took a deep breath and let it out as a whistle. He scanned his notes.These were only the French connection, never mind the shit happening over here. He let out another whistle. And Donald had suggested that somehow he quietly worked on this independently. Impossible! Reading his notes once more he drew a line under them before writing underneath in much bolder letters.

'WHY ME'?

Similar to a man in France, at that moment he felt like the loneliest man on earth.

Chapter 6

A Safehouse in South London, England

Jane stood in her bedroom looking out of a window at the semi wild garden beyond. Today hadn't gone to plan but there was nothing she could do about it, it wasn't a disaster and if anything the death of Pete Collier may even work in their favour. Roger sussing the fob connection demonstrated what a danger he could be to the organisation's plans. He had a mind like nobody else she knew.

The explosives hidden in Porton Down would now be uncovered. She had no choice but to pass on what Roger had told her to her counterparts in MI5 and MI6. They would instigate a search and that would be it. No spectacular explosion, the explosives, hidden for years would be found. The fact that there would be no explosion, for her, didn't really matter. The very fact that they had been planted at all will shake the establishment to the core. The only downside was that now, with no spectacular explosion, the same establishment will be able to cover it up, pretend that it never happened. The Great British public will never know. For that reason the organisation will not be happy.

And it will all be Roger's doing. The organisation had wanted him dead a long time ago but Jane had fought that and, to date, they had granted her wishes. They had done their best to shake him up but not to physically harm him in any way. What happened today may change their view for the future. The car bomb had been her idea. The bomb had been designed to do limited damage, nothing else. Not to kill. Her hope was, and with her nudging him, that Roger may consider retiring. That the apparent risk to his life simply wasn't worth staying with the NCA anymore. 'Don't try and die a hero', she had prompted but he had simply ignored her. Bloody stupid stubborn man. Well there was nothing more she could do, she couldn't shield him anymore.

Roger, from now on you're on your own.

The Royal Lancaster Hotel, Lancaster Gate, London, England

Fatima sat in a lounge chair by the window clock watching. The one thing the organisation taught everybody was to be punctual. Eight pm the letter had said, for eight pm she had ordered room service and now it was ten seconds to. There came a tap on the door. Fatima looked at her watch. Dead on eight.

"Room service".

Tingling Fatima went to the door. She hoped it would be the little Asian girl. It was.

"Pitgam".

"Axsti", Fatima greeted.

"Axsti".

The girl dressed in an immaculate hotel uniform wheeled her trolley over to the table and proceeded to place the aromatic delights onto a crisp white cloth. The final touch was a vase with a single flower, a red rose or as Fatima knew it, Gole Sorkh. Smelling its scent made her feel strangely heady.

The girl didn't speak, but taking her hand led Fatima to the table and gently eased her onto a chair. One by one she proceeded to lift the glistening silver covers revealing an array of colourful and aromatic dishes served in traditional Persian tableware. The display led Fatima like a wide winged bird back to Persia. She recognised each and every dish, they were the favourite dishes of her parents. She could even visualise her mother making them. Her senses were out of control, she was no longer in a London hotel. She was in the mountains that were her childhood. She felt gentle hands caressing her head. Fatima didn't feel as though she were in heaven, she was in heaven.

Chapter 6

New Dawn Hotel, Bayswater, London, England

Aayan stood in the small reception area of the New Dawn Hotel. The receptionist was looking for her booking.

"Found it, she smiled".

Aayan smiled back. It had been a long time since she had smiled like she was smiling now. She had to pinch herself. She really was here, she could scarcely believe it. Not only was she in an exciting western city. London, BBC London. She had a job, a well-paid job as a doctor at a private hospital, a salary, just over a year ago, she would have considered pure fantasy and a flat, which in the photographs she'd been shown, resembled a palace.

It was all a far cry from her village, Jidhi in Somaliland. War and famine had devastated what little was there. Here in London there was so much, her eyes felt as though they were bulging at every new scene. There was so much to take in.

She wondered at how she had ended up here. The start of her journey now seemed a millennium away. With her country's new ties with Ethiopia and the deteriorating situation with Somalia, her father had risked both their lives and smuggled her into Ethiopia. Once there, her father had volunteered her for a medical charity. She had been welcomed and after a few months even started to learn basic medical practice. Out of the blue, she was approached by a woman who asked if she would like to train as a doctor and work in a Western city. She'd said yes, thinking it was a joke, until the very next day the woman, along with a native of her home country, arrived to pick her up. She'd been driven to a small airfield where she met two other women. Like her, they had been promised a new life in the west. Throughout the flight they had been blind folded and not allowed to talk. When they'd touched down they found they were in terrain that was featureless desert, except that underground there was a quite incredible medical facility. A facility with modern hotel style living quarters. Rumours abounded as to where they were and the origin of the facility but the most common and ones that refused to go away were that they were somewhere in Libya and that where they were, was left over from the second world war.

Aayan had no idea how long she was there. They never saw daylight and had to adhere to a strict timetable but never was life there oppressive. Quite the opposite. Apart from medical skills, whilst there she learnt both French and English and she now considered herself fluent in both. Indeed since arriving in London she considered at times her grammar to be more superior to the natives. Whilst training she'd had to regularly take exams and always passed with flying colours. Everything she was taught seemed to enter her head and stay there. Before she had never had a good memory. Somehow that had changed. After, no idea how long, she was told there was an opportunity at a hospital in Kensington, London. She'd never heard of Kensington but had heard of London because of the BBC World Service. BBC London, it was how everyone she knew in Somaliland got their news.

To work in the UK, she was told she would have to pass two more exams. The ones she'd taken at the underground facility were recognised by the UK. The certificates were all headed 'Faculty Of Medicine of Tunis', and the certificate that opened the main door for her, IELTS. She never questioned her certificates but suspected they were not in Tunisia and definitely nowhere near Tunis. All that mattered to her was that she knew she was a competent medical professional. From wherever the medical training facility was, she was taken to Cairo, Egypt, where she took an English health service exam called PLAB1. She'd almost achieved one hundred percent marks and was fast-tracked by her sponsor to take PLAB2, the practical exam at the GMC building on the Euston Road. Her results she was told would arrive in a few days' time and for the time being she was to stay in the hotel where she was now.

Aayan was confident that she had passed PLAB2 and that she would find having to wait very frustrating. A car, after a bizarre ten second meeting with someone outside the GMC, someone who she could no longer remember, had brought her to her hotel. Before she'd got out her driver had given her a padded envelope. She'd been worried at first that the hotel hadn't got her reservation. A reservation made by the organisation. What organisation? Either her contacts didn't know or wouldn't say. She didn't really care and to her relief the receptionist found her reservation. Her room was all paid for.

"Why are you visiting London"? the receptionist asked casually, not really interested.

"I'm a doctor". I'm starting a new job here".

The receptionist looked up. "The last person staying in your room was a doctor starting work here. In fact, we seem to get quite a few doctors. We must be doing something right". The receptionist laughed. Aayan smiled, took her key and left to find her room. Inside after putting down her bags she sat on the bed and opened the envelope the driver had given her. Inside she found money, notes, lots of them. Counting she found there was £500 and a welcome letter. £500, the woman from dusty Jidhi was going to enjoy herself. Never in all her life had she had so much money.

A Street Somewhere in EC1, Islington, London

It was near to midnight before Nick and his two colleagues felt they could leave the scene in Islington. The suspect's house was burnt to a cinder and the two adjacent houses were in no great shape either. It was obvious after the investigation was over they would have to be demolished. There had been no secondary device, no booby trap explosives and from what they could determine no one had been at home when the incendiary device had triggered. The EOD were pretty confident that the device hadn't been triggered by a remote control, therefore it must have been a timer, though they were yet to officially find the source. Work on doing that would start in the morning. Thank god doing that wasn't their responsibility. The thought of sifting through the mess before them, would for him anyway, be a thing of nightmares.

Back at the NCA's temporary offices Nick said goodnight, or good morning as it was pointed out to him, to the two officers who had accompanied him and before leaving himself went to check if there was anything left for him on his desk. There was, but nothing that couldn't wait till tomorrow. Tomorrow it looked like, would be another grind. Great.

Picking up a plastic bag which contained his uneaten sandwiches for the day, he made to leave. However a sound coming from Roger's office stopped him. Treading softly he popped his head round Roger's door. Out of the corner of his right eye he saw a movement. It was a CCTV camera moving, somebody was watching, he hoped it was a good sign. He felt an involuntary shiver. Offices at night had a strange atmosphere and camera's moving only made it worse. The sound that had delayed his departure he found was Roger. His boss was slumped in his chair, fast asleep and snoring. Nick smiled, gone midnight and he's 'asleep on the job'. Tomorrow he'd let his boss know. Laughing to himself Nick walked back up the corridor passing dimly lit offices, some with people still working in them. The NCA never sleeps, or was that London? As Nick checked, out one of the security officers apologised for the action of their colleague. 'He's been working here for years, I can't believe it.' Nick listened, 'years'. Had he been a plant or had the corrupt officer been approached and won over whilst working. It would be the million dollar question. If he had been a plant you were looking at then years, and that scared him as it would everybody else.

"My boss is asleep in his office". Nick felt it only right that he let security know. There was little point in guarding the guy during the day only.

"We know, don't worry, we're keeping an eye on him". The security guard pointed to a monitor. There was his boss, just as he had left him. Mouth open, slumped in his chair.

"Somebody ought to wake him, let him go to his bed".

The security guard made a face. "I was afraid you may say something like that, I suppose I'll have to go".

Nick grinned, "Do it gently", and laughing climbed into his car. As he drove off, in his mirror he saw the security officer making his way in the main building. He should have been relieved but his only thought and one that stubbornly wouldn't go away was that he hoped the guard was on their side and not with the so far, invisible enemy.

The Next Morning

DVLA offices, England

There was no red sky and therefore no warning that morning. Darkness faded into grey and that was it. That was the new day, a new grey depressing day. As a consequence for most people it was a depressing start but not for the IT team and the digital forensics specialists working to discover the source of the hack at the DVLA and put everything right. Restore the system back to how it had been and to put up a firewall that would prevent anything like this from happening again.

At just after midnight and without touching a keyboard, suddenly, as if by magic, all the false images of animals, clowns, and famous people simply disappeared to be replaced by the original. The correct photo. Mal data disappeared before their eyes to be replaced by the original, correct data. They had no idea who was doing it or how they were but hundreds of thousands of corrupted listings, before their very eyes were restored to their original settings.

When the process had finished a large team of IT employees frantically checked and checked again and five hours later the DVLA database was declared, at least tentatively, safe. Back to normal. Uncorrupted, as it had been before the hack. A call was made to the secretary of state for transport reporting the good news. The same to the head of the NCA, Jane. The head of MI5 and Stephan Sands the Home Secretary. All were advised that these were initial findings only and that a forty eight hour gateway at least should be allowed before making any formal announcement. Not listening to advice, the two ministers contacted the prime minister and told him their good news. Further discussions were held and the government, desperate for good news, decided, again going against professional advice, to announce the good news to the nation.

Calls started to be made to the UK's media.

Two Marsham Street, London, England

Stephan Sands, the Home Secretary had had a sleepless night. It was possible that he may lose his job over the DVLA farce. His was a proud family with a long and proud history, always in the upper echelons of society. Receiving the sack would be seen by both his parents as a stain on the family and absolutely unforgivable. Therefore a call with the news that the hack had been thwarted, 'thwarted', the word he used to inform the prime minister not one used by the IT professionals, had come as an immense relief.

That relief had been short lived when both the head of MI5 and of the soon to be disbanded NCA had together requested an urgent meeting and as a result, at six am sharp the three of them were having 'dishwater' coffee in his office. The reason for the meeting, he was soon to discover was to start the debate about having a national identity card, one that would be almost impossible to forge and a strongly protected database. The debacle with the DVLA's database proved that the Ministry of Transport should not have the responsibility for what had become the nation's unofficial identity card. That now was the time to discuss having an official identity card, just like other countries. The head of MI5 pointed out that they were having to deal with more and more malicious attacks from abroad. Individuals put on the streets of the UK often using forged identity documents. That they were put there with the sole intention of creating terror and chaos and not just by Islamic terror organisations. That Russia too was attempting to do the same. A dedicated identity database would help them in this battle and who better to start it than Jane, head of the NCA who sometime in the next couple of years would be out of the job.

Stephan Sands listened, most of his job involved listening to advice and he hated the fact. He preferred to listen to his own advice. He didn't disagree with the two sitting in front of him but the thought of putting this to the prime minister filled him with dread. From the start he knew it would be a complete waste of time. That budget restraints would blow the idea out of the water before it even got going. Millions, perhaps hundreds of millions of pounds spent just to save the odd life or two. The prime minister would see it as wasting his time and the consequence? Almost certainly, when the time came a demotion maybe to the back benches. He rubbed his forehead in nervous frustration.

There came a knock at the door. His day was just about to get a lot worse.

NCA's Temporary Offices, Gladstone Park, Cricklewood, London, England

It was just past five am when Roger Denton of the NCA woke. He immediately fumbled for the remote control. Finding it on the floor he turned on the TV and searched for BBC1. World Business Report. To his relief the face of Sally Bundock filled the screen. Normality, he craved it and Sally delivered it to him. Almost jumping out of bed, Roger almost ran into the kitchen, filled the kettle, spooned instant coffee into a mug and ran to the bathroom. After relieving himself he poured water into his mug and returned to the bedroom. After adjusting his pillows he positioned himself comfortably and took his first sip of coffee. Looking at the screen the time read 5.14. He took another sip. He had another forty six minutes of Sally and he was going to enjoy every bloody minute. Forty six minutes of normality, bliss and he was going to enjoy three cups of coffee, more bliss. After his third coffee he would shower and in his own time he would take the lift to what would undoubtedly be chaos.

Considering he'd had hardly any sleep, he felt remarkably refreshed. His body was probably running on adrenaline only but that wasn't a bad thing. Thankfully nobody had phoned him in the early hours. And one possible reason why he was feeling good that morning , he had in his head the day planned out. Whereas with recent mornings, events had dictated his day for him. Today he'd made up his mind, he was going to tackle the chaos on his own. First he'd go and visit the Hilton, then if time allowed, Mr Peter bloody Fitch. The investigation was becoming too big to handle. He wanted to go back to the beginning. Old ground yes, but maybe something, something important possibly had been missed. And if anybody was going to find it, it would be him.

Roger timed his three coffees perfectly. By the time he had nearly finished his third, Sally had gone off air and BBC Breakfast was starting. He made to slide out of bed when the next report stopped him.

"Breaking News", the presenter read from a piece of paper. The paper meant it really was breaking news. "The BBC has it on good authority that the recent hack of the DVLA database has been dealt with by an IT team sent in by the Home Office and from all accounts there should be no more sheep, or any other animal for that matter appearing on UK driving licences".

"I'm sure President Putin and Kim Jong Un will be pleased", quipped the female presenter sharing the couch that morning.

"That's all we have at the moment. We are seeking confirmation and clarification from both the Ministry of Transport and the Home Office, and as soon as we have it, we'll bring it to you. Now for the rest of the news".

Roger wasn't listening. He'd leave things to die down then he'd contact JJ from MI5. See if he could shed some light. If their digital intelligence team really had cracked it, they could possibly help solve their little problem. Perhaps even restore the doctored CCTV images they were dealing with. Solve that and he was confident they'd be able to identify who they were dealing with and from there find out who was behind the recent chaos. Instructing Alexa to play a mix of Rod Stewart he made his way to the bathroom. 'Baby Jane' was the first song that played and half knowing the words, Roger Denton of the NCA started to sing, and loudly.

In an office somewhere in central London a man dressed in jeans, a T-shirt and fleece smiled broadly. He called to his colleagues.

"Hey you two, listen to this".

A man and a woman entered the room. Their colleague, sitting, turned up the volume. Rod Stewart's voice could just be heard in the background but drowning out everything was the voice of Roger

Denton. All three started to laugh and the two standing started to dance. Baby Jane finished and the three waited to see if there'd be anymore. They weren't to be disappointed. 'Do Ya Think I'm Sexy', was the next song. A cheer went up as the unmistakable voice of Roger Denton made an enthusiastic start to the song. The three joined in and the dancing exaggerated. In his shower Roger gyrated to the music whilst singing his heart out, blissfully unaware that he had an audience of three.

Two Marsham Street, London, England

After a knock at the door, a senior civil servant stepped in.

After nodding to his two guests, the man glanced at a note he was holding in his left hand.

"Sorry Stephan but we've had a note along with a request from the BBC and a number of other agencies". He had a look at his watch. "You might want to turn the news on, BBC 1". Stephan did as the man suggested, a small white dot on the screen expanded to show the familiar couch along with the equally two familiar presenters. The male presenter held a piece of paper and a caption appeared on the screen. 'Breaking News'.

The four watched the same broadcast as Roger Denton. At the end of it, Stephan turned the TV off and threw the remote control at the wall. The back came off and the batteries spilt out onto the floor.

"Fuck, fuck, fuck". The three watched on in silence. They were used to this but this morning's performance was much more animated than usual". A phone on his desk rang. The Home Secretary picked it up. It was his secretary, Pamela.

"Stephan, I've got the prime minister for you".

Fuck.

A House Somewhere in Swansea

In a small simple lounge in a small simply furnished room Kaveh watched the 'breaking news' with a meek satisfied smile. The prime minister he'd been told was going to fabricate a story, his government taking credit for the cleansing of the DVLA database. Complete rubbish. The organisation had ordered him to pre-empt the prime minister by sending a simple message to the main British media. The BBC had been the first and he was pleased. Everyone, where he came from, respected the BBC. After the BBC he had contacted ITV and after ITV, four national newspapers. He had used a cell phone given to him by the organisation. After the calls he had been instructed to destroy it. He'd made to do so but the phone had already destroyed itself, it had literally dissolved. Grabbing his packed case he opened the front door. A taxi was waiting. He knew it would be, the organisation was always on time. In no time they were on the M4 leaving Swansea behind. Kaveh couldn't help feeling sad. He'd enjoyed his time in Swansea. And he had no idea where the organisation was taking him now. He knew the driver wouldn't tell him. She'd welcomed him with the greeting Axsti when he'd climbed in and he knew that that would be the only word spoken between them. He risked a glance in the driver's mirror. On seeing her eyes he visibly relaxed. His driver was Persian, the same as him.

The Royal Lancaster Hotel, Lancaster Gate, London, England

The first thing Fatima sensed when she awoke was the scent. A sweet fragrance, similar to pine, her inner being knew well. It was from the haoma plant, her parents used to create a drink from its stems. She remembered the drink being something special. Even as a child she was strictly forbidden to spill any. Slowly Fatima opened her eyes, daylight filled her room. It must be morning, somehow she had lost an entire night, she could not recall getting into bed. And somebody had turned the lights off. There was nothing unusual in that except she could not remember doing it herself. Leaning on her elbows she scanned the room. It was perfect as though room service had serviced it. Not a thing was out of place. For the first time since opening her eyes Fatima realised she was lying on her bed, completely naked and on it, not under the covers. And the reason for the scent of the haoma, haoma flowers were scattered all across her quilt.

She lay back, closing her eyes as she did so. The scent of the haoma was overpowering. It was somehow taking control and she didn't care. Let it. She didn't care. In fact she wanted it to. Somehow she desired it. Yes, desire. She was full of desire. A light, a gentle light, a warm light appeared from somewhere, eyes still closed Fatima watched transfixed. There was someone inside the light. She was desperate to see who. Slowly a face started to appear, a familiar face, a face that held her attention. Fatima recognised her, it was the Asian girl from the night before. She remembered the aromatic, delicious food that she had served. How it had made her feel so good. She remembered the girl's touch. How it had transported her deep into heaven. She was in that heaven now except that there was something else. She felt desire, desire to see more of the Asian girl, desire to enjoy her own body. Slowly Fatima let her hands fall over her own breasts, Squeezing gently she moved them to her nipples and started to squeeze with her fingers. She let out a low moan digging into the bed with the souls of her feet.

She wanted to see more of the Asian girl, Fatima desired her body. Never had she felt such a strong desire. The light faded to a warm glow and the Asian girl raised her arms slowly revealing everything Fatima desired. Fatima let her right hand leave her nipple. With her left she cupped the whole of her breast and squeezed. Again she let out a deep moan. With her right hand Fatima started to caress her inner thighs, moving ever so slowly toward her vulva. On reaching it she squeezed then stretched apart the outer lips of her vagina. With three of her fingers she started to play with her clitoris. All control had now left her. All she desired was to reach climax. Her left hand left her breast and entered her mouth, Her tongue started to explore. With her right hand Fatima started to rub hard and fast. Then with a deep, deep, deep guttural groan almost the entirety of Fatima's body left the bed before collapsing, arms and legs spread wide. For several minutes she lay still enjoying the scent of the haoma though now the fragrance was having the opposite effect. It was calming her, telling her to relax.

Without warning Fatima sat up, as though a switch had been flicked. She needed to shower, to get dressed. Today was the day she was leaving the hotel and moving into her house. A car would pick her up at one in the afternoon. Before that she must dine at the hotel. And she was no longer Fatima. She must no longer think of herself as Fatima. From today she must only think of herself as Ariana. One day, a voice in her head was telling her. She would return. Return as Fatima and from that day onwards she would only experience joy. Entering the bathroom she stepped into the shower. As the water flowed she could feel Fatima washing away.

From here on we will only use the name Ariana. Ariana, Fatima's real name but with an invented past.

MI5, 12 Millbank Street, London, England

In an office without a view a number of agents were investigating a list of construction companies. Companies that were involved with the construction of the FEL facilities at Porton Down. The head of the NCA had reported the possibility of explosives being hidden somewhere in the construction. A report that after a short period of doubt was now being taken seriously. One company stood out, a limited company at the time, it had since been deregistered. There were three directors listed with Companies House but somehow their details had been deleted. Their registered address had been an accountant in Catford and checks had discovered that they too were no longer trading. There had also been an operating premises listed. A team had investigated that and found the building had been destroyed in a fire. Why hadn't they known? Many questions were going to be asked if explosives were found at Porton Down. All the construction workers would have to have passed BPSS and EBS checks. These were now being checked. In the meantime however, to prevent the possibility of further loss of life it was decided to temporarily close the Dstl, (Defence Science and Technology Laboratory) facilities at Porton Down, relocating them to their more secret premises under Portsdown Hill, overlooking Portsmouth in Hampshire.To a certain extent there would now take place the rather bizarre development of the EOD investigating the FEL's own premises. The place where the EOD would send evidence to be forensically checked.

Whilst the history of hundreds of employees' backgrounds was being checked the FEL's facility at Porton Down was being evacuated in a calm and orderly manner.The cover was that there may be a construction defect and, that on health and safety grounds, it had to be checked before staff were let back in. Each employee was reminded that they'd signed the Official Secrets Act and news of what was happening was not to get out.

By ten am the first team from the EOD were beginning to search the premises. It was a huge job and everyone involved was very aware that a detonation could happen at any time.

Chapter 6

Place d'Armes, Calais, France

Capitaine Vendroux awoke to find daylight streaming through his window. Like Ariana in London, he too woke with a built in desire. However the capitaine's desire was quite different. His only desire was for his head to stop hurting. Gingerly he got out of bed. He vaguely remembered where he was, a hotel somewhere off the main square in Calais Nord. His bedroom window was a skylight and standing on tiptoe he peered out. He was afforded a view of the square and on the far side, behind the ancient English built watchtower, he could just make out the Cafe de Paris. The place of his sins the night before. It was all coming back to him. Capitaine Vendroux groaned. How was he going to get through the day?

Once in the bathroom, he stuck two fingers down his throat and retched. All he could bring up was bile. Putting the toilet seat down he sat, dropping his head between his legs. Something he was taught whilst serving in the military. After a couple of minutes he began to feel better. Feeling brave enough to stand up, he turned on the shower and stepping out of the uniform he'd slept in, he turned on the water. He was immediately sprayed with streams of ice cold water. Letting out a yelp he stepped back, slipped and landed in a heap on the shower floor. Cursing he knelt before pushing himself up till he was standing once more. By now warm water was welcoming him. Leaning his head back, the capitaine delighted in the water's healing touch. When he stepped out he was feeling almost human.

He looked at his watch, he'd forgotten to take it off in the shower. Thank god it was waterproof. The time read nine minutes past nine. Merde, he was going to be late, bloody late. Finding his phone he rang the gendarmerie. Colette answered.

"Colette, I'm catching up with some paperwork at home. I'll be in, around eleven. If anyone needs me, tell them to feel free to give me a call". He put his phone down, he hoped he sounded convincing.

In her office, Colette laughed. Their capitaine's antics had been captured on several mobile phones and were all over social media. Last night had spread like wildfire around the gendarmerie. Most views reinforced the original and that was that their new capitaine was a complete dick head. Others felt more sympathy. It proved that he was human.

Lieutenant Beaufort was relieved. He hadn't returned to the gendarmerie yesterday afternoon and was not looking forward to having to provide an explanation. His capitaine's antics had very much let him off the hook. Better still, he'd take advantage of his capitaine's absence that morning. Going to Colette he asked for the English officer's name who had been trying to contact him. Colette after several bouts of laughter jotted down a name. 'Roger Denton, National Crime Agency and two numbers, a landline and a mobile.

"Merci", the lieutenant after examining them, folded the paper and placed it in his back trouser pocket.

"Before you go lieutenant", Colette stopped him. "Jean, you know, one half of the couple who think they saw Capitaine Maubert, well…". Colette couldn't bring herself to finish the sentence. "Well he phoned for the capitaine this morning. I told him he wasn't in yet and asked if he wanted to speak to me or you. I thought he'd say yes of course but he didn't, he said he'd wait for the capitaine to come in. In fact he was quite stand offish".

The lieutenant shrugged his shoulders. "That's what comes with dealing with kids". The lieutenant left Colette's office sporting a grin. Privately though he was worried. This didn't bode well.

In her office, Colette watched him go. She knew the lieutenant well, he couldn't fool her. He was worried. She thought back to Jean's call for the capitaine and his blanking of her. It didn't bode well at all.

NCA's Temporary Offices, Gladstone Park, Cricklewood, London, England

Roger Denton of the NCA, after checking on the progress of his various teams, and with Nick went to security to book out an agency car. After filling out the paperwork he was given a BMW. Though shiny on the outside the interior looked as though it had seen a considerable amount of action. If the car was leased, the NCA would have a considerable forfeit to pay. Roger smiled to himself, he would like to be a fly on the wall during that conversation.

Leaving the NCA compound Roger drove around the block until he came to the Chinese supermarket, Wing Yip, just a few minutes away. He drove the car into the underground car park where he got out. He had no intention of driving the car into central London, someone would almost certainly be tracking his every move. If they really wanted to, they could find him using face recognition but he really didn't think whoever it was would go to that much trouble. That they would only track his movements if it was easy, such as a tracker in a car. From the underground parking he took the stairs into the shop and out of the front door.

After crossing the Edgware Road he followed the road south until he arrived at the stop where he could catch the 189 bus to Marble Arch. From there he planned to walk along Park Lane to the iconic Hilton. The bus to his surprise was busy and he had to stand most of the way.

Alighting at Marble Arch instead of following Park Lane Roger walked through Hyde Park. Despite the sky being heavy with greyness, the park managed somehow to deliver a sense of exuberance refusing to let anyone passing through it to give in to depression, no matter what they were going through. For Roger the park offered positivity, whereas yesterday he'd perhaps, for the first time in his career, felt that he was defeated, nowhere to turn and without a friend in the world. This morning, he'd woken up with a plan, a mission, let small steps lead to big steps and see where the big steps lead. He may not have friends but he had colleagues, learn to trust them Roger, until you know not to. This was the complete opposite to Donald's advice, which was to trust no one from the beginning, but he preferred his world to his. Imagine living life trusting no one. Donald had admitted as much in their meeting at the Lamb and Flag. He'd tasted it and didn't like the taste. He had to trust someone or the burden became too much. He trusted Jane and he trusted Nick. And he trusted the man he was about to meet, Ishaan, head of security at the world famous Hilton hotel on Park Lane.

Before crossing the Lane to the hotel, Roger gave Nick a quick call. He'd only spent five minutes with him before he'd left and he wanted an update on the night before and to update Nick on what he was doing today. Nick had nothing much to report except that something was going on with both the FEL and the EOD. Forensic testing of explosives would be 'indefinitely delayed', whatever that meant. Digital forensics were apparently getting nowhere, so nothing new there and every time they investigated any phone number of interest, the result was always the same when dialled they got the same laughter they'd experienced with John's mobile. All those days, that felt like years, ago. There wasn't much Roger could say except to keep trying, sooner than later whoever it was would make a mistake. They always do. He then told Nick about his plans for today. To see Ishaan at the Hilton, and if he still had time, Peter Fitch. If anyone wanted him he told Nick they must come via him and he was to let no one know of his movements. You're the only one Nick he had said before ringing off.

'Indefinitely delayed'. Roger guessed it had something to do with the exchange he'd had with Jane yesterday. Strange she hadn't updated him. He tried calling her but her phone went to voicemail. That could only mean she was in a meeting with a minister or with another of the agencies. He trusted her to call him in good time. With one last look at the skyline surrounding Hyde Park, Roger turned and taking his life into his hands crossed Park Lane to arrive at the entrance to the Hilton hotel. Rather than phone Ishaan, Roger announced his arrival at the reception desk. He wasn't sure what sort of reception he'd receive but he needn't have worried. Several minutes later Ishaan appeared, all smiles. He wore a crisp cut dark suit and the whitest shirt Roger had ever seen. The collar was cut away as was the modern fashion. He certainly fitted in with the hotel's clientele and Roger guessed that was the idea. Observing him, Roger felt distinctly underdressed. A stereo-typical detective wearing a worn out suit with worn out shoes.

Shaking Roger's hand Ishaan signalled to the lifts. "You should have told me you were coming, all the public areas are really busy. It's either my office or the Sky Bar. Roger thought for just two seconds.

"The Sky Bar". Seconds later the two men were travelling up in the lifts where not long ago several people had mysteriously disappeared.

"The cameras are working now". Ishaan nodded to the glass eye in the ceiling. "Pity they weren't before".

Roger stared at the circle of glass. "Tell me again, Ishaan, why wasn't the lift CCTV working"?

"It was being upgraded". The lift doors opened and Ishaan held out his arm to allow Roger to step out onto the Hilton's highest floor. "Coffee"?

Roger looked longingly at the bar, "Actually would you mind if I had a beer? Just a half, an IPA if you have one".

If Ishaan had an opinion he didn't show it. "IPA"?, he asked the young man preparing the bar.

"Bottled only, it's very good".

Ishaan raised his eyebrows, Roger nodded. "Perfect".

After receiving his beer, Roger walked to the window overlooking Hyde Park. He stared at the metropolis beyond. With so many cameras, London despite its size was a very hard place to hide in and yet, at the same time, it was so easy. You could be anyone you want in London. In many other capital cities the ethnicity tended to be singular, indigenous but London was so cosmopolitan. Your skin could be any colour and you were one hundred percent a Londoner. Nobody looked out of place and that tended to make his job very difficult. A foreign nation with mal intent could place an agent or agents in London and they would immediately blend in. Ishaan joined him, his coffee had taken longer.

"A penny for your thoughts".

Roger took a deep breath, "I was debating how hard it is to hide out there". He waved his hand at the window.

Ishaan answered immediately. "I would have said with all the CCTV and ANPR, that it was nigh on impossible".

He was right of course, the trouble was all they had were images of Peter bloody Fitch and he was always either at home or teaching at his precious school. To Roger, Mr Fitch led an incredibly boring life, too bloody boring to be true. He was always somewhere or his car was always somewhere where it could be verified. It was all too bloody neat, too bloody perfect.

"A penny for your thoughts again".

Roger turned to look at Ishaan. "Believe me you don't want to know Ishaan. Tell me who's the company who does your CCTV"?.

A company the hotel has used for years, long before I started here. Before you go I can give you their details if you like. They're Reading based".

Roger nodded, "Yes please, just routine". Both men knew that was a lie. Taking a sip from his beer Roger turned to look across the bar. "That's where our target, John was sitting"? Roger pointed his glass towards a seat close to the bar's centre.

"Yes".

"And what the CCTV did have of him, at one point he was staring over there". Roger moved his glass in the direction of a window seat.

"Yes and that's where, as an ex blue top, I become suspicious. That seat on the CCTV is showing up as empty. The bar at the time was busy and yet that seat and table were vacant. The window seats are nearly always the first to go and yet, throughout the time your target and agents were in the bar the seat remained empty. Nobody in the bar made a move for it. Normally when a window seat becomes vacant, someone will immediately take it over. In the CCTV footage we have, nobody does which suggests to me...".

"Somebody was sitting there", Roger finished off for him.

"Yes".

"Listen, Ishaan, you haven't heard this from me but we just don't have the resources to check every room in your hotel". Ishaan didn't look surprised.

"To be honest I'm surprised you even considered the idea".

Roger laughed, "Being an ex-copper you know our resources or lack of them".

"I do", Ishaan smiled. "It's my biggest memory of working with the Met".

"But I would like to, if you have no objection, send a digital forensics team in. See if they can come up with anything".

"You have the paperwork"?.

"We do".

"Then be my guest, and I'll be happy to assist where I can".

Roger actually blushed. "Well I was going to ask if we could do this on the quiet".

"On the quiet"?.

"Without your management knowing".

Ishaan shook his head, "Sorry that's a step too far, but if you're worried I'll smooth it over with them. Give them an explanation that will suit their doctrine if you see what I mean".

Roger looked at the floor, "I do, and thank you". He'd taken a chance and Ishaan had as he'd expected kicked it into touch. It was a distinct possibility that one of the top management may be involved and therefore as far as he was concerned the less they knew the better.

"I may even be able to secure a couple of rooms for them". It was a demonstration that Ishaan was showing willing.

"That would be lovely, thank you". Roger had stopped blushing. Saving any more blushes at that moment, Roger's phone rang. Checking, he saw that it was Jane. He gave a look that Ishaan recognised. This was private. "Sorry, I've got to take this". Roger apologised.

"Don't worry, I'll go and get that information you requested, you have the bar to yourself". Ishaan walked to the bar to return his empty cup and after giving Roger a look disappeared in the foyer with the lifts.

"Morning, Jane". Roger scanned the bar, except for the barman he did appear to be alone. Returning to the question of trust he wondered if the barman was trustworthy or was he a plant? A bartender was a very easy plant and in a position that enabled both eavesdropping and influence. A real fly on the wall but with distinct benefits. The barman didn't appear to be showing interest but then professionally trained operatives never did. As a precaution, Roger walked to a window area where he was pretty sure the barman wouldn't be able to hear him, nor would the nearest miked camera. "Morning, Jane", Roger repeated.

"Roger, Jane. You rang me. Sorry I was with Stephan". Roger knew she meant the Home Secretary.

"How is the poor man"?.

Jane let out a loud laugh. "Huh, our friend hasn't had a good morning". Jane related how the head of MI5 had badgered her into attending an early morning meeting with the Home Secretary, to try and persuade him to seriously think about introducing a national identity card. That the hacking of the DVLA's database, the country's unofficial national identity register, proved that one was needed. MI5 had been pushing for this for decades but successive governments had always drawn back from the idea. A) because of the cost and b), because it would almost certainly be unpopular with the electorate. She then went on to detail how the PM had been planning to take credit for the restoration of the very same database via a press conference at number 10, only for the news to be leaked by no one knew who, to the morning broadcasting stations. If that wasn't enough I had to tell him about poor Pete Collier, and the possibility of a bomb being hidden somewhere in the newly built FEL's premises at Porton Down. When I left him he was not a happy man. Porton Down cost close to two hundred million pounds and at the moment, it's a dead duck. We've had to evacuate it whilst the EOD carries out an investigation and that could take weeks, possibly months. I'm not sure he's had the guts to tell the prime minister yet". Jane laughed again, this time Roger with her. Once again he found himself wishing he could be a fly on the wall.

"But the DVLA Jane, that's good news at least isn't it? If our guys have cracked it, that's a huge step in finding out who is responsible surely". He heard Jane laugh again.

"Cracked it, ha that's a joke, the system righted itself. The hack from what I've heard so far, was almost certainly programmed to come to an end after a period of time. Our teams at the moment haven't the foggiest idea how it's been done. Of course that's not what the prime minister wants the nation to believe and what he will say at his press conference is that our digital experts have dealt with the hack and are at this very moment improving security so that a hack like this never occurs again. I fear not long in the future our dear prime minister is going to have egg all over his face. The hack is almost certainly a demonstration of power, along with what they've done to us. We're all just waiting for some sort of demand. Who from and what it will be is extremely worrying and keeping many of the best minds in the security services awake at night".

"Bloody hell what a mess", Roger remembered Donald telling him as much when they had first met. 'This is big', were his words. In his eyes this was fast going from being big to bigger.

"I couldn't agree more", there was resignation in Jane's voice.

"Going back to Porton Down Jane, is that why Nick has told me our explosive device investigations have been put on hold"?.

"Probably". Jane admitted. "If it helps I'll push them to the top of the list. For now, top priority and sensitive investigations will be carried out at Portsdown Hill, though the powers that be are very worried about this as Portsdown Hill, officially anyway, doesn't exist. They're even considering re-opening Fort Halstead but that's already been half stripped which means more money".

"Shit, another bloody mess".

"Again I agree". Jane concurred for a second time. "Where are you today Roger? I know you're not in your office".

Roger told her. "I'm actioning the old adage of 'going back to basics', clearing my head to see if I can see the wood for the trees".

"Fair enough. Well, take care, Roger and keep me informed".

"I will", but Jane didn't hear him. She had already rung off. Roger returned his phone to his jacket pocket. Looking up at the ceiling, he noted that two cameras were trained on him. The barman was busy restocking. Hands in pockets he moved around the bar. This was the place where John was last seen alive. The next sighting of him was of his head only, delivered by courier, Roger scoffed, to his house. Two questions, how was John taken out of the hotel, dead or alive and where was the rest of his body. In fact where were the bodies of all the severed heads that had turned up, not one body had turned up, just the heads, oh and their genitals. A body wasn't that easy to hide, where were they disposing of them? In random sites or in the same place. He had to assume they were being buried, otherwise the smell of decay would give their position away. His mind returned to the chair in the corner window. Who had been sitting there? The two Arab women he was sure he'd seen waiting for a lift? But on the CCTV the nearest chairs to the chair in question had been occupied and those people had already been identified and checked and had valid, as well as innocent, reasons for being there. Who had been sitting in that corner chair? Why had someone gone to so much trouble to make them disappear and where were they now? He remembered what Donald had told him about the femme fatale in France, could it possibly have been her? As he pondered all of the possibilities Ishaan re appeared carrying a number of papers.

"I'm not going to offer you a penny for your thoughts anymore".

"Don't offer, as I'm not at liberty to say".

"Which means you have something at least".

"Yes", Roger gave a rueful grin, "except it was given to us, and not in a nice way".

Ishaan handed Roger the papers he was carrying. "Well I hope these will help, that's the details of the company that installed and maintains our CCTV. There's also a list of contacts, people who work for the company that we deal with and have worked with in the past. And I'm giving them to you nicely". His sarcasm was lost on Roger.

Roger took them, glanced at them and after folding them placed them inside his inner jacket pocket. "Thanks, can we take a walk outside"?.

Ishaan's face questioned why but he didn't ask. "Of course, I could do with some fresh air, too long spells of electricity gives me a headache".

Once more the two took the lifts that held so many secrets. If only they could talk. Outside the two men found the same wall they'd leaned against when taking a break from watching the CCTV.

"It's bloody cold" Ishaan complained, "this better be quick".

"It will be", Roger took out a pay as you go phone from his coat pocket. He handed it to the surprised Ishaan, "Don't ask any questions, you can guess why I'm giving you one of these. My number is programmed into the contacts". Roger held up another pay as you go phone.

"It better have credit".

Roger grinned, he appreciated Ishaan not asking why. "It has, and plenty. From now on Ishaan if you have anything for me, please call me using that. If it's simply routine then call me on my usual". Roger held up his smart phone. "You can guess by me giving you that, that we're up against it. The sad thing is I'm running out of people I can trust".

"Well you can trust me".

"They all say that". Both men grinned. "And you're asking me to trust an ex-officer of the Met"?.

"YES". Both men laughed louder.

Suddenly Ishaan looked serious. "If you're back here, investigating our CCTV after the bombing of…"

"Gas explosion". Roger reminded him.

"Yeah right. After the bombing of your HQ, you must believe that what took place here at the hotel is either connected or if it's not with everything else going on, bloody important to something".

Roger kicked the wall with both feet, one after the other. He looked straight at Ishaan. "Honest answer"?.

"Go on".

"I don't know. I have no evidence, just the feeling in my gut".

"That's a good place to start".

Roger smiled, "someone else sort of told me that".

"Am I in good company"?.

Roger smiled again, "You are, very good".

Ishaan rubbed his hands. "It's bloody freezing, look unless there's anything else, I need to get back".

Roger nodded, "Fine I'll try and get a team booked to go through your CCTV tomorrow, are you sure you want to offer them rooms. They're monsters".

Ishaan shrugged. "They work for the NCA, of course they are". Ishaan turned to go. Roger touched his arm.

"Ishaan, a word of advice. If ever you have work done on your building. No matter how small. Run a security check on them, if you need help with it just ask. we'll check your CCTV people". Roger tapped his chest.

Ishaan looked quizzical.

"And don't ask why, just take my advice".

"Is it good advice"?.

"It's excellent advice".

"Ok then". Ishaan threw a mock salute and made his way back to the gaping hotel entrance. Roger watched him go. His gut was telling him that Ishaan was a good man. He bloody well hoped so. As Ishaan disappeared inside Roger looked up at the hotel towering above. The day of the sting operation, the day when everything started to go wrong felt like years ago when in fact, it was only days. How he wished he could turn the clock back. After one last glance at the hotel, he once more took his life into hands crossing the busy Park Lane. Immediately after reaching the other side Roger's phone went. He didn't recognize the number.

"Roger Denton".

"Roger, it's Doug".

"Doug"?.

"From the pub next to your house you idiot, you left something here from the other night, you need to collect it".

"Left something"?

"Yes, bloody hell, do I have to spell it out"?.

The penny dropped, "no, sorry, I'll be up later. Doug, how did you get this number"?.

There came a loud sigh. "You gave it to me, remember? You also gave me a key so I could look after your house when you're away. You gave me your number in case anything happened. Well it has as you know, I didn't do a very good job did I".

"I'll be up later".

"See you then". Doug rang off.

Roger looked at his watch, it was nearly midday. Shit he wanted to see Peter Fitch, he'd better get his skates on. He was about to wave down a taxi, a challenging task at the best of times, when his phone rang again. This time it wasn't his smartphone. It was his 'burner', his pay as you go. This must be important. Answering, he ran for the nearest entrance into the park. On Park Lane it had been close to impossible to hear Doug speak and Doug had a soldier's voice.

"Hello".

"Hello, don't say a name". A typical Donald introduction, Roger was getting used to them. "I thought it best to wait till you were outside. You never know who may be listening". How did he know? Roger looked around wildly even though he knew it was a complete waste of time. "Can you hear me"?.

Roger stopped running. "I can now".

"Good, I thought I'd let you know that I've had a pathologist's report back. It makes for interesting reading. First, it's almost certain that your head was cut whilst the victim was still alive. The genitals too. It is his belief that they were cut off first and stuffed in the poor bugger's mouth before they dealt with the head. There the barbarity ends. Whoever did this was a professional, almost certainly a trained surgeon". Roger made to speak but Donald stopped him. "There's something else, something our pathologist has no explanation for. He found a small drill hole in the victim's head. On examination, he found that the pineal gland was missing, that it had been removed. A very professional job. As I said, he has no explanation as to why". This rang a bell with Roger, he remembered now that Ismail, the poor bugger whose head was delivered to his wife had received the same treatment. "We both know that Mr Haver's head isn't the first. I told you about the migrant's head at our little tete de tete before, and since then your pathologist discovered the same thing. My man says the removal of the gland can be easily missed, therefore…"

"It may be prudent to have all the other heads re-examined".

"You've got it, not only to find out about the gland but to see whether your guys can realise whether all the victims were decapitated whilst still alive".

"Which would suggest an Islamic radical connection".

"Not necessarily, Islamists were butchers, remember? They weren't surgeons". Roger had to admit Donald was right. "But it is, I feel worth finding out whether the heads that are still in France, received the same treatment. Where I sit I can do nothing about that, you guys can".

"I've got to contact a guy in France".

"I know, well butter him up, see if his gendarmerie is willing to finance a second examination. If it becomes necessary, I'll see that the money gets signed off from here". Where's here? was Roger's immediate thought.

"Have you any idea why whoever is doing this would want the pineal gland"?.

"None at all", Donald was emphatic. "It may be the work of a mad man but I fear not".

"What about the rest of the bodies? We have the heads but not a single body. As yet we haven't really investigated where they might be". For a few seconds Donald was quiet, he was obviously thinking.

223

"I told you about the 'red market', maybe you should start looking there".

"Where's there"?.

"That's your job, signposts, remember? Where are you going now"?.

Roger told him he could see no harm in doing so.

"Ah the incredible Peter Fitch, able to be in several places at the same time. Well I hope you're not wasting your time".

"I won't know till I've been".

"No you won't". The phone went dead. Roger had wanted to know the pathologist's charge for his examination of D.C. Haver's head and whether he really was going to charge his credit card. He could phone Donald back but he knew it would be a waste of time. Gazing into the park Roger reflected on their conversation. Not once had Donald mentioned the recent explosions and he must know about Porton Down, the site was of national importance. Vital to the defence of the UK and yet not a word. Instead this fixation on the severed heads and France. France, he must phone there.

Using his smartphone, he phoned Nick back at the NCA's temporary offices. Explaining it as a hunch, he asked him to contact the Met's pathologist, working on their case, asking him two questions. With the heads that they had, could he check for the pineal gland and in his opinion were the victims decapitated whilst they were still alive.

'Lovely', was Nick's one comment. "Anything else"?.

"I'm off to interview Peter Fitch".

"Where are you hoping to find him? On the moon"?.

"Very funny". This time it was Roger's turn to ring off. Looking at his watch he ran back to Park Lane, raising his hand hoping to attract a taxi. Remarkably he did, one, almost as though it had been waiting, pulled over. After climbing in, the driver moved off. Roger saw him examine him in the mirror.

"Where to"?.

Chapter 6

Gendarmerie Nationale, Calais, France

It was close to midday when Capitaine Olivier Vendroux arrived at his gendarmerie.

"Did you get all you needed to do, done sir? Colette called out whilst wearing her sweetest smile.

"Yes, thank you, Colette". The capitaine swore he could hear somebody laughing but looking round he could see nobody.

"These are the people who have called you this morning". Colette handed the capitaine a neatly typed piece of paper.

"Thank you Colette, can you please bring me up a fresh coffee, noir not blanc".

"Of course".

"Merci, Colette". With that the capitaine made his way slowly up the stairs to his office. Once inside he examined himself in the mirror. His uniform looked fine, he had changed but his face looked terrible, not helped by cutting himself twice, whilst shaving. There came a knock at the door and Colette, not waiting for an answer, entered with a steaming cup of freshly brewed black coffee. She placed it, taking care to do it quietly, on his desk.

"Capitaine I have Jean Fournier, the young man on the phone. The one who came to see you yesterday, remember"?. He's already phoned three times this morning".

The capitaine frowned. This was all he needed. "Ask him to phone back in half an hour will you Colette, let me get myself together first".

"Of course, capitaine". Colette shut his office door, loudly enough, she knew, to do a little damage to Capitaine Olivier Vendroux's fragile head. Back in her office she picked up the phone. "Hello Jean"?.

"Oui". His voice was deadpan.

"The capitaine has asked me to ask you to phone back in half an hour".

"D'accord".

"Is everything alright Jean"?.

"Fine, don't worry". The way Jean said 'don't worry', did worry Colette. The way he said it, sounded both sarcastic and malicious.

"Ok, if you're sure, Jean", but Colette found herself speaking to thin air.

Tenerife, Canarias, Spain.

Pierre de Fauw, dressed as though he were royalty, stood alongside a number of dignitaries in front of a bank of television cameras. They were on the outskirts of Los Cristianos and behind them standing in recently landscaped, beautifully landscaped gardens stood a glistening white, modern three storey building. It was a brand new hospital, local television was about to report. Built with private money from a company owned by the man from Belgium, Pierre de Fauw. Not a penny had been asked for from the local authorities. All they'd had to do was find and gift the land, along with generous tax breaks for the next ten years. The hospital which even had its own harbour would operate as both a private as well as a public affair. Residents of Tenerife would benefit from the facilities whilst those with money could pay handsomely to recover in the sun. The hospital suited everybody's needs and Pierre de Fauw was something of a local hero.

With a fleet of ambulances passing slowly behind them, the television cameras started filming, a couple even broadcasting live. To an enthusiastic round of applause Pierre cut the richly coloured ribbon. The hospital was declared open and would start receiving patients the very next day. To highlight the point, doctors and nurses in crisp white uniforms paraded alongside the ambulances. After giving a number of interviews Pierre was whisked to 'la alcaldia', for a civic reception and slap up meal prepared by some of the Island's top chefs.

After finishing his meal and the shaking of many hands Pierre was driven back to the Island's main airport where his private jet was waiting. His next destination was the CQF - Calais-Dunkerque airport at Marck, France. It should be a smooth flight the captain announced and with any luck the flight shouldn't take more than four hours. They should arrive around nine pm. The hostess offered Pierre a bottle of champagne but he waved it away. Coffee only followed by water, lots of it. He had a big day tomorrow and he needed to be ready for it. Before they had flown over the last of the Canary Islands, Pierre was already asleep. It had been a good day, a bloody good day.

Pembridge Square, Bayswater, London, England

Her new home, Ariana discovered, was in Bayswater not Notting Hill where she had originally been told. Nonetheless it was still magnificent. The square where her new home was situated boasted a landscaped garden at its centre, a quite beautiful garden, which as a resident she had permission to enjoy. Not that she needed it for at the rear of her property was a magnificent garden. Beautifully landscaped and though well-manicured it could no way be described as formal. Where appropriate the flora had been allowed to wander as it wished. A brand new conservatory allowed one to enjoy the garden no matter what the weather. Nearly all of the houses in the square were painted white and Ariana's was no exception. The house or rather villa she was later to find out, if you included the attic rooms, was four storeys high. It had a stucco frontage with huge bay windows and chequered marble steps leading up to a huge burgundy coloured door. Colonnades on either side supported a ridiculously high porch.

The height apart from the basement and attic was carried throughout the house. Never had Ariana experienced such high ceilings, not even in Orme's house. The house throughout was richly decorated and it was obvious that money had never been an object. In attendance at the house were three full time servants, two chefs, a part time gardener who lived in the basement and a full time security guard who was relieved by another when needed by others employed by the organisation.

Though Ariana had never lived in the house, she knew everybody who worked there and each room down to the most minute detail. It was as though she had lived there all her life and that she had been responsible for the recent renovation. All memories of Fatima were gone, she was Ariana, or at least until the organisation chose otherwise.

Le Week-End Cafe/Bar, Sangatte, France

The owner of the cafe where Jean worked watched as his young waiter made yet another call using his mobile. That must have been the sixth that day and every time each call had lasted little more than a few seconds and after each Jean's face had dropped. There was something seriously wrong, the owner could see it. His waiter's whole manner that morning had been robotic, he was simply going through the motions without offering any personal touch. It was so unlike Jean who normally had a word for everybody. It was almost as if he was carrying the weight of the world on his shoulders. At first he had thought it may be the worry of him becoming a father but his young lady, Camille had phoned him this morning to say she was no longer in hospital, that she was now safe at home. Jean, after the call, lasting roughly half an hour, had been back to his old self. So it wasn't that. Something else was worrying him. He decided as his boss he needed to know. Whatever it was, it was affecting his work.

"Jean", Jean looked up to see his boss waving at him. "Jean, come here a minute will you". Jean did as he was told, collecting a couple of finished glasses as he did so. When he was close his boss placed one hand on his left shoulder. He looked at his young waiter straight in his face, almost as though he were his father. His expression was one of kindness, concern. "Young man, what's worrying you? You look miserable and yet you've just found out you're going to be a father. You should be dancing and singing, not moping around as though you've just lost your bollocks". And you haven't been off of that bloody mobile of yours. I don't mind you making a call now and again, but every half an hour". The owner's voice trailed off. He'd made his point, now it was for Jean to give him an explanation.

"Pardon", Jean's head dropped. "Sorry" he repeated, "...but I can't tell you. It's a problem, my problem and it's personal. Can I please make one more call? I promise it will be the last one today".

The owner stared at him hard. Finally he removed his hand from Jeans shoulder and grabbing a cloth, started wiping a glass. "One more", he agreed, "but that's it. After that I want you smiling and singing to the music like you usually are. The weather is depressing enough and with you, with a face like that....". The owner did an exaggerated copy of Jean's expression. " Some of my customers are close to suicide".

"I promise". Jean actually managed to smile.

"Good well do it out back, not out front. It doesn't look good you being on your bloody mobile every few minutes".

"Merci", Jean, phone in hand rushed through the door beside the bar and down the corridor to the yard at the back. Holding his breath he dialled. He felt sick, in fact every time he'd made a call that morning, he had felt sick. And every time he'd got through to that interfering woman in league with the dodgy, he was sure, lieutenant. This time was no different, that woman answered. "Can you put me through to Capitaine Vendroux please".

"I'll try, is that you Jean? Is everything ok"?. Jean could sense the worry in her voice, so she should be. Interfering old cow. "Yes everything's fine, can you just put me through please".

"Certainly I'll just see if he's available, hold the line please Jean". Music played through the earpiece. Jean waited, fingers crossed so tightly they hurt. "Just putting you through Jean".

Silence followed. Jean could hardly contain himself. "Hello, Capitaine Olivier Vendroux".

NCA's Temporary Offices, Gladstone Park, Cricklewood, North London, England

Nick, along with many of the NCA's teams were watching the prime minister's press conference. It was being broadcast live. He was extolling the professionalism and work by the teams investigating the hack at the DVLA and how that everything was now back to normal. Their work was, he was at pains to point out, not yet over. Their job was now to ensure such an event never threatened the security of the nation again. After five minutes the microphone was passed to an official at the DVLA. She went on to explain what was to happen next. The procedure for replacing corrupted licences.

Most of the team were incredulous. Many were, in a remote way, involved in the investigation. They had heard nothing of any break-through, this could possibly help them with so many issues. In particular the digital forensic operators were very put out and they started making calls. Nick tried phoning Roger but frustratingly his phone was off. This was important, he couldn't leave it. He called Jane. Jane answered.

She quickly put Nick straight. She essentially told him what she had told Roger. That there was no breakthrough. The problem had sorted itself. The prime minister's line was a bluff, pure spin, for political as well as popular gain only. This will come back to bite him, "Keep your teams investigating Nick. There has been no breakthrough".

"This will get out sooner or later, and when it does there will be a political crisis. But let us not be the cause, Nick. Make sure everybody in your building is aware of that. Many of us would like to see the PM fall because of his own lies, but that's not our job. It's really important that everybody understands that. If I find somebody in my agency has leaked what I've just told you, I'll have their flesh boiled from their bones. Understood Nick"?.

"Understood". He was about to ask something else but Jane had gone. Nick took a deep breath, bloody hell, what a bloody mess.

Wellingborough, Northamptonshire, England

Roger had decided, rather than taking the cab to his car parked under the Chinese supermarket, to take it instead all the way to Wellingborough. All of the way the cabbie hadn't attempted to say one word, a near miracle, leaving Roger with his thoughts. He kept thinking of Donald's apparent obsession with the heads, the pineal gland and the red market. He wondered what the Met's pathologist would come up with. Whether his findings would concur with Donald's man. The fact that D.C.Havers had had his genitals and his head removed whilst still alive, played on Rogers mind. Every time he considered this, his mind went back to John, his ex-colleague and friend. Had the same procedure happened to him? Had he been still alive when his body was mutilated. He remembered opening the box containing his head and immediately felt sick. Rather than vomiting the feeling in his stomach quickly turned to anger. He was more determined than ever to get the bastards who did this.

Rather than ask the driver to take him directly to the school, he asked to be dropped at the Columbia Hotel which was only a five minute walk to where he wanted to be. After booking a single room, he went up to wash after which he was ready for Peter Fitch.

The remarkable thing about the school where Peter Fitch worked was that it was very unremarkable. There was nothing about it that stood out. Ordinary, very ordinary was how he'd describe it. The one thing that caught his attention was the number of CCTV cameras. There were far more than he deemed necessary and they all looked fairly new. Via an intercom on the front gate, he introduced himself and his reason for being there. He even had to show his ID card to a camera before he was allowed through. After the gate he made his way to the well signposted reception. There were more CCTV cameras along the way, he made a mental note. At reception he found the school head waiting for him and she didn't look best pleased.

"This is verging on harassment", she accused Roger before he had even had a chance to introduce himself.

Glancing apologetically at the receptionist, Roger gently suggested to the head that they have a quiet word in her office. For a moment it looked as if the head was about to refuse Roger's suggestion before she apparently changed her mind and told him to follow her. With a wink to the receptionist, he did as he was bidden.

Roger found her office to be surprisingly personal. It was airy, delicately decorated with plenty of greenery and nearly all the photos, of which there were many, were of friends and Roger supposed, family.

"I do have a life outside of my school and I like to be reminded of it", the head sounded defensive.

"As do I", Roger replied using his best smile. His reply was a lie of course, he had no life to speak of outside the NCA.

"Of course". It was the nearest, he knew, he was going to get, to an apology.

Roger handed the head his card. "Roger Denton, may I sit down"?.

"Please do, Caroline Carter, Mrs", Mrs Carter forced a smile.

Roger folded his legs and leaned back, he wanted to create an impression of informality. To break the tension. "I assure you I'm not here to persecute your teacher, Mrs Carter, but I do have a problem and I do need to get to the bottom of it. To be honest I think someone or somebody is using Peter and I want to see if he has any idea of who it could be. Why have they chosen him? Believe me, I don't think for one moment he has done anything wrong, but someone is trying to implicate him with some very serious offences". As he spoke Mrs Carter visibly relaxed.

"Can you tell me what those offences are? You must understand that I'm responsible for the safety of all of the children here".

Roger shook his head, "I'm sorry Mrs Carter, I can't do that but believe me if we ever thought Peter was a risk, you'd be the first to know".

The head didn't look convinced.

"I assure you, Mrs Carter, we do not believe Peter is responsible for any of the crimes someone is trying to associate him with. If I thought otherwise, he'd already be out of here".

The head looked a little reassured. "Well if you want to see him, it'll have to be now. He's just about to finish class. At that moment a bell rang and teenagers began to fill the corridors, the sounds took Roger back to his childhood, the last time perhaps when he was really happy. It was all he could do to hold back the odd tear.

"Before you fetch him, Mrs Carter, can I ask who did your security here, your CCTV for example".

"Why do you want to know"?. The suspicion was back. Roger had to think on his feet.

"Only that it looks very good, I'd like to recommend them to a few people".

Mrs Carter looked pleased at this. "I'll get my secretary to dig out their details, now I'd better go and grab Peter before he leaves, wait here please Mr Denton". Roger was just about to say, 'Roger' please, but the head was too quick. She was already out of earshot.

Gendarmerie Nationale, Calais, France

Capitaine Olivier Vendroux, really didn't need this. Not the way he was feeling. What did that little prick want now? He'd already wasted close to an hour of his time yesterday. At first he'd tried to persuade Colette to put the bloody pain in his arse off until tomorrow but the little jerk was too persistent. He took the call.

"Capitaine Olivier Vendroux". A very nervous sounding voice spoke at the other end.

"Capitaine Vendroux, it's Jean Fournier, I came to see you yesterday, you asked us to. Me and Camille. But I came alone, do you remember"?.

The capitaine took a deep breath, at the same time massaging his head. Of course he remembered, how could he forget. He took another deep breath.

"Are you still there"?. Stupid little twat, of course he was.

"Yes, Jean, I remember. What is it you want"?.

Jean started to blurt out his story. In response to the capitaine warning him to keep what he knew a secret, he related in a tumble of rambles what happened after Capitaine Maubert's funeral. He and Camille after being sent away by himself, going to the capitaine's widow's house where they also met the lieutenant and the lady who worked in reception. Camille that was it and how the lieutenant had warned them not to speak to anybody about this. Especially you, Capitaine Vendroux. I should have told you yesterday, I'm really sorry, Jean finished.

The capitaine listened in growing horror. He thought he'd put a lid on the whole affair, evidently not. If the organisation got to hear what had happened, especially after their warning on Mont d'Hubert, he was dead meat. Not only that, his second in command and his secretary, the two closest to him in the gendarmerie were conspiring against him. What about the rest of his gendarmerie? Was anybody loyal to him? What had been a dull ache on his brow had now become something of a bomb ready to explode at any minute.

"Capitaine, capitaine, are you still there"?.

That little prick was still on the line. The reason for his biggest headache ever, he'd get them both for this. Why couldn't they have kept their stupid little mouths shut.

"Capitaine"?. Jean was beginning to worry.

"Yes, yes. I'm still here. Thank you for telling me. I'll deal with it. You haven't told anybody else"?.

"Non".

"You're quite sure"?.

"Oui", Jean was starting to tremble.

"Well make sure you don't", the capitaine realised his mistake and softened his tone a little. "Thank you for telling me".

The capitaine was gone. Jean stood, still holding his phone. Had he made a dreadful mistake? He wasn't sure, he was already starting to regret it. Regret everything. Making love to Camille on top of Cap Blanc Nez that night, regret not going to the gendarmerie sooner, regret going to the gendarmerie at all. Regret telling the victim's widow and daughter, regret telling the lieutenant and Colette the lady, the nice lady in reception and now telling Capitaine Vendroux who they'd already told. Merde what a fucking mess. In his anger, Jean kicked a waste bag full of empty cans across the yard.

"Merde, merde, merde, merde", he shouted out loud, punching a wall. "MERDE, he yelled out in pain as his hand made contact.

The owner, wondering what the hell was going on, ran out to see for himself. He found Jean crumpled on the floor in a flood of tears.

He gently lifted the boy, for that was what he was, to his feet. Jean to him was the son they'd never had. To see him like this was bringing tears to his own eyes. He must not let that happen.

"Come, Jean, come and sit down", with his arm around Jean's shoulder he led him back into the bar and sat him at a table in a corner at the back. Several of the clientele, all regulars looked over. The owner silently asked them to look the other way. Sitting holding Jean's hands he called for his wife to pour a beer. His wife, concern written all over her face, placed the glass in front of their waiter who had his head resting on the table. "Come on Jean, drink up, things can't be that bad, if you think they are, you're among friends here. You know you are. You can tell us, and if we can we will try and help. If necessary protect you". The owner had no idea why he'd added the last bit, for some reason he had felt it necessary. He couldn't explain why.

To everyone's relief Jean slowly lifted his head and taking hold of the glass as though his life depended on it, took three long sips of his biere blonde.

"Merci", then he started to talk, he came out with everything, What he and Camille had witnessed whilst making love in his car on Cap Blanc Nez, their first visit to the gendarmerie, their meeting at Capitaine Maubert's house, his second meeting with Capitaine Vendroux. His struggle with what to do. His recent phone call to Capitaine Vendroux and how now he thought he'd just made a terrible mistake and that he may have put the lieutenant, the lady receptionist, himself and worst of Camile and his unborn baby in grave danger, deadly danger. The owner, his wife and several of those near enough to hear listened with their mouths open. Nobody spoke, nobody knew what to say. Nearly everyone was in shock.

Chapter 6

With silence dominating the background music took over, a new song started to play. Tahitialamaison by Keen' V. Hearing it Jean lost it, yelling he swung his arm across the table sending his beer flying. The whole cafe was once more shocked into silence, nobody realised the significance of the song that was playing. Who is it that controls fate? you may be asking yourself again.

Back at the gendarmerie in Calais, Capitaine Olivier Vendroux was considering his future, not just his future but his very life. His lieutenant, his secretary and his predecessor's wife and his daughter were evidently suspicious of him and if they went to a higher authority he was dead meat. A friend of his had gone to a great deal of trouble to get him this post and he had completely fucked it up. He now recognised that his pompous overblown pride had ruined what was seen to be within the organisation a prestigious posting. Why? He had no idea, he still believed Calais to be a dump. There was something big under that bloody cliff top, that's all he knew. He also knew that if the organisation considered him a risk his life on this earth was finished. The organisation didn't accept risk. If they thought there was any, they dealt with it and fast. The capitaine looked around his office. It wasn't really his office, it was still Capitaine Maubert's, he had never really left. He could even still smell him. Capitaine Maubert was imprinted on the building. He'd never stood a chance. Coming to a decision he kicked back the chair and grabbed his case. There was no point in running from the organisation. Many had tried and very publicly been found. If he was going to go out he'd go out with a bang. He'd enjoyed last night, even though he'd suffered for it today. 'Soigner le mal par le mal', (the French equivalent of hair of the dog), he was going to test that saying tonight, boy was he determined to test it. Jogging down the stairs he waved to Colette, "Bonne nuit my loyal one". And the capitaine was gone.

Colette looked on in astonishment as did several gendarmes. 'Dick head', one commented and everyone laughed.

A Comprehensive School, Wellingborough, Northamptonshire

Roger Denton of the NCA, for the first time, was looking at Peter Fitch in the flesh. The others had been right. He looked as far removed from a violent criminal as was possible. Under a suit jacket that had seen better days, he wore a yellow tank top and underneath that a blue shirt with a frayed collar. His shoes, though well-polished, really could do with renewing. Roger doubted the man before him owned another pair. His skin was pale and his face reminded Roger of a mouse. Everything about Mr Fitch was subservient, he wouldn't last ten seconds under interrogation, which was why everyone else who had seen him decided that he was a victim and not a criminal. Roger's first impressions were the same and after an hour's chat, Roger, like everybody else who had interviewed him, felt exactly the same way. He couldn't imagine this man treading on an ant never mind committing murder. As he had told everyone else who had interviewed him, Peter Fitch repeated to Roger that he could think of no reason at all why he had been targeted and Roger believed him. Still it had been worth coming up to see for himself. Now he was happy to chalk Peter Fitch off. Roger gave Mr Fitch his card, just in case he did think of something and after shaking hands watched his suspect leave.

"Well, he seems happier than he did when I told him you were here, congratulations". Mrs Carter had been waiting outside. She handed Roger a small square piece of paper, almost certainly taken from a notepad. "I've written down the details of the company who installed our CCTV, you asked for their details. If you need anything else, here's my card. I've written my mobile number on the back". Caroline Carter's smile this time was genuine.

Roger, thanking her, took the paper and without looking at it folded it and placed it in his wallet.

"Now I really must be going, I mustn't impose on your hospitality any longer".

"You don't want a coffee before you go"? The smile was still there. Caroline Carter was a completely different woman than the one earlier.

"Roger shook his head, "I'd love to but I really have to go, duty calls".

"Now that I do understand", Caroline Carter laughed, "I'll see you out".

Ten minutes later Roger was back at the Hotel Columbia. After grabbing a half from the bar he was sitting on the side of the bed in his room. Reaching into his inside jacket pocket he pulled out the sheets of paper given to him by Ishaan. Typical of Ishaan, an ex-detective there was an overload of information. What he really wanted was the company name and address. He soon found it, Ishaan had been right, they were based in Reading. Taking out his wallet he removed the note Caroline had written for him. Roger stared at both, they were the same company. Was that coincidence or something more sinister?

Pembroke Square, Bayswater, London

Just as she was retiring to bed, Ariana received a call. It was Henrietta Sands. She was desperate, with everything that was going on, her husband was rarely home and when he was, he was in a foul mood. He was also tending to drink which had the effect of him being even worse in the morning.

She so enjoyed their day's outing. Would Ariana indulge her and come over for lunch. She was quite an accomplished cook and loved entertaining but rarely got the chance as Stephan was always having to or be entertained in some stuffy restaurant. Please, she had almost begged.

Ariana happily accepted. This would take her a step closer to her target and a step through far more subtle means than taking the usual, more risky approach. She felt sorry for Henrietta and for the first time felt a little guilty but then again, she was only doing her job. She must not let the feeling of guilt affect her work. Lying back, the feeling of guilt had gone, instead she felt a pang of excitement. She'd had some big assignments in the past but this one was by far the biggest. Her target was one of the most powerful in the British government. What was it she wondered that the organisation wanted her to get from him? She couldn't wait to find out. Nestling her head on the pillow her breathing started to slow. Ariana let out a slow contented sigh, the scent of the haoma flowers one of her servants had scattered on her bed took her back to Persia. The beginning of everything.

The Columbia Hotel, Wellingborough, Northamptonshire

Roger Denton sat on the side of his bed staring at the two bits of paper in his hands. Was he looking for something that wasn't there? He was a detective, elimination was a big part of his job. Turning on his smartphone he called Nick. Nick, finding it hard not to ask too many questions, went over what had happened at base, which wasn't much. The prime minister's broadcast was discussed and Nick told him about his conversation with Jane. Roger confirmed that he already knew what Jane had told him and apologised for not letting him know. Both men were critical of the prime minister, agreeing that his announcement could well backfire and if it did it would have the result of making the intelligence agencies look incompetent, they would get the blame no doubt. They could never make a public announcement telling the truth, to inform the Great British public that the prime minister had lied. No, instead they would be held up as a scapegoat and that the politicians would, to cover themselves, almost certainly promise yet another pointless review.

The pathologist hadn't come back yet, Nick told him, hopefully he would tomorrow. Roger then broached the subject of the CCTV.

"Nick, it's probably nothing but will you do a company check for me. It's a private company based in Reading. They fit CCTV and quite possibly a lot more, I've no idea. Find out what you can about them and let me know, will you". Roger then reeled off the company name, FE Security and the address in Reading.

"Will do, want to tell me why"?.

"Not yet Nick, just do it, will you"?.

"Of course, it shouldn't take long".

"Don't prejudge Nick, now you've said that it'll probably take days".

"It won't, I'm touching wood. Sir, there's something else, security are stressing out about your car, they say it's been abandoned in that Chinese supermarket's car park. You know the one near us".

"You mean Wing Yip".

"That's it".

"Not abandoned, Nick, left there, tell them to pick it up will you, I don't need it". There was a pause.

"How are you getting around"?.

Roger laughed, "Flying horse, you're asking too many questions Nick".

"Fair enough, I haven't got any more".

"Pleased to hear it, I've got to go".

"What time are you back"?.

"That's another question, Nick".

"Sorry, you're right, it is. I'll take it back".

"Night, Nick". Roger rang off. Right, he had to get going. He had no intention of spending the night in the hotel. He needed another taxi but wasn't going to ring for one. Buttoning up his coat he left the hotel, taking a right into the town centre. Anyone watching would simply think he was going for a pint or a meal. Before leaving his room, he'd ruffled up his bed to make it look as if he slept in it, used the soap, squeezed out some of the shower gel and turned on the shower for a few seconds. He'd departed leaving his key in the door on the inside. As far as the hotel would be concerned he'd simply left early.

It didn't take Roger long before he'd found what he was looking for. A taxi office. Because of the distance, he had to wait for half an hour. The taxi delivered him to Milton Keynes train station where after a twenty minute wait he took another taxi. 'Where to'?, the driver asked. Roger gave him the name of a road in Bushey, he was going home.

Cafe de Paris, Rue Royale, Calais Nord, France

Capitaine Olivier Vendroux, was out of uniform, He wasn't going to make the same mistake twice. He'd been greeted as though he were an old friend by some of those drinking in the cafe. Several had been there last night and showed him what they had filmed. 'You're famous capitaine, famous in Calais', one or two declared and a few more expressed that they liked the fact he was human. 'Not like that stuffy Capitaine Maubert'. 'He would have never been seen, mixing with the likes of us".

Something of a party atmosphere started to unfold and the capitaine joined in abandoning wholeheartedly his position in the town. He was going to party as though it was his last night on this earth, and he didn't care what anyone thought. By eleven pm he was starting to get out of control and those who before were enjoying his company were starting to be wary. The barman too was keeping a watchful eye on him. From experience he was pretty sure this wasn't going to end well and the capitaine's behaviour was also starting to make some of the cafe's customers look a little uncomfortable.

The last straw came when the capitaine lunged at a girl trying to buy a drink at the bar. Putting his arm around her waist, he pulled her towards him searching for a kiss, at the same time grabbing her left breast. The girl let out a shriek and several customers jumped in to help pull him off. The barman and a colleague dashed out front and picking him up threw him into the street.

"You're barred, don't try coming back". shouted the barman. Inside, the owner was on the phone to the gendarmerie. He described what had just happened.

"Your capitaine has just assaulted a female customer. We have it recorded on our CCTV and there are many witnesses. You need to send someone".

"We're on our way, five minutes, no more".

"Merci, be quick. Your capitaine is out of control".

"We're on our way".

Outside the capitaine staggered to his feet. After making a one finger salute to the cafe, with a winding walk he crossed the road to the square that was Place d'Armes heading for the hotel where he'd stayed the night before. He never made it, from the shadows appeared two men. Walking either side of him, they lifted him up under his arms and effortlessly carried him to a waiting car. After throwing him in the back seat, the two men got in either side of him. The car sped off heading for the port and Calais Plage.

The capitaine started to struggle, shouting. One of the men slapped him on the side of the face.

"Tais toi".

The capitaine gave a look of surprise, before and without warning starting to vomit.

"Merde", the two captors in the back cried simultaneously. One slapped the capitaine again.

It was actually three minutes before a gendarmerie car arrived at the Cafe de Paris but the capitaine was nowhere to be seen.

If he turns up again, do not hesitate to give us a call, the gendarmes said and drove away planning to search the streets for Capitaine Olivier Vendroux. He had to be somewhere. Fucking dick head.

As the car with Capitaine Olivier Vendroux drove along the Calais seafront two cars pulled out in front and three behind.

Above them in his penthouse Pierre de Fauw was gazing out to sea, reflecting on what a great day it had been. Perfect almost. He was blissfully unaware of what was happening in the street below. Never assume everything's perfect Pierre.

The procession of cars at an easy pace, so as not to attract attention took the coast road, the D940 passing through Sangatte. As they passed Le Week-End cafe no one took any notice. It was simply normal traffic. Steadily they started the climb to Mont d'Hubert and Cap Blanc Nez. As they did so, one of the cars at the rear did an overtaking manoeuvre. It was deliberate, to give the impression to anyone watching that this wasn't a procession but simply regular traffic with an impatient driver amongst the spread out line of cars. At Mont d'Hubert, the car with Capitaine Olivier Vendroux turned left into the car park for the restaurant on the summit. All the other cars continued on the D940 towards Wissant except the last car which also turned left into the car park. Travelling in this car, a man and a woman, after parking, got out. The woman, shivering with the cold, headed straight for the restaurant. The male, who had been driving, after looking around gave a discreet signal. The car with Capitaine Olivier Vendroux drove around the back, two men dressed in chef's outfits opened a wide door to the service area. The car manoeuvred inside. After closing the door, the two opened a door to a huge walk-in freezer. Slowly the car entered and the two men quickly closed the door, after which they returned to their duties in the restaurant kitchen. Inside the freezer, a woman in a white coat picked up a fire extinguisher and squeezed the handle. No powder came out but the rear wall of the freezer slowly slid open. On the other side, a road descended deep underground. The driver slowly edged the car forward. Once fully onto the road, the freezer wall slid shut. The driver then edged the car slowly along the underground road designed for WW2 armour, deep under Mont d'Hubert. The car came to a halt in a wide domed parking area. Somebody in the chamber opened the right hand rear passenger door. They leaned inside.

"Welcome to hell Capitaine Olivier Vendroux".

Coulogne, Near Calais, France

Lieutenant Beaufort was at home. Unable to relax ,he was pacing up and down his lounge. So stressed was he, he hadn't even started the beer his wife had poured for him. His obvious stress was beginning to stress her as well and hoping to help, she put on one of her husband's favourite singers, Florent Pagny. He'd always told her his music helped him to think and it was very obvious to her that he was doing nothing else but thinking now.

'Savoir Aimer' started to play. It didn't have the effect of making him sit down but he did stop pacing up and down. He suddenly noticed his beer and picking it up, went to the French windows and stood staring out at the garden. His wife, standing behind him, placed a hand on each of his shoulders, then rested her cheek. Like this she started to sway to the music. The lieutenant didn't move a muscle, he knew his wife was there and he was enjoying her closeness. Any other time, he would have turned and danced with her, this evening however his mind was elsewhere.

Colette had told him about Jean's visit then the capitaine's bizarre farewell, clocking off a good hour earlier than he was meant to and this after he turned up a couple of hours late this morning. Now he was receiving reports that the capitaine was once more in the Cafe de Paris. What the fuck was the matter with the man and where did he and Colette stand now? Not only did he feel responsible for his wife, he also felt responsible for Colette. Had he put them both in danger? He sincerely hoped not. And what about Jean and Camille? According to Colette, Jean had blanked her. Why? What was going through his head? Merde, what a fucking mess. In his mind he worked back through his day, his meeting with Jean-Paul the pathologist. Angleterrre kept raising its head, somehow that country was connected with what was happening here. He remembered that an officer in the UK had been trying to contact his predecessor and had spoken with Capitaine Vendroux. He needed to speak with that officer. It was a plan of action and he desperately needed one. But he didn't speak English, there were phones that could translate but the only one in his gendarmerie was in the capitaine's office and there was no way he could use that. Did the officer in the UK speak French? Almost certainly not.

"Cheri, do we know anyone who speaks English"?.

"Non, pourquoi?"

"No reason", shrugging her off, the lieutenant reached for his phone.

"Who are you calling"?.

"Colette". His wife wasn't listening. She was dancing by herself.

The lieutenant, requiring peace and quiet, moved into the kitchen. Opening the fridge he cracked open a fresh beer and poured it into his empty glass. Taking a sip he waited to see if Colette answered. It was seven rings before she did, he was counting.

"Colette, ca va"?.

"Just", Colette answered. "I wish I knew what was going on Lieutenant, nothing's been the same since that storm, and now this".

"I know. Listen Colette, I want to follow through on a few things. I want to contact that guy in the UK".

"Roger Denton", Colette, helped. She'd told him god knows how many times.

"Yes, do we have anyone in the gendarmerie who speaks reasonable English? Somebody we can trust"?. He hated having to ask that.

"There's Mirielle, she went to university in England. Her English is good and we're friends outside of work.

"Perfect", the lieutenant felt a rise of excitement pass through his veins. He liked Mirielle, she never complained. He had no idea she spoke English. "Do you think she'd mind if you called her now? Ask her if she'd mind calling someone in England with me tomorrow, say in my office at nine thirty. That's eight thirty in the UK, but they're the same as us. The detective will be in early".

"I'll try her now". Colette rang off. The lieutenant hadn't even had time to return to the lounge when Colette rang back.

"Mirielle's fine with it".

"Brilliant, merci Colette, I love you".

"You're married lieutenant". Colette was gone. Feeling happier he returned to the lounge where his wife was still dancing by herself to the music of Florent Pagny. Toi et moi was playing. Taking her in his arms they started to dance together. Mouthing the words to the song, the lieutenant felt a sudden rush of emotion. One that he had never experienced before. Tears started to roll down both cheeks and within seconds he was sobbing uncontrollably. Knowing not to ask any questions, his wife pulled his head onto her shoulder and proceeded to caress his neck. They both realised the moment and before they both knew it they were making love on the lounge floor. Not sex, this was love, made with a tenderness that both had never experienced before. At the end, both were crying. They'd reestablished a closeness that had long been forgotten, forgotten with the trials of life. As they lay on the carpet, the lieutenant's phone started to ring.

"Whoever it is, can fuck off". His wife clenched her legs around him so her husband couldn't get up. The act led to another bout of love making.

In the gendarmerie, the gendarme in charge of the night shift put the receiver down in frustration. The lieutenant wasn't answering. He didn't know who else to call. Their new capitaine had allegedly assaulted a woman in the Cafe de Paris. Apparently there was CCTV and dozens of witnesses. The media was already ringing asking questions and now their capitaine had somehow managed to disappear. They'd checked his accommodation and he wasn't there, now they were ringing round the hotels but so far nothing. Merde, what a fucking mess.

Hervelinghen, Near Mont 'Hubert, France

Jean and Camille lay in bed at Camille's parents. Jean with Camille's head on his shoulder lay with one hand on what he hoped was her womb. If he was honest he wasn't really sure where that was. In bed together at Camille's parent's house was a first, as up until now they hadn't been allowed to sleep together under their roof. However seeing as how their daughter was now expecting Jean's child her parents could see little point in continuing that rule.

You'd have expected their conversation to be about their baby, but it wasn't. It was all about Capitaine Maubert and Capitaine Olivier Vendroux. Jean was now convinced that he'd made a terrible mistake and in doing so had betrayed the nice woman and the lieutenant. Not only that he'd blurted everything out at his place of work in front of around half a dozen people. His boss had told everyone there to keep their mouths shut, but would they? He didn't think so.

Chapter 6

They decided between them that in the morning one of them would have to telephone either the nice lady or the lieutenant. "Now get some sleep Jean'" Camille ruffled his hair gently. Soon her hand fell onto the bed and she was asleep. Jean lay still, his eyes closed, but he was awake, wide awake. How could he sleep?

Neither heard Camille's phone. People were busy sharing videos, videos of an incident in the Cafe de Paris. Everyone agreed, what a fucking mess. And most agreed, what a dick head.

A Street in Bushey, London, England

Roger Denton of the NCA had asked the taxi to drop him off at Bushey railway station. From there it was a fifteen minute walk to the street which used to be his home. He wasn't sure how he was going to feel, seeing the rubble that was once his home. In some ways he now regretted ever coming back. It was too late now, there was something waiting for him at the pub. Maybe he was being over cautious playing games but he couldn't get rid of the feeling, a very strong feeling that he was being listened to, as well as being watched, and so too some parts of his investigation. Just as Donald had suggested, he wanted to investigate under the radar, preferably on his own. Coming from the station, he was this evening entering his road at the opposite end as last time. The advantage of this was that he could enter the pub without having to pass the rubble that marked where his house used to be. Keeping to the shadows he could see just one van parked, guarding the rubble. He could just make out two men sitting inside. Not taking any risks Roger entered the pub via the nearest door. Inside the pub was pretty quiet and Doug spotted him immediately.

"What will you be having"? Roger chose a large glass of merlot over a beer. He was tired and it had been cold outside, he needed to warm up and a mellow red, he was confident, would do just that. "There you go", the landlord, Doug, placed a large bulbous glass on the bar in front of him. "If you don't mind me saying Roger you look bloody shattered".

Roger cupped the glass in both hands, and after removing one, slowly tipped the glass towards his mouth. He had chosen well, the red stuff was just what he'd needed. Replacing the glass on the bar he smiled at the waiting landlord.

"I'm homeless, carless, womanless, friendless and soon I fear, jobless. On top of that somebody is screwing with my head and I'm bloody cold".

The landlord, Doug, grinned. "Nothing to worry about then, and that'll warm you up", he nodded to the wine. "Does anyone know you're here"?.

Roger shrugged his shoulders. "I hope not, but who knows".

"Who knows", Doug repeated. "Have you seen that van parked outside your house"?.

"Hmm,hmm", Roger confirmed without moving his mouth from his glass.

"The van's marked with the logo of some gas company. They're bomb investigation. I took a photo of the clowns and sent pictures to some of my old buddies. Two of them recognised them immediately".

"Only two? Not much of a memorial for my old house is it".

"Oh there's been more, to start the site was crawling with them".

"That's all right then", Roger held out his glass for a refill. Doug took it, replacing it with a fresh glass. He started to pour.

"You're not driving are you"?.

"I told you, I'm carless".

"What happened to your car? You used to have one, I remember seeing it parked outside your house".

Roger pulled a face. "I'm not at liberty to tell you".

"Ah one of those, ok, where are you staying? You know after...", Doug motioned to the window behind Roger. The window that looked onto the pile of rubble that was once Roger's home.

Roger tipped his glass allowing more of the wine to slide down his throat. "I'm not at liberty to tell you that either".

"Ah, nice then, a bit like Big Brother then"?.

Roger nodded, "I'm sure someone somewhere will be placing my bits on line". Again he pulled a face.

"Fanny Denton", that's what iId call a posting if it was me. You have to admit, it has a ring about it". Doug went to serve another customer, chuckling as he did so.

Roger turned, leaning his back against the bar. Funny he remembered, someone else had said something similar. He couldn't remember who. Were pictures of him naked in his underground bunker really circulating without him knowing? Not that he cared. He stared out of the window. A middle aged couple sitting just in front of it, to his amusement, did their best to avoid eye contact. It had started raining outside and, for the first time, he noticed that there was a floodlight, probably for security, illuminating the rubble. As the rain got stronger, he unintentionally counted the drops as they hit and ran down the glass. His mind was picturing his last evening in his house, Ane Brun was singing All My Tears. He remembered the moon, its rays penetrating his lounge. There'd been something magical about that moment, the moment before......... He turned back to the bar, he couldn't face looking out of the window any longer and tonight there was no moon, just an inky blackness, as though a lid had closed on his coffin.

Doug came back and in one hand he was holding a menu, "In case you're hungry".

"I'm not".

"Have a look anyway", Doug shoved it at him. "Something inside might take your fancy, go and sit at a table".

"Doug's expression and tone of voice told Roger that Doug had a reason for wanting him to do this. He took the menu.

"And hold it tight shut", Doug whispered through clenched teeth, before letting go.

The penny dropped, bloody hell, he must be tired. "Got ya", Roger took the menu, choosing a seat with a small round table beside the door which opened to the hallway leading to the toilets. Opening the menu on his lap he saw there was a small brown envelope. Pretending to read he let it slip onto his lap and between his legs. Then lifting his right thigh he slid the envelope under his leg and into his pocket, at the same time removing a tissue. To finish the sham he wiped his nose. Walking back to the bar he ordered another wine and a lasagne.

"Be careful, that wine can creep up on you, and if you don't mind me saying, you don't look in any fit state to handle it".

Roger looked wistfully at the array of bottles sitting on the ornately carved wooden shelves on the wall behind the bar. "I'll make it my last one".

Doug gave him a sympathetic smile. "Ok, go and sit down, I'll bring your lasagne over".

"Before you do that, do you have a number for a taxi"?.

"Where to"?.

Roger grinned, a partly alcohol fuelled grin. "I'm not at liberty to say".

"Bloody hell, are you playing truant or something"?.

"Something".

Doug pulled a face, Fuck you, I'll get you a card, hang on". Seconds later he was back holding a crisp white business card. His expression had changed, he looked full of thought. "Roger, have you got to go back tonight? I mean, are you under some sort of control order, curfew"?.

Roger took the card and watched, rather like a dog looking for a treat, as Doug poured a fresh glass of merlot. "Nobody has said as much, though they will be recording my coming and going, why do you ask"?.

Doug finished pouring and there being very little wine left in the bottle, poured the remainder into a glass for himself. He shrugged, "Why don't you stay here? I mean, I don't know what your plans are for tomorrow. It may not be convenient for you, but you're welcome to kip down here. I have two spare rooms upstairs, reserved for staff. I used to take staff from Europe but Brexit's put an end to that. Bloody pain Brexit. Anyway you're welcome to kip in one of the rooms, they're both ready. One looks out onto the street and one over…", again Doug motioned to the window.

Roger turned Doug's offer over in his head, it was a complete surprise and very tempting. And no one would be watching him have a slash. "You're sure Doug? What about your wife"?.

Doug took a sip of his wine. "She won't mind, you wally. Say yes and I'll have her bring your lasagne up to your room".

"Well if you're definitely sure, I'll say yes, thank you Doug".

"Don't be daft, we're both ex-services. We look after each other. Nobody else bloody does".

"Here's to that". Roger raised his glass.

Doug touched him on the arm, "Come on, I'll get my wife to show you the rooms".

Ten minutes later, Roger was alone in his chosen room. His choice was the one overlooking what had once been his home. At first he'd thought he'd hate the idea, but somehow gazing on the mess that had once been his home he found comforting. Almost as though he was holding the hand of his house, relieving it of its pain as its soul made its way up to house heaven. Completely irrational but that's how it felt. There was a knock on the door and Doug's wife entered with his lasagne and chips. Placing it on his bedside table she asked if he wanted another wine. He did but this time Roger resisted. He would need a clear head in the morning.

"Ok then, I'll say goodnight then. Oh and Doug said to let you know that there's CCTV all around the pub and that it's recording. He'll let you know if anyone comes snooping. Sleep well". With that, she shut the door. Roger watched her go, she'd passed on Doug's message as if she was passing on a football result. That's what comes of being married to someone with military experience, you become entwined with the life or their life experience and all that comes with it. Some wives and no doubt husbands too, could handle it, many though couldn't. He was a good example. In danger of feeling sorry for himself, Roger, sitting on his bed, placed the plate with his meal on his lap and started to eat. It was good, better than he'd expected and yet he'd eaten in the pub many times in the past and the food had always been good. Why wasn't it going to be this time? After he'd finished Roger placed the dirty plate in the wardrobe, he couldn't stand the smell of old food. Undressing, he took out a pay as you go phone and the envelope from his trousers. Getting into bed he sat up and took a sip of wine. It wasn't so enjoyable now, red wine had a way of letting him know he'd had enough or was it his body? Either way, he didn't fancy any more and getting back out of bed, to avoid further temptation, he placed the wine glass on the windowsill. Looking out at the remains of his house, he noticed the gas van was still parked outside and that two men were still sitting in it. Almost certainly Jane's doing.

Getting back into bed he tore open the envelope. Inside there was a small scrap of notepaper headed 'Hampshire Constabulary'. On the paper, neatly written was a phone number along with an exclamation mark. Nothing else.

Picking up his pay as you go, Roger dialled.

After six rings somebody answered. "Mr Denton, is that you? Do you know what bloody time it is"?

"It's not that late is it"? In truth Roger had no idea what the time was. "Yes it's Denton. D.I. Johnson"? Roger was unhappy they were revealing their name on the line. Anyone with an interest and listening may pick them up. He kicked himself for not warning him in his note.

"No I suppose not, nearly eleven, hang on. I'm in bed, early night. Let me go into the next room or I'll wake my wife". Roger waited, he must live in a big house for it was a good two minutes before D.I. Johnson was back.

"Ok, sorry about that".

"I'm sorry for calling so late, listen don't mention yours or my name whilst we're on the phone again".

"Bloody hell, what's going on, why all the secrecy, pay as you go and all that? I know you guys are having a shit time, is it anything to do with what happened to your offices? Or what we've been investigating? The murder in Langstone? As you know, that's pretty well wrapped up, at our end anyway. I know you guys have still got a lot to do".

Roger was looking at the windowsill, he was regretting leaving his glass there. He should have thought through what he was going to say before he rang. He was getting bloody careless. "Yes I know, you rang me remember, several times. It must be important"?.

D.I. Johnson was frustrated the man from the NCA hadn't explained why they were speaking on pay as you go phones but decided not to ask any more questions. "Well, I don't know, I think it could be, one of my...".

Roger cut in. "Don't tell me anymore, not over the phone. I need you to tell me face to face. Can you meet me tomorrow"?.

"Yes, if you wish. What will you do, come to the station"?.

"No, not there. It needs to be somewhere private, a pub or something but one we can easily check we're not being followed or when we talk, not being listened to".

Fuck, what the hell was going on? Had they, by investigating the Langstone murder rattled a hornet's nest? "I think I know just the place. It's called The Harrow. It's at a place called Steep, near Petersfield, just off of the A3. It's not easy to find, do you want directions"?.

"No don't worry I'll find it, what time"?

"They've only got parking for around half a dozen cars so best get there before midday, that's when it opens.".

"Ok, eleven forty five".

"Earlier if poss, I'll be there from eleven thirty, if there's room I'll park badly, taking up two spaces thereby saving you one".

"Ok, thanks, see you tomorrow".

"I look forward to it, bye". D.I.Johnson rang off. Roger continued sitting up. Why had he agreed to that? Reserving two car spaces. He didn't have a car. Exhausted, he decided to sort it in the morning. That's when he was at his best.

Below, Doug was in what used to be a walk in storage cupboard. Now it was his amateur security hub. The views from all of his cameras were played out on a large monitor. Camera four on the front left corner of his pub was trained on the road towards his neighbour's ruined house. Manoeuvring it, he managed to get the whole of the van parked outside. He zoomed in and saw the two men inside waving back at his camera. Shit.

Mont d'Hubert, Near Calais, France

'Welcome to hell'. Capitaine Olivier Vendroux heard the welcome through a fuddled brain. Hell, it couldn't be any worse than how he was feeling now. He retched and once more vomited in the back seat. His two passengers quickly got out.

"Useless piece of shit". one exclaimed.

"Let's take him to pieces, the other cursed, and slowly".

"And make him watch us do it, just like the Egyptian did to Armani".

Another voice spoke, it was Baptiste, the operative who had played the Calais gendarmerie so well. "We don't do anything until tomorrow. Pierre is paying us a visit, we will ask him what he wants to do. We have a problem on our hands, sadly that piece of shit can't just disappear. One capitaine dead and his replacement missing. Too many questions will be asked if they're not already. No, we have to really think about this".

"Well we can't send him back as if nothing had happened, he'll ruin everything". The driver of the car joined in the conversation.

"I know, I know, we have to think".

"Useless piece of fucking shit", the first passenger to exit the car shouted at the capitaine. "Merde, it stinks in there". The man drew back quickly, spitting at the floor. The smell had gotten onto his tongue. Another man approached, Antanois. The day to day manager of everything under Mont d'Hubert.

Baptiste turned to him. "Antanois, what do you suggest"?. He knew though Antanois was working through his own punishment that he was still a favourite with Pierre, that Pierre trusted him, and to his credit the operation here under Mont d'Hubert ran very smoothly. Like clockwork, in the main due to Antanois' management. His replacement in contrast, residing in their farmhouse just outside Escalles hardly did a thing. He was virtually nothing more than a glorified look out.

Antanois looked in at the disgraced capitaine. He appeared not to be bothered by the smell. He looked up the small group with Baptiste. "If you want my advice, put him in one of the chambers under Cap Blanc Nez. Perhaps one of the ones nearest the waste cavern, the smell from there seems to seep through the walls into the ones close by. They're also untreated, just hollowed out chalk. As a result they're cold and damp. "Leave a bucket in there with him. If he's sick now, later he'll have the shits too. A single bucket will soon sober him up and then he'll suffer from the cold. He'll soon be wishing he was dead. But he'll be wishing for a nice peaceful death like we give our nightly cargo. We will of course not grant him his wish, Pierre will think of something appropriate, I'm sure".

"What time is Pierre due tomorrow"?.

"Pierre never gives us a time but knowing him it'll be around ten in the morning, possibly earlier". Antanois answered Baptiste's question.

"It'll be earlier if he watches the news". Silence fell as everyone considered Baptiste's observation.

"Well there's not much more we can do for now except lock that waste of space up. There's no way we can safely get a message to Pierre, we'll just have to wait till the morning. I'll get someone to get a waste bin from the kitchens, we can transport him in that". Antanois moved off to fulfil his suggestion.

"Right, let's get him out", Baptiste barked at the two men who had accompanied the capitaine from picking him up in Calais Nord.

"I'll do it", the first passenger to have got out of the car reached in and grabbing Capitaine Olivier Vendroux by the hair, pulled hard. There came a scream as pain replaced the feeling of nausea. As he was dragged out and onto the floor of the cavern the other passenger aimed a kick at the capitaine's abdomen. Capitaine Olivier Vendroux doubled up in pain as the foot made contact splaying more vomit across the floor and under the parked car.

"That's enough", Baptiste barked. "We've no idea what condition Pierre will want him in. That's not for us to decide. You never know, he might, after all, let you two play football with our dear capitaine here".

"I bloody hope so, piece of shit". Spittle landed on the capitaine's face. He didn't notice, the capitaine was too busy wishing he was dead.

Chapter 6

The Hare and Hounds Pub, Bushey, North London, England

It was five o'clock when Roger Denton of the NCA woke. He had no idea what he was going to do that day except visit D.I.Johnson at a pub near Petersfield in Hampshire. He had committed the name of the pub and the village where to find it to memory, now he wrote it down. After making and drinking a coffee he got in the shower. Drying himself off, and after turning the light off, he looked out of the window. The van was still there. Poor buggers, he could still remember the days when he was often chosen for the graveyard shift as it was called. He hoped he would never have to go back there. After shaving, he scribbled a note of thanks and placed it on the bed. Carrying his shoes in his hands he tiptoed down stairs to the bar. He knew the public doors would be shut but he'd spied a back door which he was pretty sure would be bolted only. If not, he'd simply have to do the age old classic and escape out of the toilet window. He sincerely hoped it wouldn't come to that. He felt bad sneaking out and hoped Doug would understand. He needed a taxi and didn't want to order one to the pub. There was a twenty four hour taxi office at Bushey station, if they didn't have one prepared to take him to Petersfield, he'd simply get the train. As he stepped onto the ground floor Roger thought he heard a sound in the bar. There was an old grandfather clock in an alcove and in between two windows, he could hear the sound of that ticking from upstairs. But this sound was different. Roger's training kicked in, after placing everything he was carrying on the steps. Keeping his back to the wall he slowly made his way into the bar.

"Morning Roger, coffee"? Doug's voice was unmistakable. "I hope you weren't going to go without saying goodbye". Roger could just make out in the darkness a mug of steaming coffee on the bar. "Proper stuff that is Roger, better than the instant in your room".

"Thanks", not sure what to say or think Roger took it. Doug was right, it was excellent coffee, freshly brewed.

"Sorry I can't put the light on but I don't want to wake the two goons in the van up".

"What are you doing up Doug"?.

Roger thought he could see Doug grinning in the dark but couldn't be sure. "I knew you'd sneak out early, not wanting to disturb us or impose on us any longer. You're a bloody idiot Roger. I'm on your side. You're in trouble, it doesn't take an idiot to see that. I don't know what's happened to your car, but I'd bet a million quid it's not an everyday repair in some garage. And the NCA provides you lot with cars, the only reason I can think you're not driving one is because you don't want, god knows who, to know where you are. You've got no transport so my guess is that you're going to the station to either track a train or book a taxi. And if it's a taxi, for the same reason I've just mentioned you're reluctant to order a taxi to my pub. You don't want to leave fingerprints. Am I right"?.

"Close".

"That'll do, now do you want my help or not? If not, you can bugger off down to the station and join the sad face brigade".

Roger sighed. "How can you help me, Doug"?

Coulogne, Near Calais, France

Lieutenant Beaufort, awoke to the sound of knocking at his front door. Loud urgent knocking. Still a little dazed from sleep he reached for his phone to see the time. Three fifty four in the morning! What, who the fucking hell could it be? Then he noticed something else. Twenty three missed calls, all from his gendarmerie. Fuck, what the hell had happened? What the fuck was going on? Leaping out of bed, as he walked he staggered into a pair of trousers and almost fell down the stairs. Peering through the glass in his door, he recognised the man and woman in uniform on, the other side of the door. They were from his gendarmerie, Capitaine Maubert had chosen them to go with Marie into the 'jungle', to see if they could find anyone who could identify the body of the girl found on the beach below Cap Blanc Nez. They were heavily involved in the 'red market' investigation, so far with no results. Beyond them were a small group of people but he couldn't make out who they were.

Opening the door, he was immediately greeted by the click and flash of cameras along with a barrage of questions from, he assumed, journalists. "Entrez, entrez, vite, vite". The lieutenant ushered the two gendarmes in. "What the fuck is going on"?.

Between them the two explained what had happened the night before. The assault in the Cafe de Paris and how since then, Capitaine Olivier Vendroux had somehow vanished into thin air. That the incident in the cafe had been caught on camera and was now all over social media. The woman involved had made a formal complaint as had the cafe owners. They had searched throughout the night, checked every hotel, gite and chambres d'hote but nothing, no sign of their capitaine. The rumour going around the gendarmerie was that realising his mistake the capitaine may have committed suicide. The media are already asking that very question and there's a growing crowd of them outside of the gendarmerie. To make matters worse, even though it was the early hours and the reports only hours old, they were already receiving tip offs that feminist groups from all over France may be planning to hold a protest march through the town.

"You may want to watch the news, sir, it's all over".

The lieutenant switched on the television, tuning in to the twenty four hour news channel. They were right, the news was full of it. There were even live pictures from outside the gendarmerie in Calais. Suicide was a word used too often and of course a comparison with his ex-boss. Thank god they didn't know the probable truth.

Give me five minutes the lieutenant told them and I'll be ready. Tell that lot outside that I'm not going to answer a single question outside of my house. That I'll make a statement when I know the full facts. And fuck knows when that'll be the lieutenant muttered under his breath.

Calais Plage, Calais, France

Pierre de Fauw had lay in bed awake too long, resisting the urge to go to the toilet. The classic old man syndrome was beginning to get him down. Not only was it a pain having to repeatedly get up in the night, it was a constant reminder that he wasn't getting any younger. Walking back to his bedroom, he was distracted by a noise outside and the rotation of blue on his one way view, tinted window wall. Walking to his window, standing naked, he gazed down at the road below following Calais beach. Several police cars and one from the gendarmerie were slowly making their way along the seafront. Nothing unusual in that maybe but shouting and chanting at them were a small but noisy group of women and more were joining them. Curious he wondered if there was anything on the local news and switching on his television went to make himself a coffee. His penthouse was open plan so he could see the television in his lounge from just about anywhere. Not even the bedroom had a dividing wall. There was no need, he never entertained in his Calais penthouse, not even women. Casually, Pierre ground some beans and then spooned the resulting powder into his cafetiere, pouring in water, he watched as the coffee spiralled around the glass. He always considered it a beautiful thing to view. Only after he had pressed the coffee and poured did he look up at the television and what he saw made him freeze. Capitaine Olivier Vendroux, their plant was all over the news. Counting to ten, he took a long sip of his coffee, it was roasted locally and was very good. He enjoyed supporting local businesses and it was also good for business. The coffee had the calming effect he desired. Panicking, knee jerk reactions weren't his style and were never good for business. What was unfolding on the news was a potential disaster for him and the organisation but the problem would have to be solved and solved it would be. He was confident of that. Through careful thought and planning. The question was, where was Capitaine Olivier Vendroux now? Never his choice for the plant, that's what came of trusting others. His team in Calais, he knew, had been keeping an eye on him and therefore he was pretty confident, unlike the authorities, that they would have a good idea where he was. He looked at his watch, a Patek Philippe, held on by a leather strap, Pierre never took it off. Four thirty, he was due to visit Mont d'Hubert. He'd been planning to wander in around ten. That morning he'd have to make it earlier but not too early, eight thirty would be fine and would demonstrate there was no need to panic. Re-filling his cup, he wandered back to the window. The commotion below had either come to an end or moved on elsewhere. He stared out at La Manche, a car ferry was ploughing its way towards Calais Port, its lights making up for the moon that wasn't there. In the distance, shining bright, he could see the port of Dover. For a few seconds he thought of Ariana and how she was managing. He had a soft spot for Ariana, she was something of a prodigy, his prodigy. He could never live it down if something happened to her. Returning to his bed he turned off the television and dimmed the lights. Taking another sip of coffee, using a control panel built into his bed he turned on his music system. The sound of piano music filled the air, Winter into Spring by George Winston. Pierre closed his eyes and took another sip of coffee, this was turning into the perfect morning.

Gendarmerie Nationale, Calais, France

It was far from a perfect morning for Lieutenant Beaufort. On arriving at his gendarmerie, he found there to be what he could only describe as 'controlled chaos'. The night manager had virtually every man searching for Capitaine Olivier Vendroux with the result that the other usual type of night crimes were having to be ignored. This had resulted in some very angry calls, some understandably from victims. The media outside was growing by the hour and it pissed him off that they almost expected fresh coffee and croissants and that he would, in the name of public relations, give it to them. And out of the gendarmerie's already stretched budget.

On his arrival, he immediately received two calls. The first on his mobile from his wife asking what the hell was going on and was he ok, in that order. The second, on the reserved land line was from the Commandant des Regions, Hauts des France, the guy who had disciplined and suspended his ex-boss, Capitaine Maubert. Lieutenant was expecting a bollocking but that didn't happen.

"Morning lieutenant, I won't ask you if everything is ok as I can see, from watching the television and from reports, that it isn't. My reason for my call, lieutenant, is to offer my help and support. First things first, have you found Capitaine Vendroux?

"No, sir, we haven't".

"Have you any idea where he might be"?.

"To be totally honest, sir, no we don't. I've only just got here and from what I know so far, every type of accommodation has been contacted, all negative. We've found his car, parked in the main square, Place d'Armes, so he must be on foot. We're at this very moment contacting all the local taxi firms but being the early hours a lot of them aren't answering their phones.

"Go and knock on their doors lieutenant, wake them up".

Chapter 6

"I know, sir, it's just man power, everyone's flat out. We've called many of the day shift to start early and nearly everyone working the night has volunteered to stay on until the capitaine is found".

"Well done lieutenant, I know it's difficult for you. What is it with your bloody capitaines and women? Is it something to do with the water they drink"? The commandant paused. Not that I'm comparing Maubert and Vendroux. Capitaine Maubert was a good man, targeted by a professional, who knows what any of us would do in similar circumstances. We all hope that we could resist the best of feminine charms but who knows. Capitaine Maubert was an excellent gendarme, the best and a family man and look, your new capitaine, I don't know what to think. He wasn't my placement, I was overruled by Paris and now look. Bloody Parigos. Look, for now lieutenant, you're in charge, and I'm sorry for that, I know it's a bloody awful situation. If or rather when you find your capitaine, the first thing you'll need to consider is how to protect him. There are a great many people out there at this moment, who would happily kill him and just as happily face justice for it. You can just imagine the media circus should such a trial take place. And be prepared for demonstrations, not just local ones. Our ears to the ground are already picking up feminists from all over La France planning to demonstrate in Calais. I can tell you that it will be a bloody nightmare for you.

Planning ahead I'm sending a brigade of CRS to help, they will ensure that there is a very public display on the streets. The feminists will shout 'provocation', but tough, let them. I'm also calling neighbouring gendarmeries to lend you their support, mainly with manpower. You're going to need it. Do a good job, lieutenant, and I'll see you right. Capitaine Maubert was always singing your praises".

"Merci commandant", the lieutenant was somewhat lost for words.

"No need. One last question, lieutenant. Suicide is a word being bandied about. Do you think that could be true"?.

"I sincerely hope not sir".

"So do I. Two bloody suicides in under two weeks, it dosen't bear thinking about if it turns out to be true. And if it is, let's pray to god he hasn't thrown himself off of Cap Blanc Nez like Maubert, poor sod. If it turns out that he has, we'll no doubt have dozens of copycat suicides. The Cap will become some sort of shrine for every bloody weirdo in the world and a great many of them come to visit".

The lieutenant listened, his heart in his mouth. This was his chance. He may never get as good a chance to tell the commandant that it may well have not been suicide, that it may have been murder. But he couldn't, he just couldn't get the words out.

"Well good luck lieutenant, you know where I am if you need me". The line went dead, it was too late, the moment had passed. There came a knock at the door, the night manager stood in the frame looking as though he'd had a gutful.

"Sir, the shit out there, the media, are starting to cause a problem, there's too many of them and a lot are asking if we can supply refreshments, especially the British.

"Ok, get a couple of Boulangeries to deliver croissants will you and see if they're able to supply coffee too, tell them to charge it to me at this address".

"Yes, sir, do you want to come and talk to them? They're beginning to be a right pain".

"No but move them into the car park will you, get them off the road. The CRS are on their way to help us, if they become too much of a problem I'll have them handle it">

The night manager grinned, "Now that I'd like to see".

"Anyway where's Hivin, the media are his job".

"Not answering his phone, sir".

"Then send someone around to wake him up, lazy bastard".

"My pleasure sir". The night manager left.

The lieutenant stood in, at that moment a much valued silence. From his office window he admired the illuminated red brick and white limestone tower of the town's hotel de ville. He never got tired of looking at it. His mind though, was on his conversation with the commandant. Why hadn't he told him, why hadn't he? He may never get another chance.

Ardres, France

Vivienne, Capitaine Maubert's widow and her daughter sat on their sofa. Both were watching television, shocked into silence by what was playing out on the local news.

At the advertising interval, Vivienne turned to her daughter.

"Where do you think he is? He can't just disappear like that?

"Perhaps he's committed suicide". Her daughter clamped her hand over her mouth. Pardon Maman".

Her mother shook her head. "Rein, but what if he's been murdered like your father may have been, do you think it's possible"?.

The Hare and Hounds, Bushey, North London, England

"How can you help me Doug?"

"I've got my daughter's car out back, she's at uni. Do you want to borrow it?, as long as you look after it. If you don't mind me mentioning it things belonging or close to you, have a habit of getting damaged".

Roger took another sip of his coffee, he looked at the rain falling on the window outside, the flapping of a creeper across the same window told a story of wind and the temperature he knew to be not much above freezing. Doug had suddenly become an angel.

"You're quite sure Doug? Yeah if you're willing, and scouts honour, I promise to take care of it".

"If you don't, bloody make sure it's a write off, so I can get a new one on the insurance".

"Scout's honour", Roger held up three fingers

"What, look after it or promise to write it off?"

"Both".

"You'll need this, and this", Doug threw him a bundle which, when Roger had separated, turned out to be an old jumper and a parka. "You'll need to wear them when driving, otherwise people will look at you. They'll be a bit big but you can pick something else up. If you want my advice, go to a charity shop and get some trousers too. Mine definitely won't fit you".

Roger rolled the parka and jumper up. Why will I need these? "

"You'll see...". Doug laughed, "...anyway you do need a change of clothes, you didn't bring any. And before you ask, I'm not lending you my underwear. It wouldn't fit anyway, mind you my wife's knickers might. Fanny Denton". Doug pushed past him, chuckling. "Come on, I'll show you your new wheels".

Roger followed the landlord out to the back yard. Backed into a corner was a small car covered in a blue tarpaulin. After struggling with some ties Doug grabbed one corner and pulled. The cover almost took off in the wind and it took the strength of both of them to prevent it from doing so. In all its glory sat Roger's new 'wheels', a Fiat Panda, probably built in the early two thousands. The paintwork was aquamarine, almost certainly not its original colour and on the front passenger door some customised artwork consisting of a rainbow and the word peace, each letter painted in a different colour.

"The same design is on your door", Doug grinned seeing the look on the man from the NCA's face. "Do you want to borrow it or not"?.

"Thank you, Doug", Roger held out his hand for the keys. Doug dropped them from a height.

"My daughter loves her, she's named her Molly". Doug could just about get his last words out for laughing.

Roger pulled a face. "I'll remember this, Doug", Roger held out his hand. "Thanks anyway". The two men shook.

"It's nothing, turn right at the end and the goons won't see you".

"Roger".

"Roger, Roger". With that the landlord ran for cover, the rain was getting heavier and the wind stronger.

Roger sat looking at the controls, the interior smelt strongly of perfume. Turning the key he said a silent prayer. The engine started without the slightest sign of resistance. Ten minutes later, he was on the M1, heading for the M25 whilst struggling to find Radio 5 Live on the radio.

Mont d'Hubert, Near Calais, France

After showering, Pierre dressed in a navy blue polar neck and beige chinos. Donning a Vetra, dark brown wool Melton jacket, he took the lift to the underground car park. There he got into a car that in his eyes would, 'blend in'. Wanting to avoid the coast road he took the D940 to the A16 where he joined it in the direction of Boulogne. Not long after passing the sortie for Eurotunnel he came off at the junction with the D243E3. Soon after passing through the hameau, (hamlet), of Haute Escalles he turned off to the right, bringing his car to a stop behind a, typical of the region, long low farmhouse. Sitting in his car, he waited. Within seconds, a man came out and unlocked the door to the garage built into the hillside. Pierre edged the car in and the man closed and locked the door behind him. Not one word was spoken between them.

Inside, Pierre got out and started removing a jumble of boxes from the wall in front of him. Once cleared, he took from its holding a powder fire extinguisher, covered in dust. Taking out the pin he squeezed. The back wall, the wall facing the garage door, started to move. Pierre jumped in and started the engine. He knew that he had just 30 seconds before the wall would start to close again. Putting the car into gear he moved the car forward, in front of him lay a brightly lit tunnel wide enough for a large vehicle. Pierre, despite the problem he had to solve, could not help feeling a tinge of excitement. The tunnel and everything beyond it was the result of almost a life's work. Work was still going on, underneath Le Mont a Crignons, delicate work that needed time. He couldn't wait to see how it was progressing. For now though he had to sort out the little problem of Capitaine Olivier Vendroux.

Wisley Services, A3, North of Guildford, England

Roger Denton of the NCA sat in his 'wheels', in the parking area at Wisley services, savouring a cappuccino and a bacon bap. He'd changed from his jacket into a baggy jumper and parka. He'd also found a men's beanie hat on the backseat which was just as well as he quickly discovered that the heating in the car didn't work. The coffee was definitely helping to compensate.

Worried what the NCA may be thinking, he turned on his smartphone and called Nick. Nick answered with the first ring.

"Worried about me Nick"?.

"Worried for you, there's a difference".

"Thank you but don't be. There's too many people, perhaps the wrong people tracking what we're doing, I have a couple of leads I want to follow up without that risk".

"Fair enough, but how do I get hold of you if I need you"?.

"I'll check in regularly Nick, I'm not going to disappear, not intentionally anyway". The risk wasn't lost on Nick but he stayed silent. "Anyway, anything new to report"?.

"Nothing to speak of, hopefully we'll hear from the pathologist today. Digital forensics have been working through the night but have come up with nothing. I think they're as baffled as everyone else".

Roger had a thought. "Nick, has anyone checked to see who installed our CCTV"?.

"No, I don't think so, isn't it normally an internal job"?.

"Possibly but check will you and did you get time to do a check on that company I gave you"?.

"We've made a start but it's a financial labyrinth trying to find the true owners. We'll continue working on it today but we may have to turn it over to the serious fraud boys. They're more used to unravelling this sort of thing".

"I'm okay with that". Roger finished his bacon bap. He'd already decided he was going to get another, maybe a sausage bap too. Why had he been so self-conscious when placing his order? Because of the pretty girl half his age serving? That he didn't want her to think him a greedy old man? Bloody ridiculous, but it was true. "Nick, while I remember I need you to send a team from digital forensics into the Hilton to examine their CCTV. I don't think they'll find anything but you never know. Ishaan is the guy in charge of security there, well you've met him. He's a good guy and will be expecting them. He's also promised to try and find us a couple of rooms, they may have to share but tough. The legal stuff is on my desk. Have you heard from Jane"?.

"No, not so far, not this morning but I'm sure I will when she discovers you were at a sleepover, a woman was it"?.

"I wish, no lasagne and a glass of wine".

"Nice".

"It was". Both men laughed

"Right I've got to go Nick, I've got a hot date".

"Good luck sir, when should I expect to hear from you"?.

"Sometime this afternoon".

"I look forward to it sir".

"Thank you", and Roger rang off. Brushing the crumbs from his jumper he exited the car, returning to the garage shop. With relief he found that an Asian man was now serving. He placed his order, adding another coffee, a bar of chocolate and a bottle of diet coke for later. Shame on you he scolded himself, the feeling of guilt lasting no more than a few seconds. No sooner had he taken a couple of bites from his sausage bap when his phone rang. He saw immediately that it was Jane. Shit why hadn't he, after Nick, turned his phone off. "Morning Jane".

"You're eating, I can tell, you sound disgusting".

"Sorry, breakfast",

"I'll forgive you", on hearing this Roger took another bite of his sausage bap, followed by a slurp of coffee some of which escaped and dribbled down his jumper. "You didn't sleep in your quarters last night". Who had told her?

"No, living underground was starting to get me down".

"Understandable, I'm insisting on leaving the safe house today, living in a Big Brother house is starting to get me down". Roger said nothing, he took another bite of his sausage bap. Two more and he'll have finished and could give Jane his full attention. "May I enquire where you stayed"?.

"No offence Jane, but no. I need some privacy".

"Roger, finish whatever it is you're eating. You're starting to make me feel sick".

"Sorry", Roger pushed the rest of the bap into his mouth and by doing so almost choked. Jane held her phone away from her, not wanting to hear the end process".

"Finished, Jane, sorry".

"So you should be, you need a woman Roger, so she can teach you how to eat".

"Many have tried, Jane".

"And failed, evidently. Roger it's entirely up to you where you stay the night, the only reason I'm asking is, if ever you're facing danger, we can, if it's possible, protect you".

"From whom, Jane"?.

"You know damn well, Roger, we have no idea". He was pushing her too far.

"I know, Jane, sorry but in a way that's exactly why I want to go absent for a little while. I don't want to be tracked by the enemy, whoever they bloody are. The NCA has fallen, you by recommending that it be disbanded, are admitting as much. Those within the NCA tasked with following my moves may well be working for the other side".

Jane remained silent, he was right of course but the organisation would not be happy not being able to keep tabs on him. For now she had no choice but to back her subordinate. She would be doing exactly the same if she was in his shoes. "Ok Roger, you have my backing, but if you feel you're in the slightest bit of danger you let me know".

"I promise Jane".

"Do you mind telling me where you're going today"?.

"I'd prefer to report back afterwards". To Roger's surprise, Jane accepted this, She then went over with him, what was happening from her end. No explosives, as yet, had been found at Porton Down. Not even a trace, if they were there they were bloody well hidden. Not even tracker dogs had come up with anything. Around twenty minutes later, Jane rang off. Roger took a sip of his coffee, ugghh, it was tepid, he liked hot,really hot coffee. He proceeded to unwrap his bacon bap, touching it he knew it was cold, bloody Jane. He was considering returning to the garage shop a third time when his phone rang. "Bloody hell, leave me alone", he shouted out loud. He picked up his phone, his screen displayed a French number calling. Coffee and bap forgotten he pressed the round green display to accept.

Pembroke Square, Bayswater, London, England

Ariana loved her new home. Every room smelt of money. Her one dislike was that she wasn't left alone for one second. There was always someone there wanting to do something for her. She had to, she discovered quickly, to tell her live-in workers if she needed or wanted to be on her own. If she didn't, she'd have someone constantly following her like a lovesick dog.

One pleasant surprise was her wardrobe. A room on its own the wardrobe was well stocked with shoes and all sorts of garments, even underwear. This personal touch she knew immediately to be Pierre's doing. For a man, he totally understood how to dress a woman and how to make her feel, as well as look good. She would have fun dressing up later. Much later, for she was booked up that day. Another thing she learned almost immediately since moving in, as the new Ariana, the organisation kept and organised a diary for her. That morning she had a meeting with a charity that supported women in the Middle East, lunch time she had a date with Henrietta and if there was time, a meeting here at her house with members from an organisation helping young people start up tech companies. This meeting her adviser told could wait till later on in the week. It would have to be, thought Ariana, she wanted to make full use of her time with Henrietta. A meeting with the lioness in the lion's den. She couldn't wait and she had no doubt it would take up the whole afternoon.

Chapter 6

Gendarmerie Nationale, Calais, France

By nine in the morning the media gathered outside the gendarmerie were getting tired and an inevitable silence had fallen on them. Asking the same questions over and over again and receiving the same answers over and over again had taken its toll, the initial excitement had worn off. That along with the cold, wind and rain, the majority had accepted they'd simply have to sit and wait. Monsieur Hivin, the one man media department had eventually shown up and the first thing he promised was a statement as soon as they had any news. No one there believed him but what choice did they have.

Inside the gendarmerie building things were very tense. Officers outside were now combing ditches, canals, anywhere where their capitaine may be hiding or lying injured. Two theories were starting to raise their ugly heads. The first that their capitaine really might have committed suicide. Realising what he'd done and the consequences, almost certainly prison, he couldn't face the future and took the easy way out. Most in uniform admitted if they faced the same set of circumstances that they would probably do exactly that. Life in prison would be worse than hell. The second theory, that following what had happened, their capitaine had been murdered and his body hidden somewhere. Either were very plausible and as the clocked ticked were gaining in status.

As the commander had promised, a brigade of CRS,(Compagnies Republicanes de Securite), riot police, had arrived and were taking up positions in Place d'Armes and along Rue Royale, running from the railway station, past the Cafe de Paris to the port. This, it was predicted, is where any demonstration would probably take place and indeed, there were already groups of angry looking women starting to gather, carrying a myriad of banners. Each sporting different words maybe but all with the same message.

Men and women too, officers from neighbouring gendarmeries had arrived to help with the search, freeing up Calais's gendarmes to carry out their normal duties. It wasn't a mess, not yet but it could easily turn into one and a very nasty one. And everyone involved was very aware of that.

Just before ten, Colette broke off from helping Monsieur Hivin with the media, in search of the lieutenant. She found him in what she still considered to be Capitaine Maubert's office.

'Sitting in this office, I feel like I'm filling a dead man's shoes. What I don't know is which dead man', was the first thing the lieutenant said to Collette after she'd knocked and walked in.

"Don't talk like that or you'll wish the poor man dead". She was right, and if he was being honest he was. It would solve a lot of problems if they found a body instead of a living breathing, Capitaine Olivier Vendroux. He didn't express his view to Colette.

"Sorry, what is it, Colette"?.

"It's probably not a good time lieutenant but you wanted Mirielle to translate for you, you wanted to phone that detective in Angleterre". Behind Colette, the lieutenant saw that Mirielle was waiting patiently.

"No, it's the perfect time, there's nothing I can do out there except get more and more stressed. Come in, Mirielle". The lieutenant waved to the young woman patiently waiting. With Colette standing to one side Mirielle entered and took a seat, Colette followed and then hesitated.

"Do you need me, lieutenant"?. The lieutenant waved for her to take a seat, "Yes, yes Colette, shut the door will you". Colette did as she was told and took a seat a little way away, by the window. The lieutenant studied Mirielle. A little over five feet tall, with a typical pale Calasian complexion and her dark hair tied back, Mirielle was as plain as they come. And yet look into her deep brown eyes and there you would find a spark for life along with all knowing. Mirielle wasn't stupid, quite the opposite and she also had the sort of personality that never offended.

"I didn't know you spoke English, Mirielle, I'm pleased that you do though".

"It's on my application to become a gendarme and therefore must be on my record lieutenant". Mirielle gave the lieutenant a smile that hinted that her answer was in humour.

"She studied languages at Cambridge in Angleterre", Colette cut in.

"Cambridge"?.

"Oui", Mirielle smiled again.

"Cambridge, and you're working here"?.

"I like it here lieutenant, I like my work, it's interesting".

"It's certainly that", the lieutenant agreed. He went on to explain what he needed her for. That she was to help him to speak to a detective in Angleterre. To translate for them both. Most importantly whatever she heard was not to be repeated outside of these four walls. She had to promise. Mirielle made the sign of the cross.

"I'm a Catholic, lieutenant, you have my word". The lieutenant believed her, out of all the officers in the gendarmerie she was the one he felt he could trust the most. For once lady luck was shining on him. "Thank you Mirielle, right let's do it, let's make the call. Have you got his number, Colette"?. Colette sighed, she had given it to him, she'd forgotten how many times. Hiding her frustration, Colette gave it to him again. The lieutenant dialled, an English ringtone soon sounded, his call was quickly answered.

"Hello", the lieutenant quickly passed the phone to Mirielle.

"What's his name"? Mirielle whispered frantically. The lieutenant told her.

"Roger Denton"?.

"Yes, speaking, Lieutenant Beaufort"?. It was obvious the English detective was puzzled why he was speaking to a woman.

"Mr Denton, my name's Mirielle, I work at the gendarmerie in Calais. Lieutenant Beaufort is here with me".

"Hello". Mirielle waved for the lieutenant to shut up.

"He doesn't speak English, I will be translating for you both".

"Nice to make your acquaintance Mirielle". Mirielle felt a shiver go down her spine, she loved English men, they were always so polite, the ones she had met anyway. Some of her friends held very different views.

The topic of conversation quickly developed into why they both wanted to speak to each other and it didn't take much longer before each discovered that the other had doubts about the operation of the office in which they worked. They were both going through a distinct lack of trust about some of the people they worked with. Both officers were reluctant to say much more on the phone, it was too risky. 'I'll come to you', the English officer had dictated. 'Not at your gendarmerie though, somewhere neutral'. They had agreed in the end that Roger Denton would travel to France, book into some accommodation, after which he would contact Mirielle on her private mobile. 'And I won't be using this number', Roger had finished. With that au revoirs were said all round and the lines went dead.

"I'll need you when we meet physically, Marielle". Marielle's eyes shone on hearing this, she couldn't wait. After she'd left the office, Colette and the lieutenant sat in silence for a while, each deep in thought.

"You must be careful, lieutenant", Colette broke the silence.

"What do you mean, Colette"? He knew what she meant.

"What the English detective was saying, to me it doesn't sound good. You're not paid enough to risk your career, perhaps even your life over something like this. This is the kind of thing the intelligence services should be tackling". The intelligence services may be involved but the lieutenant didn't reveal this to Colette.

"I'll be careful, Colette, I promise".

Colette looked doubtful, "As long as you are lieutenant, don't try to die a hero".

The lieutenant laughed, an obviously fake laugh. "I won't, I promise".

"Just don't you eat those words". A loud knock at the door prevented any further conversation.

"Sir, there's a riot in Rue Royale, I think you need to come down, it's mad".

"Merde", the lieutenant jumped up and followed the young gendarme down the stairs.

"Colette returned to her office, her phone was ringing. Running she picked it up.

"Colette"?.

"Oui".

"It's Jean, Jean Fournier".

At the Wisley services on the A3 in England, Roger Denton of the NCA, after the call, was debating whether to tackle the now very cold bacon bap. He'd thought of something else too. His passport was in his desk drawer in his office at Gladstone Park. "Bloody hell, he swore out loud. Picking up the phone he called Nick.

"Nick I need a favour"

Following a short exchange of words, Nick was gone, after reluctantly agreeing to Roger's request for a favour. On something of a high Roger decided to attempt the bacon bap. After one bite he decided it was disgusting. Not bothering to get out of his car he threw the bap on the passenger's floor. Turning on the ignition he put the car into gear and manoeuvred out onto the A3. Right Mr Johnson, let's see what you've got for me. Whatever it is, it had better be good.

Mont d'Hubert, Near Calais, France

Pierre de Hauw pulled up in the main reception area, deep under Mont d'Hubert. Several people were waiting for him, after a communication from the operative in the farmhouse.

"Morning all," Pierre greeted those waiting as if nothing was wrong. One by one he shook hands with everybody.

"How's business Antanois"?.

"We can't cope, we have more orders than we have parts. The new establishments, especially in the UK are helping but it's not so easy for them as it is for us to find new product. They're still relying on us to supply them. We really need another soup kitchen, eight to ten a night simply isn't enough". Antanois spoke as though he were simply talking about standard goods, only of course he wasn't.

Pierre looked through the window of the sales office. Fourteen staff were either on the phone or responding to online orders. All disguised as travel agent enquiries. They'd already expanded their sales operation and were going to have to do so again. Merchandise was the problem, at the growing pace of new orders they simply weren't able to meet with the demand. There were also his special needs for the facility under Mont a Crignons. He couldn't take the risk of simply sending out another van in the guise of a soup kitchen, the authorities would simply shut it down. He may though frame it as English do-gooders doing good. The authorities would be reluctant to touch them. It wouldn't look good. He made a mental note to get it done.

"Let me sort that, Antanois", Pierre slapped him on the back. "You're doing an excellent job here, I'll have a word with others, see if I can get you back into your farm-house". Antanois's face lit up.

"Merci, Monsieur de Hauw, merci".

Pierre turned to Baptiste. "Baptiste we have a little problem and it needs sorting quickly".

"We do, and before you ask sir, we have him here".

"Who? Capitaine Vendroux"?. Pierre looked visibly relieved.

"Yes",

"Where is he"?. Antanois answered this.

"In a cell near the waste area. It's not nice down there and he was in a hell of a state when he came in".

"Was he"?, Pierre looked pensive. "We can't discuss this out here, Antanois, can we go into your office". It was a statement not a question. Pierre along with Baptiste followed Antanois into a room adjacent to the sales office. On the walls were posters of Lebanon from the days when that country had been a popular tourist destination. Pierre let Antanois take his normal seat behind his desk. "So tell me, what do we do? Any ideas"?.

Baptiste and Antanois looked at each other, it was Baptiste who spoke. "He can't simply disappear and if we put him back out there he'll almost certainly give us away, it's a real 'Catch Twenty Two'.

"Agreed", Pierre leaned back in his chair, so far that it was resting only on its back two feet. "We're going to have to let him go but we'll have to wipe certain parts of his memory".

"Is that possible"? Baptiste looked doubtful.

"Maybe, but we'd have to somehow ensure it would be permanent, we don't want it coming back sometime in the future".

"We could, sometime in the future, make him disappear quietly, until then we're going to have to keep an eye on him". Baptiste naturally fell into his security role. Pierre smiled.

"That goes without saying, for the immediate future we have a couple of operatives in the gendarmerie at Calais that can do that for us".

"True, Pierre, but they're low level and after this, he'll almost certainly be taken to Paris".

"Where the organisation can keep a better eye on him, Baptiste".

"True, I suppose, but it's a big risk".

Antanois cut in. "Do you want me to get him cleaned up"?.

"No", Pierre didn't hesitate. "No, if we're going to put him back out there, he's going to have to return him in the same state in which we brought him in. If we clean him up people will start asking questions. Let them assume he's been sleeping rough".

"Which he has been, bloody rough". Baptiste laughed.

"Right, Pierre stood up. "Get someone to check on him, Antanois, will you? I don't want Monsieur Vendroux to die on us".

"He won't, sir. I have someone sitting outside".

"Have you, make sure he's paid well or give him a day off after".

"I will".

"Good now Baptiste, I need you to take me to the lower levels, I need to visit the 'research and transition' area. I'll discuss with our team there our little problem with Monsieur Vendroux and his memory or lack of it".

Whilst Baptiste led Pierre to the lower levels, Antanois went to check on Capitaine Olivier Vendroux. Inside his cell the stench was hardly bearable. Not only was there the odour from rotting human flesh next door, there was the smell of fresh human vomit as well as the unmistakable stench of human diarrhoea. Antanois peered into the bucket, there was only vomit.

"He's shit himself", the man tasked with guarding the capitaine explained.

Antanois turned to look at the capitaine who was slumped up against a bare chalk wall. He stared angrily at Antanois.

"Why don't you bastards just get on with it. Shoot me or something, haven't you had enough fun"?.

Antanois chuckled. "Fun you call it, the fun has been of your own making. You my friend have created one hell of a headache. Anyway, we're not going to let you die. After a few modifications, you're going back to your miserable life outside". If the capitaine looked surprised he didn't show it. He was nursing a thumping headache and a familiar feeling was beginning to rise up from his stomach. Moving his knees apart, he bent over spewing vomit over the floor.

"You disgust me", Antanois spat in the direction of the capitaine. He turned to the man guarding him. "I've been told not to have him cleaned up".

"Thank God"!

Gendarmerie Nationale, Calais, France

"Hello Jean". Colette put her hand to her head, Jean Fournier was the last thing she needed right now. ""How can I help you"?.

"I'm sorry Colette", Colette listened as Jean rambled on. He was one mixed up young man and suffering badly. All because, through no fault of his own, he and his girlfriend had witnessed a possible murder on Cap Blanc Nez. After admitting to Colette what he had told Capitaine Olivier Vendroux in the interview held in his office, he then went on to explain his phone call the following morning and his revelation of what had taken place at Capitaine Maubert, widow's house. "How you and the lieutenant told me not to discuss this with anybody else, especially not him. The capitaine was so nice to me during the interview. Afterwards I changed sides. I thought that you and the lieutenant may be les meurtriers' and the capitaine the good guy. After my call, I realised I'd made a terrible mistake. And now this…". Meaning Colette assumed the farce around the disappeared Capitaine Vendroux.

"You have been rather silly, Jean", Colette wasn't going to let him off that easily. "You may have put us, Vivienne and her daughter as well as yourself in serious danger. Who knows what these people are capable of".

"I know and my girlfriend is pregnant, she and now my baby are at risk too, and it's all my fault". A baby, Colette, immediately felt sorry for him.

"Look Jean, the best thing you can do is go back to work, pretend nothing has happened, just keep an eye out for anything unusual. Let the lieutenant try and sort things out. He has his hands full at the moment. No one knows where the capitaine is. The gendarmerie are trying to find him before the feminists do". There came a pause, an uncomfortable pause, Colette sensed there was more to come and she was right.

"My boss has given me a couple of days off". Colette stayed silent, there was more to come. She knew it, and she knew too that it wouldn't be good.

Jean told her of him breaking down at his place of work, Le Week-End cafe/bar at Sangatte, and how he had spilled everything to his boss and his wife along with several clients sitting nearby.

Colette held her head in her spare hand. The bloody stupid little boy, baby or no baby if he was here standing in front of her, she'd slap him. How she managed to hold back her anger, she just didn't know.

"Whatever you do Jean, don't tell anybody else, you must promise me".

"Ma vie". I promise. Colette wanted to believe him but he was so bloody weak.

"I have to believe you, Jean. Do not let us down. I have to let the lieutenant know but at the moment he has enough on his plate. When I have told him, he may well want to talk to you".

"That's fine". It'll have to be, Colette bit her lip.

"Where will you be? On the two days you have been given off".

"Here at my girlfriend parent's house".

"Where's that Jean? I need their address".

"He's not going to come here is he"?. Colette sighed, she was beginning to lose her patience.

"Just give me their address, Jean, if you have a problem how are we going to help if we don't know where you are"?

Jean gave her their address along with the landline number.

"Don't disappear, Jean, will you, we haven't the manpower, and stay safe", Colette was about to ring off when she added something else. "And congratulations, Jean, to Camille too".

"Merci". Jean's voice was faint. Colette rang off. She placed her head in both hands. The stupid, stupid little boy and now he was going to be a father. God help their child. Anger rose within her and completely out of character Colette swung her arm hard across her desk, knocking everything on it flying across her office. Several people in reception looked through her interior window in surprise. Shocked at herself, Colette quickly returned to her usual gentle manner. Raising her arm to those outside, looking in, she mouthed the word, 'pardon'.

Picking things up, she hoped the lieutenant was having a better time than her. Which, of course, he wasn't.

The Harrow, Steep, Hampshire, England

It took Roger Denton just over forty minutes to reach Petersfield and without the use of GPS, another thirty minutes to find The Harrow. The detective inspector had been right, the pub really was tucked away. As luck would have it ,the D.I. hadn't needed to double park. When he arrived there was still one space left in the small parking area out front and alongside the outside toilets. It was a small space and his NCA BMW would never have fitted but his new 'wheels', the Panda fitted in nicely.

He had to tap on the D.I. 's car window, his meet hadn't expected him to arrive in an aquamarine, early two thousand Fiat Panda with a rainbow and the word 'PEACE' painted either side. Roger's attire didn't help either.

The Harrow, Steep

"Don't ask", were the first words he said, realising the look of aston-ishment, (I'm being polite here), on D.I. Johnson's face.

"I won't if you don't want me too, but I'd really like to know".

"Well you're not going too".

"Ok".

"Nice pub, anybody follow you"?.

"D.I. Johnson shook his head,"If they did they'd have had to have been disguised as sheep or cows. Anyone following you on these lanes and you'd soon know it".

Roger had to admit he was right, anyone following him and he'd have soon known it. D.I. Johnson had chosen well. Hands in pockets, he looked at the pub. Half tiled and attached to a small row of cottages, The Harrow didn't appear as if it had changed at all since it was built, which he was to learn later was the 16th century, when the Tudors ruled England. He relayed his thoughts to the D.I.

"It hasn't changed inside either, there's hardly room to swing a cat".

"Best we sit outside then, we don't want people to hear what we have to say".

"I'll drink to that". As the D.I. said this the doors to the two bars were opened and a small group of people waiting outside disappeared within. "The pub's full now, we'll have to sit outside." Roger wasn't sure if the D.I. was joking or not.

"Look, you grab a seat and I'll get the drinks".

"You won't need a menu, it's on the wall by the bar. I'll have the soup". Soup, who had soup these days? The D.I. read Rogers thoughts. "Try it, I've been coming here since I was a kid some forty odd years ago. The menus never changed, neither has the soup. It's like the one your grandmother or great grandmother used to make. When the pot never left the stove, you just kept adding to it".

Roger was doubtful but he promised he'd try it. Inside, he discovered D.I. Johnson hadn't been joking. There were a dozen people inside and there was hardly room for anyone else. He ordered two soups and two pints of Swift One, a locally brewed pale ale delivered straight from the barrel behind the bar. Outside, he found the D.I. sitting under a covered area attached to the pub.

"Thanks", the D.I. took his pint. Both men took a sip of their beer before talking. "Do you know when I retire…", D.I. Johnson broke their silence. "….I'm going to travel Britain looking for unspoilt pubs like this". Roger had to agree, it wasn't a bad idea. "They're becoming harder and harder to find, unspoilt pubs", the D.I. continued. "Large bloody breweries tend to take them over and instead of leaving them as they are, they cover the original feature with imitation. What's the point? Roger had to admit that he agreed one hundred percent with the D.I. In their short time at the Harrow, he was growing to like the D.I. In a police station you would never see this side of someone. Roger was just about to broach the subject, which was, why was he here"? when the soup arrived. He didn't regret having taken D.I. Johnson's advice. He'd never tasted soup like it and the bread that came with it. By the end he was full, something that never normally happened with soup. After their dishes had been cleared, Roger asked the question. He was conscious that the time was moving on, and he had to get to France.

"So, what have you got for me"?.

The D.I. took a long sip of his beer. "It's to do with those twelve Albanian children you told me about".

Roger's ears pricked up. They were the main reason he was going to France. "Go on".

D.I. Johnson told Roger what the journalist at the Portsmouth Evening News had told him.

"Is this guy reliable"? Was Roger's first question after he'd finished.

"One hundred percent, he's never let me down in the past, and according to him, so is his contact in the navy".

288

Roger considered what he had just heard, if this turned out to be true and if it got out, the news would almost certainly bring down the government. It was shocking. He remembered his meeting when he and Jane had visited the Home Secretary after receiving the results of the DNA tests, of Donald, or Jason as he had called himself back then, at their meeting in the Lamb and Flag. Jason, telling him that the British government had done a 'dirty deal' with France.

"I can hardly march in accusing the Navy but as migrants are the NCA's domain, you can". The D.I. looked inquisitively at Roger, he could see that what he had just told him had shaken the man from the NCA. It was obvious he was troubled.

"You won't reveal your contact"?. Roger was fishing.

"No sorry but I can ask him questions on your behalf".

Roger had expected nothing else; trust was everything in police work. Break it for short term gain and it could set you back years. "Not for now, can you jot down the name of the fort for now". Not having any paper the D.I. turned over a beer mat and scribbled it on the back. Roger took it and placed it in one of the many pockets in his parka. He stood up. And after thanking the D.I. , apologising for having to rush off, and promising to be in touch, Roger left for his car. D.I. Johnson remained seated. He was in no hurry, in fact he was planning on having another but not until the man from the NCA was out of sight. As he drove past Roger waved which the D.I. returned. Out of earshot two men, watching, exchanged words. On seeing the rainbow one exclaimed, 'Bloody poofters', his companion objected. 'Live and let live, live and let live, they're not doing us any harm'. Unaware that he was causing so much comment D.I. Johnson returned to the bar.

Back on the A3, Roger reflected on what the D.I. had told him. He was mistaken if he thought the NCA could suddenly walk into a naval base. Perhaps Jane could force something? The fort in question was on Portsdown Hill, where had he heard that name before? It would come to him. And then there was the question of Paris, why, if the bodies of the children were here, had the gendarme in France told him that the bodies had been transferred to a morgue in Paris and that it was now a French investigation? It just didn't make sense. He couldn't wait to meet lieutenant what's-his-face. Sensing he was on to something, he phoned Nick.

Before allowing Roger to speak Nick blurted out, "I've got your passport sir and I'm on my way". He sounded stressed.

"Great, Nick, ETA"?.

"Half an hour if the M25 behaves itself, which it rarely does".

"Great, thanks Nick, I'll see you there". Roger turned his phone off, he had already stayed on it too long. Half an hour was what it would probably take him to reach the Cobham services on the M25. Things, for once, he felt, were beginning to work out his way.

Chaillot, Paris, France

Marcel Leclerc, looked at the scrap of paper in his hand and then at the street ahead of him. This was definitely the street address but surely there was no way a morgue could be located here. Chaillot was where some of France's richest people had houses and the street was a good example of this along with a couple of five star hotels. He was beginning to regret now that he hadn't asked his friend in Calais, Lieutenant Beaufort, why he was so interested in this morgue. He thought it would be quite simple, but now on seeing the street he was beginning to have doubts.

He'd chosen to do his friend the favour on his day off and therefore he wasn't in uniform, Silly, but somehow by not wearing his uniform, it felt rather as though he had lost a suit of armour.

He found the exact address halfway down the street. It was a side door in an access to a guarded parking area. The number was clearly displayed on a brass plaque but there was no name and Marcel could see no access for ambulances. More curious than fearful he rang the bell, also brass. In fact he noticed the brass bell button was dark, unpolished, polished not even through use. This entrance was hardly used. He was just about to give up when somebody, a woman, opened the door.

"Please come in, sorry for your wait".

Marcel did as he was bid and found himself in a small reception area, with a heavy oak desk and an ornate lamp, also brass.

"Can I help you"?. The lady, Marcel guessed in her early sixties, walked around to the other side of the desk, flicking off dust as she went.

Marcel took out the scrap of paper, he wished now that he had made more of an effort and transferred his note onto something that demonstrated a little more class. I'm looking for a morgue, it's for a friend", he read out the name and the address. "I think I'm at the right address".

"You are", the lady confirmed,"Just a minute, do you mind waiting Monsieur"?.

"Marcel, Marcel Leclerc, and no, not at all".

"Monsieur Leclerc. I'll just go to find someone who can help you, s'il vous plait, take a seat.". The lady disappeared down a corridor and shortly after he heard her, or he assumed it must be her, taking a flight of stairs. Marcel looked at the chair, like the desk, it was covered in dust. Something wasn't right, he decided to get out. He tried the door but he found it locked, there was only way that could have happened, it had been locked electronically. Looking up, he realised he was being watched. Not by a standard security camera, this one was minute, hardly visible. He felt bile rising to his throat. There came the sound of footsteps approaching and their sound wasn't the same as the lady's. These were much heavier.

Two men, both smartly dressed, appeared in the reception area.

"Can we help you"? The taller of the two spoke.

"I'm here on behalf of a friend, he's asked me to look up this place for him", he handed the man who had spoken his scrap of paper. The man took it and read the address.

"Morgue, is your friend looking for someone? Does he think there may be a body of a person here he's looking for"?. They were legitimate questions and Marcel had no answer.

"I don't really know", Marcel knew how stupid his answer sounded, he cursed himself for not being more prepared.

The taller man looked at him straight in his face. "Your friend asks you to look up a morgue and you don't ask him why? I need to see your ID, Monsieur"?

"Leclerc, Marcel Leclerc", Marcel handed over his Identity card. The man took it but didn't give it a second's glance.

"And your mobile phone please". This time the shorter of the two men held out his hand. Marcel was about to protest but very quickly realised that to do so would be fruitless and could anger the so far, very polite men. He dropped it into the man's open palm.

"Merci", for the first time the taller of the two, examined his identity card. "Now Monsieur Leclerc, I'm afraid you must come with us, we need you to answer some questions". Before Marcel knew it the two men had grasped his elbows, one either side. He recognised that the two were very well trained, the best. There was no way he could escape. "Come with us please". The two men started to march him along the same corridor down which the lady had disappeared. At the end they too took some stairs, but unlike the lady, they were not taking the stairs to an upper floor. They were descending into what Marcel assumed must be the basement. And as horror films tend to depict, basements are where bad things normally happen. The taste of fear was beginning to salivate in Marcel's mouth. Beaufort, what have you got me into?

Chapter 6

Cobham Motorway Services, M25, Surrey, England

Roger saw Nick drive in. To the average member of the public, it was just another car, but to Roger it was so bloody obvious. An exceptionally polished BMW driven with exceptional sureness. You might as well stick a sign on the roof saying, 'Hi, I'm from the NCA'. Pulling out of his parking space, Roger quickly fell in behind his colleague and pulled up beside him when he stopped. Nick's look of disdain was almost comical when he looked across at the aging hippie driving a ridiculously silly, painted car followed by a look which combined both horror and surprise when his colleague recognised him. Roger motioned for Nick to wind down the window.

"I'll get the cappuccinos, Nick, you sit tight, AND NO sarcastic remarks". Nick mouthed, 'as if' and pressed the button to bring the window back up. It was bloody freezing outside. As his boss disappeared to get the coffees, he studied the car that Roger had arrived in. What the fuck and started to laugh out loud. When Roger returned with two large coffees, Nick had just about recovered. After thanking his boss for his coffee the first thing he asked was -

"Where the fuck did you get that, and those clothes. You look like Tom Good out of the 'Good Life', in fact no, Tom Good is a lot smarter".

"Don't ask, Nick", then Roger grinned. And in an exaggerated French accent added, "I'm travelling in disguise".

"Well you need to change your trousers, you look like you've just mugged a tramp but couldn't bear the thought of removing his bottoms".

"Very funny, Nick. Did you bring my passport"?. Reaching across, Nick opened the glove compartment and handed his boss his passport. Roger took it and placed it in a large pocket.

Watching, Nick couldn't help warning, referring to the Parka. "Don't lose it in that".

"Don't worry, I won't".

"I guess you managed to get hold of that gendarme who you have been crossing messages with".

Roger took a sip of his coffee and quickly put it down, it was too hot. "I did, and this might be a complete waste of time but after talking to him for a few minutes on the phone, I don't think it will be".

"Has Jane signed this off"?.

"No".

"She'll go nuts".

"I'm doing this off my own back, Nick, using my own money. I'm not going to claim anything. I'll phone Jane later and tell her I'm taking a couple of days off".

"What? in the middle of everything that's going on"!

"She's suggested I look at retiring Nick, and after everything that has happened to me recently, who can blame me wanting a couple of days to myself"?.

"True", Nick had placed his coffee on the dashboard causing the windscreen to steam up. "How did your meeting go"?.

Roger told Nick some but not all that D.I. Johnson had told him. Enough to whet his detective's natural curiosity. "This is why I'm going to France, Nick, I need to find if there's a connection. I'm going to phone Jane later, tell her what I've found out. She might be able to help in gaining access to where we're not normally allowed to tread.

"Blood hell, sir", Nick took a long sip of his coffee. If what you say is true we're going to have to tread really carefully. We're going to be treading on a lot of people's toes if we're to investigate thoroughly. Departments and people who do not take kindly to having their toes trodden on".

"I know, Nick, that's why I need Jane's help with this".

"So you're going to ask her for a couple of days off and then land her with what you've just told me. I'm sure that conversation will go well". Roger returned a rueful smile.

"I can't say I'm looking forward to it. Anyway, have you got anything new to report"?.

"Actually I have, you may want to steady yourself". Roger gave him a look and then grabbed his coffee, he'd forgotten about it. "We've had the pathologist come back to us, specifically in answer to your questions. I'm afraid you were right, it looks as if all had had their genitals removed and stuffed in their mouths whilst they were still alive and the decapitation of their heads finally killed them. Bloody awful, and John who we lost in the Hilton, had been badly beaten as well, really badly beaten. And in answer to your second question, all had had their pineal gland removed except for John Mitchell, and the reason for this, though it's only a theory at the moment is Mr Mitchell had been so badly beaten, he'd suffered brain damage. The pathologist surmises the pineal gland, because of this may have been of no use to whoever was responsible. Though no one we talk to has the foggiest idea why anybody would want to collect pineal glands. Their function is limited and much of what they do can be copied using drugs".

Roger took a long sip of coffee, it was tepid now, disgusting. He was trying to stay cool. He was trying to avoid picturing John in his final moments, the bloody bastards from hell. He was even more determined now to catch who was responsible. And prison would be too good for them. God help them if he caught them he'd kill them with his bare hands and prison would be worth it.

"Are you alright, sir"?.

"We've got to get these bastards Nick, if it takes our last breath on this earth to do it".

Nick finished his coffee. "I agree with you sir, I just wish I felt that we're making inroads somewhere, and I don't"

"Whoever they are will make a mistake sooner or later and when they do, we'll be waiting for it".

"I bloody hope so sir".

Roger sucked in air. "Anything else"?

"Digital forensics are booked into the Hilton tomorrow, to start on their CCTV system, I'm not sure they'll find anything though. They've got nowhere with everything else and that charade at the DVLA. Our guys have told me that they haven't got a clue how to prevent it from happening again".

"I almost wish it would, that way we'll get rid of the idiot running the country".

"Cheers to that sir, if it did what or whose photo would you want on your licence"?.

Roger thought,"My father's".

Nick hadn't expected that and searched for the right response. Roger rescued him.

"Have you got anywhere with the CCTV company? And have you checked who did ours"?.

"We've passed it over to fraud, we're nowhere near qualified to investigate that tangle. They're confident though that they'll soon unravel it. Find out who owns them. One thing they have said, whoever it is, is overseas".

"And our CCTV"?.

"That's easier, a company called Rowlands though they're now in administration".

"Probably because we haven't paid them". Roger said dryly.

"Probably. They were a startup company this year, so sad. They did some work at our old offices but the guy who procured them died in the explosion so we can't ask him why he took them on. They will have undergone the usual checks".

"Which we now know, mean fuck all".

"You have a point, sir".

"Anything on Porton Down"?.

"I've heard nothing sir".

"Ok, I'll find out from Jane, what's going on there. Anything else"?.

"JJ rang from MI5, wants you to give him a ring, not urgent," he said. When you have a mo".

"Ok, anything else"?.

"That's pretty much it sir, sorry I haven't got anything more positive".

Roger waved his passport at him, "This is positive, Nick. Thank you". Roger opened the door.

"My pleasure, sir, what ferry are you booked on"?.

"I'm not, I'm taking the tunnel". Roger froze. "Shit I haven't booked a ticket".

Mont d'Hubert, Near Calais, France

Baptiste, with Pierre descended to the lowest level under Mont d'Hubert. To arrive at this point they'd had to pass through several levels of security, pass cards, pass codes, finger prints, palm prints, face recognition and iris scans. The final descent was by lift, there was no other way and the lift could only be accessed via what to the average person looked like a dead end tunnel, with nothing of interest. The lowest level had only dimmed lighting. Infrared cameras were at every few feet controlled by a security office deep under Mont a Crignons. There were no tunnels in the lowest level, just one open space, egg shaped, with rows of supporting pillars. There were no employees, no humans on this level, it was for access only to the heart of Mont a Crignons. There was access on other levels to Mont a Crignons, all tightly controlled as well and each entrance cleverly disguised as natural chalk. Security was always tight, should an unwanted get near but nothing like the lowest level.

At either end of the egg-shaped cavern, set in the chalk wall was a huge iron door. Pierre walked to the southern door. After an iris scan and punching in a code Pierre had confined to memory the large iron door slid open. The two men passed through. As soon as they had done, the large iron door closed behind them. To open it again would require a different code. They were now in a twelve foot square cell with an identical door ahead of them. To the right attached to the wall was a metal bench. Baptiste went and sat on it, he had never been this far before and knew this was as far as he would get. Pierre, using a different code, also ingrained in his memory, opened the second door. Without looking at Baptiste he passed through. The door closed behind him and Baptiste was left alone with one dim light and four infrared cameras, all trained on him. He couldn't see them but he knew they were there. Holes in the ceiling, a dozen of them. If anything should happen they would pump gas into the chamber and he would pass peacefully to another world. He had been trained for and was prepared for this. And if there was a risk of unwanteds accessing the space the chalk above would collapse, making unauthorised entry virtually impossible.It was the ultimate security, preventing the secrets under Mont a Crignons from ever reaching the outside world.

Gendarmerie Nationale, Calais, France

Lieutenant Beaufort wiped the sweat from his brow. He had never policed a riot before and what he had experienced had shocked him. The demonstration had started peacefully enough but had soon become violent and shockingly violent. Women too, he'd never experienced anything like it. Intelligence suggested that the demonstration had been infiltrated and taken over in the main by extremists attached to anarchist groups. These people were looking for any excuse to have a go at authority and Capitaine Olivier Vendroux by assaulting a woman had given them the perfect excuse to do this.

Chapter 6

The search for the capitaine had had to be, in all but name, temporarily called off. Resources for now were needed elsewhere. Everyone in policing prayed he wouldn't stumble into the hands of the demonstrators. If he did, judging by what was confronting them, there'd be very little hope of him making it out alive.

"What worried everybody was that the demonstration, after several hours, showed no sign of calming, and if it was still the case by nightfall, the CRS warned him, all hell could break loose. To Lieutenant Beaufort, it already had.

Eurotunnel Terminal, Folkestone, England

Roger Denton of the NCA, sitting in a queue for Le Shuttle, reminded him of why he never chose to visit the continent by car, especially since Brexit. He'd now been queuing for close to an hour and he couldn't imagine a worse way of wasting your life. And this after paying a premium rate as he hadn't booked in advance. He found it hard to understand why the British public accepted it. For a few months he'd worked in Munich, in a joint operation with the German Kriminalpolizei, Kripo for short. Whilst with them, they'd told him a joke about the English. 'If you put twenty Englishman in a circle, what would they do? ' The answer, 'queue'. Remembering this, Roger, couldn't help smiling, they were so bloody right.

It did though give him a chance to phone Jane. He told her what D.I. Johnson had told him. At first she'd been suspicious as to the reliability of the source before agreeing, through her own sources, to see what she could find out. She was doubtful though whether she'd be able to obtain a warrant to search the fort under naval control on Portsdown Hill.

Still nothing had been found at Porton Down. There was pressure to re-open the site from the men in 'grey suits'.

Roger was honest with Jane about his plans for visiting France. 'If I do this off my own back…', he told her,"… by taking a couple of days off, it won't have to involve you or the NCA. 'You won't have to sign it off".

A maverick, Jane had called him on hearing this, to be exact a 'bloody maverick' but she gave Roger her blessing. 'Just be careful and KEEP ME INFORMED'. Gaining Jane's blessing meant a lot to Roger, he felt a lot more comfortable now he had her blessing and she hadn't quizzed him for details. Just a general overview.

After Jane he phoned Donald. Once again Donald answered on the first ring.

"Don't repeat our names". Donald, Roger was learning, always started a call by saying this.

Roger told him about his meeting with D.I. Johnson, about the twelve bodies along with two adult males being taken to a fort under naval control on Portsdown Hill. I told you about our government doing a dirty with the French, Donald reminded him.

"Yes but why then, when I spoke to Calais did the capitaine there tell me the corpses had been taken to France"?.

"I'd have thought it was obvious, to throw you off the scent. It wouldn't surprise me if they were taking their orders from London, with the blessing of the French government of course".

Roger had to admit that this made perfect sense. Nothing this government did surprised him anymore. He then told Donald about his planned meeting with the lieutenant, second in command at the gendarmerie at Calais, and that the lieutenant felt that there was something not right with their new capitaine. That he was trying without asking questions to change the track of their current investigations.

"You haven't heard the news then"?.

"No, I've been driving and the bloody radio doesn't work".

Donald told him about the capitaine's behaviour, the subsequent riots and the capitaine's mysterious disappearance. Shit, Roger was surprised Nick hadn't told him about this.

"Have you booked your accommodation Roger? The place is filling up with journalists from all over the place,if you don't do it soon, I doubt you'll get anywhere".

"I'll do it as soon as I get off the phone with you".

"Ok, one thing. We've checked your Lieutenant Beaufort out and as far as we can see, he's genuine. A good honest officer who wants to do the right thing. That's rare these days, keep him on our side, and if you wish, give him my number. He might not always be able to get hold of you. Me, he will. But tell him he must use a pay as you go, in France they're called 'portable jetable'". If he doesn't, this number will no longer work, I know the number of his mobile, so warn him".

"I will, I still have a spare".

"Ah yes from the flat". Roger ignored him.

"I might give him that".

"Well if you do make sure there's lots of credit on it or while you're over there, buy a French Sim card".

Roger went to answer but Donald had rung off. How the bloody hell did Donald know the Lieutenant's mobile phone number? He'd also wanted to ask about his pathologist charging his card. And Donald hadn't asked him about the Met's pathologist's report, how strange. Bloody man, why did he trust him? He had no idea, he just did. Cursing he topped up his last remaining pay as you go phone with £50.

Passing passport control, he was asked the purpose of his trip. What a bloody stupid question, what had it to do with Border Force? He wanted to say, to shoot Macron, but simply answered it was for a few days break in France, 'good wine and good food'. Well avoid Calais, the woman examining his passport warned.

"It's all kicking off there".

Roger thanked her and after being waved through by the French, joined another queue waiting to board a train. As he waited, staff in high vis jackets were tapping on the windows of those queuing. It was to warn travellers not to visit Calais. Great thought Roger, that's exactly where I was planning to stay.

Mont d'Hubert, near Calais, France

After passing through the second iron door, Pierre stepped into another cavern, this one circular. This cavern was very simply lit with typical builder's style caged lamps, a loose wire connecting them. There appeared to be no way out other than returning via the iron door. Pierre knew otherwise, he knew the pattern of the hewn chalk off by heart. He approached the wall to his left and pulled out what looked like a tv remote. First, with the red light at the tip he scanned his thumb and after, punched in a ten digit code. What had looked like solid rock started to move to reveal on the other side a simple barely lit tunnel.Pierre stepped through the opening and started walking. He knew it would take a good half an hour before he would arrive under Mont a Crignons. Along the way, there were regular stencilled signs, several with the swastika. The wording was German and left from when Rommel's troops had last occupied the complex. The tunnel had remained hidden for years until the organisation had rediscovered it. What had developed since was his baby though the organisation would argue it was theirs. He didn't really mind, they were working towards the same goal, he just hoped that he wouldn't die of old age before that goal was reached.

Chapter 6

Hotel L'Escale, Escalles, France

Roger had found the hotel on an internet hotel comparison site. Donald had been right, all the hotels in Calais were fully booked. Where he found himself now though was delightful. The hotel was reasonably modern, with a pool and situated in a small village at the foot of a hill he now knew to be called Mont d'Hubert. Close by and visible from the hotel was Cap Blanc Nez. With everything that had taken place, the name Cap Blanc Nez had often been central and now here he was as dusk settled, gazing up at it. He might even drive up this evening and experience the place for himself. Get a feel for it.

The one downfall, he felt extremely underdressed, as the hotel was quite smart and when he enquired about the pool, the receptionist commented. 'We ask all of our guests to have a shower before using the pool'. He needed to get some clothes. The receptionist spoke good English and Roger made up a story of his bags having been stolen and enquired where he could buy some, just to get buy for the next few days. Don't go into Calais the receptionist warned him, it's a 'cauchemar', (nightmare). Instead, using a map, she circled a couple of retail parks on the outskirts of Calais, or you could go to Boulogne she suggested, 'the centre is nice'.

After thanking her, Roger went to his room, showered and swapping his fleece and jumper for his only shirt, made his way to the hotel restaurant. He fancied a swim but hadn't packed his bathers. That morning he'd had no intention of visiting France, let alone staying in a hotel with a pool.

The menu thankfully was translated into English and he chose 'La soupe de poissons' to start, followed by 'Le risotto de noix de st-jacques, champignon et bacon'. Wanting to drive afterwards, he restricted himself to just one glass of muscadet, recommended by the waiter. He decided to forgo dessert. After paying the bill Roger finished with a coffee back in his room. He felt good, he'd eaten well today, including his baps for breakfast. Some things the English excelled at.

On turning on his tv, he found the last occupant had been tuned to the local news channel. Sitting on his bed with his back leaning against the headboard Roger watched as an obviously very excited reporter relayed what was happening in Calais Nord. The scenes were shocking, the CRS were engaged in running battles with mainly female demonstrators. Projectiles were being thrown, cars overturned and shop and cafe windows smashed. All because of one Capitaine Olivier Vendroux. The man who had dismissed his enquiry. And now after very publicly assaulting a woman in a bar, he had gone missing, You couldn't make it up. Watching the French authorities take something of a hammering he decided to contact the lieutenant's interpreter. Watching what was unfolding on television, he wondered if the lieutenant was going to be able to find the time to meet him tomorrow. He needed to let him know that he had arrived in France and to let him know where he was staying.

Mirielle answered on the first ring. "I'm waiting for the lieutenant to call", which explained the swiftness of her response. Roger told her that he was in France and where he was staying. "You're better off there than here", she told him. Roger enquired, with everything that was going on whether it would still be possible to meet tomorrow. "To be honest with you, detective, I have no idea. I will ask him and will call you back".

"Thank you, Mirielle".

"De rien, you're welcome detective".

"Thanks again". Roger rang off. He hadn't the heart to tell Mirielle that he wasn't a detective, that strictly speaking he wasn't a policeman either. After the call, he reflected on calling it an early night. No, he wanted to experience Cap Blanc Nez. Sod it, if it was dark. Capitaine Maubert, the capitaine who had been trying to contact him, had met his death on Cap Blanc Nez in the dark. He wanted to experience similar conditions, test his gut feeling. His gut at that moment was telling him something wasn't right. The fact that a second capitaine, Maubert's replacement, was now missing, only reinforced that feeling.

In the hotel car park, he found three youths laughing at his car.

"She's called Molly", he told them. The three looked at each other, each shrugging their shoulders. Standing out of the way they, allowed the man from the NCA to reverse. Watching the Englishman drive off they broke into laughter once more.

Roger was surprised how steep the drive to the summit of Cap Blanc Nez was. So steep was it, the road was forced to zigzag its way up similar to an Alpine pass. At the top, Roger turned into the car park below a towering monument in the style of an obelisk. A monument remembering the 'Dover Patrol'. Roger had no idea what that was. Apart from his, there was only one other car in the car park. He was surprised how windy it was on the summit. Where he was staying, in the village of Escalles he had hardly noticed it all. Getting out of his car, he was thankful he had brought the parka. Zipping it up as he walked he approached the edge of the cliff. Even in the dark the view was magnificent. The English coast was clearly visible and there were views along the French coast line both to his left and to his right. The sea below in the darkness looked very foreboding. He couldn't imagine wanting to take his own life by jumping off where he was standing now in the dark. Not even in broad daylight. It must be a horrendous way to die. Roger stared down at the sea crashing against the base of the cliff. And out there somewhere is where the now world famous severed heads were first spotted. And the young girl, her body was found on a beach at the base of the cliff. Cap Blanc Nez held a lot of secrets, secrets that needed to somehow be exposed. He would ask Lieutenant Beaufort his thoughts when they met. He hoped it would be tomorrow. The waves below like flames in a fire were mesmerising and the sound powerful. It was surprising then that he heard something behind him.

A Safehouse Somewhere in South London, England

As dusk settled, Jane was sitting on the sofa in the lounge watching the BBC 24 hour news service. Two people tasked with keeping her safe were watching the news with her. She was fed up with being part of a crowd, tomorrow she'd move back to her own house. Living here was suffocating her and making her work for the organisation very difficult.

The main news story was the disappearance of the man in charge of the gendarmerie in Calais and this after allegedly assaulting a woman. 'Allegedly', Jane smiled to herself. They were so bloody politically correct in this country. It was obvious, his assault was there on screen, for everyone to witness. There was no 'allegedly' about it. Shocking pictures of the protests unfolding in Calais Nord followed.

Jane thought of Roger, he was out there somewhere. She wondered where he was and what he was doing. She ought to tell Orme. She knew the organisation had some sort of base just outside of Calais. Contacting Orme whilst staying in a safehouse wasn't easy. Even with a double. The safehouse meant there had to be a lot of planning.

Tomorrow she will move back into her own house. Even if MI5 forced the Met to post a guard, it would be better than this.

Mont d'Hubert near Calais, France

It actually took Pierre forty minutes until he reached a blank wall deep below Mont a Crignons.

Above him were several floors where, one day in the future it was planned that mass 'transition' would take place. Their first subject in this process, after years of research and experimentation, was a French girl called Marie. By working with the gendarmerie she had become a risk to the organisation and had been picked up with a view to selling her body parts on the red market. However following a review it had been decided that Marie could better serve the organisation alive as their first complete transitional guinea pig.

Returning to Pierre. Taking out the remote control device, Pierre this time scanned the index finger attached to his right hand, followed by a much longer code. The hidden door could not this time be operated from the outside, it had to be operated by a guard in the control or security room situated on the floor above. Receiving the scan and code an operator there entered another code. After a ten second wait a section of wall slid back and Pierre stepped through. He now had a five minute walk until he was under Mont de Sombre, the hill adjacent. On the surface the German bunkers had been blocked up by the local authorities, unintentionally doing the organisation a great favour. As the shorter tunnel ended, Pierre took a deep breath, he was almost there. This time he scanned the index finger on his left hand and punched in another code. After a ten second wait another door hidden in the rock face slid back. Once again Pierre stepped through, this time into a perfectly round chamber. A large black disk hung from the ceiling above and, hidden above this rays of light were being beamed at precise and regular intervals around the chamber. On the floor in the centre was a simple painted circle. Standing in this and looking directly at a swastika painted on the wall ahead Pierre raised his arms as though offering his surrender. Concentrated beams of light started to scan every part of his body. Pierre didn't move, to do so meant the scanning process would be aborted and have to be started again. Three failed attempts and the process would be completely aborted and access forbidden, even for him, Pierre. The scan succeeded and a hologram of a computer keyboard appeared just in front of him. Pierre punched in another code stored in his memory, and another door, concealed within the rock, slowly opened. On the other side a brightly lit tunnel stretched into the distance. This time an electric buggy, similar to that used by golfers, would be his transport. Disconnecting it from its electricity supply Pierre got in and after putting the buggy into gear pressed his foot on the right hand pedal. The one other pedal being the brake. Ten minutes later he was at the end of the tunnel. He could now taste his excitement, on the other side of the wall, deep below Mont de Couple, hidden from the outside world was his baby and to, a great extent,the organisation's raison d'etre.

Pembroke Square, Bayswater, London

It was getting dark and lights were being turned on all over London. On returning home Ariana couldn't help but notice that her house was almost lit up like a Christmas tree. Every window appeared to have a light shining inside. As she approached the front door it was opened for her, her servant offering to take her coat and scarf. Ariana would have to get used to this, she was used to doing things for herself. Having everything done for her by somebody else she was finding exhausting. The irony of it.

"What time would you like dinner, madam"?.

"I don't, thank you". Ariana was stuffed, Henrietta had excelled herself.

"I'll ask chef to prepare you some snacks, just in case you're hungry a little later. Ariana knew it was fruitless to say no thanks and agreed to the uniformed servant's proposal.

"Thank the chef, won't you".

"Of course, anything else, there's a fire lit in the lounge"?.

"Excellent, I'll retire there".

"Anything to drink, madame"?.

Ariana thought, everything about this house is Persian, obviously for her benefit. She'd put them to the test.

"Aragh Keshmesh".

The servant appeared completely unphased. "Certainly, small or large glass"?.

Ariana thanked him and retired to the lounge where a fire was roaring. A couple of minutes later, another servant appeared with a large brandy glass, half full. Ariana placed the glass under her nose. Exactly how she remembered. She took a sip, enjoying the burning sensation as the dark liquid slid down her throat. It was good, better than good, it was perfect. Thanking the servant who had brought it, Ariana dismissed her, telling her she wanted to be alone.

"As you wish".

Sitting back in her chair, she cupped the glass in her hand and stared into the flames. Everything about this house reminded her of Persia, not Iran, Persia. There was a big difference. And not just of Persia, of her early life, family life in the mountains. She knew it was no accident but how did they know. The organisation, how did it know and why were they doing this for her now"? She pushed her thoughts to the back of her mind. She'd find out in good time. There was no point in wondering. Back to the present.

She'd had a great lunch courtesy of Henrietta and an enjoyable afternoon. The house she lived in with her husband was in Pimlico, therefore close to Westminster, in a typical Thomas Cubitt designed square. Inside the house was as Ariana saw it, typically English. Grand but understated with paintings on the walls of life in England as it once was. There were very few photos on display, and those that were displayed tended to be of parents and grandparents. Ariana could see nothing that was current.

Henrietta had tried to please her by attempting to cook a number of Persian dishes and she hadn't done a bad job. She had, Henrietta confided in her, bought a recipe book especially, but frustratingly hadn't had time to practise as she would have liked to have done. In the afternoon, over several glasses of cream sherry the two women had talked and laughed. With careful steering, Henrietta revealed more and more about their marriage, what it was like being married to the home secretary and increasingly about her husband's job, his likes, his opinions and his dislikes. In return, Ariana told Henrietta about her life, prepared for her by the organisation, and her charity work, especially helping women to escape, many were victims of abuse in the middle east, especially where she was born, Iran.

In their time together the two women had got to find out a great deal about each other and their liking and respect for each other was equally shared. In her professional capacity Ariana had learnt a great deal about her target, Henrietta's husband, and as a result, her seduction of him and the total dominance that was to follow was going to be so much easier.

After three glasses of Aragh Keshmesh, Ariana was starting to feel the effects from the alcohol and retired to, what her servants referred to as her 'private quarters'. Climbing into bed she felt exhausted. London was a city that did that to you like no other in the world. Pierre had warned her this was the case. He was right. During the night, Ariana awoke needing the bathroom. Getting out of bed, she found herself feeling extremely light headed. Not the feeling you get from drinking too much alcohol which is the very opposite. In fact she felt so light headed, if she opened the window she swore she'd be able to fly high in the sky, just like King Solomon's army, though without the need of a carpet. Returning from the bathroom she sat for several seconds on the edge of her bed. Her bedroom was full of scent, she hadn't noticed before but now she did. She recognised the smell, spreading her hands on her quilt she knew where the scent was coming from. During the night someone had scattered her quilt with the flowers of the haoma. Gathering the flowers in her hands, Ariana pressed them into her nose. Immediately she was flying like the Huma bird high above the sacred mountains of Persia. So elated was she, like the Huma bird she never wanted to come down to earth. Smiling, Ariana fell back onto her bed, a deep peaceful sleep taking over everything. The outside world would have to wait for her.

Cap Blanc Nez, near Calais, France,

The sound made him jump. Looking at the sea below Roger realised how vulnerable he was. He swung round. Behind him stood an elderly couple. The only place they could have come from was from the lone car in the car park. The car he'd registered had English plates.

"We were admiring your car", the woman smiled, speaking in English.

"Lots of character", the man, her husband Roger assumed, added.

"Thank you, actually it's my daughter's, I've borrowed it for a few days", Roger had no idea why he felt the need to lie.

"I said it looks like a girl's car, didn't I Henry".

"Yes she did". Henry confirmed

"Magnificent isn't it". The woman stepped forward until she was standing beside Roger. "We've been coming here for years, we love it. We prefer it at this time of year and in this weather as you tend to have the place to yourself. In summer it tends to get really crowded.

"The trouble is, since what happened here recently, you now tend to get loads of weirdos. Ghoulish tourists I call them". This was Henry's input.

"Why are you here"?. The woman looked up at him.

Roger thought, why was he here? That night. "I'm visiting Calais but with all the trouble I've come out here, I'm staying at the hotel below, L'Escale".

"So are we", the woman exclaimed. "Aren't we Henry".

"We are".

Roger groaned inwardly.

"We love it here", the woman repeated. "From here, in the dark, you can truly appreciate the power of the sea".

"And how dangerous it is", added Henry.

Fifteen minutes later, after ordering a cognac at the bar, Roger was in his room. He'd left Henry and his wife standing on the cliff edge admiring the power and the threat of the sea. His brief excursion had made him realise how stupid he had been. Henry and his wife had crept up on him so easily. If they'd harboured mal intent, the slightest push and he'd have been over the edge and certain death. His detective's brain led him to the suicide of Capitaine Maubert. He wondered casually if there were any witnesses, had no one questioned whether it had may have been murder, not suicide at all.

Finishing his cognac, Roger switched on his mobile. There were no messages, it was though the world had forgotten him. He wished. No, he didn't, he was hoping he'd find a message from the lieutenant or Mirielle. No doubt the demonstration was still keeping them busy. Turning on the television, he switched off the light. Settling down, he was looking forward to watching the news. In ten seconds, Roger Denton of the NCA was sound asleep.

Hervelingham, Near Mont de Couple, Wissant and Mont d'Hubert, France

Jean and Camille, sat in bed together watching outside their window, dusk descending over Mont de Couple. They'd spent the whole day in Camille's parent's farmhouse. Despite their fears there'd been no threat from person's unknown. The day had passed by quietly and they'd spent most of it watching the disorder in Calais Nord on Camille's television.

"We can't do this again tomorrow" Camille decided as darkness enveloped the mont. "We need to get out Jean, we can't hide every day and, after tomorrow you have to go back to work. Your boss has only given you two days off".

Jean looked doubtful. "I was hoping that woman or the lieutenant would get back to me".

"Jean, there's a fucking riot in Calais, what do you expect, for them to ask the rioters to stop, so they can give you a quick call"?.

Jean realised how stupid he had been and grinned an embarrassed grin. "I suppose not".

Camille hit him with a pillow. "Idiot Jean, tomorrow we're going out, for a little while at least".

"Where do you want to go"?.

Camille had a determined look on her face, Jean had seen it many times before and knew whatever she suggested they were going to do. No wouldn't be an option, not unless he was prepared for an almighty row.

"Let's face our demons Jean. Let's drive and park on Cap Blanc Nez. In the same place we saw what we saw. Do this for me Jean".

Jean was horrified at the thought but Camille was determined, he had no choice but to oblige her. "Ok, let's do it".

Camille flung her arms around him, kissing him firmly on the cheek. "Merci Jean, merci." Jean gazed out of the window at Mont de Couple. 'See you tomorrow, Cap Blanc Nez' his mind spoke. 'Just bloody behave yourself'.

Mont de Couple, near Wissant, France

This time the wall at the end of the tunnel opened automatically. There was no need for scans or codes, he was expected. Gently, he manoeuvred the buggy inside and got off. He was in a fairly large room, well-lit and spotlessly white. Hanging on one wall were a number of white coveralls with a face mask and a filter for breathing. Knowing that he was being watched, Pierre put one on. As soon as he had finished he faced, on this occasion, an obvious door. The door slid open and Pierre stepped through into a much smaller room. Like the cavern a little earlier there was a circle on the floor. Pierre stood inside it, stretching his arms out wide. A fine spray from walls, floor as well as ceiling filled the chamber. The spray lasted just thirty seconds but it was a full minute more before the microscopic droplets gave in to gravity. As before, a quite obvious door slid open. Another room, the same size as the last. Pierre stepped in and waited. The door closed behind him. At first it appeared that nothing was happening until, after a minute or so, Pierre started to feel warm. The temperature was rising. Without warning another door ahead opened. Pierre stepped through into another identical room, he knew this to be the last. As before there appeared to be nothing happening but Pierre knew he was being scanned. Without warning, the door ahead opened and he stepped through to be greeted by two men and a woman, all wearing the same coveralls.

"Welcome, Monsieur de Hauw". The man in the centre of the three spoke, his voice, because of the suit, sounding mechanical. All three held out a hand, which Pierre shook in turn. 'Please, follow us Monsieur'. The three led Pierre through something that is best described as straight out of a science fiction novel. Suspended walkways passed above pools of still water, water with vapour rising indicating the water was heated. Heated to and maintained at a strict temperature the spokesman explained. There were, he added, twenty four identical domes with pools. The walls were of natural chalk but had been carefully smoothed so that they shone. Suspended from the ceiling, just as in the earlier chamber, was a large black disc. And just as in the chamber earlier, beams of light shone from the top of the disc at precise and regular intervals. All of this was very impressive but most impressive of all, depending on your point of view was what was floating in each pool. In each pool there were thirty six perfectly round spheres, made of almost crystal like glass and in each sphere, somehow suspended in the centre was what was very clearly a human brain.

Gendarmerie Nationale, Calais, France

Lieutenant Beaufort was exhausted. Never in all his career had he seen such blatant lawlessness with little or no regard for the people who owned the businesses that were destroyed. Innocent people who had nothing to do with what the rioters, for rioters were what they were, to call them demonstrators was an insult to people who peacefully fought for a cause. Innocent people who had nothing to do with the antics of Capitaine Olivier Vendroux. Who indeed were almost certainly as angry and as disgusted by his behaviour in the Cafe de Paris as the people who caused so much mayhem.

With the temperature dropping fast and hotels in the town full, the demonstrators, rioters, call them what you will, had finally dispersed. Many of his officers, already exhausted, had volunteered to stay well into the night to protect the shops and cafes that had their windows smashed in; the CRS too had agreed to retain a presence in and around Calais Nord to discourage anyone in mind of creating further disorder.

Tomorrow a clean-up operation will begin. Another one. Not long ago the good people of Calais were licking their wounds and clearing up following 'the storm of the century', now the residents and business people of Calais Nord will be doing the same again. The lieutenant felt sorry for the Mayor who had worked tirelessly to make Calais somewhere people would want to come and visit from both sides of the water. And now this, anarchy in the streets of Calais played out on both national and international television along with the capitaine of the gendarmerie blatantly assaulting a woman in a local cafe. What sort of image would the town have now?

Grabbing a coffee from a machine, the lieutenant moved about thanking his men who were slumped on chairs, many on the floor all equally exhausted. All had the same question in their minds. Where was their bloody capitaine? Several expanded the view that the rioters had done Capitaine Olivier Vendroux a great favour. The demonstration or riot had distracted them from the search for him, he could be miles away by now. All were determined at the first opportunity to find the bloody dickhead. Finding Capitaine Olivier Vendroux would be their number one priority. Their gendarmerie desperately needed a success story.

To the lieutenant's surprise Colette appeared in reception, he thought she'd gone home.

"Lieutenant, have you got a moment? In my office"?.

The lieutenant followed her to her office. Through her interior window he could see more of his gendarmes arriving looking exhausted. Outside, a handful of media were settling down for the night. The majority were still making a nuisance of themselves in the centre of town.

"Colette, have we arranged for refreshments to be delivered to that lot outside"?.

"Oui, filled baguettes and coffee, the Mayor, by the way told me to bill him".

"Did he". The lieutenant actually managed to smile. "In that case, order the same for our men and women out there, will you, Colette".

"Of course, I'll do it immediately after".

"Ah yes, what was it"? The lieutenant stopped gazing through the window and concentrated on Colette".

"The English Detective, Roger Denton, he's here in France. He's staying at the L'Escale hotel at Escalles. He's spoken to Mirielle and wants to know if you can still meet with him tomorrow. He must have seen the news. Do you want me to tell Mirielle to pass on a message

316

to say, with everything that's happening at the moment, it's simply impossible. I'm sure he'll understand".

"NO", the lieutenant stopped her. "No, it's important that I meet him. I know it's late and I don't know if she's still on duty but get a message to Mirielle will you. Ask her to message the English detective advising him that I still plan to meet, and that we'll call in the morning to arrange a time and place".

"Will do", Colette wondered about telling the lieutenant about Jean's phone call earlier but decided to leave it till the morning. The lieutenant had enough on his plate. She refrained from telling him that Mirielle was waiting in her car outside for her. With the riot she hadn't felt safe driving home alone. She'd ask Mirielle to send a text to the English detective. Now to order in refreshments for the gendarmerie. Courtesy of the Mayor. Colette could not help but grin.

Mont de Couple, Near Wissant, France

After the pools Pierre was led through a corridor with walls, rather like an aquarium, of glass water filled tanks. And like a fish tank the water was being oxygenated, though Pierre noticed, rather like champagne the bubbles were extremely fine and not rising from one corner but throughout the tank. Bobbing in the water were what looked like grains of rice, except unlike rice they were coloured grey with a reddish tint. There were hundreds, maybe as much as a thousand to each tank. From the ceiling the spokesperson pulled down a plate of glass placing it over the facia of one of the tanks. The interior was instantly magnified to such an extent that one 'grain of rice', was enlarged to around the same size of a small lemon. With the aid of magnification the form changed from a simple grain of rice to a pine cone.

"We currently have over fourteen thousand of these little beauties," the spokesman boasted, "shipped from all over Europe. Soon with the new units coming into operation, well you've just visited one I believe, in Tenerife and there's two just about to start operating in the UK. There will no longer be the need to have them shipped. And shipping is always difficult, on average we lose almost eighty percent during transportation. Such a waste".

After Pierre had asked several questions and received satisfactory answers he followed the three into another unit where more coveralls were hanging from hooks on a wall. Here the four of them removed the coveralls they were wearing after which they entered another unit to start the process with which Pierre had entered but in reverse. After finishing the laboratory procedure the next chamber was completely different, it almost resembled a hotel reception with several corridors leading off. One was even headed 'lounge area and bar' and another 'prayer chambers'. Here Pierre said goodbye to the two accompanying the spokesperson after which he was led down the only corridor not signposted to what looked like a security office. On one side of the room sat a desk and a number of very comfortable looking chairs, an area obviously used for meetings. There were also several cabinets, all made of wood and on one, a low cabinet there was even a tray of decanters and another tray with an assortment of glasses.

On the opposite side, facing, were a bank of at least twenty television screens, below which on a sloping panel were a set of controls and four microphones on a bendable stem. Four office style chairs fixed to the floor sat in front of each microphone. Some of the screens were blank but most were active. From this room one could spy on any part of the 'village' under Mont d'Hubert and the even more secretive complex under Mont a Crignons.

"Drink Pierre"?.

Chapter 6

Pierre knew exactly the drinks on the tray. "Arak, if you have it". Pierre knew he did.

"I'll join you", the man poured a dark liquid into medium size brandy glasses. Handing Pierre his glass the man raised his. Here's to the final outcome".

"I'll drink to that". Pierre raised his glass. "So how are you Atbir and how are we progressing? When will we be ready to start delivering the final outcome"?.

Atbir proceeded to go over in some detail the progress they were making, as for being ready to start delivering the 'final outcome, two years, if things go very well, maybe eighteen months.

Pierre was happy with Atbir's answer, he'd expected him to say double that, maybe even five years. Things were progressing far quicker than either he or Orme had dared hoped for. And Atbir was the epitome of caution, he was incapable of exaggerating. He was also descended from the 'originals', and therefore trust was never in doubt.

"And our first project is ready for testing".

This was news to Pierre, he knew that a suitable subject had been found and was being worked on but he had no idea that they'd progressed to such an extent that the doctors involved deemed that the experimental subject had progressed to being a test subject.

"We can take a look at her if you want". Atbir moved over to the bank of television monitors, motioning for Pierre to come and sit beside him. After typing on a keyboard the largest screen burst into life and there in the centre of the screen sat a girl, mid-twenties, Pierre judged, peacefully reading a magazine, A pile of newspapers sat on a small table beside her.

"This is Marie", Atbir spoke as though the girl on the screen was his very own daughter and in many ways Marie was. Atbir genuinely cared for her even though the television monitor was the closest he'd ever come. "She was picked up because she had become a danger to the operation under Mont d'Hubert. We were going to treat her as standard merchandise but Dr Kailash, recognised that she could be an excellent test subject and because of her background and position in the Calais community, possibly a very valuable asset. Especially if you want to step up production under Mont d'Hubert, which we need to".

Pierre looked doubtful, he had his concerns. The operation here was too valuable to risk for the sake of haste. "You're sure we're not rushing things Atbir"?.

"It's not my decision, it's Dr Kailesh, but I trust him just as you trust me".

Pierre watched the girl on the screen, she looked so peaceful, contentment written all over her face. He instantly warmed to the girl. As he watched a woman in nurse's clothing walked in. She handed Marie a mug of something. Marie took it, offering the nurse a broad smile, after which the nurse retired.

"You see, Atbir gestured. The girl, Marie, is quite happy. She has had the procedure and as far as we can tell, there are no signs of harm, Her brain is functioning normally.

Pierre still looked doubtful.

"Would you like to speak to Dr Kailash? Marie is his baby".

"That would be helpful".

Atbir punched in some numbers. Marie disappeared and a man with an elegant sculptured face appeared on the screen, he was smiling. "Pierre, it's good to see you even though it is on screen".

Pierre smiled, him and Dr Kailash or Rome Kailash went back years, to the beginning almost. "Good afternoon to you Rome, do you know it's the afternoon"?.

"I have a clock". Dr Kalash, or Rome lifted a clock off the wall and presented it in front of the camera.

Pierre laughed, "that's a very old clock Rome, couldn't the organisation have found you something a little more up to date"?.

Dr Rome Kalaish grinned. "Sometimes old or if you want, tradition is best, you should know that. It's what the organisation is all about. The most reliable clock is the stars and by reliable, I mean they don't have to rely on a battery or a winding mechanism. Origin, if you can find it and use it is always the best way".

"And are those the principles you've used with this girl Marie, possibly our first 'test subject'"?.

"To some extent, yes. That would be correct".

"Are you sure, it's not too soon? Are you sure your experiment with this girl won't go wrong and she ends up leading the authorities back to us"?.

Rome shook his head. "No, quite sure. Look Pierre, she's the first, the first test subject and there will be many more after her. Being the first, there's always a chance that something could go wrong, and we aren't going to be able to control her, influence her, yes before she is released but not control her which of course has its risks. But lead the authorities back here? Not a chance, we have wiped all knowledge of this place from her brain. As far as the girl, Marie is concerned she has been staying in a gite. She needed a break. And if the authorities follow it up, the booking was made online, from the girl's computer, using her bank card. And the gite has a code security lock, therefore the renters never set eyes on her. Anyway the authorities will have no reason not to believe her story, you're worrying over nothing Pierre".

"I hope you're right, Rome".

"I am", another smile.

"When are you planning on releasing her"?.

"Tomorrow, around lunchtime, in Ardres. We've read what we can of her brain and she has a strong desire to go there, it's very evident".

Pierre could guess why but he didn't say anything. "Rome you say you can wipe part of her memory, you're quite sure"?.

"One hundred percent, why? Are you still worried? You needn't be".

"It's my job to worry", Pierre gave a nod of thanks to Atbir who had just refilled his glass. "No, we have a problem, Rome, and I think I'm going to need your help. But you have to be two hundred percent sure that a memory can be eradicated, that nothing can lead back to us".

"More than two hundred percent sure, double that, what's your problem? And how can me and my team be of assistance"?.

Pierre explained, in some detail about Capitaine Olivier Vendroux and the problem they now faced, that he had become a severe risk to the organisation. As it turned out Rome had seen the saga with the capitaine play out on the local news. Watching, he'd had no idea that Capitaine Vendroux, was an organisation operative.

"Where's the capitaine now, do we know? I'm not sure how we can be of assistance".

"We have him, he's under Mont d'Hubert. Antanois is looking after him". Pierre couldn't help smiling at the term, 'looking after".

"I see".

"And you can see our dilemma. If he disappears we'll have half of all France's gendarmes descending on Calais looking for him and they may even re-investigate the death of Monsieur Maubert. That would mean us having to close operations under Mont d'Hubert for months and we simply can't afford to do that".

"So what do you propose? What are you asking me to do Pierre?"

"Wipe part of his memory, like you've done with the girl and all memory of how he got posted to Calais. All knowledge of the organisation must be eradicated from his mind".

"And when are you wanting me to do this PIerre"? Dr Rome Kalaish was beginning to worry.

"I really want him back in circulation tomorrow. His return will quieten everything down. Capitaine Vendroux can face the French justice system and we can get back to normal".

No reply, on the screen Rome sat with his elbows on both knees, his head between his legs. Finally he looked up. "It's a big risk, Pierre. Sure we can eradicate the parts of memory you require, but getting his life balances back to how they were will be impossible in such a short period. I can give no guarantee on how he's going to behave once he's back. He could go completely crazy".

"If he did, Rome, that may play into our hands. The gendarmerie too. They could then claim that the capitaine had a mental problem".

"Judging by what I've seen on television, I would say he has already".

"I don't disagree with you there, so will you do it? I'm not going to force you, Rome".

"Meaning if I say yes, if it all goes belly up, I'm the one to blame".

Pierre grinned, "No I didn't mean that, do you want me to order you to do it"?.

"Yes please".

"Then I order you".

"Thank you, then I'll do it. Can you wheel him over straight away"?.

"We can, but before we do, you need to know one thing". Pierre described Capitaine Vendroux's general condition. "We can't clean him up Rome, he has to go back out as we found him. If we clean him up, the authorities will start asking questions. Send him back in the same condition in which he spent the night and they'll assume he's been sleeping rough".

Rome looked hard at the camera. "Thanks a bloody lot Pierre, now piss off".

Pierre laughed, he wasn't sure if Rome heard him as the screen went blank. With the help of Atbir , Pierre contacted Antanois, explaining that Capitaine Olivier Vendroux was to be prepared for Mont a Crignons, that he must not be cleaned up in any way and that he must not be damaged or conscious when he's delivered. A specialist medical team from Mont d'Hubert will have to facilitate the delivery. Pierre gave Antanois the names.

That done, Pierre felt he could relax, Atbir with the bank of screens proceeded to give Pierre a tour of operations under the three hills, Hubert, Crignons and Couple. But Pierre though watching wasn't listening. His mind was wandering back to the beginning. When Orme had somehow found the original Nazi plans of the colossal underground complex. He knew it had taken her years of searching to find them and since then, she had never revealed to him how she eventually discovered their location or where that location was. When they had first entered the labyrinth underground, everything, except the underground medical facilities had been chambers and tunnels of exposed hewn rock. It had taken decades to get to where they were now and everything had been achieved in secret. Patience had been their bible.

The purchasing of the restaurant on the summit of Mont d'Hubert was vital before work could begin. After that a series of farmhouses had to be purchased, all with concealed but direct access to the underground complex. Nearly all of the tunnels from the farmhouses after construction had finished were filled in, with one or two remaining open for emergency access. All of the tunnels leading from the outside to the complex under Mont de Couple had been filled in or blocked off. And the gun emplacements and shelters on top of the hill had been blocked off by the civil authorities and turned into a reserve for bats. The perfect cover for what was happening beneath. Nearly all who were involved in the construction, especially under Mont de Couple, were aware that when they'd finished, they'd never be able to leave. Some would die in their underground world, though all, especially the 'originals', hoped to still be alive, to be there at the 'final outcome'. Only the 'originals' knew what the term 'final outcome', meant.

It was nearly midnight when Pierre returned to his penthouse looking over La Manche, and spent almost an hour in the shower before he was ready for bed. At first he found it hard to sleep, his mind was too active. Tomorrow was another huge day, there were too many of them at the moment. He'd love to be able to discuss his fears, his hopes, even everyday life with someone else, a friend, but he had no friends. He had only contacts, hundreds and hundreds of them, all doing his bidding. But none, none knew or even questioned how he was feeling. Despite his wealth, despite his power at times he desired the simple life that was on display everyday, everywhere around him. That life, he knew was light years away and as a consequence he often felt as though he were the loneliest man in the world.

Rolling over he faced his window wall. Lights outside played patterns in the glass. He imagined Ariana was there looking in. Ariana, how he loved that woman. It almost broke him sometimes that he could only love her from a distance. That he could never tell her his true feelings. All he could do was help her experience Persia, fly her in her sub consciousness back to where she came from. After all, although she didn't know it, she was one of the most important originals. Royalty in fact, a queen in the way a bee would be.

Chapter
—7—

The Following Morning

Hotel L'Escale, Escalles. Near Cap Blanc Nez, Mont d'Hubert and Wissant

The sun was shining. Roger Denton of the NCA couldn't believe it. There was a golden orb shining with a bright blue sky. Someone must have been saying their prayers forcibly enough for God to answer them. After having a shower he switched on his phone. There were several messages that could wait and one that couldn't. It was from Mirielle. He looked at his watch, seven thirty. It would have to wait, for a little while anyway. He needn't have worried. Ten minutes later his phone rang, it was Mirielle. Such was his haste to answer Roger dropped the phone, cutting Mirielle off.

"Shit", he exclaimed out loud in frustration not to mention exasperation, "shit, shit, shit".

"Bonjour Monsieur Denton, what did you just say"?.

"Sorry Mirielle, I dropped the phone".

"You just said shit didn't you"?.

"Yes and sorry I dropped the phone". He heard Mirielle along with whoever was with her laughing on the other end.

"You know Detective Denton, when I was at Cambridge studying languages, I think the word you have just said is the world's most recognised word,certainly among the students I was with anyway".

"What does that say about English culture"? Roger had recovered.

"A great deal, it's good to be recognised internationally. Anyway detective, you should be proud of your language. Some organisations estimate there to be close to a million words in your language whereas with French it's around one hundred thousand. You have many more ways of swearing than we do".

"I'm not sure that's a good thing".

"Cherish it detective, anyway we are digressing. I have Lieutenant Beaufort with me and he wants to meet, today would be good".

"Today would be good, in fact, more than perfect for me".

"You can't have more than perfect detective, perfect is perfect. Us French like our lunch, our lieutenant proposes lunch, but not in Calais. He hopes you understand but he's worried about being followed. He does not want to be seen with you. He hopes you understand and are not insulted.

"Perfectly, and I totally agree with him, where does he suggest? I'm staying at the...", Roger picked up a brochure in the room. "...at L'Escale, do you know it"?.

"Yes and yes detective, we know, you told me, and yes we know it. The lieutenant suggests we meet at a restaurant called La Sirène. It is literally on the beach. Rue de la Plage, Audinghen. Your GPS will take you there". Roger refrained from telling the translator that he wouldn't be using GPS. He would find it. "It's not very far from where you are staying, detective. We aim to be there for one o'clock".

"Perfect, I'll see you there".

"See you", Mirielle rang off.

Looking at his watch, it was gone eight. He'd ring Nick, he should be in the office by now.

"Morning, Nick, I'm just calling to see if you have any updates for me."

"I'll know when I arrive in the office, no one's phoned me during the night so I guess everything's the same as yesterday. We know fuck all" Nick sounded weary.

Roger quickly realised his mistake. "Sorry Nick, I forget there's a time difference. I'll call back around lunchtime".

"Yes sir, I look forward to it". Nick put the phone down.

Breakfast was a buffet, simple by UK standards but perfectly decent. After he'd finished he returned to reception. Yesterday the receptionist had circled where he could buy some clothes without going into Calais centre. Now he wanted to know where he could find a restaurant called La Sirène. 'The Mermaid' the receptionist educated him and on a different map, provided by the local tourist office, circled the restaurant and drew arrows on how to get to it. It looked simple enough. Now to buy some clothes.

Gendarmerie Nationale, Calais, France

Lieutenant Beaufort actually felt good that morning. It's amazing how your body responds when you need it to. His teams too looked to be in a good mood. They all looked up for it. The intelligence services had detected no new plans from the feminists or anarchists groups and therefore the CRS that morning had packed up and left to be replaced by his gendarmes. The process of clearing up was well underway and, by daylight, a great many of the shops had already been boarded up, waiting for a glazier. The mayor was due to visit the area around ten with a badly leaked promise of financial help for the area. Many of the journalists had started to leave. Anything after yesterday, their bosses surmised, in comparison would be boring news. If Capitaine Olivier Vendroux was found they could purchase pictures both still and moving. It was hardly worth spending money on a maybe. There was always something else happening elsewhere that was more important. Capitaine Olivier Vendroux was already old news.

At eleven am, the Commandant de Regions, Hauts des France called, wanting to speak to the lieutenant. He was full of praise for both the Lieutenant personally and his gendarmerie. So pleased was he that, as a show of thanks he was awarding the gendarmerie one thousand euros, specifically to be spent on their Christmas party, which wasn't far away. As for the lieutenant, he was putting him in temporary charge until a suitable successor could be found. And if the lieutenant passed his final exam, maybe a successor from outside wouldn't be needed. A promotion from inside may be more appropriate.

With all the good news, the lieutenant was really looking forward to lunch, as was Mirielle.

From her office, Colette watched the visibly open display of exuberance by most of the uniformed officers including the lieutenant. She was conscious that she still hadn't told him of her conversation with Jean. Unlike most of the others she couldn't share their shared positive energy. The more she thought about Jean's call the stronger her feeling of foreboding. She needed to speak to the lieutenant but now was not the time.

Hervelinghen, near Mont d'Hubert, France

Jean and Camille were ready for the world. Bouncing off each other, they'd decided no longer were they to consider themselves victims. Together they were going to face the world and everything it threw at them. No longer were they going to hide. Neither wanted to admit that perhaps a bright blue sky, and a sun that had gone missing for days, reappearing had anything to do with it.

After a late breakfast, they were both ready. Jean's car started first time. It didn't always, a good sign. And just after half eleven, they were on their way. Ahead of them, in the distance, as they drove, the sea in view could have easily been mistaken for the Mediterranean. Cote de Opale, the Opal Coast, was what this stretch of coast was called and that morning the sea was demonstrating why. After passing through Escalles, Jean's car tackled the climb to the summit of Mont d' Hubert without protest. Another first. At the top, he took a left, pulling into the carpark that served Cap Blanc Nez. Because of the good weather Cap Blanc Nez that morning was busy but to their relief no one was in 'their' parking space. Their special parking space. A space from where you could see the edge of the cliff and the space where they'd been parked when they'd unwittingly watched the murder of Capitaine Maubert. They were sure their space would have been taken, another miracle or so they perceived. Turning off the engine Jean switched on the radio. As the music started he lay his right hand on Camille's stomach. Camille, with both hands held his and moved it slightly. She knew where her womb was, and now Jean with his hand was protecting their future.

La Sirène, Rue de la Plage, Audinghen, France

Roger pulled into the car park for La Sirène restaurant around twelve thirty. The lieutenant had chosen well, there was no way you could follow someone without being seen. He found it hard to believe that England was just across the water. Where he was now, felt like a million miles away. It was truly beautiful. The receptionist at the hotel had told him that La Sirène was a family affair and that it 'represented everything good about the sea'. Parked here, Roger could see why, there was even a fishing boat parked on the approach road.

Finding clothes that fitted as well as suited had been surprisingly easy. In under an hour he had chosen outfits for three days. He recognised none of the labels and when trying them on had felt distinctly French. Never mind we all have our cross to bear, he laughed to himself. Secretly he felt they made him look good, younger even. For lunch he'd chosen a pair of light blue trousers and a blue polo neck. Simple but effective especially when sporting a new pair of highly polished brown leather ankle boots.

He only had to wait ten minutes when two cars, one following the other, pulled into the car park, pulling alongside and coming to a halt either side of him. Out of the car on his left stepped a youngish woman, Roger guessed Mirielle. On his nearside, a tall man in, Roger estimated in his mid-thirties, almost certainly Lieutenant Beaufort. Both he noted were in civvies and driving typically untypical cars of the French gendarme. Roger had done his homework and he was right. Mirielle had come in her own car and the lieutenant in Colette's.

Introductions were brief, after which the Lieutenant whispered something to Mirielle. Her response was a light giggle. Roger raised his eyebrows in question.

"My boss is commenting on your desire not to be followed, to uphold a certain level of anonymity and you turn up in a car like that". Mirielle chuckled again.

"Well, you'd never expect to find a policeman driving that would you"?, Roger defended his car.

"True", Lieutenant Beaufort smiled, it was one of the few English words he knew. True, truth.

"She's called Molly".

"You English are crazy". Mirielle was laughing again. Roger couldn't disagree.

To anyone watching, the meeting couldn't seem more natural. A group of friends getting together for a fisherman's lunch. Which was a shame for no one was watching.

Inside, the lieutenant chose a table by the window, it was hard not to. The view was magnificent, but Roger was looking at something else. A framed photo on the wall as you came in. The photo was of two men and a woman standing beside a classic car. The three looked to be in conversation. Roger recognised the car, it was rare, an Aston Martin DB4 Vantage Sports, he also recognised two of the people. One was his ex-colleague and friend John Mitchell and the woman Maureen Fowlis. He remembered John telling him how they had met. So this must be the place. The lieutenant and Mirielle, noticing the English detective wasn't with them doubled back to see what had caught his eye.

"I know these two", Roger whispered, touching the glass. "He...", pointing at John, "...has been murdered and she has gone missing. Can you ask the owner how he got this photograph"?.

Mirielle repeated what the English detective had just told her to the lieutenant, who in turn called the owner over. On asking him the question, he looked embarrassed.

"The car is beautiful and I wanted to show people the class of customer I have. And it's a very beautiful photo, is it not? It looks great hanging there".

Roger had to admit it was, and it did look good where it was hanging, it caught your eye.

"Are they friends of yours"?. The restaurant owner spoke English.

"Those two are", Roger pointed, "I don't know who he is, do you"?. Roger pointed to a tallish, immaculately dressed man with a mop of tousled curls.

The lieutenant replied in French, Mirielle translated. "That man with your friends is Pierre de Hauw. Everyone in this area knows him"

Pierre de Hauw, Roger thought hard. Where had he heard that name before? It wasn't long ago, of that he was certain. He made a mental note.

NCA's Temporary Offices, Gladstone Park, Cricklewood, London, England

At just gone midday, Nick got a call from security.

"Sir, we've just received a parcel. From memory, it looks very similar, if not identical, to the one addressed to your boss, Mr Denton. The one he made such a fuss about".

"Is it addressed to Roger"?.

"No sir, this one's addressed to you, to a Mr Nicholas Hunter. We're holding the delivery driver here, you may want to come up".

"I'm on my way". Nick dropped what he was doing and sprinted out of the door. Minutes later he was with security at their front yard. Sat in a small office was a man in uniform, looking extremely nervous. To Nick he didn't at all look like someone who was attached to a sophisticated criminal organisation. Parked outside, still with the driver's door open was what he presumed to be his van. It was painted red and had the Parcelforce logo.

"The parcel's in here sir, it's been scanned for traces of explosives, there aren't any".

The security guard led Nick into a walk-in cupboard, he pointed to a square parcel sitting by itself on a shelf. Nick didn't need to pick it up, he saw instantly that it was identical to the one Roger had received containing D.C. Haver's head. And he was pretty certain a head was inside this box, but whose?

"And it's addressed to me"?.

"Yes sir, look". The security tapped the address label.

Nick examined it, not wishing to get too close. The guard was right, clearly printed, was his name. 'For the personal attention of Mr Nicholas Hunter. Shit. Why him?

"I need to make a phone call, two minutes". Nick stepped outside. He tried Roger first but his phone was off. He tried Jane only to find hers was off too. Shit, shit, shit, what was he to do now?

Mont d' Hubert, Near Calais, France

Marie stepped into the car, it was a beautiful day and she was looking forward to it. She'd had such a wonderful break and felt so refreshed. Now she was looking forward to seeing her friends in Ardres. It had been such a long time, too long. The taxi driver told her that he couldn't drop her outside the door as he knew the road and it was difficult to turn. If the lady didn't mind he'd drop her at a turning area a little way before. It was only a five minute walk after that. Marie didn't mind at all. With everything agreed including the price, the car took off. Immediately Marie fell asleep.

A little way behind Marie, Capitaine Oliver Vendroux was being brought to the surface. The plan was to drop him off in a secluded area close to Bleriot Plage, very close to Calais. People will assume he'd been roughing it in the sand dunes. A van was brought close to the entrance. Inside the rear wall of the fridge opened and through stepped Capitaine Oliver Vendroux, smelling like an open sewer and looking much worse. The one person walking him through felt repulsed, he wanted to be sick, he'd been told to hold the capitaine's arm until he was safely in the van. Not bloody likely. No way was he doing that. Anyway the capitaine was as meek as a newborn baby. Those waiting stepped back as the capitaine passed. With the walk-in fridge door closed, the service doors were opened, the van door was open, waiting for its human cargo.

The sunlight had an effect on the capitaine that no one was prepared for, or expected. His eyes felt as though they were on fire, burning fiercely. Never had he experienced such pain. He screamed and kept screaming, his arms flailing wildly. Taken by surprise, everyone escorting him froze. The capitaine started to run, scratching at his eyes. Customers entering the restaurant watched in horror. "

Shut everything down, a security guard shouted. "Get that van out of here. SLOWLY, SLOWLY, no one panic".

Ardres, France

Vivienne, taking advantage of the weather, was preparing her garden for winter. With everything that had taken place recently she hadn't given it the attention it needed. She found tending her garden therapeutic. As her husband had liked to lose himself in hard rock, she liked to lose herself in her garden.

She was on her knees aerating the soil with a trowel when she heard the front door bell. It must be her daughter, she'd gone shopping. She was quick, Pulling off her gloves and leaving them on the grass, Madame Maubert entered the house. The doorbell rang again, this time rather impatiently. 'I'm coming, I'm coming' she whispered to herself, why wasn't her daughter using her key? Too much shopping no doubt.

"Where's your key"? She started to say and stopped in her tracks. "Oh"!

In front of her, smiling brightly stood Marie. She looked the picture of health, except for her eyes. There was something wrong with her eyes. There was something missing. It was almost as though she was there physically but not mentally, perhaps even spiritually.

"Hello Vivienne, do you mind if I come in"?.

Before Vivienne could answer Marie brushed past her and was inside.

La Sirène, Rue de la Plage, Audinghen, France

The reputation France had for food was demonstrated effortlessly by La Sirène. Roger, guided by his hosts, had ordered dishes he'd never heard of and each turned out to be delicious. More than delicious, with each mouthful, he didn't want the food to leave his tongue for his stomach.

Whilst eating both sides discussed the missing children. The lieutenant revealed his meeting with the pathologist in Boulogne and what had been discussed. I have a recording of his examinations with me, he told Roger. They were in his office back at the gendarmerie and could kick himself for not bringing it. He promised to get it to Roger so their experts could make what they could of it. He also told Roger how the pathologist had told him, his personal theory, the red market, how he'd been threatened by an officer of the GIGN, therefore the state. How he'd been given an address in Paris to give to anyone who made an inquiry. Just as Capitaine Vendroux had done with Roger. He must be in on this somehow, both men agreed.

The lieutenant told Roger that he had a friend checking out the address in Paris for him. He hadn't heard from him yet and would phone him before they'd finished their meal.

Roger in turn explained what a detective had told him in the South of England and about the severed heads that they were holding. He asked the lieutenant if their pathologist could check the following with the heads of the children they still had under their care. Were the decapitations, in his opinion, carried out before or after death, and had they had the pineal gland removed. Neither the lieutenant or Mirielle knew what a pineal gland was. Looking it up, translated into French, the English detective was referring to the glande pineale. They still hadn't a clue what it was and Roger, even with Mirielle's help, found it hard to explain.

The lieutenant made a call to Jean-Paul. It was always first names now though in return the pathologist always referred to the lieutenant as lieutenant. Never using his first name. The lieutenant went over what the English detective had told him along with his two questions.

"I'm at lunch now", Jean-Paul told him. "After what happened, I always take lunch, something I never did before. I've lost all interest, lieutenant. These days I'm just going through the motions until I retire. On full pension", he added.

The lieutenant couldn't help feeling sorry for him. Jean-Paul had always been the consummate professional and now it was obvious that the state didn't give a shit.

"I do not think the heads were taken off while the children were living but I shall double check when I get back, and I'm sure I would have noticed if their pineal glands had been removed but again, I will double check after lunch. Let's all hope that I don't discover that the heads were removed whilst the poor little things were alive".

"Yes, let's hope so", the lieutenant added for everyone, there was a tear in his eye.

He briefly related their conversation to Mirielle who translated for the English detective.

"The trouble is….", added Lieutenant Beaufort, "…I don't know who I can trust anymore".

Mirielle translated. Roger jumped on it. "Neither do I, I have exactly the same problem". Mirielle translated. Roger thought. "Actually I think there is someone I can trust, he told me to trust you. He also told me that I can give you his number but that you must use a pay as you go phone, 'portable jetable'".

Mirielle started to translate but the lieutenant's mobile rang. Mirielle and Roger waited for him to finish his call. But he didn't. Jumping up from the table he started running for the exit, phone still pressed to his ear. Mirielle watched, disbelieving as the lieutenant spun his car round and sped up the hill as if his life depended on it.

Seeing what had just happened a waiter approached. "Would Madame and Monsieur like the bill?

La Morgue, Centre Hospitalier, Boulogne Sur Mer

There was something wrong, the lights were turned off and having no windows the morgue was in darkness. Where was everybody, there should be at least three of his staff working. As long as they got the job done he was fairly free with the hours when his staff worked. But there should always be at least one person in attendance. Even at night. Work in his morgue never stopped. Especially mid-afternoon.

Passing his office, he entered the main theatre. He turned on the lights. Everything was neat and tidy, nothing was out of place. That is, as far as he could see. He went to the bank of drawers where the bodies were stored. He opened a wide but shallow drawer. Used for body parts, it's where the children's heads were stored. The drawer was empty. Quickly, he moved to another drawer, the one that contained the body of the girl found on the beach near Escalles. That too was empty. He quickly opened another drawer. One that he knew contained the body of a young man killed, only days ago, in a motorbike accident. The body was still there. The heads and the bodies of the children had been specifically targeted. His blood ran cold. He heard a noise. There was someone else with him in the morgue and he knew it wasn't one of his staff.

Cap Blanc Nez, Near Calais, France

Jean and Camille sat in Jean's car, listening to music and enjoying the view. The Cap was pretty busy, people attracted by the fine weather. Both were starting to doze off when the volume on the car radio seemed to change, it was getting louder. The song too suddenly stopped and another song started to play. A song they both knew well, 'Tahitiala-maison' by Keen'v. They looked at each other, dread in each other's eyes.

They heard screams outside and people started to run as though they were trying to avoid something. A louder scream came from behind their car, a terrible blood curdling scream that came straight from the depths of hell. More people started to shout and scream, running for their cars. Almost paralysed with fear, Jean and Camille hardly dared to look, but look they did. Without warning a person they both knew well ran past their car, arms waving wildly, sometimes scratching at his eyes. All the time 'Tahitialamaison' played loudly on the radio. People watched in horror as the capitaine, looking as though he'd been dragged through a hedge and smelling much worse, ran full pelt towards the edge of the cliff.

"He's going to jump", a woman screamed and jump the capitaine did, leaping with full force into the air. The lasting memory most people had was of his scream as he disappeared beneath the cliff edge. The capitaine died with the force of hitting the water. He felt no relief, there was no sweet smelling garden to welcome him, simply flames replaced by more flames and his eyes never stopped burning.

As the capitaine hit the water, 'Tahitialamaison' stopped playing, replaced by the sound of the DJ's voice. Camille looked at Jean and burying her head in his chest started to cry.

Chapter 7

La Sirène, Rue de la Plage, Audinghen, France

Roger paid the bill.

"I'd better go, find out what the hell is going on. And I had the nerve to call you English, crazy.", Mirielle couldn't hide the disappointment in her voice. It was obvious she had enjoyed their little outing.

Roger remembered something, he pulled out his wallet and removed Donald's card.

"Just in case I return to England without having the chance to meet with your lieutenant again. This is the name of the man who asked me to pass on his details. But if you ever have cause to phone him, you must use a pay as you go phone, otherwise the number will cease to exist".

"A burner phone",

"Stop being so American".

"Well it's easier than saying pay as you go", Mirielle defended herself.

Roger ignored her, he was busy writing Donald's details on the back of the restaurant bill.

He handed it to Mirielle, who took it, read it and immediately started laughing. It was not the reaction he had expected. Not in the slightest. He started to put his wallet away.

"What is it? Why are you laughing"?.

"You obviously didn't do Latin at school"?.

"Who does these days"?

"Well maybe you should", Mirielle pushed his chest. "I think this guy is joking you. Donald Anas. Anas is Latin for duck. Donald Duck".

The entire

Bloodied

series

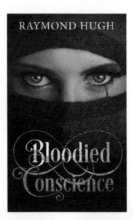

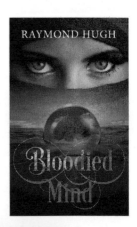

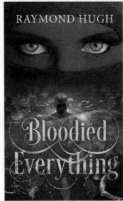